AN ABANDONED BILLION DOLLAR PLUNDER.
A FORGOTTEN SACRED PILGRIMAGE. A CURSED FAMILY LEGACY.

The Curse of Cortés

GUY MORRIS

GUYMORRISBOOKS.COM

ISBN: 978-1-7357286-3-6

Published by Guy Morris Books

Copy editing: Joel Pierson

Cover design, illustration & interior formatting:
Mark Thomas / Coverness.com

To my son Joshua for all of the stories, adventures and comics that we read and experienced together. Curse of Cortés is about the redeeming power of family even during dark times.

Prologue

Desolation of Xi'

12,872 BPE (Before Present Era)
Western Caribbean near modern-day Honduras

Creation tradition of the Polpul Vuh:

Here is the story of the beginning, when there was not one bird, not one fish, not one mountain. Here is the sky, all alone. Here is the sea, all alone. There is nothing more. No sound, no movement. Only the sky and the sea. Only Heart-of-Sky, alone. And these are his names: Maker and Modeler, Kukulkan, and Hurricane. But no one speaks his names. There is no one to praise his glory. There is no one to nurture his greatness.

Then the Creator said, "Let it be done," and it was done. The earth emerged from the sea. Plants put forth shoots. Wild animals came to be.

During the first creation of the world, man was made of mud. Man could hold no form, and so he was forgotten. In the second creation of the world, man was made of wood. But man had no soul and could not praise the gods. So, it was decided to destroy these wooden people.

As a young apprentice, Hun Hanahpu spent years making his own personal copy of the sacred scripts and ancient prophecies. As the last of the prophetic bloodline, his death will bring the end to an epoch of wisdom and enlightenment.

If only he had recognized the omen of Bolon-Yokte sooner, but the mystifying light appeared suddenly, and then within weeks left unimaginable devastation. Although in truth, no action or sacrifice could have held back the judgment, yet it took an act of rebellion against the high priest for Hun-Came to lead his followers to the mountain caverns of Altun Ha. Without adequate preparation, the hunger and dissension of the refugees spread rapidly until the day the mountain shook violently, and a scorching hurricane forced them deeper into the cavern darkness.

By the time he emerged from the mouth of the cave days later, a thick blanket of charred rubble spread across the entire landscape. Entire forests of mahogany and cedar had been incinerated into cinder and ash. Black smoke filled the sky until there was no sun, and his lungs burned to breathe. Then came the cold, torrential rain to saturate the charred hillsides, dissolving the barren mountains into giant, deadly lahars of noxious mud, reshaping the land until it became unrecognizable.

For the survivors, the natural spring within Altun Ha has become the sole source of fresh water. Many have already died, while others suffer from skin pustules, coughing blood, or severe burns left to fester. Without food, Hun Hanaphu expects that few of them will prevail through the coming months.

"Stroke," Ghana's deep voice yells out, pulling him from his pensive recollections. "Stroke … stroke."

His eyes fall to the oarsmen, who grunt and strain against the choppy seas. Perched at the bow of the larger canoe, he turns his gaze ahead in disbelief and utter horror.

Except for the ridge crest of the divine mountain, the entire sacred city has disappeared beneath the waves. Where there once was a vast wetland of villages, seaports, croplands, and trading routes, he sees nothing but filthy ocean. The vibrant sights, sounds, and exotic aromas of ships, markets, and children has been replaced by the heart-shattering slosh of waves and the stench of death. Even the sacred mountain has transformed into a desolate, ash-covered island. A whole nation has been swallowed from the earth. His heart implodes as tears track over the thick grime covering his tattooed face, while trembling hands clutch his jaguar cloak to fight the sudden cold. Agonizing grief even stifles his willingness to breathe.

"There's no one left to save," says his faithful servant Ghana.

"Why are we here?" growls a large oarsman. His thick arms fold in order to appear intimidating, if only to mask the fear in his eyes.

"Tell us the truth, shaman," shouts another.

He scans every eye and takes a deep breath. He cannot lie to men who have lost everything.

"We're out of food at the survivor camp." He confirms what they must already suspect. "The crops have burned, and the jungles are charred to the ground, barren of life." He points to fish floating on the water. "The rivers and oceans that once fed us with plenty now offer only death."

He gestures toward the second canoe traveling close alongside them. "I have asked my twin brother Xibalque to lead a team to find the temple maize stored in the caves above the ridge."

The sailor unfolds his arms, accepting the slim chances of finding maize as worth the high risk of death. Hun Hanahpu hesitates, unsure he wants to admit his personal motives for braving such peril.

"For myself alone, I vow to search for the Bac'tun Tae, the star calendar, and salvage what I can of the sacred ancestor scripts." He chokes down the shame of his confession.

Excited whispers spread. "You risked our lives for that cursed talisman," shouts the oarsman, once again defiant with his arms crossed.

Others also cast derision, claiming the ancient religion had failed them, the chief priests had failed them, and that he had failed them. Unable to erase the truth of their misery, Hun Hanahpu holds his tongue to endure the accusations. His elongated skull, once a symbol of pride and status, no longer holds any meaning; only survival matters now. When he has heard enough, he raises his right palm and then waits patiently for each man to return the gesture.

"Bolon-Yokte has torn open the sky and ripped out our very hearts while they still beat within us," he cries with a genuine lament, gritty tears staining his cloak. "We share the same agonizing pain."

A couple of men begin to weep, comforted by their companions.

"Our epoch has ended." His voice catches. "Our entire world has ended." The words pierce his heart like a searing lance. "And we are the cursed souls to bear witness to such horrors."

Survivors of the unimaginable, some of the men stare into the void with silent, bitter tears, while others pound their chests to drive out the inner acid of torment. Only one truth still binds them together.

"As long as two of us remain alive, they will call us brothers, and as long as we remain brothers, they will call us the Xi' of Matwiil," he shouts with deep emotion.

"We are Xi," they respond with a battered sense of identity.

Slowly, one by one, with each man committed to his purpose, they pick up their oar to row inside a small bay, once a busy seaport. Bile builds in the back of his throat from the smell of sulfur and decay that hangs in the damp, acidic air. Approaching the shore, a mournful vibration resonates within his chest and rings between his ears. Both canoes creep toward a shredded, singed tree sticking out of the shallow water near the shore.

Ghana grabs at the tree limb but then lurches backward, falling into the others with eyes wide. "It's alive."

As he grabs the branch, Hun Hanaphu senses a mild tingling emanate from its roots that resonates the mournful lament into a piercing pitch of a hundred thousand voices crying in unison, pulsating within his chest, tingling to his fingers and toes, echoing harshly between his ears, growing louder and deeper like a massive, swarming hive of human suffering.

He lets go of the branch and tosses the bowline around the limb to tie the canoe. Even without touching, he can still sense the abiding mournful chorus vibrate in the thick, choking air.

"What is that?" asks the oarsman, his eyes wide with fright.

For a long moment, no one answers. "Souls wailing in the anguish of *ba*, tormented death," whispers Ghana.

Hundreds of thousands of souls had vanished beneath the crusty rock and rancid sea. It's an unworldly, dreadful place of Xiba, the catacombs of the Xi'.

Overcome with waves of clammy chills, Hun Hanahpu's stomach tightens into a knot and then tightens again. Pale and dizzy, cold sweat beads down his face until he lurches over the rail of the canoe and vomits into the murky, rank water. When the spasms calm, he recalls the final passage of the ancient prophecy.

The earth will blacken before a terrible flood. Hurricane will make a great rain.

Witnessing a fulfillment of prophecy more horrendous than any man ever could have imagined, he prays for the courage to lead his frightened men. After he spits out the bitter residue, he wipes the putrid drool on his bare arm.

"Let's get going, while we still have light."

Chapter 1

A Cursed Legacy

Punta Gorda, Isla Roatan
June 15, 7:04 a.m. | 143 hours to Mayan chaa

The Garifuna call it *asandiruni*, a premonition, a déjà vu of some forgotten struggle pushing at the edge of our consciousness, or a *gubida* ancestor spirit whispering a secret wisdom into our dreams. No longer willing to give ground to such superstition, Sophia Martinez shakes off the lingering unease from last night's dream and races to catch up with the others; she's late.

She slips into the back of the agitated crowd as it moves away from the colonial First Macedonia Church and grips the hand of a childhood friend, silently reminding herself to be present in the current heartbreaking moment, not drawn back into the old traumas.

"How's the mood, Mona girl?" she whispers.

"Angry and hot, Sophie girl," retorts Mona. "The whole island be fed up with children dying."

7

In front of the *Dugu* procession, flowers cover a wooden coffin, spilling over to fill the bed of a 1980s Ford pickup. Sixteen-year-old Timothy Morales died of a fentanyl overdose last week, the thirteenth victim this year.

"I hear you, *mi' itu*," she agrees. "The heart can only break so many times."

"Ya, girl, and then it burns hot for justice," gripes Mona as her face contorts with tears.

Behind the pickup, Timothy's mother wails loudly, needing support from her family and friends just to keep walking. A local band plays traditional Garifuna percussion laments while the entire Punta Gorda community chant and dance to evoke their gubida ancestors for comfort. But Sophia no longer calls on her gubida or believes in other superstitious nonsense. Her spirit guides abandoned her long ago, leaving her to heal her own wounds, make her own way, and find her own truth. Orphaned as a child, any notion of a faithful ancestor carries a deep sense of betrayal.

"Somebody needs to do something before this plague destroys the island," she bemoans.

"You be somebody, girl," says Mona. "We all be somebody, but you know as I know dat many will mourn but few will rise up. We be Garifuna. We pray for strength to endure da pain."

Mona lets go of her hand to dance out her grief. "Endure with me, itu."

Encouraged by Mona, and driven by the drums, Sophia channels her own sorrow and rage until her petite, shapely frame gyrates with the powerful rhythms. Her amber blouse, blue jeans, and beloved red sneakers blur into a swirl of color. Beads of sweat roll through her pixie-cut hair until the salty taste of sweat and tears reaches her full lips.

The Dugu ends at the congested Colonial Era graveyard east of town, where testimonies, prayers, and singing will last for hours until the *Beluria* feast, which can last another day or two. With her respects paid, she kisses Mona on the cheek and slips back to her Jeep. The cruise ship will arrive soon, and she has one more stop.

Over the island crest road of Spanish cedar, mahogany, and fishtail palms, Sophia heads toward the pungently aromatic natural mango forest east of

Parrot Tree. The enormous canopy of big-leaf trees offer shade from the hot sun, allowing the intoxicating smell of rotting mango to hang in the air like a perfume so thick, she could eat it with a spoon. She inhales deeply to rejuvenate her spirit. When she notices the mango shack open up ahead, she impulsively skids to a stop. The stand owner has been sick for several weeks.

"Ya, Ms. Sally," Sophia says. "Good to see you feeling better."

The typically chatty old woman responds with a peaceful smile and a silent nod. Odd can be commonplace on Roatan, so Sophia mirrors the behavior with a grin. After paying extra for a couple of mangos, she blows the spiritual healer a kiss before climbing back into her Jeep.

"You will need to have faith, girl," Sally's voice whispers from right behind her ear.

Sophia snaps her head around, startled. The old shack looks empty. Stepping out of her Jeep, she checks behind the stand to see nothing, not even fruit. Sally must have ducked into the narrow jungle path, yet she sounded so close.

An icy chill slowly creeps down her spine. The only person ever to use that phrase was Sophia's Papá, Antonio. Then it strikes her like a bolt of lightning, the reason for her bizarre dream, and her emotional reaction at Dugu, and then Sally's odd comment—her Papá disappeared twenty years ago today. Maybe Sally wanted to honor him with his words, but even so, that was too eerie. The phrase unleashes a cascade of emotions and memories she's worked years to erase.

Determined to hold on to a more positive attitude, she pushes down the agitation and hits the gas pedal. A cruise ship will arrive soon, and she can't be late again. With a click, she cranks up the radio volume until Ziggy Marley buzzes over the worn-out speakers. Love is My Religion.

Sophia weaves through French Cay and Mahogany Bay toward the Port of Roatan. With a well-practiced zigzag through the crowded streets and back alleys of Coxen Hole, she skids to a stop outside Victoria's Café, owned by childhood friend Liz Beth McAllister.

"Ya, Liz Beth," she shouts, running into the café. "I'm running late, girl."

"Ya, itu," the large, busty black woman snorts, setting her usual latte and lemon scone on the counter. "You be late for your own weddin', girl."

A loving affirmation, considering Sophia isn't even dating. "Well, you know," she replies with a grin, "if he can't wait, he's only bait."

Both women break into laughter as Sophia dashes back to her double-parked Jeep. After taking a huge bite of scone and washing it down with a sip of café, she hesitates before pulling away.

At the end of the block, a stranger leans up against a wall smoking, with a tattoo on his neck, his cap worn backward, and baggy pants showing his shorts. His dark sunglasses follow the young girls wearing their swimsuits and sarongs. A drug dealer, maybe even the murderer who sold tainted fentanyl to Timothy. Once unthinkable on the island, death by drug overdose has become a parasitic plague, fed by the cash flow of tourism. Like many, she blames the police corruption of Captain Primo Boyles. Every business complains, but the problem only grows worse.

As if the devil could hear her thoughts, a local patrol car pulls around the corner. Aware of the watchful eye, she pulls away, pointing at the drug-dealing pervert. With a long slam on her horn, she gestures to the boy that she has her eyes on him. Startled back, the punk drops his cigarette, which scorches his shirt. His curses fade behind her as she heads to the port with a smug grin. She's only half Garifuna. Her Spanish half still has a temper.

A few minutes later, she skids into a parking space behind the Town Center Terminal, where an enormous Royal Caribbean cruise ship waits at the end of a long wharf. Hundreds of eager faces line the ship railings, while others wait below for the ship gangway to lower, anticipating the best diving, snorkeling, sport fishing, ziplines, and cantinas in the Caribbean. She finds it ironic how vacationers always experience the idyllic island lifestyle on a rushed urban schedule.

A faded sticker on the side of her Jeep reads Isla Roatan Tours. Over the past twelve years, she's built a small business as the leading cruise line tour coordinator for the Honduras Bay Islands. The last of her family namesake, her ancestors arrived on Roatan with a 1531 Spanish massacre of the indigenous people. Since then, a Martinez has played a key role in nearly every island saga.

No one personifies Roatan or its remarkable history better than Sophia does. Roatan flows through her veins, resonates in her sultry accent, shines in her mocha skin, and still whispers dark *asandiruni* in her dreams.

Turning off her engine, she pauses, surprised to feel the car still moving. Several hundred birds take to the air as palm trees swish and buildings sway. Frozen to her seat, she watches a corner of the Cruise Ship Town Center collapse, shooting a flying stone to hit the back of a running dockworker, knocking him to the ground. Sophia ducks as debris slams into her grill and other nearby cars, setting off alarms that add to the noise and turmoil. She lifts her gaze in time to watch the canvas awning of a nearby café pull away from the building to fall on top of early diners. Patrons scream as they hit the ground with the sound of shattering glass. The rumbling grows louder as stucco cracks and older wooden buildings rip apart.

Sophia grips the steering wheel so tight that her knuckles drain of blood while the Jeep bounces on the buckling pavement. An earthquake shakes the island in a terrible tantrum. Several people at the ship's railing take out video cameras to capture the unexpected excitement. To her utter astonishment, the ship gangway continues to lower as if they still plan to unload the tourists. The foolish, stubborn action triggers a more frightening thought.

"*Hijole*, oh my God, *Abuelita!*" she exclaims. The oldest, most bullheaded woman on the island lives in the oldest, most fragile building on the island—Sophia's home.

Turning over the engine, she bumps out of the bulging parking lot, past broken buildings and over rippled roads to race the thirty-two kilometers home. Efforts to call the house prove useless; there's no signal. With each kilometer, an anxiety grips her chest until she can barely breathe. Carmen came to live with Sophia after her mother died of cancer, only months after her father disappeared without a trace. She was eight and terrified. They've relied on each other ever since, even when they drive each other crazy, which is most of the time.

Turning onto a dirt road, Sophia hits the gas to climb the hill, skidding to a halt only inches from the old basalt wall. The historic Martinez cabana sits nestled under the shade of an enormous banyan tree high on a ridge with a terraced view of Punta Gorda to the north and the old pirate shantytown of Oakridge to the south.

Sophia exhales relief to see the front of the home look undamaged, until she spots the sagging roofline. Charging through the front door without thinking of the structural danger, she finds photographs, antiques, and seventeenth-century heirlooms scattered on the floor, many of them damaged. The stone fireplace and the kitchen have fallen outward, leading to a partial roof collapse.

"Abuelita, Abuelita," she calls out. "Where are you?"

"In da back," a frail gravelly voice replies in a thick accent. "Get out da house, girl."

Difficult to describe, Carmen's accent layers Jamaican with hints of Ivory Coast and old Spanish. Rapid and guttural in tone, she swallows her vowels, mumbles into her gums, and fluidly mixes English with Spanish and Garifuna. For outsiders, she's almost impossible to understand.

Sophia hurries down the hillside steps onto the terraced garden to find her Abuelita or little nana, Carmen Morales, covered in dust near a pile of salvaged dry and canned foods. Sophia leaps over the debris to embrace the diminutive old woman.

Not affectionate by nature, Carmen gives in with a patient pat. "My time be coming soon girl, but no today."

Sophia hates hearing that inevitable truth, even from a woman over a hundred years old. Still holding firmly onto Carmen, she turns to get her first real view of the damage, nervously running her fingers through her short hair out of habit.

Charcoal and brown basalt rock lies scattered across the terrace. Darkened lumber and sun-bleached roof tiles look like sticks and chips dropped over the ragged rubble. The fireplace has tumbled deep into the terrace garden as if trying to escape. A layer of black soot radiates out from the stone to sprinkle the grass and garden. Toward the driveway, the bedrooms appear undamaged, at least for now, but an aftershock could weaken the home further.

An enormous shudder of apprehension rolls through her shoulders, imagining the cost of repairs draining her meager savings. The sudden anxiety of losing her home tightens her gut. The crumbling stone cabana is all that remains of the five-hundred-year Martinez family island legacy. The thought of living anywhere else feels like acid eroding at her soul.

"Nah, don't worry, girl. A way will come to rebuild da house," Carmen reassures her as if reading her mind.

She gives Sophia a quick squeeze and then scuffles back to rummaging. A resilient old *buyei*, or spiritual teacher, Carmen has seen earthquakes, hurricanes, civil wars, famine, and lifetimes of tragedy.

"Da dead be dead, but da living gets hungry," Carmen repeats one of her many weird sayings with a wink. "Now go find da cooking pots," she says, pointing to a section of rubble.

"Dis be why a woman need *waguri*," complains Carmen. "What did you do to Emilio?"

Here comes the marriage talk again. Sophia sighs. "I didn't do anything to Emilio. I told you that we wanted different things. We're just friends now."

While not a Garifuna, Emilio shares many of Carmen's superstitions, a big reason why Carmen likes him, and a key reason why they no longer date. Sophia refuses to live under those outdated, misogynistic views of a woman's place, wanting to see herself as emancipated and enlightened, or at least on the path.

"Maybe you smell bad," says Carmen.

Sophia rolls her eyes. Carmen believes the longer a woman waits past age sixteen to marry, the more men treat her like fish sitting too long in the market. Sure, she would like a relationship, but only with the right man. Most of the men on the island are lazy, superstitious pirates looking for an easy road to nowhere. She's holding on to the hope of a spark, a little mystery, or perhaps even the improbable, a hero. Like her home, it's a crumbling hope.

After an hour of stacking dishes, bowls, pots, and pans, Sophia turns to the old fireplace. Under a pile of sooty basalt, she spots something unexpected, a crude limestone box with no markings. Scaling over the rubble, she reaches down for the heavy stone and slides off the top. The box contains a filthy

the connection to her discovery other than yet another unexplained family tragedy.

"This has nothing to do with Franco," she retorts. "I'm not giving up a chance to repair the family home because of a crazy old ghost story told by an even crazier old man." Sophia trembles, not in the habit of defying Carmen so directly.

Carmen turns with a profound sadness in her eyes. "I may be old," she mutters, "but I know what I know, an' I know da dead be coming for more dead until da *iñara* be destroyed."

The old buyei turns away to shuffle up the terrace steps toward a neighbor, one of her itu nu gossip sisters, leaving her circle unfinished. Carmen isn't telling her something. Abuelita has never trusted Rafé, and for good reason— the man is a raving lunatic. Yet her eyes showed a genuine fear when she spoke of the family curse and of Franco.

After losing both of her parents as a child, it was easy to believe in an angry spirit with a grudge. For years, she was afraid to even fall asleep. By her teens, the legacy became a vague, depressing cloud hovering over her life. Unrelenting fear kept her from taking chances until she withdrew deeper and deeper. As a young woman, she vowed to move beyond the baseless superstitions and overcome the worst of her own self-doubt. While she still struggles with good days and bad, she refuses to believe in curses, ghosts, or other shadows of ignorance, especially that absurd family legend. Bad choices, bad company, or bad timing, there's always a rational explanation for bad luck.

More than the money, if she can get an unbiased, historical assessment of the artifacts, then maybe she can dispel generations of mystery and stigma. Either way, Carmen will brood unless something is done to contain the unleashed evil. Sophia removes the items from the stone box to hide them in an old backpack kept in her Jeep. After replacing the lid, she puts the box in the middle of the cleansing circle. With a sprinkle of lighter fluid and a match, she sends a ring of black smoke into the sky, blown off by the growing breeze.

With any luck, Carmen will see the smoke as a sign of respect or maybe capitulation. Either way, the superstitious old buyei will avoid the box as long as it sits inside the circle of fire and ash. With any luck, the tactic will buy enough time to dispel this damnable legacy and find a buyer for her mysterious relics.

From an overhead banyan tree branch, a local stray cat named Ziggy flips his tail, watching. "Don't look at me like that." She frowns. "You know that woman is loco."

Chapter 2

Darkness of Dementia

Isla Barbareta, Honduras
June 15, 10:18 a.m.| 140 hours to Mayan chaa

C hico Lavoie whistles subconsciously while he tinkers on the engines of his flying oasis, a 1961 Grumman seaplane that has seen better days. Heavy corrosion on the fuselage blends into the red paint, now more of a sun-bleached rust orange. Black streaks trailing the engines testify to chronic oil burning, giving the plane a garish Halloween look. While she may not be pretty, she still floats, and flies, well, most of the time. The rest of the time, she's a perfect lagoon man cave.

Wiping oil from his hands, he lights up his bong, kept on the plane at the insistence of his wife, Mari. Still holding his breath, he reaches for a cold Pacifico from a scuffed-up cooler tied down with bungee cords. Chico learned to fly as a teen, when he joined the Honduras Air Force, but an accident left him with a medical discharge, a chronic limp, and an overgrown waistline. Without a valid pilot's license, he transports supplies between islands on the cheap. Raised by his father, Hector, he grew up on Isla Barbareta, a privately owned island several kilometers east of Roatan. Hector has been the island caretaker for the past sixty years. Chico doesn't make much money, but he pays no rent to live in paradise, an almost-perfect life. Almost.

The one screaming, insane exception to his tropical nirvana bolts from a dilapidated shack at the end of the cove to run down the beach toward his six children playing in the sand. Well, *run* isn't the right term; shuffling with an intent to go faster would be a better description. Rafé Martinez, the skinny, leather-tough, naked old goat screams warnings to flee the devil's fury. When he gets closer to the children, they squeal and giggle as they scatter in every direction. To them it's all a bizarre game. They accept the crazy, wrinkled old man who sometimes forgets to dress, as family.

"Simon," Rafé calls to Chico. "Cut the bridge. Hide the women. Set the traps," he shouts. "The dead come for more dead."

He looks more agitated than normal. Rumored to be over 112 years old, no one really knows, but Rafé has lived his entire life on Barbareta as an outcast.

Chico blows out his stinky breath with a cough. "Go put on some shorts, old man."

With the children still hiding and giggling, Rafé turns back toward the bluffs at the far end of the beach. When he gets there, he stops to look around, perplexed, as if uncertain where he is or how he got there. Slowly, he turns back toward his shack, ducking and swatting around his head as if a bird were attacking him, but there is none.

"Poor bastard," Chico mumbles. "Earthquake must've spooked him."

His chest vibrates from a flip phone in his shirt pocket. "Hola, Chico Air. We get it there because we care," he answers the call with his standard line, a funny irony given the condition of his plane and lack of insurance.

"Hi, Chico. Are you busy tomorrow?" Sophia's voice cuts in and out from a weak signal.

"Hey, Sophia," he greets. "I was just thinking about you." Rafé's last living relative, Sophia, still uses Chico Air on occasion, although much less these days.

"Let me check my schedule." He clicks mute for a moment and takes another sip of beer before clicking mute again. "*Si*, for you, I can move other jobs. Where are we going?" he asks, expecting the usual trip to Utila, where she manages tour operators.

"Belize," she replies. "Can you make it that far?"

"Belize?" he repeats. "Yeah, yeah, sure, I'll get fuel. Hey, girl, you need to come visit Rafé, like soon, okay?" He changes the subject.

When Sophia was young, she would visit Rafé often to fish or explore the cays. Her visits would always calm the old man down. As his dementia grew worse and her business expanded, the visits became less frequent.

"Why, what did he do now?" she asks.

"Hell, I don't even know where to start," Chico replies with a snort and takes a sip. "Maybe the earthquake shook something loose, but *el loco* is driving me to drink."

"Really, Chico, scapegoating Rafé for your drinking?" she replies.

"No, it's true. I'm drinking right now just watching his naked ass run down my beach." He takes another sip of beer. "Just come visit your uncle, okay, and bring new shorts."

"Pants again?" She sighs loudly. "Okay, fine, just meet me at sunrise."

After the call ends, he leans back in his seat to finish his beer and load another bong. *That was weird. Sophia never goes to Belize.*

Chapter 3

Deception (Engaño)

One man in a thousand years will rise from nameless obscurity to change the world. Emperor Chi, Cyrus of Persia, Alexander the Great, and Ghengis Khan each left a legacy of violent conquest, cultural rejuvination, and expansive empire. During the late fifteenth century, the Mayan prophet Chilam Balam foretold that after the Thirteenth Baktun, or December 21, 2012, would come a rebirth, a new epoch, and a new empire. Juan Perez de Menendez vows that it will be his empire to rise up.

As the chairman of media empire Evolucion, encompassing television, radio, online and traditional print, Juan Perez de Menendez exerts an incomparable influence over Latin American minds and hearts, and he intends to exert a share of that influence today.

Waiting for his meeting, he can't help but admire the Old World charm of Los Pinos, Mexico's Presidential Palace. More extensive than the White House grounds, Los Pinos retains the quaint elegance of a colonial age, destined to be replaced. In a full-length reception mirror encased in a 17th century gold frame, Juan admires his reflection. A fit man in his fifties, coiffed in a tailored suit, silk tie, and gold Rolex, which provides a perfect contrast to his burnished skin, dark eyes, strong jaw, and gray temples. Always a charmer, he casts a brilliant smile. His new look suits him. A year in isolation from cosmetic surgery will prove well worth the pain.

Double-wide layered mahogany doors with a polished brass plate reading *President of the United Mexican States* open with a soft whoosh. Director General Tomas Flores enters the room with the confident stride of a skillful politician, in tailored pinstripes and alligator shoes.

"Señor de Menendez, welcome to Los Pinos," Tomas greets as the two men shake hands.

"Director General Flores, good to see you again," he replies with a polite smile.

Patting the younger man on the arm, he grips the tender muscle in a subtle show of force. Slim and effeminate, Tomas winces before he forces a smile. In his early forties, politically astute, and articulate, Tomas boasts an unblemished reputation in the sleazy business of politics. Yet, Juan Perez knows a dirty secret. Behind the immaculate façade lies a Machiavellian traitor with a depraved appetite for boys. To this day, the politician remains unsure who owns the video evidence held over him or precisely why. The master Machiavellian has been outplayed by el diablo himself, tamed into a silent and cowardly submission.

"El Presidente will see you now." Tomas holds out his arm. "This way."

Escorted into the massive polished mahogany office, President Arturo Lanza rises from behind an enormous carved walnut desk to greet the influential tycoon, an old acquaintance from university days and elite social circles. Encouraged by his anonymous handler, Tomas had invited Juan Perez to help frame a compelling keynote for the Latin American Summit on Sustainable Growth (LASSG).

"Señor de Menendez, thank you for coming," says Lanza with a firm handshake.

"El Presidente, wonderful to see you again. You're looking well," he lies; the man looks stressed. "I trust you're looking forward to Cozumel."

In planning for over a year, the Cozumel event has evolved into an invitation-only occasion limited to presidents, prime ministers, generals, admirals, and senior business executives throughout Latin America. LASSG has become the pivotal occasion to attend if you are anyone of true importance or power, promoted as the Latin American equivalent of the Bilderberg meetings in Europe.

"To be honest, I grow concerned that Evolucion has hyped the event beyond what may be achievable," Lanza complains.

Politicians often fret over negative press. By oversetting expectations, Juan Perez has given himself the subtle advantage of a positive influence. In fact, the entire Evolucion media empire has promoted LASSG as the start of a new era in Latin American unity and prosperity. News stations publicize the event as a pivotal point for the entire continent. Morning radio programs discuss the economic impact, and even travel channels feature the unmatched paradise of Isla Cozumel, Cancun, and the Yucatan Riviera.

"Several leaders are wavering on attendance," says Lanza. "It would look bad, no desperate, for me to keynote a half-filled summit."

President Lanza has a lot on the line. Since the accusations of bribery came out during the El Chapo trial, his reputation for corruption has grown worse. The infamous war on drugs has cost over 250,000 lives since 2006, leaving both the people and the economy hemorrhaging. The Panama and Paradise Paper leaks continue to create wave after wave of investigations. Lanza needs a distraction, a way to pivot the public attention.

"El Presidente, your opportunity, I dare say your destiny, awaits you on Cozumel." Juan Perez whispers like it were a precious secret. "You must project the image of a world leader above the stain, moving forward to prepare a better future for the people." He lays out a perspective that has Lanza listening. "Cozumel will be a historic event, marking a new dawn for all of Latin America."

Tomas stands back with arms crossed, chin lowered, and his eyes locked on every facial expression of the president. Perhaps he admires watching a true master at work.

"What about the attendance?" Lanza pushes back again.

"Nonsense, they are merely seeking a motivation," he replies with a humble bow. "We will make a personal call to each hesitant leader, and together we will stress the critical importance of their voice during this historic event. We can emphasize the value of their image standing alongside other leaders. Then we will offer them what they want, influence over the media messaging within their own country."

Juan Perez knows four ways to manipulate a politician: donate big, create a positive photo op, discreetly bribe, or extort. An expert in all forms, he knows never to extort when you can just as easily pander.

"We should be honest," he warns. "Neither Evolucion nor history will be kind to those who decline."

"Excuse me, gentlemen," Tomas redirects. "The summit committee is waiting. Perhaps we can continue this conversation afterward over cigars and cognac."

Tomas opens the door into the executive briefing room, where a dozen senior staffers wait patiently. Tomas addresses the committee. "Ladies and gentlemen, we enjoy the honor to have El Presidente join us today with a special guest."

Polite applause follows the introduction as Tomas continues. "As you know, LASSG begins in four days. Today we will walk through the complete agenda and logistics, starting with General Panera for an update on security."

General Francisco Panera nods his enormous head, stands up to face the group, and clicks on a map of Isla Cozumel. A large man with a muscular barrel chest, Panera sports a massive black mustache that dominates the heavy wrinkles of his face, in sharp contrast to his crisp uniform.

"As you know, we chose Cozumel to ensure the absolute safety of Latin American leadership," he says. "Mexico and Brazil will share naval patrol against assault by sea. Mexican Air Force will patrol the skies while Colombian

Air Corps will support air traffic control. Lastly, Peruvian troops will back up Mexican security at all checkpoints."

As he speaks, the general uses a laser pointer to highlight locations on a map. "Every hotel or building within a half-kilometer perimeter will be swept."

"How will you handle the press?" asks Tomas.

"Excellent question," responds the general. "Every correspondent will be preapproved and go through multiple security screens. Access will be limited to specific social events or scheduled interviews and will require an escort when not in their rooms." Panera lays out a very strict format. "The entire island will remain on lockdown during the three days of the summit."

Perfect, thinks Juan Perez. The second day of the summit will be the summer solstice on June 21, called the *chaa* by the Maya. Various countries' leaders will host elaborate indigenous celebrations on the beaches, starting with a Ricky Iglesias concert the night before and building up to the moment of dawn. Evolucion will cover the concert and chaa ceremonies live.

"Well done, General, well done," President Lanza compliments.

"Ladies and gentlemen," Tomas interjects, "before we go into other logistics, I would like to introduce our special guest. Each of you knows Señor Juan Perez de Menendez, chairman of Evolucion. I have asked Señor de Menendez to share his vision for LASSG, which I believe you will appreciate." Tomas stands to initiate polite welcoming applause.

Juan Perez scans each eye in the room. With a humble bow of his head, he accepts the admiration. Several of these men and women have met him in the past. So far, none reacts to the subtle change in his appearance, so he enjoys the moment as a personal triumph. After enduring a series of painful reconstructive surgeries, he spent countless hours memorizing personal histories, watching videos, practicing speech patterns, relearning how to walk and laugh. He has emerged from his cocoon more magnificent than ever. Anyone can steal a digital identity, and a gifted actor can deliver a powerful performance, but it takes a true genius to usurp an entire empire.

"Today, my friends," he states with a warm smile and open palms, "we

Chapter 4

Worthless Fakes

Old French Harbor, Isla Roatan
June 16, 6:15 a.m. | 120 hours to Mayan chaa

D awn peeks over the Eastern Caribbean with a splash of tangerine that unrolls across the sky until it blends into burnt orange that gradually bleeds into dark gray at the southern horizon, where Hurricane Stephanie dominates the skyline. Sophia arrived at the dock early, hoping to avoid the peering eyes and lose lips of wildfire island gossip.

As promised, Chico and his rusted tin can wait at the end of the dock. She's flown with Chico her whole life, yet the past few years, boarding his plane produces a twinge of dread as if she's daring death. At the hatch door, Carmen's paranoia unexpectedly paralyzes her mid-step, preventing her from putting one foot in front of the other. A high-voltage panic attack jolts through her system on the fear that she's endangering Chico. Over her shoulder, she carries the backpack with the mysterious cursed relics. *Curses aren't real*, she tells herself, but her feet won't move, and she can't seem to exhale. The panic deepens.

Staring at her from his seat, Chico blows his stinky weed breath out of the cockpit window and cranks the clamorous, smoking engines to life. The deafening noise and smelly smoke shakes off her momentary paralysis. With a deep breath and a quick step on board, she closes the hatch and takes her seat as copilot. Three deep breaths later, she slowly opens her eyes.

"You okay?" Chico stares at her with a worried expression.

"I'm fine," she responds, turning away her eyes. "How's Rafé?"

Chico pulls the seaplane away from the dock, nudging the throttle until the old engines groan with a rumbling roar that sounds like they could explode any second. Sophia braces as the plane skims over the water until the wings lift into the oncoming wind and she lets out a sigh of relief.

"I've never seen him so bad," Chico yells over the noise. "He was up all night chanting."

"Chanting?" she repeats.

"I don't know what else to call it," Chico clarifies. "The old goat sounds like a dying toad." He banks the plane northwest. "So, why are we going to Belize?"

"Supplies to rebuild." She tells him the truth, but not the whole truth, unsure what she wants him to know until she knows more herself, and even then, she prefers to keep family secrets private.

"Yeah, sorry to hear the news," he shouts.

With a glance over the side of the plane, Sophia struggles with Carmen's ominous warnings. It would be easy enough to drop the entire bag of relics over the water to sink them in the deep as Carmen insisted, but that would be a surrender to superstition over knowledge and allow fear to defeat hope. Her questions would forever stay unanswered, and she'd never learn the truth behind generations of a dark legacy. As the last of the family namesake, she may be the last chance to remove the stigma. Then she thinks of Sally's reminder to have faith and her need to rebuild. *The dead be dead, but the living need a place to live*, she thinks to herself, mocking Carmen.

With renewed resolve, she stuffs her bag under the seat and grips the armrest as turbulence jostles the plane. Pushed by tailwinds, they soon land in the Bay of Campeche. Anxious to escape the rattling, smoking beast, Sophia scurries to find the main street and hail a cab.

*

Museum of Belize, Belize
June 16, 7:25 a.m. | 119 hours to Mayan chaa

A brass plaque at the entrance explains that the British built the Belize Museum in 1857 as a prison when both Belize and Roatan were under British colonial rule. Sophia lifts her gaze up to the massive iron gates with anticipation, takes a deep breath, and then follows the entrance until it opens onto a two-hundred-meter-long central courtyard enclosed by two-story colonial brick buildings with guard towers.

Early for her appointment, she visits the permanent Mayan and Olmec collection on the second floor. It doesn't take long before the Buena Vista Vase, discovered in the caves of Altun Ha, captures her attention. Admiring the exquisite artistry of one of the oldest artifacts ever found, the design features the mythical Hero Twins, Hun Hanahpu, and his brother Xibalque, dancing over Hun Came, the Lord of Xibalba. One of the Hero Twins holds a blade shaped exactly like hers, which feeds her hope that she may have found the repair money.

"You must be Señorita Martinez," a voice intrudes, holding out his palm. "I'm Dr. Ricardo Colon, the museum curator for pre-Columbian antiquities."

Engrossed in the mask, she hadn't noticed the middle-aged man approach. A trim of gray hair around his ears, a tad shorter than Sophia, he wears a silk tunic, Italian shoes, and a costly Breitling wristwatch.

"I am." She smiles, accepting his hand. "Thank you for agreeing to meet with me."

With a condescending scan to her red sneakers, blue jeans, and mint-green cotton blouse, he turns. "Of course, this way please."

After a quick, self-conscious check of her breast and clothing, she follows him into a small, crowded office packed with boxes and artifacts. Glass walls face the corridor with vertical blinds that remain partly open. Closing the door, he takes a seat behind the desk, holding out a palm for Sophia to sit. Pictures of Dr. Colon with various politicians and celebrities cover the rear wall behind him. He clears a space in the middle of his desk with a light and a magnifying glass.

"Señorita Martinez, you spoke of a green obsidian dagger," he begins. "The only known ancient mines for green obsidian are near Teotihuacan, Mexico." His tone sounds skeptical.

"Yes, I found several things inside a stone box that was hidden inside a basalt wall built in 1811," she clarifies.

She places several color printouts on his desk, photographed with her cell phone, magnified, and printed in eight-by-ten profile.

"You didn't bring the items with you," Dr. Colon says. "I can't help you." He pushes the printouts back with a disdainful look.

Sophia leans back in her chair, disappointed and embarrassed. "Transporting antiquities across borders is illegal. I hear stories of corrupt customs agents and museum directors who confiscate items and then sell them on the black market." She bluffs, knowing her backpack sits under the copilot seat on Chico's plane. As an orphan, she learned intuitively to distrust strangers.

"If you're not interested, I'll keep my appointment in Cancun tomorrow," she lies, with no other appointments planned. "Thank you for your time." She stands to leave, afraid for a heartbeat that he won't take the bait, and a little ashamed at her manipulation.

"Wait, please, sit," he exhales in a huff. "I'll give you a generalized opinion based on an inadequate examination."

The curator takes back the photos and lines them up in the center of his desk to examine only one at a time. She glances up to notice a camera above the spot and two more cameras in the ceiling corners. He's taping the meeting and her images. She shrugs it off as museum security, but something about this man gives her the creeps.

"What's this?" he asks.

"The stone box I found with the relics," she explains.

Without comment, he tosses the paper in her direction and then scans the next image.

"Looks like a sixteenth-century compass in a damaged hexagonal casing. Worth ten thousand pesos in a curio shop," he dismisses, tossing the photo at her to examine the next one in the stack.

Her jaw clenches from his arrogance and condescension.

"Looks like a leather book, badly damaged and filthy. Pages appear to be covered with something, but hard to tell what," he postulates, squinting at the image under the magnifying glass.

"Blood," she says. "Someone covered the pages in blood."

After Carmen fell asleep last night, she examined the items by candlelight, especially the macabre book. Someone had smeared the pages with blood and then etched over the blood. Writing covers every edge, with some text written upside down or backward. To a superstitious mind, it would seem creepy, cursed even.

The curator grimaces. "How do you know?"

She hesitates. "Family folklore," she says, omitting any mention of curses, spirits, or lost caverns.

He grunts. "Have you read the book? Who is the author? What does it say?"

"It's written in Spanish, I think, but very hard to read," she admits.

He grunts again, tossing the paper and moving to the next image. The curator takes much more time to study the tortoise shell with its odd symbols, placing the photo under the illuminated magnifying glass.

"These markings are not Mayan," he notes with curiosity. "Do you still have this shell?" He looks her in the eyes.

"Yes, of course," she replies. "What is it? What does it say?" She has a few questions of her own.

The curator leans back in his chair to take a deep breath, tapping his fingers on the desk. Placing the image of the shell to the side, he doesn't answer the question, raising her suspicions.

"Ah, the dagger," he says with wide eyes.

Even as an image, the object has a timeless artistry, featuring a slight

S-shaped double crescent with one side the handle. The etched design of the handle is polished smooth, as if worked for a generation, with inlaid blue jade in a stylized serpent motif or glyph. Green translucent volcanic glass looks sharp with dried blood still visible.

"Could be pre-Olmec," he mumbles. "The blue jade inlay looks Guatemalan." His eyes narrow. "Tell me about your family legend. How were these hidden?"

While he waits for her answer, he reexamines the tortoise shell image.

"With all due respect," she replies, "I'm here to learn reliable facts from you, not dwell on unreliable island folklore."

Dr. Colon sits back, folding his arms. "I insist. It may offer clues to their origins."

With a sigh, she selects her words carefully. "An ancestor discovered a sea cave in the early eighteenth century. Within the caverns, he found these artifacts near the bones of a Spaniard. After taking the artifacts, he hid the entrance to the cave. A hundred years later, another ancestor hid the relics in a wall. Now I'm trying to learn their origins and perhaps why they were hidden."

Dr. Colon draws the hint of a smirk as he leans forward. "Where do you live again?"

Sophia hesitates, distrusting him more with each breath, unsure exactly why. "Isla Roatan."

His smirk widens. "Who else has seen these?" he inquires, looking at the dagger image.

"Just family; you're my first of three museum stops." She lies again. She had hoped to learn a history or value, but so far, she's learned nothing. Even worse, he's lying to her or holding back. She's unsure if she should be angry, insulted, or worried. He takes a long time reexamining the dagger image.

"I can bring the items back," she offers. She wants him to be interested; needs him to be interested.

"That won't be necessary," he states. "I have no interest. Without providence, it would be impossible to confirm their authenticity."

He hands back the photos and stands to open the door.

"I don't understand," she protests, confused by his answer.

"They're worthless fakes," he responds with a sneer, "created to support a hoax like your mysterious family legend. You have no providence."

"Why would someone hide fakes in a wall?" she objects.

Upset by her tenacity, he raises his voice for others to hear. "I'm sorry Señorita, I don't consider your artifacts authentic. I must ask you to leave at once." He stands by the open door with an air of condescension.

Sophia stands to leave, staring him down as she exits. Without another word, he closes the door behind her. Stunned and baffled, she stands in the hall, trying to understand what just happened. Peeking through the slim blinds of his glass wall, she notes his printer roll out the images taken from the ceiling camera. He pulls up his smartphone, comparing the dagger image to something on the phone, but she can't tell what. When someone turns the corner down the hall, she has no choice but to move on.

Back on the street, she shudders to purge his negativity. "Smug little *pendejo*."

She can always try another museum, but that could take weeks or longer to fit into her tight schedule, not to mention the expense. Dr. Colon left her with more questions than answers and more of a sense of shame than redemption. *A hoax, he called them a hoax.* She feels humiliated. She's lived her whole life under a cursed stigma, a shadow that the family blamed for every misfortune or bad choice, only to learn it was likely a hoax. While a part of her wants to accept his discouraging explanation, it doesn't feel right. Why would Papá abandon her over a hoax?

Disheartened, and with few options, she hails a taxi. She needs to shop for roofing supplies using the last of her meager savings. Not the outcome she had anticipated, she takes a deep breath, and wills herself to endure like a good Garifuna.

Chapter 5

Speak of the Dead

Belize Harbor, Belize
June 16, 9:44 a.m. | 117 hours to Mayan chaa

The trip to Belize was one of the bumpiest Chico can remember, and the flight home against the coming storm will be even worse. After a few hours of refueling, checking oil, and inspecting the engine, supplies begin to arrive on an open flatbed truck. Choosing only the lightest items, he carefully distributes the weight, tying down the cargo with surplus military netting, and then sending the remaining supplies to the next cargo ferry that leaves for Roatan in a week.

With the deliverymen gone, he wedges into the pilot seat, lights up a bong, and opens a Pacifico. The tinny voice of Bob Marley's "Don't Worry" squeaks through the frazzled speakers. Minutes later, just as he begins to relax, Sophia storms on board the plane without a greeting, locks the hatch door, and drops into her seat, despondent.

"Okay, let's get this rusted junk in the air," she gripes. "Hey, wait, where's the rest?"

He blows his breath out of the cockpit window, ignoring her hurtful insult.

"On the next container ferry for delivery next week," he responds. "I have a weight limit, and we have a head wind." He primes the engines until they blast to life with a rumbling, popping growl. Sophia steams for a moment and then drops it.

"How did it go?" he shouts above the noise.

"I got a reality check," she replies.

He takes the hint, construction can be discouraging, but senses it could be more. Sophia has flown with him since childhood, often giggling, yet the woman next to him looks afraid, nervous, holding tight to the lumpy seat with white knuckles. There must be something else.

Outside the channel, Chico pushes the throttle until the fuselage slams hard against the choppy swells, rattling the frame. The extra weight may be too much for the old bird. Not gaining altitude, his plane can't take much more battering, yet the iron buoy directly ahead poses the greater danger. Pressing hard with his feet, he strains his back to pull the yolk with a long, loud grunt until they creep into the air only feet above the channel marker.

Sophia lets out a loud breath as Chico chuckles nervously, afraid to think of how close he came to leaving his family fatherless. He reaches for a sip of his beer to celebrate, but the celebration doesn't last long as the heavy winds that had chased them to Belize now ram against him on the way home.

"Chico, before we go back to French Harbor, I should stop to check on Rafé," shouts Sophia.

"Hey, that's great news," he shouts back with a smile. "He'll be glad to see you."

"You sure?" She raises an eyebrow. "The last time I visited, he called me Isabella."

"He calls me Simon half the time." Chico chuckles at his own joke, but Sophia doesn't laugh with him. Maybe the damage to the family home stirred up more than money problems. As if reading his mind, she changes the subject.

"How well did you know Papá?" she asks with a slight tremble in her voice.

Surprised, he hesitates. "We were close friends, like brothers."

"How did he die?" she asks.

He takes another sip of his now-warm beer, wishing he could relight his bong instead, uncomfortable with the sensitive topic. "You know," he sputters, "some say he drowned or was dragged to sea. Others say the sharks got him." He tries to change the subject. "Hey, when will the cruise ship return?"

He doesn't want to dig up the painful details of Antonio's death. Both Antonio and Rafé went missing, but only Rafé came home. The search expanded, and volunteers even showed up from the mainland. While some of them were looking for Antonio, others were after the legends of family treasure. No one told poor little Sophia that part. As far as she knew, the whole world was there to find her padre.

"Why does Carmen link his death to the family curse?" she asks.

He takes his final swig, tossing the empty bottle out the window. "Hell, I don't know," he retorts. "Something about revenge of a ghost, or a buried secret, but I never understood the story."

He lies. Antonio was obsessed with the family legend, convinced there was a secret treasure guarded by an evil spirit somewhere on Isla Barbareta. When they were young, he and Antonio used to explore the island, looking for the entrance, but never found it.

"You mean the ridiculous ghost story Rafé told me as a girl?" Sophia casts him a doubtful look. "Come on, Chico, you sound like Carmen. I'm looking for real answers here."

He shrugs, unsure what else to say. Rafé and Antonio both believed in the curse. Chico has never had a reason to doubt them.

"Why was Rafé accused of killing Papá?" She turns in her seat to face him.

"Who told you that?" He's seen Sophia depressed and withdrawn, but never so inquisitive. No one has spoken of that particular rumor in years. He reaches for another beer, but she stops him.

"It doesn't matter. I'm asking you. Why did they suspect Rafé?" she demands.

He groans, not wanting to tell her the story, yet he always knew she would ask someday. With a loud exhale, he grips his sweaty palms around the yoke. "Two days before they disappeared, Antonio and Rafé were in Coxen Hole, buying supplies. I mean, weird gear like long ropes, light sticks, clamps, iron pegs, you know, stuff like that. When they paid with a gold doubloon, the island rumors spread like a wildfire, I mean like blazing."

"A doubloon?" asks Sophia.

"Yeah, I know, right?" he agrees. "They said they were exploring."

He shifts in his seat, stretches his neck, and feels his shoulders tighten from stress. Sudden turbulence batters the nose sharply downward, forcing him to fight to regain altitude. Sophia jostles in her seat and ties her broken belt straps.

"Exploring where?" she insists.

"They wouldn't say, but the night before they disappeared, Antonio and Rafé stayed up drinking, so Papá and I joined them. Antonio got drunk and may have said too much." Chico confesses something he never told the police.

"What'd he say?" she asks.

"That he found the secret without the key," he responds.

"A key to what secret?" She wonders aloud.

"I asked the same thing, but Rafé cut him off," he replies. "Next morning, they were both gone before dawn. Rafé returned three days later in the middle of the night, soaking wet, disoriented, and covered in blood, blabbering like a maniac about the abyss. The search for Antonio lasted another two weeks, but we found nothing."

Memories flood back as if it all happened yesterday, the loss of a good friend, the turmoil of the search, a conflict with intruders, and the shame of failure. Another sharp patch of turbulence masks a shudder passing through him.

"You didn't answer my question," pushes Sophia. "Why do people say Rafé killed Papá?"

Chico hesitates, biting his lower lip. "Rafé was the last person to see Antonio alive," he pauses. "And because the blood on his clothes was not his own blood."

Thankfully, Sophia hands him a beer and sits back to stare out the window, lost in her own gloom. He fights the turbulence and the dredged-up guilt and regret of a lifetime ago in the awkward silence.

Chapter 6

Priceless Omen (*Tamax Chiʾ*)

Cenote Cocodrillo, Isla Cozumel
June 16, 2:15 p.m. | 112 hours to Mayan chaa

Careful to stay on the reinforced planking, Juan Perez steps inside the semidry sinkhole connected to an unexplored section of the enormous Cenote Cocodrillo. Cenotes are underground limestone river caverns that interconnect for thousands of miles under the Yucatan peninsula, reefs, and islands. The known Cocodrillo Cenote measures 3,342 meters starting at a southeastern reef, yet he stands within a new and unknown section.

"Señor de Menendez, I've made a once-in-a-lifetime discovery," declares Dr. Petrie Gerhard with his thick French accent, and still wearing his wetsuit.

A fugitive of Interpol, the nerdy Frenchman has developed a vast Latin American network of looters and corrupt museum directors. A rural Cozumel landowner recently found a new sinkhole on his property and made the fatal mistake of notifying someone in Gerhard's network.

"Why am I here?" demands Juan Perez.

"Allow me explain. During 1566, Fray Juan Pizzaro wrote of an Inquisition discovery within a lost cenote on Cozumel near the Temple of Ixchel. Normally, the Mayans built temples over cenotes to reflect the ancient myth of a sacred mountain over a natural spring leading to the underworld of Xibalba. Very few temples were built within a cenote itself," explains Gerhard, pushing his thick glasses up his thin nose.

"What did you find?" asks Juan Perez more forcefully.

"The tomb of the creator," replies Gerhard, his voice quivering as he hands over a small, stone stelae with a glyph. "Kukulkan, or as known by the Aztecs, Q'uq'umatz."

Juan's heart skips a beat. An obsessive collector, he has amassed thousands of priceless artifacts from across the continent that fill a private museum. Passionate about pre-Columbian empires, he would normally consider such a discovery to be incredibly good fortune, but these are not ordinary times. Within days, the military will descend on Cozumel, and there will be no time to excavate the tomb. Besides, if the Inquisition found the tomb, then little of value would likely remain.

"There's more," says Gerhard. "According to Fray Pizzaro, the Mestizos were looking for the lost library of Chilam Balam, and reportedly took thousands of ancient idols and scripts before massacring the local village. But their horde never made it to Merida because their ship was lost in a hurricane and never seen again."

A student of the prophecies of Chilam Balam, Juan Perez senses his pulse quicken. If the items never reached the Bishop of Yucatan, then they were not destroyed by the fires of the Inquisition. Yet, as Gerhard noted, they were lost. "Get to the point."

The archaeologist reaches for his phone to show several images.

"A ceremonial dagger with the same glyph and one of the ancient scripts came into my network this morning in Belize," Gerhard explains. "Quite fortuitous timing. Without the stelae, I would not have been able to confirm the source, but they are the same."

Intrigued, Juan Perez absorbs the images. Fortuitous timing indeed, the ceremonial dagger of the creator would be priceless, the sacred obsidian blade of a mythical god. Elegant and clean, the dagger shows a sense of eternal purpose. So close to the chaa the timing must be an omen of unequaled significance, a confirmation of his destiny.

"Tell me about the owner," Juan inquires flatly to hide his excitement.

"A single woman who lives on Roatan," says Gerhard. "I checked with our police contact Boyles, and she lives with an elderly woman in a derelict cabana with no security. An easy target," Gerhard teases. "But there's a twist."

"What twist?" he asks.

"Do you recall twenty years ago, when I investigated the legend of a cursed family treasure on Roatan?" Gerhard reminds him of the incident.

"I recall you found nothing, and one of my men died," he snaps. "What's your point?"

"It's the same family," Gerhard replies. "The daughter of the missing man found the dagger hidden with a journal. I'm thinking," he pauses, "maybe the book could have a clue to the treasure."

"Rubbish folklore, Doctor. Only the blade of the maker matters; the blade is the treasure," insists Juan Perez, dismissing the sideshow distraction.

To buy such a rare relic would require weeks of lawyers, negotiations, and banks. The business model developed by Gerhard has a touch of brilliance. The Frenchman gets a tip from his network of corrupt museums and black-market dealers. The tipster sends an address with security details, which may include a payoff to local police. Juan deposits funds into a Cayman account. A mercenary team secures the item by stealth or force, if necessary. The museum or tipster has no traceable ownership on record, a smooth operation.

"Who else knows about this hole?" he asks, changing the subject, pointing to the cenote.

"Besides the landowner that Shay needlessly shot, no one," retorts Gerhard.

At the mention of his name, the large, shaved head of Shay Golan rises up and pivots toward the nerdy archaeologist with a snarl. Gerhard and Golan hate each other. Shay couldn't care less about temples, and Gerhard sees Golan as a dimwitted savage.

A huge man, the bastard son of a Syrian antiquities' smuggler and his Somali whore, but trained by Hezbollah, Shay Golan commands his most successful relic-recovery team. Sweaty and filthy, the Syrian lowers a three-meter-long watertight container onto a motorized water sled within the cenote. Nearby, divers set up for a rebreather-gear dive that should give them up to five hours underwater.

"I found an unopened sarcophagus three meters underwater, built before the oceans rose, which makes the temple at least nine thousand years old," Gerhard continues to babble.

"Did you finish the sonar readings? How deep is it? Where does it end?" Juan Perez interrupts him. The only reason he approved this project was access to the cenote range.

Gerhard nods. "Readings indicate the cenote extends at least ten kilometers and may even interconnect to the mainland at Tulum."

He can hardly believe his good fortune, an inspired improvement over the original plan.

Giving the doctor a wary look, Shay steps in front of Gerhard to face Juan Perez and lowers his voice to a throaty whisper. "Bury Buluc Chabtan now, and clean the site," he warns in his thick Syrian accent.

"Don't dare presume to instruct me," Juan Perez hisses, forcing Shay to back off, his head lowered.

"You have forty-eight hours to find the death mask," he tells Gerhard.

Shock and disappointment washes over the archaeologist's face, as if the greedy fool seems oblivious to his ultimate fate; he just got a forty-eight-hour reason to live.

He turns to Golan. "Send a team to Roatan tonight," he orders. "Find the woman, and bring back my blade."

Ruthless and without a conscience, Shay nods his acceptance of the mission. "I'll go myself."

With a glance to the dive team well underway, he turns to climb the ladder with Shay behind him like a guard dog.

"Wonderful news, Dr. Gerhard, but attract any local attention, and I'll bury you with the tomb," Juan Perez calls back over his shoulder.

Within moments, the high-speed luxury Sikorsky S92 helicopter lifts above the jungle clearing and banks toward the ocean. He pours a shot of tequila and throws it back. Plans are proceeding even better than expected, as if his acension were indeed part of the prophecy. Just as Chilam Balam had foreseen the arrival of Hernán Cortes in the last epoch, the prophet saw his arrival for the coming epoch.

Chapter 7

Locura de Loco

Isla Barbareta, Honduras
June 16, 2:34 p.m. | 112 hours to Mayan chaa

Sophia grips the rail, propping her feet against the console, the terror of a violent death saturating every taut muscle. After a long, turbulent flight, Chico's rattling albatross descends into the large inner lagoon of Isla Barbareta. Approaching low, they skim over coral reefs until it clears, then they hit the water hard, jolting her forward and shaking the fuselage furiously. Slowing quickly from the extra weight, they drag a trail of black smoke into the pristine lagoon. She opens the cockpit door as the shallow draft plane moves into position close to shore.

Chico cuts the engines, drops the anchor, and breathes a deep sigh of relief with an involuntary chuckle. "Bumpy flight, huh?"

On the beach, dressed in soiled shorts and a tank top, Rafé sharpens his fishing knives with dark, weathered skin sagging over his bones. When he sees Sophia in the cockpit, he drops his knife to wave his arms wildly. "No, no, go away!" he shouts. "Dead come for more dead. Sophia, go away, go away!"

Hearing the same macabre phrase that Carmen used yesterday makes the hairs on her neck rise up. With a hard swallow, she ignores the sensation. Turning to Chico, she smiles. "Well, at least he knows who I am today."

Chico winces. "You sure you want to do this?"

She stares at the wrinkled lunatic acting like a weathered, windsock scarecrow. There may be secrets locked deep inside his cobweb of nonsense. Not satisfied with the idea of a hoax, and still desperate for real answers, she's even willing to consider a few crazy ones. With her curiosity aroused and her eyebrows furrowed, she picks up the backpack.

"No, I'm not sure," she confesses. "But I am determined. Let's go poke *el loco* and listen to the *locura* that spits out."

Chico pulls out his bong from a side panel. "You go ahead." He loads the bowl. "I live *locura de loco*."

*

Isla Barbareta
June 16, 4:04 p.m. | 110 hours to Mayan chaa

It takes Sophia hours to calm Rafé enough to focus even a little. She can't remember ever seeing him so agitated, tearing her heart to pieces. Rafé had always been her connection to Papá, her link to being a Martinez, and now she's losing him too.

Laying the artifacts on the sand, she hopes he might recognize one of them. Although it's a longshot, she doesn't have many shots left.

"Rafé, focus," she directs. "I found these in the stone wall Montego built. Why were they hidden?"

His eyes widen as he stalks the items until he backs away, suspicious.

"Rafé, why did Montego hide these in a wall?" she asks again.

Rafé walks in a circle, softly snapping his fingers, twitching his neck. "To keep a secret."

"What secret?" Sophia asks. "A secret to the key?" She remembers the comment mentioned by Chico that didn't make any sense.

"No." his eyes grow wider. "A secret to the grave," he moans, walking away then compulsively turning back again, pacing in the same sand circle. The conversation spirals, trying to pin down who's grave.

Holding up the tortoise shell with symbols she asks, "Rafé, have you ever seen these?"

Placing it in his hand, he quickly gives it, back nodding with a scowl. "On the wall."

"Yes, I found them in the wall," she repeats. "Why were they hidden?"

Rafé shakes his head. "On the wall to desolation."

Twitching his neck and rolling his eyes, he fixates on the journal before snatching the book, carefully thumbing through the pages. Rafé can't read, so she's not surprised when he tosses the book back to the sand with a scowl and returns to his circular track.

"Do you know that book?" she asks.

For a flash, it appears that he understands her question and struggles for the right words. "A testament of hades," he whispers with a haunted look in his eye.

His response shudders her with an unexplainable icy chill. Unsure how to interpret his macabre answers, she changes the subject.

"Rafé, what happened to Papá?" she pleads. "Tell me the truth."

Shaking his head, unwilling to talk, he turns away with a growl, hunkering his shoulders.

"Rafé, I won't get mad. Tell me the truth," she asks again. "What happened to Antonio?"

"Antonio, Antonio," Rafé starts to weep and shudder. "Such a dark despair." With a growl, he shuffles away.

She's lost him. After hours of wrestling with his incoherent answers, she slowly accepts the museum theory of a family hoax, or worse, a hoax fed by generations of dementia. Perhaps family dementia is the true curse of the Martinez, a cursed fate she may one day unwillingly inherit.

Fatigued with trying to make sense of Rafé's locura, she takes a walk to calm her agitated nerves. Troubled over his worsening condition, and no closer to any real answers than when she started, she looks for a positive point of view. Even if the items are fake, she can still sell them to a tourist curio shop, although for much less money than she had hoped to earn. Even if the whole family legend were a hoax, at least that's a more rational explanation than a curse.

Still uneasy with Carmen's irrational superstition, she hides the backpack in a nearby dry rock crevice, where her childhood diary still waits inside a zip-top bag within a now-rusted Little Mermaid lunchbox. Secrets that she never shared, and maybe wounds that never healed, locked away. The relics will be safe here until she finds a buyer.

By the time she returns, she finds Rafé snoring loudly in his hammock. On his cluttered table of old food, fishing gear, canoe anchors, and pepper-spray cans, she finds a crumpled piece of yellowed paper with scratches that like look like the shell symbols. Strange, in all of her visits to Rafé's hut, she's never seen this odd piece of paper. As Rafé continues to snore, she desperately wants to reach inside his head to unlock his lost memories. Leaving the yellowed paper on the table, she sets down the new swim trunks and lets the ancient uncle sleep.

Any hope of solving the family mystery has evaporated, and she's still unsure how to pay for the rest of the roof. She had hoped that new information would ease the pain of growing up the orphaned daughter of a cursed family, but the box of junk has offered no explanation for generations of tragedy. She needs to put this morbid distraction behind her. The cruise ship will return tomorrow.

After a short chat with Mari, a brief game of tag with the kids, and a promise to visit more often, Chico flies her home to French Harbor. She'd spent far more time than expected on Barbareta, when she should have been home helping to prepare for the crane. Last night during the burial feast, she shamelessly played on Emilio's lingering feelings for her to gain his assistance with the crane team. She neglected to mention that she would be in Belize half the day, now the entire day. She'll have some serious groveling to do. Only instead of the vindication of historical truth she had hoped would justify her deceit, she returns with the shame of a generations-long insanity-fed hoax.

Martinez Family Home, Isla Roatan
June 16, 8:01 p.m. | 106 hours to Mayan chaa

By the time Sophia pulls back into her driveway, the industrial crane crew has already packed up to leave the site before the coming storm hits. Hurricane Stephanie churns a few hundred kilometers to the south, stirring up trouble. As the rumble of the heavy diesel falls down the hill, she steps onto the terrace to receive sharp, cold glares from both Carmen and Emilio.

Filthy and exhausted, sweat glistens off Emilio's shaved head, dripping off his scraggy blond beard. Sooty grime coats his bare chest as evidence of his promise kept, despite her lies. Awash with guilt over deceiving a friend to chase after a hoax, her stomach tightens.

"I'm so, so sorry. I forgot to tell you that Chico agreed to fly me to Belize for roof supplies," she explains. "The first delivery will arrive tomorrow."

Neither responds, turning their back on her, continuing to work, giving her the cold shoulder. A classic Carmen move she actually deserves this time.

"Then, on the way home, Chico mentioned that Rafé had a bad reaction to the quake, so I stopped to check on him. Wow, I've never seen him so agitated," she plays the sympathy card.

Emilio continues to work in silence, avoiding eye contact as Carmen lifts her head to glare suspiciously. Disgrace churns her stomach. Instead of finding answers, she came home more confused and distressed. Putting on her best smile, she steps over to give Emilio a long hug, knowing his grunge will ruin yet another blouse.

"Thank you so much, Emi. I owe you big time." She gives him a kiss on a dirty cheek. "Let's talk about promoting the dive festival next month." She attempts to buy his absolution with a tease of extra business.

He averts his eyes, still angry or perhaps disappointed by her obvious ploy. "Yeah sure, anytime."

Emilio had collected stones by size, organized wood into reusable or firewood only, and then stacked roof shingles. Instead of random chaos, the hillside terrace looks like a well-organized construction site, ready to rebuild. Emilio even revived the cleansing circle fire for Carmen, the flame once again smoldering down to ashes. *A good man*, she thinks. Maybe *waguri* would be a good thing for her. Then again, if she doesn't love him, would it be fair to either of them in the end? She circles a lap around the same unending argument where no one wins and she ends up alone.

A crack of thunder jolts her nerves and ushers in a sudden gust of wind before the sky opens into a downpour. "*Prisa*," she shouts. "Everybody in the tent." She had set up a temporary tent yesterday under the banyan tree.

Breaking into a run for the steps, Sophia unexpectedly slams into three commandos who violently shove her backward onto a pile of roof tiles as they charge down onto the terrace.

"Where are the relics, where is the dagger?" demands a large barrel-chested mercenary with a thick foreign accent, his targeting laser dancing on her stained blouse. "Now!" he shouts.

Her mind freezes, thinking the relics are fakes and they aren't even here, but her quivering lips won't speak. As she stalls, a bright flash of lightning exposes Carmen scurry to the cleansing circle and strain to lift a nearby rock. Defiant in spirit, her old arms tremble from the weight.

"*Asuera da inaruni y amuru*," she shouts an incantation to spit the curse on the intruders.

A second soldier spins to shoot Carmen's tiny frame twice, jolting her backward against the terrace wall, dropping her frail body to the ground.

"Noooo!" screams Sophia, scrambling to protectively fall on top of Carmen, expecting bullets in her back any second.

In another flash of lightning, Emilio swings a nearby spear gun to shoot a bolt through the neck of Carmen's killer, dropping him instantly. In a terrifying heartbeat that plays out in agonizing slow motion, the first intruder turns to shoot Emilio in the chest and thigh. His body twists as it falls, smacking his head against a pile of lumber and dropping him limp to the ground. A third man puts on gloves to grab the hot stone box and rapidly retreats into the downpour while the foreign commando grabs his dead comrade to throw him over his shoulder.

Paralyzed and unsure what to do, Sophia's eyes fill with a second downpour as Carmen's warm blood soaks her blouse.

"I lie 'bout many things," Carmen wheezes.

"Don't speak, save your strength," Sophia pleads. "I'm gonna get help."

Pulling out her phone, she panics to find the signal down again, jabbing at the keys as if her intensity will make them work.

"Find da son o' Olivier, who be da son o' Joaquin, who has da key. Rafé know—" Carmen stops breathing, and her lifeless eyes stare into the downpour.

Devastated, Sophia falls onto Carmen's bloody chest in quivering, heaving sobs until she remembers Emilio. Crawling over the wet, sooty grass, she finds him unconscious but still breathing, with warm blood spreading over his chest and pants. Using his belt, she ties a tourniquet on his leg. Then, locking her hands around his thick chest, she struggles to drag his limp body up the terrace steps. Unable to get his whole body into the Jeep tail bed, she uses bungee cords to tie him down.

"Come on Emi, don't give up on me now," she pleads.

Soaked to the bone, her clothes stained with the blood of Carmen and Emilio, her heart pounds uncontrollably as she speeds recklessly down the hill toward Coxen Hole. The torrential downpour continues to unleash its fury while the echo of Carmen's voice rings loudly in her mind; *the dead will follow her.* She prays that Emilio won't be next, terrified beyond words that he may be dead already.

Chapter 8

Voices from Beyond

Woods Hospital, Waiting Room
June 16, 11:46 p.m. | 103 hours to Mayan chaa

Still stained with soot and blood, Sophia looks like a drowned swamp rat, staring listlessly at the tile floor of the hospital waiting room. Emilio has been in surgery for hours. Without a sense of time, her mind remains stuck on the moment of Carmen's death, replaying it repeatedly. Suffocating from shame and remorse, she rocks back and forth in her chair. Unable to wash the image of Carmen from her mind, she wants to wail but swallows it down. She learned as a child to shove down her feelings until she felt numb, suspended in time, detached from the overwhelming pain as if watching herself from a great distance, a state of emotional survival.

Both Carmen and Rafé warned of coming death, so there must be a rational explanation, but it eludes her. If the relics are part of a hoax, how could Carmen's warning come true? Dazed and in shock, her thoughts spin relentlessly as she rocks back and forth. "Get control of yourself, girl."

Dr. Augusto Morales emerges from emergency surgery wearing a clean white doctor's jacket. Tall, lean, and still boyishly handsome in his forties, his shoulders sag, looking drained. Approaching her with heavy sympathetic brows over dark, compassionate eyes, he pulls her out of the seat for a tender embrace.

"Sophia," he whispers. "Thank God you're okay."

One of the few doctors on the tourist island, Augusto is also a great-nephew to Carmen and a good friend of Emilio. Resting her head on his chest, she's afraid of what he has to say next.

"The whole island hurts for you," he whispers, still holding her. "I sent medics to get Carmen. Don't worry; we'll take care of everything."

She nods her appreciation into his chest, still numb and distant.

He pulls back. "Thank God you brought Emi in when you did." He changes the subject. "We removed two bullets and stabilized him, but he lost a lot of blood, and his head hit something hard, so there's a lot of swelling. He's not out of danger."

An incredible weight lifts, knowing Emilio hasn't joined the dead yet. She exhales, unaware she'd been holding her breath.

"I don't know how to thank you." Her voice cracks.

"You can start by telling me what happened," Augusto replies.

On the drive to Coxen Hole, her mind traced the events since the quake. "I'm not sure where to begin," she responds. "It started the day of the earthquake. One minute, Sally was telling me to have faith, and then—"

"Wait," Augusto stops her. "When were you talking to Sally?"

"Yesterday, at her stand, before the earthquake," she replies.

Augusto turns pale, stepping back. "Sally passed away four nights ago; I was with her. We still have her body in the morgue." His frightened eyes widen with confusion and fear.

Sophia stands back mystified, running her fingers through her hair. "No. No, that, that's impossible," she argues. "I, I bought mangos. We, we spoke."

She suddenly realizes that she never actually saw Sally speak but only heard the words, and the mangos were no longer in her car, she had assumed stolen.

Sally's odd behavior and remark now give her a chilling tremble. The night her father disappeared, nothing made sense except that her world would change forever. Disconnected, almost out of her body, she senses her world changing again, and the idea strikes terror to her bones.

"I, I can't talk right now," she says, spinning to the exit. "I need to go."

"Sophia, wait," Augusto calls out. "Captain Primero is looking for you."

Captain Primero Peter Boyles lost his father in the search for her papá and has blamed her cursed family ever since. Boyles must be how the strangers found her home so easily.

Walls begin to close in as she calls back from over her shoulder. "Tell him you never saw me. I was never here."

Chapter 9

Family Secrets

Martinez Family Home, Isla Roatan
June 17, 12:41 a.m. | 102 hours to Mayan chaa

On her way home, Sophia passes the ambulance taking Carmen back to Coxen Hole. Choking down her emotions with a heavy gulp, she pushes the pedal harder until she pulls into the drive of her home, now draped in utter darkness, no power, no life, shattered, empty, and without Abuelita. A perfect metaphor for her life.

Frozen in her seat, the rain pounds on the canvas roof while Carmen's last words replay endlessly in her mind. She doesn't believe in curses, but it's unclear what to believe. The murderers came for the stone box, or rather for the fake relics she left on Barbareta. By now, the thieves know they killed Carmen for an empty box, so they'll be back. They violated her most sacred place, her family home, and now she's vulnerable. If she stays with Mona or Liz Beth, she could endanger them as she did Emilio.

The only way the killers could have known about the relics was through Dr.

Colon. The little snake lied to her. If the items are worth killing over, then they are not fake. If not a hoax, what makes them worth someone's life? It doesn't matter; her disrespect led to Carmen's death. A toxic brew of rage and remorse swells within her until her back arches and she succumbs to an uncontrollable torrent of sobbing while the rain pounds the car windows and canvas roof.

Sometime later, dehydrated, spent, and more desperate than ever for answers, she wonders how to find the unnamed son of Olivier who was the son of Joaquin. Who are Olivier and Joaquin? What does the son have a key to open? Mention of a key reminds her of Chico's comment. Rafé may have known about the key once, but his memories are lost. She resents having to deal with all these dark family secrets at such a dreadful time.

Family secrets—the thought triggers a sudden epiphany. Grabbing her emergency flashlight, she enters the weakened home and heads directly to Carmen's bedroom. Cold, drafty, and structurally dangerous, it's still one of the few dry spots in the storm.

Opening an interior doorway, she stands back, waiting for something to fall. The crammed, chaotic wall of moldy junk stays in place. Carmen had promised to clean the room for more than a decade, and that promise was decades overdue. The old Garifuna threw nothing away, so to find anything specific in the packed curio shop of family enigmas will take a bit of luck. Instead of a closet, the door leads to a small adjacent bedroom, once her nursery. Already full of family history when Carmen moved in, the room now looks like an archaeological dig.

A sudden noise at the other end of the house shoots a bolt of terror through her chest as she holds her breath, listening carefully and lifting her flashlight. A lurch from the darkness sends Sophia leaping backward against the wall with a scream until Ziggy saunters into the light beam whining, soaking wet, and rubbing against her leg.

"*Hijole* Ziggy," she retorts. "You scared the life out of me."

She reaches down to rub his neck. "So, I guess it's just you and me now."

Saying the truth aloud chips away at her already-shattered heart. Too dehydrated to cry, she exhales a shuddering sigh.

After lighting several candles, she pushes the bed next to the wall to clear the floor. Opening a bottle of tequila that survived the quake, she pulls a few long swigs, setting the bottle close. As rain pounds the windows and the winds howl down the hall, whipping the tarps placed over the open roof, Sophia searches Carmen's closet of lost secrets. One by one, she opens every box, bucket, drawer, chest, trunk, bag, rag, and urn. In one box, under a pile of old newspapers, she finds a surprise gold coin stamped 1669 *Rey Felipe de Espana*.

She's not sure where these coins came from, but the extra money is a godsend. The coin was under a stack of old newspapers from the days and weeks after Papá disappeared. Volunteers came from all over the region, but it turns out many were searching for the lost Martinez treasure—something Chico forgot to mention. The papers featured several theories of what happened to Papá, including lost caves, accidental drowning, a shark attack, or the speculation of murder.

One article laid out the long history of Martinez tragedies, starting with the death of three of Paulo's four sons who went in search of the treasure, the murder of Paulo's grandson Montego, multiple disappearances including Papá, and repeated cases of insanity like Rafé.

"Ziggy, get this," she reads. "After Rafé Martinez returned home alone, he was unable to explain his ordeal or how he found his pockets full of gold and gems. His convenient claim of amnesia only fuels the rampant speculation of another murder over the lost Martinez treasure." She raises an eyebrow. "Another detail Chico forgot to mention."

Sophia reminds herself that she doesn't believe in curses, blaming bad timing, bad choices, or bad company. Yet, reading about the dark tragedies that have overshadowed her family for centuries, all laid out in print, suggests otherwise.

A few hours before dawn, she finds what she's looking for tucked away in a small trunk. A book Carmen bought decades ago when Papá was still alive. Sophia recalls Abuelita proudly showing the book to everyone before storing it away. Odd because Carmen couldn't read, but the subject adds even more to the mystery.

Ice Age Origins of the Mesoamerican Calendar by Dr. Estefan J. Martinez.

Sophia notices the common surname of Martinez, a revelation since she grew up believing she was the last of the family namesake. Tucked between the pages of the book, she finds another surprise, the faded photograph of a young bride still in her early teens, standing next to a thin man in a chair, wearing an ill-fitting suit. The back of the photo identifies them. *Joaquin and Carmen Martinez, Wedding Day, June 21, 1919.*

Sophia stares at the photo, shocked and puzzled, not only confirming that Carmen had once been married, but to a Martinez. What happened to Joaquin—how did he disappear? Is he the reason Carmen has so much animosity toward Rafé? Could Olivier be the son of Carmen and Joaquin?

Too many questions without answers rumble around her tequila-saturated head. Exhausted, she curls up next to Ziggy, wondering what to do next. Ever since arranging the trip to Belize, she has felt driven to step beyond her comfort zone in order to find answers, but so far, her efforts have only raised more questions and led to death. Now, Carmen's dying wish pushes her even further out of that comfort zone to find a lost relative with a mysterious key.

Frightened, devastated, and perplexed, she wants to honor the dying wish of a dear gubida, except that she has no idea how to fulfill that wish. With her eyes fixated on the old photo, the turmoil, stress, and tequila conspire together to slip her over the edge into a hard, lurid sleep.

Chapter 10

Narco Jesuit Conspiracy

Polanco Park, Mexico City
June 17, 1:13 a.m. | 101 hours to Mayan chaa

Lucia Alvarez-Vasquez looks camera-ready less than an hour after the middle-of-the-night phone call. A well-known investigative journalist, she projects the modern Latina woman—sophisticated, intelligent, and informed. Her camera operator José Juarez, on the other hand, gets to wear his usual oversized T-shirt, sweatpants, and sneakers. She bites down a twinge of jealousy.

Emergency, military, and local police vehicles have cordoned off the exclusive Chapultepec District condominium, adjacent to national parks, Aztec ruins, and exclusive shopping. Crime for these communities typically means an occasional drunk driver or double-parked Mercedes. The elite watch news of violence elsewhere, but never imagines it on their doorstep. Even at this late hour, dozens of high-rise drapes are open, with anxious eyes that peer down at the emergency lights and the small crowd on the boulevard.

Neither local law enforcement nor the military will comment, keeping the media away to contain the narrative. The unofficial rumor involves a murder-suicide, with the victim's names withheld. It sounds too convenient and rehearsed. Federales don't normally cover a murder-suicide.

Lucia paces back and forth like a caged jaguar when an ambulance driver exits the building with the seventh body bag, the fifth child judging from the size. She darts to intercept him.

"Excuse me, Channel 9 News," she announces. "How was the de Aguilar family murdered? Were they tortured? Where was the bodyguard? Who gave the killers access?" She lobs the questions at him, not waiting for answers, hoping he'll crack.

The driver waves her off. "Just the family, you'll need to wait for the police report," he says, moving past her to load the body, closing the van door behind him.

A minute later, he drives away with lights on but the siren off. A police officer moves in her direction, so she turns to walk away as José turns off his light.

"Well, that was a waste," José complains.

"Actually, it's what he *didn't* say," she replies, but sees José doesn't get it. "He didn't deny the victims were the de Aguilar family."

José gives her a *so what?* look.

"Salazar de Aguilar, the CEO of Banco de Mexico Nacional, owns the entire thirty-fourth floor and lives there with his wife and five children. I interviewed Señor de Aguilar last year for an article on bank fraud. Last week, the International Monetary Fund placed Señor de Aguilar under investigation for Nacon money laundering linked to leaks from the Panama Papers. Señor de Aguilar started his career at Fossack-Monseca, the law firm where the Panama Papers leaked." She grins at her capacity to connect the dots.

"You have a death wish," replies José.

"What? There could be a real story here," she argues.

"I cover celebrities, entertainment, business news, and the environment, and if I'm lucky, a little soccer. A murder-suicide is borderline," he reminds her while he packs his gear. "I don't cover corrupt politicians or cartel violence because I love my family, and I enjoy living."

Lucia dismisses the remark. "Salazar de Aguilar and Arturo Lanza are personal friends. I think Nacon is sending Lanza a message."

"You're not hearing me," he snaps. "You need a new cameraman."

Lucia eyes him with disappointment and considers arguing with him but knows it would be a waste of time. The cartels have intimidated media into silence, leaving most too afraid to seek the truth, much less speak it.

"Then go home to your woman," she retorts. "I'll find someone with *cojones*." She regrets the crude insult at once, but before she can apologize, he turns.

"Screw you," he replies. "I'm your third cameraman this year, and they agreed to give me a raise to take the job." He inhales to contain his irritation. "Look, Luci, I really like you, but how long do you think the network will keep you on if you keep putting people in danger?"

Part of her knows he could be right, except that Señor de Aguilar is the fourth executive assassination in six months linked to the Nacon cartel, a Panama Papers leak, or President Lanza.

"I'm sorry for what I said," she offers. "I actually envy your family." She reaches to shake hands. "No hard feelings."

José hands her the data card from his camera and continues to pack, his decision firm. "No hard feelings," he finally responds, "but seriously, Luci, watch your back."

"You sound like my brother," she scoffs.

As José drives off, Lucia turns back to the police line. No more ambulances wait for bodies as the police disperse the thinning crowd and shades close on darkened windows. Nacon violent intimidation of the media dates back decades, including the murder of her father to gain control of his Juarez television network. Since then, the number of murdered journalists has risen from dozens into thousands. Even worse, evidence points to a deeper corruption beyond media into banking, energy, the military, and politics, which implies a secret infiltration model borrowed from the Jesuits, an enormous insider coup of influence across Latin America financed by drug profits.

Midnight mayhem may be a recent experience for the elite of Mexico City, but she grew up as a victim of cartel violence, traumatized and paralyzed by it. She can no longer turn a blind eye. The war against Nacon corruption cost her a family, a childhood, and a marriage. Except for her brother Xavier and her career, she has little left to lose, and she's willing to ditch the career.

An inside voice agrees with José that she should leave this one alone. Another voice cries for justice, regardless of the cost. Sadly, she knows which voice will win, the one that always wins.

*

Teotihuacan Condominium, Mexico City
June 17, 3:02 a.m. | 99 hours to Mayan chaa

Exhausted by the time she gets home, Lucia collapses onto the couch, agitated and restless. Something spooked her tonight, but she can't pinpoint what, which makes it worse.

A chronic insomniac and confessed news junkie, she impulsively picks up her TV remote. She preprogrammed every news channel from Mexico to Bolivia into a split screen with eight pop-up windows, each programmed to a default country. Computer hard drives, tablets, and monitors connect to an encrypted Wi-Fi and a commercial firewall.

Other local channels report the fake story of a murder-suicide, while her story connected the family de Aguilar to the IMF, Panama Papers, Nacon money laundering, and President Lanza. Chances of her editor publishing her version are slim to none.

The second big story of the night comes from an online paramilitary news site Xavier hacked into months ago. The US Navy found a Malaysian freighter drifting three hundred miles northwest of Panama, two-thirds submerged, with a massacred crew. Recovered bridge security videos show an unmarked helicopter take a single container. Contents of the container are unknown but assumed to be drugs or guns.

On a blank notecard, she writes: De Aguilar murder cover-up, and then on a second card writes: Malaysian ship sunk for container.

Dozens of similar note cards, photos, and newspaper clippings, each connected by yarn, fill the wall of her living room. Pinning her new cards to the wall, she uses yarn to connect them to other events. Stepping back to view the latest updates, she can see obvious clusters and patterns but not a central theme. She may need to give in, admit defeat, and use Xavier's data-analysis program. Even worse, she'll have to admit that he was right. The only thing worse than an overprotective older brother is a *smug* overprotective brother.

From a channel based in the Yucatan, another story catches her eye, the unexplained disappearance of an influential community leader on Isla Cozumel. An important international summit will happen on the island in a few days. The death of a civic leader tickles her instincts. Creating a new card, she pins the note to the wall, unsure how to connect the event.

Lying back on the couch to examine the wall patterns, exhaustion wins over, seducing her asleep while stilled dressed in her clothes, again.

Chapter 11

Pimping Out Plunder

Plunder Lust, Los Rojas Reef, Panama
June 17, 7:08 a.m. | 95 hours to Mayan chaa

A ubiquitous cigar hangs from between the teeth of Miguel Martinez as he monitors the underwater excavation from a rack of video screens mounted to the bridge balcony of his rusted, battered 150-foot salvage ship, *Plunder Lust*. The tall, thirty-something California Latino blends in perfectly with the jungled coastline of the Caribbean Panama, with his dark wavy hair, persistent three-day stubble, and sunglasses to hide his sensitive hazel-green eyes.

"Cannon one ready for hoist," crackles Jackson over the worn-out speakers. "Cannon two coming up next."

Dr. Jackson Healy from the University of California Los Angeles (UCLA) leads the underwater part of the excavation, hired against his wishes by the project director.

"No, Jackson, you need to get the netting farther up, under the cannon.

Shimmy it. Sweep the sand away, no, no, sweep the sand," Miguel barks into the mic.

"Dude, really? Your brain may be rotting like the underside of your boat, which looks pretty sad, by the way," retorts Jackson, his thin electronic voice squeaking over the frazzled speaker.

"Whoa, snap," jokes Hansen Brunk, ex-US Navy Seal, and *Plunder Lust* salvage master. Hansen finishes the string grid over the wreck. He found a coral cluster yesterday that could be a ship's bell, but only three cannons so far, fewer than the twelve they expected.

"Hey, leave poor *Plunder* alone, and pay attention to the cannon," retorts Miguel. "We're behind schedule."

After making a name for himself several years ago with a fifty-million-dollar gold and silver discovery off San Tomas Island, fierce legal battles between Mexico and Spain left him with little except a cargo of debt in a sea of legal sharks. A few months ago, one of those sharks put a lien on his ship, demanding faster payment. In a slightly inebriated act of desperation, he caved in and agreed to contract the Plunder and her crew for an entire dive season.

"Hey, people on da deck, we be drifting again. Work da windlass, people," shouts Moses, his deep Jamaican voice reverberating on the deck speakers below.

Moses sits inside the cross breeze of the bridge, avoiding the blazing sun and nursing a Cuban cigar. Anchored only feet away from the deadly Los Rojas reef at the mouth of the Chagres River, the growing swell constantly pushes the ship toward the razor-sharp rock.

The only person on the deck below, project director Dr. Darcy O'Sullivan, ignores Moses in order to check out the one floating cannon. Wearing her typical faded men's Levi's, Paul McCartney T-shirt, and a straw fedora, she looks like a sexy Irish pixie in grunge.

Miguel removes his cigar. "Yo, Doc, it goes faster with a crew."

"Piss off about my crew," quips Darcy in her lilting English accent. "And tell Captain Moses to tweak his own bloody windlass."

The feisty, petite redhead pivots to find the wayward deck crew, while Miguel replaces his cigar with a chuckle. The indomitable Dr. Darcy O'Sullivan, the true reason he agreed to pimp out his ship for an entire year. They've been having a long-distance, on-and-off, as-the-wind-blows romance for three years. She's an amazing woman, and he's crazy about her, but he worries that working together will ruin their relationship. On the other hand, he had no choice.

"Hear that, Moses?" interjects Xavier in his thick Mexican accent. "Dr. O'Sullivan wants you to tweak yourself."

Xavier Alvarez, ship's security officer, and ex-CISEN Mexican intelligence, rubs a handkerchief over his sweaty, shaved head as he intently monitors his computer screen.

"Ya mon, too many women on da boat be bad mojo," grumbles Moses, climbing out of his chair to make the windlass adjustments himself.

Xavier laughs. "Really, amigo, you once captained a floating brothel."

Captain Samuel Paul Moses, simply called Moses by his friends, has never been mistaken for a man of God. Moses grew up on Jamaican fishing boats until age sixteen, when he took a high-paying job racing high-speed drug boats around the Eastern Antilles. When he grew tired of bullets whizzing past his ears, Moses took a job with a casino-brothel offshore of the Cayman Islands.

"Das how I know, mon," says Moses lowering his voice. "Das how I know."

A direct descendant of one of the surviving crew aboard Henry Morgan's final voyage, Moses grew up on Morgan folklore, and a key reason Miguel hired him. Besides, after twenty-six years at sea, Moses knows every hiding spot or corrupt harbormaster in the region.

"If women are such bad luck," deadpans Xavier, "you better warn the skipper."

"No, no, no, I kill you in da bunk wit' a snake," Moses threatens in a husky whisper. "What say on da bridge, stay on da bridge, mon, everybody know dat."

Xavier and Moses burst into laughter as Miguel chuckles, wondering if Moses knows he can hear them from the balcony.

A loud weather panel alert directs his attention to a satellite image that shows Hurricane Stephanie changing direction toward Panama. He bites down on his cigar in a scowl. He dated a woman named Stephanie once, a bipolar ice queen. A storm with the same name could be a bad omen. A superstitious man, he hates bad omens. With any luck, the bitch will change her mind again and head north.

*

Plunder Lust, Los Rojas Reef
June 17, 7:16 a.m. | 95 hours to Mayan chaa

For the first few weeks of the project, Darcy clung to the idea that the discipline of her science team would rub off on the "lost boys" attitude of the *Plunder Lust* crew. She realizes now that was wishful thinking. In fact, the opposite has proven true. Way behind schedule, she only has three weeks left to prove they've found Morgan's lost fleet or she will lose the full-year extension, and without that extension, she has no hope of earning tenure.

With a doctorate from Cambridge, an undergraduate from Yale, and a decade of fieldwork, she made the rather fateful choice to excavate five empty pirate ships. Unimpressed with her choice, the Cambridge tenure board now questions her readiness. Even more distressing, her late father, an onerous and lonely man who never married after Mum passed in childbirth, made her full inheritance conditional on achieving tenure. Even in death, he imposes his iron will on her life. She will need some of that iron to get her project back on schedule.

Grabbing the ship's intercom, she presses the button for the mess hall speakers. "Dave, Brenda, Juniper. All hands-on deck. Now," she orders.

Standing by the hatchway door, she glares down each tardy crewmember as they exit. Brenda Kerrigan bounds out of the hatchway first. The ambitious University of Arizona anthropology major with olive skin and piercing blue eyes looks like an athletic Katie Perry who inherited her competitive drive from a career US Marine father and four older marine brothers.

"Sorry, we were choking down Ben's shit shingles," she excuses, taking her position by the desalination tank.

"To be fair," interjects Juniper Burns, who steps out after Brenda, "maybe that's how truckers make quesadillas in Florida."

With the posture, etiquette, and social awareness of a liberal East Coast family, the Smith University graduate deflects all personal questions with a smile.

"Don't listen to Ms. Pleasantville. Nobody makes quesadillas with Cheese Whiz and ketchup," quips Dave Willis, the ship's lead engineer, who emerges last, throwing an unfinished slice of quesadilla in the trash. "Trust me, even the ship rats won't eat it."

An MIT engineer with a snarky attitude, Dave could make four times what Miguel pays him if only he were willing to go work for his dad in the subzero wind chills of Chicago. Dave read about Miguel's success in *TIME* and wrote him to ask for a job. Unsurprisingly, Miguel hired him. Dave wedges into position at the controls of the crane hoist that connects to the cannon sitting within bright-yellow, heavy-duty flotation balloons.

On the ship's transom, Dr. Mai Chin extends her tiny frame out over the water with one leg wrapped around a stanchion in a way only a flexible, twenty-six-year-old yoga expert could manage. With a graceful sweep of her hand, she snatches a sonar torpedo from the water. The youngest of five daughters to a founding Google billionaire, Mai earned advanced degrees in electrical and software engineering; a true genius escaping Daddy's shadow.

Three hundred meters out on the bay, strapping young ship hand Hugo Hernández slowly sweeps a second sonar tube followed overhead by Mai's customized drone, nicknamed Oliver. Using an experimental combination of LIDAR and sonar, they scan the bay for the last of five lost ships.

Darcy gives a thumbs-up signal. "Okay, Mr. Willis, let's bring our baby aboard."

"One ugly baby, coming up," he replies, hoisting the eight-foot-long, 2,400 pounds of iron, coral, and muck out of the water balloons. Swaying in the growing breeze, the cannon looks like an enormous encrusted, cancerous cigar in slings.

"Beautiful!" exclaims Darcy.

A brief cheer ends when a rogue wave lifts the hull toward the reef, lunging the heavy cannon at a deadly speed toward the ship.

"Hit the deck," shouts Miguel in the same instant that Brenda tackles Darcy onto the hot wooden planks, knocking the wind out of her as the cannon swings inches above Brenda's head. The rattling clank of the seaward anchor chain pulls the ship away from the reef but swings the cannon wildly back over the water before stalling to swing back again.

"Dave, drop it," shouts Miguel.

"Dave no!" screams Darcy, pushing herself up from the deck.

It's too late. Dave can't slow the momentum. The unbalanced strain bends a control rod on the massive hydraulic hoist. The heavy iron clump misses the balloon nets and splashes into the water, followed by curses squelched over the frazzled speakers.

"Bloody hell." She slaps the railing before shooting Miguel a sharp glare over another setback, as if the whole project were under a curse.

*

Ocean Floor Shipwreck, Los Rojas Reef
June 17, 7:38 a.m. | 95 hours to Mayan chaa

"Holy crap," calls Jackson. "What are you guys drinking up there?"

The uncontrolled plunge hit the wreck site hard, instantly clouding visibility for a dozen yards. There's a momentary silence.

"Bourbon. I'll have one waiting for you," replies Miguel in a calm voice. "Sorry about that, boys. It looks like we have a hoist problem. Mr. Willis will be busy on repairs for a while. What's your status? I can't see a damn thing on video."

"Like a dust storm in Oklahoma down here, but I've seen worse," Hansen responds in his East Texas drawl.

"You're kidding," interjects Jackson. "I can't even see my own hand. Dude, I'm done."

Hansen watches the hippie scientist ascend above the silt toward the surface.

"Hey, Skipper, I can finish netting cannon two until my air runs out," he offers.

"Roger that," responds Miguel. "Thanks, Big Rig."

Already behind schedule, Dr. O'Sullivan will whistle her teapot over this mishap. As an expert in underwater salvage and demolition, Hansen enjoys the archaeology gig more than he expected. Instead of blowing things up, he gets to investigate what happened long ago. Exactly the kind of low-stress work he needs after sixteen years of combat and special ops.

With his hands, he finds the cannon, along with a small, fragile object that seems out of place next to the heavy, encrusted iron. Pulling it closer to his mask, he studies the aged shard of darkened tortoise shell with odd markings. His dive timer pings. With the unexpected find in hand, he floats to the surface.

Chapter 12

Son of Olivier

Roatan Hospital, Isla Roatan
June 17, 10:28 a.m. | 92 hours before Mayan Chaa

The tropical sun blazes into her eyes from high over the hillside, ripping Sophia from a grief-stricken sleep, dreaming of Abuelita. Both Ziggy and the storm are gone, yet her mood remains a noxious blend of depression and desperation. Fretful over another attack, she quickly changes out of her bloody clothes, runs her hands through her pixie hair, and heads back to the hospital.

After rounding the block to check for the police, she parks behind a dumpster and sneaks in through the rear entrance. Inside the hospital, she learns that Emilio had slipped into a coma during the night, the distressing news only adding to her overwhelming guilt. After taking a quick shower in his room, Sophia spends the next hour at his bedside, talking to her friend and using the hospital Wi-Fi to search for Dr. Estefan J. Martinez.

"Hey, Emi, I think I found him. A UCLA professor of archaeology and anthropology, author of several books on the Mayan astronomy and calendar."

At that moment, Mona sticks her head in the door. "Sophie girl, Corporal Green be parking." One of the corrupt police thugs.

"*Gracias, itu*, stall him," requests Sophia, quickly packing her things.

Taking Emilio by the hand, she squeezes gently. "Emi, I owe you my life, and I will never, ever forget," she whispers. "I have to go to America to find some answers, so you hold on my friend, just hold on, and I will come back."

With a kiss on his forehead, she slips out the hospital's rear entrance.

*

Martinez family home, Isla Roatan
June 17, 12:08 p.m. | 90 hours to Mayan chaa

Sophia's heart stops as she opens her front door to realize that someone has ransacked the house. What the earthquake didn't destroy, the intruders tossed aside. The murderers had returned for the artifacts, and once again left empty-handed. They could return again, or even worse, be waiting nearby. With a shuddering wave of dread, she quickly packs a travel bag and changes into one of Carmen's vintage dresses, leaving behind her ruined red sneakers.

An hour later, with hands trembling and heart racing, she sits near an exit on the afternoon ferry to La Ceiba. Her head covered with a scarf, hiding behind large sunglasses, she tries her best to blend in with the tourists. Muscles tense, her fingers clutch her travel bag, suspicious of each passenger, and unable to shake the sense of someone watching. Always uncomfortable traveling alone, she feels forced by fate and a death bed request.

Hailing a cab from the wharf, she finds a local coin collector willing to pay cash for Carmen's last gold doubloon. To her pleasant surprise, the coin was extremely rare and worth more than she expected, although she is sure he cheated her. After another cab to La Ceiba International Airport, she pays cash to board a redeye to Los Angeles via Mexico City.

Consumed by so many shocking revelations, and overwhelmed by remorse over Carmen and Emilio, her anxieties play tricks with her mind, making her constantly look over her shoulder. She left without telling anyone, not even Mona. Only now, alone on an airplane to a foreign country, does she come to realize that she has never been more alone in her life.

Seated by the window, she clutches her bag under a blanket and tries to sleep, but she knows true slumber won't come. Shivering and unsure what she will discover, she vows to honor Carmen's last wish to find Estefan and his mysterious key.

Chapter 13

Lords of Ascension
(Aruk' Yuum)

Túumben Epoca, Northern Cayman Trench
June 17, 1:58 p.m. | 89 hours to Mayan chaa

Juan Perez carefully watches the Sikorsky S92 approach his eighty-five-meter mega-yacht *Túumben Epoca* (Epoch Arising) shuttling the last set of guests for the final presummit council meeting.

Checking the interior cabin video, he wants to make sure the visitors arriving are the ones he expects, wary of surprises. Admiral Valdez from Colombia, General Chavez from Bolivia, General Basque from Brazil, Peruvian Admiral Velasquez, and Mexican General Panera; the last five of the nine military council members. The economic council and other advisors already lounge in the ship's luxurious salon. For several years, *Túumben Epoca* has served as the unofficial headquarters for a secret government in preparation. Tonight's meeting will be the last before the chaa.

The custom ship features a helipad, a six-zodiac garage, Jet Skis, a swimming pool, a spa, a gymnasium, a gourmet kitchen, a theater, and twenty luxurious staterooms with a 350-square-meter master suite. Hidden behind the state-of-the-art bridge wall are the target controls for an Uran-E ASM anti-ship missile system. Under the hull sits an empty ten-meter sub bay. Unfortunately, he was forced to scuttle the last sub in the Cayman Trench to eliminate the isotope evidence.

He lights a cigar as his encrypted cell phone buzzes from Shay. He sent the Syrian imbecile back to Roatan after the complete failure of his last mission to retrieve a single artifact. He should have shot Shay on the spot after he lost a good man over an empty box, but there will be time for that later. Other loose ends must wrap up in the next three days, and Golan still has a purpose.

After a deep drag, he answers. "Do you have the blade?"

"No, and we tore the house apart," Shay admits. "The bitch wasn't at home or at the hospital, but we tracked her to La Ceiba. She boarded a flight to Los Angeles an hour ago."

"Los Angeles," he bellows, surprised by the development.

Given her experience at the Belize Museum, she may be seeking a US buyer. Unable to sneak the artifacts through US customs, she must have left them behind somewhere.

As if reading his mind, Shay continues. "I leaned on Boyles to learn that the woman visited a lunatic uncle on Isla Barbareta yesterday. Let me send a team under darkness. We either find the blade or we take the old man."

"Do it. The chopper will pick you up in an hour," Juan Perez orders. "Call our contacts in LA to have a local man shadow the woman. Bag her when she's back on our territory. Between the bitch and her uncle, one of them will break."

What started as an easy target has grown into an expensive, multiteam endeavor at the worst possible time, but he can't allow an American university to own the most sacred artifact ever found. It would be sacrilege and rob him of a priceless portent of his destiny.

He changes the subject. "What about Cozumel?"

"We buried Buluc Chabtan," Shay reports. "And lost two divers."

He had ordered Shay to sabotage the rebreather gear to ensure the divers did not return. Early in life, he learned to eliminate witnesses, all of them. Golan may look forward to the pleasure of silencing Gerhard at the right time, and yet the fool still considers himself safe.

"Give Gerhard until morning. If he hasn't found something, then clean the site," he orders, ending the call.

He inhales several deep breaths to recenter his persona, consciously putting on the mindset, the humor, and the charm of the man like an actor donning a costume. It gets easier and more natural each time, and soon it will be his dominant persona. He's maintained dozens of personas over the years, part of a never-ending masquerade, a chameleon infiltrating into the enemy camp. Soon, only the persona of Juan Perez will matter.

Stoking his cigar, he descends the spiral staircase into the central ship salon, as massive as a luxury hotel and just as elegant, greeting his new arrivals with a gracious, warm smile. "Gentlemen, the future will soon be ours. Tonight, we celebrate!"

Dressed in Armani casual attire, a linen shirt, and silk trousers, he acts magnanimous, holding an open palm toward the plush armchairs and lounges. "Please, mi amigos, make yourselves comfortable."

Young women serve cocktails, expensive cigars, and gourmet hors d'oeuvres. Speakers play festive indigenous music as other women mingle to flirt. Tonight will be the last chance to inspire his men before the flames of anarchy scorch the continent. Excitement mingles with pride over how far he has come from his humble beginnings.

"Señor," General Panera steps up and bows his head to lower his voice. "I need a word in private, *por favor*."

"Of course, General." He shakes the large hand. "Excellent job yesterday. Island security appears impenetrable." He leads them toward the aft deck pool for privacy. "What's on your mind?"

"The US Navy has discovered the Thai Maersk," the general begins, lowering his gaze in shame for his failure to sink the ship completely. "In response, the US has raised Defcon and ordered sonar sweeps of the Gulf. They are urging

Lanza to cancel the summit. While I convinced Lanza to rebuff the Americans, he has ordered a search of the island reef. Discovery of Buluc may be at risk."

Out of necessity, General Panera knew the original plan to bury Buluc Chabtan under a reef. Out of the same necessity, Panera has no clue that the plans have changed.

"Nonsense, Buluc remains safe," he says with a chuckle. "Search the reefs, and sweep the oceans." He sips his cocktail unconcerned. "Do whatever it takes to make Lanza and other attendees believe the oceans are safe, but we must have full attendance at the summit."

Panera's face distorts in confusion, wanting to ask a question but unwilling to cross a line. He sees no reason to inform the general of the new details, and in fact, keeping him in the dark may be the only thing keeping him alive. There can be no witnesses or loose ends.

"Yes, of course." Panera bows his massive head. "I will make it so."

"Good." Juan Perez smiles and then pats the large man's shoulder. "Now let's join the others before they gossip that we are planning a coup."

A trusted member of his war council, the nine warlords of Bolon-Yokte, General Panera, along with eight other military men maintain control over a vast sleeper cell militia. Other attendees represent his economic council of senior bankers and CEOs, each one eager to assume total control of a Putin-style oligarchy system. Each man has been groomed, corrupted, and absolutely under his thumb. Like him, they each share a mixed-blood ancestry with a cultivated loyalty to their indigenous birthright. Fervent passions he has skillfully sharpened into a powerful unifying vision.

"After the chaa, there will be widespread anarchy and economic uncertainty." Señor Tito Pena leads a discussion, sporting his ubiquitous Harvard tie. By tomorrow, the Banco de Mexico Nacionale board of directors will elect Tito to replace the recently deceased CEO Salazar de Aguilar.

"Buluc Chabtan will bring widespread bloodshed," interjects Juan Perez, testing them. "Let the crisis escalate, and allow the blood to flow in the streets. Eliminate only those who build a following, but wait for the second signal; sleeper cells must execute together. The world must see us as salvation to restore peaceful order. If we feed this perception, neither the US nor the UN will risk more than harsh words or temporary sanctions."

Looking each man in the eye, he searches for unquestioned loyalty.

"Today, gentlemen, you are among the most powerful men of your nations. Soon, we will combine our forces to become one of the most powerful nations on Earth. Separate, they dismiss us on the world stage, but united we will demand respect. Separate, we are the remnants of invader colonies. United we become a new world power," he bellows the themes of his vision.

Chests swell, nostrils flare, and grins grow wide under sunglass-hidden eyes. He has dreamed of this moment since his youth. When others scorned him, he turned his rage into subversion. When his enemies pronounced his demise, he resurrected to eliminate them. Placing his palm gently on the shoulder of each man, he feeds on their energy.

"Never again will they treat us like a small banana republic to be intimidated by our European or American masters," he boasts defiantly to nodding heads.

"No longer will the name *Latin America* identify us with an invader. Soon, world maps will feature the continental empire of Xibala, home of the Xi' peoples," he shouts. *"Ko chaa túumben!"* On the solstice, we arise.

Spontaneous applause sweeps the men up in the anticipated glory, wealth, and power. *"Ko chaa túumben!"* comes the full-throated response.

For over twenty-five years, he's built a vision to unite the continent from Mexico to Argentina under a single flag and his rule. An investment of billions to develop sleeper cells within military, police, industry, banking, and government will soon pay off. Decades of maneuvering elections and corporate boards, blackmailing or seducing politicians, eliminating or outright buying the media. Armies of hackers and surveillance experts form an illicit, dark-web criminal and security network.

Even as a boy, when others spat on him, he dreamed big—a place in history big, world-changing big, millennia-long legacy big. He will change maps, change minds, and change the global balance of power. Tired of hiding his face, feeling ashamed of his identity, he will no longer be invisible, forgotten by the world but vows the world will celebrate his life.

Soon, with the sacrificial blade of the maker as a confirmation to his destiny, he will fulfill the rebirth of Chilam Balam, and bring the darkness of Bolon-Yokte. He will rule over an empire for an epoch of prosperity.

Chapter 14

A Lethal Loco

Isla Barbareta, Honduras
June 18, 12:33 a.m. | 78 hours to Mayan chaa

Unable to sleep, Chico wanders onto the beach to enjoy a midnight joint. All the talk about Antonio's death and curses has left him unsettled.

Leisurely shuffling his bare feet in the cool sand, a sudden commotion erupts at the far end of the cove in Rafé's hut. Floodlights brighten the hut, followed by loud groans, dull metallic clangs, and at least one crash. Then the lights go out again. Baffled by the disruption, Chico speculates a poor crab must have strayed into the shack, until three gunshots echo across the lagoon. Rafé doesn't own a gun.

"Hide the gold, hide the women," screams Rafé. "Hide!"

A moonless night, too dark to see, Chico can only hear the sound of staccato military voices blending with more gunfire flashing in the dark. Squeals draw him around to see Mari and the kids huddled on the porch.

"Back in the hut," he whispers. "Stay low."

Left with a limp from his flight school injury, he hobbles as fast as he can toward Rafé's hut, until it occurs to him that he's rushing in the dark toward men with guns. Slowing to a standstill, Papá Hector startles him when he bolts from his hut with a flashlight and a 1960s vintage M21 sniper rifle, useless without a night scope. Papá collects antique weapons, and some of them even work.

"What's going on?" he whispers, hunkered down, scanning the black lagoon.

"Someone's attacking Rafé," Chico guesses.

"Wait, what?" Papá replies. "Why?"

Before Chico can even guess, the rev of a large outboard motor interrupts them, followed by a blast of machine-gun fire into the shallow lagoon water. Howling erupts from the shore as the boat races toward the coral reef. They must have hit Rafé.

They can't see the craft, but the engine leaves a phosphorescent trail in the propeller wash. Papá raises his rifle to fire but misses. With a deep exhale, he tracks the wash and fires again. Nothing. Then he carefully tracks the wash and takes a third shot. A second later, the engine whine falls off to idle, and the trail twists into an arc. He hit someone, but then the engine revs up again, twisting back toward the channel. Out of range, the boat still moves dangerously fast toward the reef.

Searching the beach with the flashlight, Chico spots Rafé thrashing to stand in the shallow surf. One hand grasps his fishing knife, while the other holds his bleeding leg. A heartbeat later, the pitch of the motor revs high for an instant, as if the prop has lifted from the water. They must have hit the reef. Then a fireball explodes over the lagoon as the flaming boat lands atop a coral outcrop.

"*Asuera da inaruni y amuru!*" Rafé shouts an old Garifuna incantation, defiantly holding up his knife.

His arm smells of petrol. He must have cut the gas line, the fuel igniting with a spark when they smashed the coral. In the bright light of the explosion, Chico spots an enormous ship sitting offshore of the reef with all lights off, stalking like a ghost.

He and Papá hurriedly nudge the cursing Rafé toward his shack. In wet, stained shorts, and a ragged T-shirt hanging over his scrawny shoulders, his head jerks in spasms. Inside the squalid shack, Chico kicks aside the clutter and lays Rafé in the hammock.

"He's getting worse," Chico complains. "You should get the tranquilizer darts."

Hector shoots him a rebuking glance.

"Just an idea," shrugs Chico, turning on the floodlights to see better.

Shading his eyes, Rafé giggles. "*Los diablos* be blinded, so I piss fire in their eyes."

Piss fire? Chico picks up a nearby can of pepper spray, which would explain the earlier howling.

"Den I whack, whack," he points to a small iron anchor on the table.

Chico notices something under the table and reaches down to pick up a pair of high-tech night-vision goggles.

Hector's eyes widen, immediately taking them. "Wow, IR 42, military grade."

Chico runs the scene through his head. Rafé must have somehow seen the men coming and waited. Turning on the flood light to blind their night vision, he pepper-sprayed their eyes when they ripped off the goggles. Blinded and in pain, he slaps them with an anchor to escape, except instead of escaping, he cuts their fuel line. Chico shakes his head, impressed. Hell, man, Rafé may be a total loco, but he's one badass loco.

Rafé continues to bleed onto the floorboards of his hut. Chico isn't sure, but it looks like the bullet grazed a thigh, a flesh wound. Hector applies a tourniquet, emitting a howl that shatters the night silence. Pulling out his cell phone, he hits speed dial and then speaker.

"*Hola, Dr. Morales, por favor, un emergencia.* Tell him it's Chico," he shouts.

They wait a few moments. "Chico, I'm glad you called," Augusto answers. "Please tell Rafé I'm so very sorry for his loss. Carmen was a light in the community. We're doing everything we can to prepare for *Dugu.*"

"Dugu? Wait, hold on," Chico stops him. "What happened to Carmen?"

The shock of the news captures their attention, as even Rafé's eyes tear up.

"If you didn't know about Carmen, why are you calling?" Augusto asks, sounding confused.

Chico heads outside for better reception, turning off the speaker. He fills Augusto in on the lagoon attack, the flaming wreckage, and the large ghost ship that has now gone. He suspects Nacon but can't imagine why they would target Rafé. Augusto fills Chico in on the murder of Carmen, Emilio's coma, and Sophia's sudden disappearance.

"Sophia was here yesterday," Chico says. "She was asking about Antonio," he hesitates, "and the family curse."

"Oh no," groans Augusto. "Not that mess again."

Augusto provides Chico with critical first-aid instructions and promises to send a med-boat in the morning. After hanging up, Chico uses Rafé's tequila to sterilize the wound before he wraps the leg. With Sophia missing and attacks on the island, he fears the situation will only get worse, just like when Antonio disappeared.

After he finally gets Rafé and the family to fall asleep, Chico returns to the beach to finish off the tequila, in an effort to sterilize his agitated nerves.

Chapter 15

Beginning of Time

A fter a muscle-aching eighteen hours, including a tedious layover in Mexico City and a sleepless, turbulent red-eye flight, Sophia endures the long line at Los Angeles International US Customs and then yet another tedious line for a taxi. After another forty-five minutes of bumper-to-bumper freeway traffic, she arrives at UCLA in Westwood with a fresh appreciation for why these people come to Roatan to recover from daily life.

After getting lost twice, she finds the Anthropology & Archaeology Department in a 1950s-era brick building wrapped in ivy and slips into the back of an old theater-style room. Much older than his book photo, Dr. Estefan Martinez now has salt-and-pepper hair that sweeps back in waves. Sitting in the back with a sense of anticipation over finding the mysterious Estefan, she has no idea what to expect. He notices her enter but continues his lecture.

"When Hernán Cortés first arrived in 1517, all the nations of Mesoamerica shared a common mythology and calendar, suggesting a shared, more ancient mother culture. While many scholars believe the Olmec were that culture, a growing body of evidence points to a much older civilization," Dr. Martinez says.

His deep, resonating voice reminds her of Papá with a more American accent. Somehow, the familiarity warms her with a sense of connection she didn't expect.

"The Aztec king Montezuma told Cortés they were living during the fourth creation of the Earth, the fourth epoch, or rather in my view, the fourth cycle of the long count calendar. If so, then in order to find the creators of the calendar, in order to find that mother culture, we will need to look much further back in history," he explains. "We need to look before the Younger Dryas Impact event of 12,900 BPE (before present era)."

A few students murmur at the suggestion. Scanning the room to gauge their attention, he gives Sophia a momentary glance before he continues. Still dressed in Carmen's vintage clothing, she feels out of place, but coming from a small island, just the ability to sit in a major university classroom excites her.

"Toward the end of 2012, many people bought into the false hysteria that the Mayan calendar pointed to the end of the world," he says with a chuckle that spreads around the room. "At least some of that hype was based on a Mayan prophet named Chilam Balam, who not only accurately foretold of the Spanish invasion but also spoke of a darkness that would descend at the end of the thirteenth Baktun, or December 21, 2012. While the world obviously didn't end, our global problems continue to grow worse at an exponential rate, so perhaps the prophecy is merely in progress." He grins.

"Either way, the enigmas of the Mayan long count are both profound and inspiring," he declares. "Profound in the mind-bending accuracy over a 5,126-year period with enough precision to predict planetary, lunar, and solar events such as an eclipse. Advanced enough to incorporate precession, the 26,000-year wobble of the Earth with an awe-inspiring .001 percent error rate."

Living on a tropical island made it hard to imagine such things. A little confused about where he's going, she's listens carefully.

"Such accuracy over so long a period of time indicates the creators must have observed the sky for at least one full cycle," asserts Dr. Martinez. "On that premise alone, we can rule out the Olmec, who didn't even exist until five hundred years *after* the start of the fourth cycle in 3114 BCE. If not the Olmec, then who created such astounding technology?"

A few students mumble, but Sophia still doesn't understand the controversy. She feels a bit of shame that she doesn't know more of her local history, and a bit of envy of the entitled students who get to study such mysteries.

"Unlike the Bible, the Polpul Vuh tradition speaks of three creations, with the first creation described as a mud people epoch, where I suspect the buildings were made of mud which disintegrated and were forgotten over time. Then came a second epoch of wooden people, or wooden structures, which according to the Polpul Vuh, was destroyed by a fire and a flood."

A student raises his hand. "You mean Mesoamerica had a flood myth like the Bible?"

"Yes, and not only Mesoamerica, but 140 other cultures speak of a devastating flood," Dr. Martinez elaborates. "But interestingly, the Mayans claim both a fire and a flood."

He rotates to play a video animation on a large overhead screen. The video opens over North and Central America with a series of meteor impacts, and then zooms in on the Caribbean region.

"Scientists have documented several major flooding events that together have raised ocean levels over four hundred feet since the last Ice Age. Imagine a four-hundred-foot ocean rise today, reshaping every coastline on Earth, in some cases by hundreds of miles, and affecting more than a half of our population. Around 12,900 BPE, during the second epoch, a meteor slammed into the two-mile-thick Canadian ice sheets of northern Quebec in what scientists called the Younger Dryas Impact Event. Enormous plasma waves, which are only possible with an asteroid or meteor, swept over half the globe, igniting all-consuming wildfires and leaving a black mat deposit of carbon, iridium, and nano-diamonds as far east as Iraq, and as far south as Ecuador and Colombia," he explains.

"When the asteroid hit the ice sheets, it threw glacial ejecta as large as sports stadiums thousands of miles, to create a half million Carolina Bays along the Eastern Seaboard. That same ejecta pummeled the Atlantic, Gulf, and Caribbean waters, to create a series of tsunamis. In Mesoamerica, the event transformed a coastal volcanic mountain range along with a vast wetland into the Honduras Bay Islands. The aftermath ushered in the worst extinction event since the dinosaurs, killing dozens of mega fauna such as mastodons, mammoths, sabretooths, and giant sloths. Even known human civilizations such as the Clovis people in America simply vanished. How many other unknown cultures also vanished?"

The film leaves Sophia in a mystified silence, surprised to learn that Roatan had once been part of a mountain range.

"Don't let anyone fool you—the Mesoamerican long count doesn't point to the end of time," he calls out with an excited voice. "Rather, it points us backward, to the beginning of time, when the myths were born during the last ice age."

The bell clangs, and the class empties quickly. "Don't forget we're off next week, and your final reports are due the following week."

Packing his briefcase, he tries to avoid eye contact with her. "Sorry, Miss, I'm late for an appointment. I have office hours today at 1 p.m." He pushes past her to race down the hall.

Disappointed, she turns to watch the professor leave and notices a man peering around the corner toward her. When she catches him, he disappears, yet he seems vaguely familiar. She dismisses the irrational sense of alarm; probably just someone checking out her odd attire. Barely a silhouette, something about his abrupt retreat triggers her anxieties a notch higher.

Chapter 16

In the Crosshairs

Jalisco Forensics Institute, Mexico City
June 18, 10.03 a.m. | 68 hours to Mayan chaa

Loud ringing startles Lucia off the couch as she fumbles to pull the cell phone to her ear.

"Hola?" she whispers, her voice still hoarse, listening to the caller with eyes closed.

"Are you sure?" She jerks up rubbing her face. "I'll be right there."

Not bothering to change from her wrinkled clothes, she races to the downtown morgue, where police have asked her to identify the body of José Juarez. The detective acts detached, as if he never expects to find the killer, claiming street thugs shot José to steal his camera gear. The scenario makes little sense. The equipment was high end, etched with studio identification, and difficult to fence. Even more peculiar was that they left cash in his pocket, high-priced lights, microphones, and other gear.

"What were you filming?" the detective asks.

Lucia hesitates. "We covered the de Aguilar massacre in Polanco Park."

"You mean the murder-suicide?" He corrects her with the official story.

"Yeah, sure," she replies.

"Who did you talk to while you were at the crime scene?" He prods further, staring at his notepad, waiting. She wonders how these questions relate to José's murder.

"Nobody would talk. Do you know why?" she asks. He ignores her.

"Did you keep any video from the crime scene?" He looks down at his pad.

"Excuse me?" she responds.

He fidgets with his pencil, nervous. "Video," he says. "Did you capture any video?"

Her instincts tell her he's looking for something other than José's killer.

"José had the data card in his camera," she lies.

"It doesn't matter," he says. Checking his watch, he turns to the coroner. "Go ahead."

The coroner looks to Lucia. "Ready?"

She nods before he slips back the sheet to expose José's pale, ashy face. Nodding her affirmation, she quickly spins away to control her shock while the detective leads her out of the morgue.

On the way home, the whole experience disturbs her for more than the normal reasons. One of them was why they called her instead of José's wife. His vow to stay alive for his family now resonates with a sadness she knows all too well. José's death will devastate them, especially his young girls. The second reason was the police fixation on the Polanco Park video.

*

Teotihuacan Condominium, Mexico City
June 18, 11:51 a.m. | 67 hours to Mayan chaa

Arriving home, Lucia discovers the door of her apartment left open, the knob damaged. Icy chills shoot through her veins as her hand instinctively slips into her purse for the Beretta 9mm Xavier insisted she carry. Her back to the hallway wall, she slowly pushes the door open with an extended left arm. Wishing her heart would stop pounding so loud, she listens for any sound of movement, hearing only silence. She swings her head into the doorway to get a glimpse and pulls back; vandalized. Her gun hand trembles as it thrusts into the doorway, waiting for a reaction. There's no response, so she risks another glance; empty. From room to room, she silently clears the apartment before letting out a heavy breath and deadbolting the door.

As her pulse slows, her rage flares. "*Bastardos!*" She kicks the couch in frustration.

The computers and data drives are gone, but they smashed the expensive monitors and screens and emptied every drawer and cabinet. With a bolt into the bedroom, she finds her jewelry tossed on the closet floor, the carved wooden box thrown on top of the moderately-priced baubles. *Why take computers, break the screens, and leave the jewelry?* With a powerful flash of insight, she realizes the call from the morgue was a diversion. She must have hit a nerve last night. Someone tipped off the cartel, maybe even her editor. Her head spins so fast, she sits on the torn-up bed before she falls.

Over a decade investigating the Nacon, hunting down the men who killed her parents, and unraveling the dangerous question of why. Now they have her hardware. If they get past the military encryption, they will know everything she knows. Instead of the hunter, she has become the hunted. Tension twists a knot in her chest while she wrings her hands on her jeans.

Why not kill her? The answer hits her like a slap to the face. They're looking for something José didn't have and something they didn't find in her apartment: the video from Polanco Park.

She runs to the bathroom to grab a vase of seashells from the back of the tub and dumps the entire jar onto the rumpled bed. Fishing around, she grabs two flash drives hidden at the bottom, and then with a dash to the living room, she takes a final photo of her card-yarn wall. Whoever trashed her place must have also taken a photo. They know too much, and she has a long way to catch up.

Years ago, she made the poor choice of flirting with the building maintenance man. It took forever to get him to leave her alone, but he once showed her a tunnel from the building basement to the building next door, built by the same developer. A little creepy at the time, but her poor judgment will now pay off. Exiting down the back stairwell and through the garage, she slips behind the furnace room to an unmarked steel door.

From the main garage level of the building next door, she sneaks a trembling peek onto the street. Two men sit in a car, watching the front of her building, likely the same men who trashed her apartment. Not finding the Polanco Park video, they're hoping to follow her, or worse.

With her heart pounding wildly, she runs to the far side of the garage and exits onto the next block to hail a passing cab. There's only one place she can be safe.

Chapter 17

Shower Seduction

Plunder Lust Bridge, Los Rojas Reef
June 18, 12:18 p.m. | 66 hours to Mayan chaa

Miguel had hoped they could avoid this turn of events. From inside the bridge, he and Xavier each hold up binoculars aimed toward the Spanish fort ruins of San Lorenzo on the bluff above the reef.

"Look to the left," directs Xavier.

"Yeah, I see him," Miguel confirms.

A cartel pirate scout has perched inside a fort gunwale, trying to act like a lazy tourist, except this tourist has a telephoto camera lens framed on *Plunder Lust* and a pair of binoculars draped around his tattooed neck. With nothing happening on deck, he takes a smoke break.

"How long has he been there?" Miguel asks.

"I noticed him yesterday," replies Xavier.

"You sure he's Nacon?" Miguel asks.

"I sent a drone over last night with a repeater cell to catch his cell calls. He reported in ten minutes ago," Xavier says. "Skipper, Shay Golan knows we're here."

"Golan, oh geez, this project just keeps getting better and better," he grumbles.

A dimwitted moron, but vicious as a honey badger, Shay Golan works for the Nacon relic raider squads. Miguel doesn't like the odds, especially anchored so close to shore with Darcy and her team of bookworms in the line of fire.

"Then get ready for *el grande*," warns Xavier. "I discovered this post an hour ago." He swings a computer monitor.

"*Buluc Chabtan ko chaa*," Miguel reads.

"What does that mean?" Xavier asks. As security officer, Xavier spends most of his time on dark-web sites, chatrooms, and other dangerous places, in order to keep the ship safe from the cartel, and he's damn good at his job.

"It's K'iche," responds Miguel. He grew up in the region, the son of two archaeologists. "Buluc Chabtan is a Mayan god of violence and sacrifice," he clarifies. "Chaa refers to the moment of dawn on the summer solstice, June 21."

Xavier folds his arms, his shaved head damp again from the summer heat. The solstice is only a few days away. "I found this post on a blog site used by our friends at Nacon," Xavier explains. "Sounds like a possible sleeper cell signal, maybe another drug war escalation."

Nacon, named after a Mayan god of war, is considered one of the world's most vicious cartels, encompassing an extensive criminal reach beyond drugs, prostitution, kidnap, and ransom. The Triad of Latin America, they have successfully consolidated weaker cartels like Zetas and Sinaloa, virtually taken over the illegal arms trade in the region, and set up a vast hacker, online fraud, and surveillance army. More important to Miguel, Nacon has financed an archaeology black market militia which has cost him plunder and lives.

"How do you want to play this one?" asks Xavier.

The threat of losing lives over a bunch of worthless historical junk ships spins like acid in his stomach. He growls in frustration, clenching his fist and then swallows his apprehension.

"We go dark, night dives only," he replies. "Keep daytime hours for lab work."

The San Lorenzo museum closes at night, which means his scout can only spy on them during the day. The tactic will buy them a few weeks at most.

"Night shifts will push us further behind schedule," notes Xavier. "What about Dr. O'Sullivan?"

Miguel groans. He'd rather deal with the cartel than tell Darcy more bad news. The further behind schedule they fall, the crankier his sweet girlfriend becomes. Working together will ruin the romance.

"Yeah, sure, okay, you're right, I should probably tell her." He turns to leave. "But if you hear a blood-curdling scream coming from my cabin," he pauses at the door, "that'll be me."

*

Plunder Lust, Captain's Quarters
June 18, 12:27 p.m. | 66 hours to Mayan chaa

Darcy abhors the onboard captain's quarters of *Plunder Lust*. Neither spacious nor romantic, the dull beige walls feature taped-up, faded pictures of luxury sailing yachts, cheeky holdovers of Miguel's barmy boyhood fantasies. With basic commercial plumbing, and a narrow glass shower stall, the room lacks any pretense at privacy.

Spoiled as a child, she grew up in a spacious private room with a large bath. Like most archaeologists, she endures the field for a season but eagerly awaits returning home. Miguel, on the other hand, has grown accustomed to his primitive lifestyle. If she does achieve tenure, part of her estate will be the manor house north of Sussex. To her utter annoyance, the sea dog doesn't show the least bit of interest in a visit. Raised in the equatorial jungles of Central America, he finds weather below seventy degrees Fahrenheit to be arctic. The man doesn't even own a coat.

Without a knock, Miguel pushes into the cabin, forcing her to squeeze toward the shower stall as hot water steams up the room.

"Hey, babe, Xavi and I were talking, and you know, funny thing, huh—" begins Miguel.

"I'm glad you're here," she cuts him off. "We need to have a bit of a chin wag."

She drops her towel and steps into the glass shower. Miguel leans against the bulkhead, his eyes frozen to her petite naked form.

"Chin wag," he chuckles. "You're so cute. Yeah sure, what's up?"

Aware of him watching, she makes sure to lather slowly and completely.

"When we start to video the daily debrief tomorrow," she begins, "I'd like you to introduce the San Lorenzo battle story, but leave out the bit about lost treasure. Don't get me wrong, it's a lovely story," she says. "But you should stick to the Lorenzo battle."

"Really? You're cutting out the best part," he replies.

"I know," she concedes, not wishing to argue. "Try to understand, both the tenure board and Panama Archeological Committee will preview the video series as part of our documentation. Any discussion of treasure will only hurt our credibility. Can we agree?" She negotiates.

"Okay, I guess, so why not let your buddy Jackson cover the Lorenzo battle," he counter-offers. "The dude's a total ham."

Stepping out of the shower, she drapes a towel around her waist, watching his gaze fall to her wet nipples, growing hard in the portal breeze. With her hair still dripping, she tries a new approach.

"Well, Captain—" She inches closer. "Because you're a well-known Henry Morgan expert." It's true. Miguel has been searching for Morgan's lost plunder since he was a boy, inspired by a dream. Most men outgrow their boyhood fantasies. In her mind, it was time for Peter Pan to grow up, but that was a conversation for another time.

"And because you first discovered the wrecks," she says playfully, placing her fingers on his arm, peering into his eyes. Also true. Miguel discovered the Los Rojas wrecks years ago but never salvaged them because he knew they contained no plunder.

"And because you tell a great story," she coos, her other hand resting on his chest, leaving a wet spot. Partly true, after a few pints with his mates, he can be quite entertaining.

"And you're rather cute on video—" She rises on her toes to kiss him, her breasts leaving large wet spots on his shirt. "And sex sells, baby," she whispers with an impish grin and a raised eyebrow. A white lie; on video, he's like a wooden mannequin and quite hilarious. He'll be the visual equivalent of starting with a joke.

Playing on Miguel's sexual psyche weakens his defenses, and with a sigh, he complies. "Okay, Dr. O'Sullivan," he gives in with a kiss. "Your video, your way, no gold, all geek."

He pulls her waist tighter for another kiss, pressing his growing excitement against her belly.

"I'm pleased to have your enthusiastic support," she smiles.

Easier than she expected. She should open all negotiations from the shower stall, especially the sensitive one coming soon. Ensuring future success, she locks the cabin door, drops her towel, and returns for another lingering kiss, nudging him backward to the bunk and climbing on top.

"Did you have something to discuss?" she asks.

His surprise instantly dissolves into passion as she pops a button off his wet shirt.

"Yeah, no, it'll keep," he replies.

Chapter 18

Meaningless Madness

Archaeology Department, UCLA, Los Angeles
June 18, 1:04 p.m. | 65 hours to Mayan chaa

With a groan, Sophia takes her place at the end of a long line of students who congest the hallway outside the office of Dr. Estefan Martinez. An hour and a half later, her turn arrives just as the professor packs his briefcase to leave again. A shudder of panic sweeps over her.

"I'm sorry, Miss, I only take appointments until 2 p.m. You can come back on Thursday, or post to my blog."

Exhausted beyond words and fed up with waiting in lines, she blocks the doorway. "I'm not a student," she says, "and this can't wait." She holds up Carmen's book. "Are you the son of Olivier, who was the son of Joaquin, who migrated from Roatan?"

His eyes narrow. "I don't mean to be rude, but who are you, and what do you want?"

She hands him the photographs. "I want to know why someone would kill for these artifacts," she says, her voice quivering.

He casts a startled glance at her, then looks down to the images. Only the image of the bloody book lights in his eyes. "Who died?"

"Carmen Morales Martinez, the wife of Joaquin Martinez." She hands him the wedding photo. "I don't know who killed her, but they came for those relics."

He studies the wedding photo, seeming to wrestle with something, then hands back the images. "I'm sorry, I can't help you," he replies, continuing to pack. "You should contact the local police to solve a murder."

"Do you still have the key to the curse of Cortés?" she asks, eager to keep him engaged. The curse of Cortés was how Papá once referred to the legend; unsure where the name originated, she's hoping it will mean something to him.

His eyes dart up in surprise. "Who told you about that?"

"Carmen," her throat catches, "before she died to protect the relics. Please, Señor, I've traveled all the way from Roatan, and I haven't even eaten since yesterday. I just need to understand why she died." Her eyes moisten, and her voice cracks, but she refuses to cry in front of this man.

"I'm sorry, Miss," he dismisses softly. "I don't believe in curses."

"Good," she retorts. "I'm looking for facts, not folklore. Do you have the key?"

He seems like a rational man, staring at her several moments, trying to decide something. "I'm sorry, I didn't catch your name," he asks again.

"Sophia Martinez, daughter of Antonio Martinez, grandson of Franco Martinez, the father of Joaquin."

He smiles. "So, you're Antonio's daughter."

Her eyes open in surprise. "You knew my papá?"

"Well, no," he hesitates. "I knew *of* him. I should explain. My son and I were in Belize when we learned of his disappearance. When I realized there was a family connection, we joined in the search. For some reason, we weren't welcomed on Roatan, so we stayed with a man named Hector on Isla Barbareta. Hector mentioned that Antonio left a daughter. I'm so sorry we were unable to find your father."

She doesn't remember him. Hundreds of people joined in the search, but Mamá kept her home. She vaguely recalls hushed whispers of shame between Carmen and Mamá over a distant family member, but she was so devastated by the loss of Papá that she paid no attention.

"How's your mother doing? Did your uncle recover?" he asks, trying to show concern but revealing that he never kept in touch. Why should he, when he wasn't welcome?

Sophia looks down. "Mamá died of cancer a few months after Papá disappeared. Rafé fell into chronic dementia."

"Oh," he murmurs, his voice softening. "I'm so very sorry to hear." With a sigh, he points to the images. "Please tell me where you found those."

Abuelita used to say that sometimes you don't know who to trust until you know who not to trust. Sally's advice to have faith rings in her mind, even more profound, knowing that she reached back from the grave to deliver the message. She takes a deep breath.

"I found them after an earthquake. They were hidden in a stone wall of our home built in 1811," she explains. "When Carmen saw them, she claimed they were cursed. Before she died, she said you had the key."

His expression changes as if he wrestles with another decision. "Come with me." He leads her down the hall toward an area marked *Secure–University Personnel Only.*

"My grandfather Joaquin gave them to me before he died," he comments on the way.

"Gave you what, a key?" she asks, but he doesn't respond.

After a few hallways, they approach a locked metal door. Entering a key code, he uses a thumbprint to gain access. They enter an air-filtered, temperature- and humidity-controlled document room with a door that automatically seals behind them. Three large lightbox examination tables illuminate the center of the room, with two walls of document storage drawers of various sizes.

Sophia has never seen such sophistication, raising her confidence and expectations. A distant relative has agreed to share something he inherited from Joaquin and keeps in a secure room. So different from her museum experience, she reminds herself to have faith.

Unlocking a wide, thin architectural plan drawer, he pulls out a double Plexiglas panel to lay on the lightbox. Between the two clear pieces of plastic are three handwritten pages about five by eight inches, obviously the missing pages torn from the end of her book. With them laid on top of the light box, she can clearly see layers of blood, and then etching over previous layers of writing. The professor pulls out several enlarged photographs of the blood-soaked pages, propping them up against the walls. Some images use ultraviolet, infrared, or other light spectrums to reveal the hidden text. Two or three layers on each page show a steady deterioration of the handwriting, changing from barely legible to an erratic scratch, as if written by an arthritic hand, or perhaps a dying one.

Unsure what she expected as "the key," she didn't expect more incoherent, bloody pages.

"What you call the key, I call insane gibberish, a meaningless madness," he explains.

"What do you mean?" she asks.

He takes a moment to think. "Well, to begin with, the writer used an illiterate level of old Spanish mixed with K'iche, but mainly because the content is quite insane and sadistic."

Insane and sadistic sounds like a prerequisite for a curse, not that she would know.

His eyes take in hers. "Trust me. I've studied these pages for many years, and I assure you there are no secrets and no keys, only the insane ramblings of a poorly educated man with immense rage and an evil imagination."

"Like what someone else might call a curse." She eyes the professor with a raised eyebrow. "What does it say?"

He smiles, shaking his head. "First, tell me what happened that made you fly two thousand miles without an appointment."

She hesitates, unsure what to share before exhaling a deep breath. "There was an earthquake on Roatan a few days ago that damaged our family home. I

99

found the relics in an unmarked stone box hidden inside a rock wall."

"Where are the items now?" he asks.

Still stung from the betrayal at the museum, she sees no harm in caution. "Hidden on a remote island." She admits the truth, but not all of it. He nods acceptance.

"When Carmen saw the relics, she warned me to rebury or destroy them or the dead would follow me." Guilt tightens in her throat, threatening tears, forcing her to pause until she can breathe.

"I don't believe in curses," she repeats to herself as much as to him. "I wanted facts, so I went to the Belize Museum, where Dr. Colon told me they were worthless fakes."

"Wait, hold up, you met with Dr. Edwardo Colon?" He bristles at the name.

Sophia shakes her head. "No, his name was Ricardo. Do you know him?"

"I've encountered his father," he explains. "I was working on a site in the region and met with the senior Dr. Colon to help translate an inscription. Within days, raiders ambushed our camp. I've always suspected Dr. Colon but could never prove it. Ricardo was working under his father." Dr. Martinez grinds his teeth. "Go on, what happened next?"

Still traumatized by the experience, she doesn't want to discuss the details. "The attack came later that same night without warning. It was raining. Three men stormed the terrace, demanding the relics, shot Carmen and then Emilio, but only took the stone box before disappearing as fast as they came. Emilio may have killed one, I'm not sure, but it was dark and over in seconds." Numb and disassociated, she stares at the floor.

"I thought you said you hid the items."

"Si," she confirms, lifting her gaze. "The box was empty. They didn't even check. The next day, they came back to tear up my house. Now I'm afraid to go home or endanger anyone else."

An attempt at a brave smile swells her eyes with tears, leaking desperation, fatigue, and grief down her cheek. Even in her own ear, it all sounds ridiculous.

"Dr. Colon lied to you," he confirms her suspicion. "I need to see the real items to be sure, but the dagger, and maybe the tortoise script could be quite old, making them valuable on the black market."

"So, Carmen's death was a robbery gone wrong?" replies Sophia.

"Perhaps, but I'm guessing Dr. Colon is a middleman to someone who wants to avoid a paper or bank trail, likely a cartel or other illegal buyer. They thought you would be an easy target. You fooled them when you moved the items," Dr. Martinez clarifies.

Relieved to hear an answer that doesn't involve a curse or a hoax, it sadly confirms that her stubborn actions led to Carmen's death. A deep aching of remorse sucks the air from her lungs. How can she ever forgive herself?

Dr. Martinez hesitates. "Either way, your life may be in danger as long as you have possession of the artifacts."

Living with the shame of Carmen's death while fearing for her life on a daily basis sure sounds like a curse in so many other words.

He considers a moment longer. "If you loan these to the university, I can arrange a modest stipend fee," he says. "Once the items are secured, we can issue a press release. Maybe it'll take the target off your back." He shrugs. "If nothing else, the university can put the artifacts in our folklore collection."

"What about those who want revenge?" she asks.

He falls silent. She's questioning his courage, and so maybe he's doing the same.

"I know the perfect team to help us once we get to the region," he replies.

Speechless, Sophia reaches out to embrace the older professor in a powerful, long Garifuna hug. Grateful, and relieved for the first time in days, she holds him until he relents.

"Dr. Martinez, I don't know how to thank you." His help may not be exactly what she expected, but it's an offer she's grateful to accept.

"You can start by calling me Estefan," he replies. "It looks like we're distant cousins."

A cousin; what a strange notion. She's not the last Martinez after all.

"Well, Estefan, if you don't mind, I'd like to start with something to eat," she suggests.

"I know just the place, the Del Frisco Grille near the beach in Santa Monica," he replies with a wide smile. "The food is good, but the service is painfully slow. It'll give us time to get to know each other and book a red-eye flight."

She smiles. His approach seems rational and logical, except for the part about taking another brutal overnight flight. Inwardly, she pulls a secret curtain over the lingering premonition that the worst is yet to come. It must be hunger.

Chapter 19

Safe House

Storage Coyocan, Mexico City
June 18, 2:42 p.m. | 64 hours to Mayan chaa

After giving the taxi driver no less than five addresses to make sure no one followed her, Lucia enters the commercial storage building in a seedy section of the city. At a unit near the end of a darkened hall, she unlocks the heavy padlock and rolls up the door. With a quick step inside, she closes the rolling door and bolts a lock from the inside to prevent any unexpected visitors. A black-and-white security screen provides a feed of the hallway. Terrified out of her skin, she stands in the darkness, watching the monitor, her heart pounding between her ears, a trembling hand gripped tightly on her Beretta.

Several moments pass before she exhales and flips a power switch to illuminate a storage space furnished with inexpensive rugs, a battered office desk, and several computers. A networked copier-printer sits next to a wire rack with several dozen boxes containing files, tapes, or CDs. Her safe house war room on the murder of her parents and Nacon corruption. Set up by her brother Xavier, pirated internet from the insurance company next door provides online access. She got sloppy by working out of her apartment; a nearly fatal mistake.

Most of the data in the boxes are originals to the flash drives in her purse. She uploaded copies to several online cloud sites under multiple fake names, another trick taught by Xavier. After booting the main computer, she steps over to a box labeled *Cartel Violence*. Lucia threw the data card in the box last night on her way home. To her knowledge, they captured nothing of importance, but someone else isn't so sure.

The raw video pans the growing crowd of concerned and frightened citizens. José covers the seven bodies carried out by the coroner, then cuts to the military guards who hold back the crowd, then her interview with the police, and then with the coroner. Nothing. The whole tape runs again and again for over an hour. She listens to every word, thinking she missed something. Then she spots him. While she's talking to the coroner, he stands at the back of the crowd, not frightened or concerned, but casually smoking a cigarette while he talks with one of the military police. After a momentary glance in her direction, he turns his face away from the camera.

The blood in her veins turns cold. She's seen his face before, a long, long time ago. He's older and heavier now, but she remembers the heavy eyebrows, the bony jaw, the scar above his left eye, and his scowl. Lucia has changed too. She's no longer the terrified little girl with her older brother's hand over her mouth to keep her from screaming. Yet, seeing his face again, even on video, triggers an intense flashback. An involuntary flurry of images saturated with a tsunami of rage, terror, and powerlessness punches her in the gut, tightens her chest, and spins her vision with a violent vertigo. Her hands and jaw clench as memories flash back uncontrolled, watching from outside her body.

Two men storm her home in Juarez, shouting at her father and mother to get on their knees. In a back room playing, Xavier forces her into a hidden crawl space beneath the floor full of spider webs. Muffled screams and gunshots precede shattered glass and the thunderous fall of bodies. The overpowering smell of gasoline dripping through the floorboards pushes her to a vent beneath the front porch. Killers drag her parents into the middle of their suburban street, leaving a bloody trail. Doused in gasoline, the short one sets her parents on fire as the house above her burns. Xavier pulls at her clothes to escape, but she can't move, her eyes fixated on the morbid scene. Unchallenged in broad daylight, the taller man turns back to admire his handiwork. She will never forget his face, the face of death, the face of the man on her video.

Her body shudders, flashing hot and clammy. The memory swells up in waves of weeping and groaning as she hunches over, trying to squeeze away the pain. It takes several moments to slow her breathing and pull away from the emotional avalanche. The same man who assassinated her parents also massacred the de Aguilar family, and now he has her within his crosshairs.

The difference between then and now is that Xavier taught her how to fight back. Using a hacked government facial-recognition application, she uploads the facial image. While that search grinds, she opens a pirated copy of an application that Xavier developed for CISEN, Mexican Military Intelligence. Very sophisticated, it has taken her two years to organize the data on her flash drives for the program to read. Opening the powerful application, she uploads the image of her wall, and then the contents of the flash drives.

She doesn't know how the application works, but it translates each note card into an event or person of interest, called a POI. Then the program connects data to each event or POI and searches online data sources to fill in the blanks. Her flash drive has thousands of video clips, AP wires, articles, and other data sources spanning decades. An hour later, the application has produced ten times as many events or POI as she expected. The pattern discovered in Mexico repeats across Latin America, reflecting a business and government takeover from within. Of the dozens of new POI to investigate, there are a few new names that catch her interest.

· *Pakistani General Basri Qamar Hayat (deceased, 49) (see profile)*
· *Felipe Roué Gutierrez (deceased, 16) (see profile)*
· *Juan Perez de Menendez (age 56) (see profile)*

The first two names are a total mystery, but the well-known eccentric, womanizing media mogul Juan Perez de Menendez both surprises and intrigues her. A friend of Arturo Lanza and just about every other leader in Latin America, his company Evolucion has been a major promoter for the summit on Cozumel, and he even owns her network.

Excited by the lead, she sends a text to her brother on an encrypted phone registered under a fake name. Xavier insists on using his dark web alias of Delores, the name of their mother. At his insistence, she set up a false dark web moniker Phoenix, because she vows to live again someday.

'Delores– Good news. Found K1. Bad news, K1 found me. At safe house running Beast App. Dead bank CEO ties to JPdM? Love, Phoenix' – SEND.

K1 was her shorthand for killer 1, and JPdM stood in for Juan Perez de Menendez.

Xavier once told her there were two types of people in the world, those who run out of a fire to save themselves, and those who run into a fire to save others. No one truly knows what type of person he or she will be until the fire erupts. Her instincts urge her to pursue this thread, no matter where it leads, even if it means running into the fire. She already knows what type of person she is, and while telling Xavier would only make him worry, she suspects he already knows.

Chapter 20

Creator's Tomb
(Mukik Kisiin)

Los Pinos Presidential Palace, Mexico
June 18, 3:39 p.m. | 63 hours to Mayan chaa

Juan Perez flew to Mexico City at the late-night personal request of President Lanza to discuss a serious matter in private. Highly inconvenient with so many last-minute details to manage before the Unity Gala, a deep suspicion compels him to ensure there are no surprises. Upon arrival, an aide escorts him to the Los Pinos gardens of flowers, fountains, and tall Ponderosa pines, where a grieving Arturo Lanza needs consolation over the bloody massacre of Salazar de Aguilar and his family.

"El Presidente, I am so very sorry for your loss. I understand you and Salazar were close friends." He consoles the politician.

The tragic murder-suicide of the national bank executive has dominated the morning headlines, with speculation that Salazar de Aguilar wanted his family spared the shame of an IMF investigation over cartel money laundering, leading to whispers of a coverup.

"Si, the five-year-old, Ramos, was my godchild." Arturo clenches his fists.

"What kind of monster would massacre children?" he asks a rhetorical question. In truth, he's known the monster his entire life, and any humanity left in his psychopathic brother died out decades ago.

"Hun Came," growls Lanza. "The demon ghost sends me a message."

He suppresses a chuckle at the moniker, but at least Lanza knows enough to dismiss the fake police reports of a murder-suicide.

"A message from the Nacon Death Lord cannot be a good sign," replies Juan Perez, sounding surprised but secretly enjoying the game of manipulation. "What do you think he wants?"

He wants to hear the coward admit the truth. Lanza was a Nacon lap dog until El Chapo exposed him for bribery. Now he refuses to cooperate, and even dared to launch an investigation to root out internal Nacon spies. An act of defiance that demanded retribution. The choice of eliminating de Aguilar served a dual purpose of striking a personal blow to Lanza and gaining control of the central bank.

Lanza hesitates, stalling on the path. "I need to know I can trust you, no leaks or stories."

"Of course, you have my complete loyalty," he lies, finding the situation almost poetic in its irony.

"I have Nacon spies in my government," he says. "Early investigations indicate there may be several, but we cannot confirm the identities. I am left with almost no one to fully trust, except perhaps you, old friend."

He may have underestimated Lanza's state of desperation. In fact, Nacon maintains multiple spies within the administration, hundreds within the government and police. None of them knows of the others, making each one expendable. After the resurrection of Bolon-Yokte, he will purge the old governments of loyalists and traitors alike. In the short term, he needs to convince Lanza to either shut down the investigation or reveal who leads the effort. He must be careful not to overplay his hand.

"Then I am humbled, El Presidente." He bows his head. "You mentioned a message from Nacon." The reason for the garden setting now becomes clear, so Lanza can be away from any listening devices or ears.

"I assume he wants me to cancel the investigation, but if so, then the investigation has already been compromised." Lanza glances to Juan Perez. "Even if I stop the investigation in secret, the murder of a close friend now makes me look weak going into the summit."

"A complex dilemma," responds Juan, taking a moment to think.

Lanza failed to confess his corruption, but instead he obsesses over his reputation. He may be able to use that ego against him.

"El Presidente, you must not allow Nacon to rob you of your place in history on Cozumel," he suggests. "You will not look weak if we use the sacrifice of Señor de Aguilar as a martyr to enflame the passions of the region. We will call upon our allies to unite against Nacon."

"I love that angle," Arturo replies.

"If the investigation is indeed compromised, as you suspect, then why not appease Hun Came until after the summit when you return empowered," he suggests. In fact, after the summit, the issue of spies will no longer be an issue.

"I suppose it would reduce the risk of Nacon sabotaging the summit," Arturo says, perhaps alluding to the classified nuclear threat.

"To cancel the summit will only make you look weak. Seize the opportunity to show strength. Let your courage set an example for others," he encourages.

Nacon has indeed grown exceedingly strong. Short of turning the streets into a bloody battleground, the governments have grown too timid to oppose them directly. Every leader in Latin America would love to see the demise of Nacon, if only they could find the infamous leader Hun Came.

"Si, si, perhaps you are correct," Lanza concedes.

It takes another hour of consoling a distraught Lanza before Juan Perez finds an excuse to exit Los Pinos. While the summit remains on track, he was unable to learn who leads the investigation.

"Señor de Menendez," calls Director-General Flores from behind, striding down the steps toward him as he approaches his waiting limo. "A moment, por favor."

He pivots to greet the senior aide, supposedly retained on a more important matter earlier.

"Director-General Flores, good to see you. I just met with El Presidente over the tragedy. Sorry you could not join us." He lies, needing the chance to influence Lanza without the chaperone.

"Si, I just spoke with El Presidente, and I need a word." He steps away from others and lowers his voice. "Why would you advise El Presidente to stop an internal investigation?"

The question stuns him for a moment, as he thinks through how to respond. There is only one reason Lanza would tell Flores about the conversation: Tomas Flores leads the investigation. Ironic that Lanza chose a man already compromised himself to find other moles. It gives him an idea on how to wrap up two loose ends with one deep cut.

He narrows his eyes and lowers his own voice. "El Presidente called me personally to seek my opinion, so I shared an honest one, Director. Given the Nacon warning with Señor de Aguilar, the internal investigations have been compromised and risk Nacon retaliation on Cozumel. I advised a delay, not to cancel. A ruse. If you do not agree, Señor, then present your case, but I do not need your permission to speak."

Tomas stares at him for a long moment, trying to read his soul. Coerced into seeking his advice by his anonymous handler, Tomas remains suspicious of who pulls his strings and why.

"I disagree, and I will change his mind," Tomas states flatly. "Removing the Nacon cancer has never been more important to the future of Mexico, a theme I noticed never promoted by Evolucion, which makes me question your true loyalties, Señor."

He holds for a beat to contain his anger and bites his tongue, telling himself to respond as Juan Perez would respond. He closes his eyes to take a breath.

"Director-General," he says, smiling tightly, "direct confrontation with Nacon only leads to death. Far too many of my journalists have perished in the wake of weak government and incompetence. My reputation is not the one you should be concerned to protect."

Tomas takes a moment to digest the response, his eyes cast down. "Señor de Menendez, do you recall what you told me when we first met on the night El Presidente won the election?"

His heart skips a beat. There were no notes in the profile regarding that exchange. He has no choice but to play the lost memory card. "I'm sorry, Director, but I am an old man with a busy schedule. Please refresh me."

Tomas steps back with a smirk. "In fact, we never spoke that night. We never met until last month." He bows his head in faux humility. "Good day, Señor de Menendez. I suspect we will be speaking again soon."

The smug politician, having caught him in a minor lie, turns back towards the Los Pinos main entrance. Tomas suspects something, and it's clear the investigation will continue. It's time to snip the loose ends.

Inside the limo on the way to the airport, he gets on the phone. "I have another urgent matter after you take care of the reporter," he says. "You're going to enjoy this one, *hermano*."

*

Cenote Cocodrillo, Isla Cozumel
June 18, 5:39 p.m. | 61 hours to Mayan chaa

Flying fast and low over the jungles of central Cozumel, Juan Perez sits inside the sound-insulated cabin of his luxurious high-speed Sikorsky S92 copter, continuing to work the phones.

"Si, President Bellerose, Evolucion cannot guarantee your reelection, but I am sure we can arrange for positive campaign coverage. We can discuss the matter further at the reception dinner."

"Perfect, Señor de Menendez. I look forward to seeing you," Bellerose replies.

He ends the call, pours a shot of tequila, and throws it back. The corrupt, racist Brazilian president will never be reelected, but the right-wing snake needed a promise of reelection support to attend the summit, and so he gave him that promise.

Across from him, Shay grinds his teeth, clenches his fist, and simmers with shame. After the fiasco of losing a man over an empty stone box, the moron lost two more men trying to kidnap an aging lunatic. Shay wants to blame Gerhard for bad intelligence, but the Syrian buffoon will pay for his own incompetence soon enough.

His encrypted cell vibrates with a known ID. He patches the signal into his noise-canceling headphones. "Good news so soon?" he asks, surprised at the quick response.

"The reporter vaporized," the voice growls.

"The *puta* makes a fool of you, hermano, just like her brother," he taunts, motivating the caller with shame.

"All the more satisfying when I find her," the voice retorts.

"What about our other problem?" Juan Perez asks.

Director-General Flores has outlived his usefulness. The investigation poses an unacceptable risk, a loose end, and Juan Perez hates loose ends.

"He took the bait," the voice reassures.

A young Nacon male prostitute has been seducing Flores into a torrid affair for months, producing hours of explicit video. Lured to a secret apartment in a seedy part of Mexico City known for gay bars and prostitutes, authorities will find the mutilated, headless body of Tomas Flores. When they search his home, they'll find a video of Tomas raping a ten-year-old boy, the same video used to blackmail him into submission, an epitaph of shame to stain a self-serving, entitled life.

"Excellent," says Juan Perez. Raped as a young boy himself, he savors the vicarious sense of revenge.

"What about Golan and the Frenchman?" the voice asks about the other loose ends.

For decades, he maintained impenetrable secrecy with a rigorous policy of eliminating any and all witnesses, without exception. Juan Perez lifts his gaze to the mindless pit bull in the opposite seat, oblivious to his ultimate fate.

"Under control, just stay focused on your problem," he exhorts and then disconnects.

As the chopper descends onto the cenote clearing, he can see Gerhard waiting with two insulated cases and a grim expression. By now, the archaeologist knows that two divers died in an accident and may perceive the frailty of his own life. Except for the stolen backhoe, the site looks clean. The men sent to refill the sinkhole stand eager to leave alive. Shay will deal with them later after the gratitude of a great meal and an evening with cartel *puta*s.

As soon as they touch the ground, Shay leaps from the chopper, bolting up to the startled archaeologist, grabbing him by the throat, and forcing him backward against a nearby tree. Glasses fall to the ground as Gerhard wiggles against Shay's apelike grip. Juan Perez walks slowly as Shay chokes the life out of the corrupt French nerd.

"So far, Doctor, your *easy target* has cost Shay three good men, a second enormous bribe to cover up a murder, and a very expensive inflatable." He speaks with a calm irritation. "The relics were not at the woman's house, nor with her feeble-minded uncle. Even worse, the woman landed yesterday in Los Angeles." He pauses a beat. "Los Angeles! I wanted this done quickly and quietly." He spits his seething anger. "I have more important matters to attend than to clean up after such bungling."

Shay squeezes tighter, scowling with an unabashed loathing. With eyes bulging and face turning blue, Gerhard points to a jade death mask alongside a darkened, elongated skull within the two insulated cases. On top, Gerhard left photographs from the museum cameras, plus new images from the underwater cenote temple, circling something on each photo, a glyph. His notes are clear on his interpretation, the serpent god, the Maker, Kukulkan. Quetzalcoatl.

Juan Perez picks up the death mask, excitedly examining both sides. An incredible jade mosaic, he doesn't object to the oddly demonic appearance, placing it up to his own face like a kid. A second before Gerhard passes out, Juan Perez signals for Shay to release the weasel. Shay steps back disappointed, while Gerhard falls to his knees coughing, gasping, wheezing, and rubbing his bruised throat. Shay pants like a beast, hungry to finish its prey.

"Give me a good reason why I shouldn't let Shay finish having fun," Juan Perez taunts.

Picking up the elongated skull, he scrutinizes it with the wide eyes of a boy. Much like the Paracas skulls of South America, a clump of the original dark-red hair remains, with cranial capacity much larger than a normal human skull.

"You hired me to find the lost tomb of the creator." Gerhard chokes between words. "You hold his skull in your hands."

He points to the mask. "The mask bears the same glyph as the blade and the temple stelae."

On all fours, the Frenchman feels in the brush for his glasses. "Together, the mask and skull contain the creator's spirit and wisdom," he coughs and stammers. "To possess the maker's power, you must possess the sacred obsidian."

Juan Perez doesn't say a word, but a spark of excitement instantly bursts into an obsessive blaze. Yes, of course he wants the power of the maker. Explained in that light, he absolutely craves it. Fixation inflates like a bomb blast to consume his imagination. Another confirmation that destiny has chosen him.

He glances to the covered cenote. From the tomb of a past epoch will come the womb for his new epoch, representing a perfect prophetic symmetry. Holding the elongated skull, the reality penetrates him that he holds the wisdom of Quetzalcoatl, the maker. Closing his eyes, he imagines himself absorbing a divine foresight.

"Shay's failure to check the damn box or take the girl belongs on him. His incompetence in snatching a lunatic is also his shame." Gerhard goes on the offensive, his voice hoarse like he had smoked a carton of cigarettes.

Golan snarls like a beast waiting for a command to kill. Juan enjoys the irony of their petty conflict. They will both be dead soon.

"You two clowns will work together. I want both the woman and her uncle snatched by tonight," he orders. "Break their wills and find my blade. Fail me again and it will be your last."

Both fools nod in silent obedience. "Get in the bird," he commands.

Shay's men load the cases onto the chopper, followed by a growling Shay and a wheezing Gerhard keeping his distance.

Buluc Chabtan lies buried, silently waiting. Tomorrow, the LASSG summit will kick off, and the entire island will go on lockdown. Only one task remains to seal the prophecy. Juan Perez pulls out a military timer device to confirm the preset entry: June 21, 6:12 a.m., the summer solstice, the Mayan chaa.

With a deep breath, he presses enter, but the system continues to read green, unarmed. With such a long distance of limestone and tunnels between Juan Perez, and Buluc Chabtan, he has a sudden panic the signal may not be able to reach the device, a factor he failed to consider in the last-minute change of plans. Until the discovery of the cenote, he had planned to hide Buluc within a tunnel of the coral reef during a night dive. The cenote places Buluc Chabtan directly under the summit and makes detection nearly impossible. A meaningless advantage if the damn thing won't light up. A panic swells in his chest until the clock sets, a countdown begins, and the light affirms red, armed.

He exhales loudly and then smashes the timer to pieces against a nearby tree, destroying the unique device connection. No turning back, and now nothing can stop him. An uncontrollable chuckle rolls into a bellowing, malevolent, and sadistic cackle. Soon, he will grip the blade of the maker, and with the power of Buluc Chabtan and prophecy, he will change the world for a thousand years.

Chapter 21

Cursed State of Mind

Dallas International Airport, Dallas, Texas
June 18, 6:16 p.m. | 60 hours to Mayan chaa

The redeye from Los Angeles left Sophia and Estefan with a long delay in Dallas until their next flight to Cancun, where they will catch a regional flight to Belize before a final leg to Roatan.

With time before the next flight, they find a café. Sophia doesn't fly much, so it feels a bit strange to notice a young man from their earlier flight periodically leering at her. She dismisses him as a pervert misbehaving, but the asandiruni continues to gnaw at her nerves.

During the flight, Estefan spoke endlessly about his theory of a lost civilization hidden under the flooded coastline of Roatan but admits to scant hard evidence. He has tried and failed to get a research permit to conduct a LIDAR scan of the Honduran jungles rumored to contain Ciudad Blanca, the lost city of the Monkey King, believing them to be ruins of the survivors. While the ancient history fascinates her, the conversation eventually turns to the American side of the family history.

"I'm afraid to say that the American side of the family endured nearly just as much tragedy as those left on Roatan," Estefan says after taking a bite of a taco plate.

"What do you mean?" she asks, eating a salad.

"Well, for example," he thinks a moment, "like you, I was raised mostly by Papá Joaquin, who was also hyper-superstitious and suffered from dementia. I never got to know my parents before they passed. My padre, Olivier, died trying to save our home from a wildfire, and Mamá Isabella died a year later from a racial road rage incident. Before he lost it completely, Joaquin used to tell me stories of growing up on Roatan and the family curse."

"*Hijole*," she reacts. "Rafé used to call me Isabella. Do you think he knew of Oliver and Isabella?"

"Joaquin and Rafé were brothers, so maybe somehow they kept in touch for a time." Estefan shrugs.

The stories only reignite her heartache over the more recent tragedies. "Carmen claimed the curse was on the Martinez name, or perhaps our lineage. When I was young, she even hinted that marriage would change my name and perhaps my fate."

"I thought you didn't believe in curses." Estefan raises an eyebrow.

"I don't," she says, "but I find it hard to believe so much tragedy in a one family could be chance. There must be a rational explanation."

Carmen had also encouraged her to destroy the relics, indicating that perhaps the curse lay on the items themselves. The book and the missing pages were split between two countries, and yet both family branches experienced tragedy, so perhaps the book is the source.

"Life can be full of tragedy. I've grown to believe that the power of a curse lies simply in the fear it produces within those who believe, and nothing more," Estefan responds.

"Maybe you are right," she concedes, acknowledging that Carmen was a very superstitious woman, yet that superstition had sent her thousands of miles to find Estefan, a man of logic.

Slowly the idea forms that a curse could be anything that holds you back from your potential, perhaps as simple as lack of self-confidence, hereditary insanity, or the foolish idea of a secret treasure. Maybe a curse is not about a name or an object, but exists solely in one's head to control someone's mind and soul.

An announcement to board their flight interrupts the conversation. Rushing to finish their meal and line up at the gate, she can't help but notice her stalker a few spots behind them. She shakes the unease as paranoia.

After boarding and sitting on the tarmac for over forty minutes, the speakers chime on again. "Huh, folks, this is the captain. We're experiencing a warning light on one of the engines, so we're going to head back to the gate so the mechanics can check the problem. I'll let you know more when I know more."

Sophia shoots a nervous glance at Estefan, who also looks anxious. *A curse is all in her head*, she tells herself again.

Chapter 22

Plunder Wonder

Plunder Lust, Mess Hall
June 18, 7:10 p.m. | 59 hours to Mayan chaa

Hansen likes to show up early for the evening project debriefs, grab his favorite seat in the corner to enjoy a frosty beer, and people watch as crew members drift in after a shower. His six-foot-seven muscular frame and US Navy SEAL training intimidates all but the most self-confident or foolish, so he learned to go out of his way to be friendly.

"Yo, David," he greets with a raised beer.

"Yo, Mount Hansen," the MIT engineer replies, carrying video equipment to set up.

Over the years, he's acquired various nicknames. He doesn't mind, as they provide a resilient camouflage for a shy, East Texas son of a Baptist preacher. Working the oil rigs in high school and then joining the navy for sixteen years on overseas combat missions with very little time left for dating, talking to women can be a little intimidating. Talking to a super-smart one has proven even harder but good practice for when the right woman comes along.

Continuing to greet each shipmate entering the mess hall, he enjoys a swig of beer with each greeting, moving quickly to his second and third beer. In between, he watches Hugo and Mai snuggle while Mai explains her theories on LIDAR to sonar signal interlacing. Hugo doesn't understand a word but enjoys the singsong quality of her voice. Mai leans against his big chest, not concerned if he understands; he's listening.

Brenda, Juniper, and Jackson banter back and forth over techniques to remove coral encrustations. With his black-rimmed eyeglasses, Jackson reminds him of Shaggy meets Waldo.

Hansen waves Brenda over to his corner. Bored with Jackson, she shrugs and joins him. "What's up, Big Rig?"

"I found this under cannon two yesterday," he explains, holding up the tortoise shell.

"What is it? Should I show it to Dr. O'Sullivan or toss it?" he asks, questioning the protocol.

"We toss nothing," she corrects him, taking it tenderly to examine. "You found this on our wreck?"

"Yeah," he confirms. "What is it?"

Brenda hands it back. "It's a script, like a Mesoamerican version of a Sumerian tablet. Before bark or deerskin codex, ancient locals would use tortoise shell for important records."

"Wow, that's cool. What does it say?" he asks.

"No clue," she admits. "Show Dr. O'Sullivan, but I would wait until after the debrief."

"Why?"

"Because that tortoise shell script has no business on a pirate ship, which makes me wonder if we're salvaging the wrong ship," she whispers and heads back to her table.

Plunder Lust, Mess Hall
June 18, 7:27 p.m. | 59 hours to Mayan chaa

Miguel follows Darcy into the mess hall, having missed another chance to tell her about the cartel scout. Just as well, he'd rather wait until he has a better plan.

"Quiet, please." Darcy steps up to a large flat screen hanging on the wall connected to a laptop. "As you know, tonight we start videotaping our daily project debrief sessions. If we are successful, National Geographic may consider the content. So please, please, people, try to be professional, and that means *you*, Dr. Healy."

The room chuckles as Jackson feigns offense.

"Before we dig into the excavation," Darcy grins at her own pun, "we'll start with a historical view of the battle for San Lorenzo. So, please welcome the man who discovered the wrecks, the owner and skipper of the *Plunder Lust*, Captain Miguel Martinez."

Only Ben claps, a little too enthusiastically. Miguel steps up to display a map of the army mule train route between Panama City and Porto Bello called the Camino Real Trail. Fifty miles west, the Chagres River ends at the rugged Las Cruces Trail.

"In 1671, Captain Henry Morgan assembled an armada of thirty-six ships and two thousand men to sack the richest city in New Spain. Old Panama City was the largest storehouse of Inca gold, gems from Ecuador and Colombia, obsidian, jade, gold, and silver from Guatemala and western Mexico. Even more enticing were the exotic new treasures of China and Japan such as Ming vases, bronzes, silks, ivory tusks, and stone carvings that arrived on four hundred–ton ships like the *Santissima de Trinidad*."

Miguel elaborates on why Panama City was so important. "Before he could sack Panama City, Morgan had to first subdue Castillo de San Lorenzo, perched on the bluffs above the mouth of the Chagres River. During a fierce and stormy ten-day battle, Morgan lost five ships, including his flagship, the *Satisfaction*," he explains.

He pops up an aerial photo of the ruins overlooking the coral reefs. "We're anchored directly over the skeletal remains of one of Henry Morgan's lost ships, maybe even the *Satisfaction* herself," he elaborates. "We're also only feet away from the treacherous Los Rojas reef that could tear the bottom off our steel hull if we slip anchor."

"Yah mon, preach," shouts Moses, nodding his head, wiggling his locks.

He considers stopping, but it feels unnatural. *They can edit, right?*

"After subduing San Lorenzo, Morgan sailed up the Chagres River until they reached the Las Cruces Trail. During a ten-day march through the thick, rainy isthmus jungle, eight hundred men died of starvation, disease, snakes, or indigenous ambush. Undeterred, the survivors conquered the fortified city in a single day, and burned it to the ground as the *Santissima de Trinidad* sailed out of the harbor, loaded with the city's best treasure."

Darcy shifts her weight. Miguel should stop there, but a little more won't hurt.

"Morgan spent the next eight weeks plundering, interrogating, and torturing citizens for their hidden caches," Miguel conveys with a light in his eyes.

Darcy's face drops into a deep scowl as her arms fold tightly. He found the line.

"To make a great story needlessly short, the sack of Panama changed history. The Spanish crown never recovered financially, and the New World opened up to the British, French, and Dutch. Arrested in Port Royale, but considered a hero in London, Morgan was knighted by King Charles II, who sent him back to Jamaica as lieutenant governor. Morgan's fateful campaign began right under our hull with the loss of his flagship, and that's where our adventure will also begin."

Darcy softens her scowl as she joins the others in weak applause, as if they expected more.

"Any questions?" he asks. An open discussion follows all project presentations.

"Yeah," Ben calls out. "How much treasure did Morgan plunder?" A tall, gangly, and gifted diesel mechanic who grew up in the back of his father's Florida truck stop, Ben soaks up the historical sessions.

Miguel looks to Darcy and hesitates.

"Morgan packed 175 mules with 750,000 gold coins, fourteen tons of silver, plus several tons of obsidian, Ming porcelain, ivory, bronzes, silks, and thousands of raw gems and jewels. Over thirty tons, plus six hundred slaves for prostitution or ransom," answers Hansen with a smug grin.

A few gasps of *wow* emerge from the group.

Xavier flashes a faux greedy smile. "Si, close to a billion dollars' US worth of wow."

"Da truth be Morgan cheated his own men," interjects Moses.

"Captain Moses is correct," concurs Juniper. "According to Alexander Esquelmelin, a biographer on the Panama raid, the surviving crew received only two hundred pieces of gold each."

Darcy stands up. "Well, as you know," she interjects, "these ships sank before the sack of Panama. Our treasure will be to learn about the life on board a privateer ship of the seventeenth century."

Hansen turns to Jackson. "So, what happened to the *Trinidad*?"

It's too late, as the wildfire of curiosity and gold fever ignites. Miguel reaches for a beer, taking a long swig to watch the show. Dave swings the camera, attempting to keep up.

"Good question," Jackson responds. "Morgan had dispatched a ship called the *Cagway*, captained by Robert Searles, to guard the Panama harbor. Neither the *Cagway* nor Searles ever returned to Jamaica. The *Trinidad* returned to port months later with lingering rumors of missing cargo, but with the burned city in shambles and many of the owners dead, the records were incomplete."

"That's cool." Hansen smiles. "It's like a mystery."

"Pirates captured *de Trinidad* years later," interjects Brenda. "Before they hanged the captain, a man named Don Francisco de Peralta, he confessed to being captured by the *Cagway*, but claimed that he escaped during a celebratory drunken orgy."

"Wicked awesome," exclaims Ben, looking mesmerized. "Bad boys, bad boys, what you gonna do," he starts to sing until the entire room shoots him a cautionary glare, his singing being worse than his cooking.

Darcy tries to cut in again. "Remember, people, we're here—"

Brenda cuts her off. "How did Morgan get away with cheating a bunch of pirates?"

"Morgan fired cannons on da beach with his men," shouts Moses, shaking his head, rustling his dreadlocks.

"Again, I concur," interjects Juniper. "Esquelmelin claimed Morgan disappeared with three ships, the entire plunder, plus two hundred slaves."

"Well sure, he needed the slaves to bury the booty," Ben interjects.

Mai wrinkles her eyebrows. "What happened to the slaves?"

"Or the ships?" asks Xavier. "Morgan showed up in Jamaica months later with a single ship, a starving skeleton crew, and no treasure. Where do you hide thirty tons of loot, two ships, and 450 souls for over three hundred years?"

"The real question," Jackson postulates, "is why would Morgan abandon the treasure once he returned as lieutenant governor?"

"Or why he burned his log books before his death?" Dave wonders aloud from behind the camera. "What secrets did he want to hide from the world?"

"Three years after Morgan's death, the city of Port Royale, including Morgan's grave, sank into the ocean from an earthquake and tsunami," Brenda interjects. "Said by the locals to be cursed by Morgan."

"Das right," replies Moses with a vigorous nod. "Das right, say it, girl."

Miguel glances to Darcy to realize she's fuming. Holding up his hands, he mouths a silent *what?* Under her continued glare, he turns to blow a loud whistle, quieting the room.

"Archaeologists have excavated Castillo de San Lorenzo for decades, yet no one has ever salvaged Morgan's lost fleet until now," he says, reasserting control. "While no one knows what happened to Morgan's booty, we do know what happened to his flagship," he states. "Our job will be to excavate the *Satisfaction* and the other lost ships of Henry Morgan's fateful fleet."

He bows his head to weak applause from the crew.

"Thank you, Skipper," says Darcy, stepping in front to keep control. "Let me be quite clear. The goals of this expedition do not include legends, myths, or folklore. Leave that nonsense for the pub, where it belongs, shall we. We're here to salvage ships from a real battle that changed real world history."

The crew sits quietly with a few residual smirks.

"So, to conclude tonight's shipwreck of a briefing, the archaeology team will meet in the main lab in one hour to review sonar scans," Darcy states. "And please, Mr. Willis, stop the recording."

Dave gives her a thumbs-up, shuts down the feed, and then gives Ben a high-five.

On her way to the lab, Darcy tries to pass Miguel, holding up his hands in faux surrender.

"I had nothing to do with that detour, but," he snickers, "the look on your face when Moses went off was priceless."

With a sour frown, she tries again to pass until she bumps into Hansen in the tight hallway.

"Hey, Dr. O'Sullivan, great debrief tonight," he says. "Totally awesome."

"Come on, they're just blowing off steam. We've been driving hard." Miguel tries to cover for the crew.

"And we'll keep driving hard until we're back on schedule," she snaps, taking a moment to regain her composure. "I don't think you understand that if we lose this contract, we lose an entire year together."

Miguel doesn't know what to say, unsure why editing would be such a big deal. "Okay, I get it, so we don't lose the gig."

With a sigh, she turns to take another route. "I'll be working late in the lab. Don't keep the cabin light on."

After she walks away, Hansen waves it off. "Don't worry, Skipper. She's Irish; piss happens."

Miguel raises an eyebrow. It's not like Darcy to stay mad, even under pressure. He probably shouldn't have pushed the story, but damn, that was funny.

Xavier steps up behind Hansen. "You said you would tell her."

"Trust me, there hasn't been a good time," Miguel deflects.

"Tell her what?" asks Hansen.

"We have a Nacon scout on the bluffs," Miguel whispers so others won't hear.

"One of Shay Golan's crew," Xavier adds.

"Moron Golan? Well, that's not good," rejoins Hansen with wide eyes.

The ship's bell chimes three times, the signal for sunset approaching. Instinctively, the trio turns toward the aft deck companionway. Stepping outside, turning toward the transom, the fresh ocean breeze blows much stronger than earlier.

"You think she's trying to tell me something?" asks Miguel, no good at reading women.

"Hell yeah, man," Hansen laughs. "Don't screw with her project."

Hansen pulls out a cigar, hands it to Miguel, then takes out a second one for himself. Miguel lights the Aston, taking several quick hits to get the embers going before enjoying a long, deep drag to savor. Xavier has his own cigar already lit, pulling a bottle from his back pocket.

At the transom, they turn to face the sunset over the mountains of Panama. The iridescent tangerine- and lithium-colored sky silhouettes the ruins of San Lorenzo.

"I don't know," mumbles Miguel. "Something's eating at her, but she won't talk about it."

"Do you *want* her to talk about it?" asks Hansen, taking a long, casual drag.

"Hell no," quips Miguel. "I mean, you know, not really. I just want things back to normal."

"I'm more worried about our friend on the bluff than your love life," Xavier reminds them.

"If we need to move to night dives, I can start tonight," Hansen offers.

"Yak, yak, yak," Miguel complains. "We cluck like a bunch of hens."

"You started it," retorts Hansen.

The group goes silent. Enough said. Moses, Ben, Hugo, Jackson, and Dave each wander to the transom, lighting up their own cigars in silence.

Xavier hands a bottle of tequila to Ben, who takes a swig before handing it to Dave, and then to others. They stand in silence, enjoying the breeze, the sunset, the tequila, and a stogie. It's a ship tradition, a time to reflect, a sacred time.

Tonight, instead of his normal reflection, Miguel stews over the various storms looming on the horizon, on the bluff, and in his cabin. Something tickles his instincts, but he can't put a finger on what.

*

Plunder Lust, Chagres River, Panama
June 18, 9:14 p.m. | 57 hours to Mayan chaa

Shoving down a twinge of guilt over her video tantrum, Darcy focuses on the new problem. They've discovered six wrecks instead of five. One wreck doesn't belong to Morgan's armada.

Juniper nudges past Miguel, hanging at the doorway with his coffee, perhaps trying to get back on her good side. Juniper had been cleaning the cannons in the adjacent lab. Using the keyboard, she opens a series of photos onto the primary screen, starting with the first cannon, now cleaned of crustaceans. Silence fills the lab.

"Morgan had seventeenth-century French or English cannons," notes Brenda.

"Exactly," replies Juniper. "Except we have a sixteenth-century Spanish cannon, fifty or even a hundred years before Morgan. I need to do chemical analysis to be certain."

"We're jumping to conclusions," dismisses Jackson. "Pirates used any weapon that still worked."

"Hold that thought," notes Juniper, pulling up the next image. "The coral cluster Mount Hansen pulled out yesterday contained a ship's bell." A partly cleaned bell shows up on the screen with a Spanish name on the brass. *El Oro de Isabella*, Isabella's Gold.

"Oh crap, I almost forgot," interjects Miguel, reaching into his shirt pocket to pull out a small envelope and handing it to Darcy. "Hansen wanted you to see this."

"What is it?" asks Darcy.

"Looks like an envelope." Miguel smirks.

Darcy rolls her eyes and opens the sleeve. A delicate seven-centimeter tortoise shell shard drops into her palm, darkened with age and inscribed with delicate markings.

"Where was this found?" Darcy asks, suddenly curious.

"Hansen said under cannon two," replies Brenda.

Darcy holds the fragment under a light-enhanced magnifying glass to study the markings.

"Well, I can rule out Mayan or Aztec." She punches a few keys to project the image onto the monitor screen for others to see.

"Hey, I'll be damned," says Miguel, leaning in. "I've seen those somewhere."

"You're joking," replies Darcy, just as surprised. "Where?"

All eyes turn to Miguel, who hesitates and then shrugs. "Okay, so I can't actually remember where, but I'm sure I've seen them."

"It doesn't matter," sighs Darcy. "We've wasted two bloody weeks on the wrong wreck."

A wave of despondency washes over her, followed by another swell that shoves people into each other with grunts and groans. As the ship rights itself, Moses swings his dreadlocks into the hatchway next to Miguel.

"Y'all need to lock down. Stephanie be headin' dis way, and da bitch be moving fast," he announces, sharing a glance with Miguel.

Darcy catches the earnest concern, raising her own apprehensions even higher.

"Where to?" asks Miguel.

"North of Honduras or we fight da swell," Moses suggests.

"Okay, people I'm putting this expedition on hold," orders Miguel. "Prepare the site. Prepare the lab. We pull hook in an hour."

Miguel turns to Moses. "Plot a course to the Port of Belize. Let 'em know we're coming."

Darcy hangs her head in frustration. *Another setback*, she thinks, refusing to look at Miguel. Certainly, she can't blame him for the weather.

An hour later, they pull the last of the six anchors and turn north toward the Cayman Trench. Standing on the aft deck, watching the dark bluffs of San Lorenzo fall away behind the ship, Darcy feels her dreams of tenure and her chances with Miguel slipping away. Falling in love with a pirate was never her plan in life, but it doesn't matter now. Soon they're going to face their first true challenge. If she can earn the annual contract extension, he won't be tempted to run. Either way, she needs to be honest soon. Regardless of the contract, or tenure, or family estates, or even his unpredictable reaction, Miguel deserves to know the truth. He's the father.

Chapter 23

Follow the Money

L ucia sizzles with excited dread. Facial recognition finally found a match. Suspected by Mexican police of being a Nacon assassin with links to dozens of murders, including her father's, the assassin on her trail is known only as Vacub Came, meaning Seven-Death. According to narco folklore, only the Nacon leader, Hun Came, meaning One Death, may use a mythical name. Her killer isn't some lowlife thug; he's the personal shadow of death for the deadliest cartel lord in the world. The news sends a shudder through her system.

On other clues, it wasn't hard to learn the deceased General Hayat was under investigation for corruption, based on a Panama Paper leak. A close friend of the Pakistani ex-prime minister, Musharraf, also under investigation, General Hayat commanded the Pakistani nuclear arsenal. While the BBC reported his death as suicide, Xavier's program links him to an assassin and a stolen ship container. Lucia's stomach tightens on the implications of Nacon acquiring a nuclear warhead.

Her second search proved more intriguing. Felipe Roué Gutierrez died as a teen during a cartel battle forty years ago. Something doesn't fit. How are a dead boy, de Aguilar, General Hayat, and Juan Perez connected? Lucia rubs her hands on her face, tired and frustrated, pacing around her desk to clear her head.

Salazar de Aguilar started his career at Fossack-Monseca, the law firm that leaked the Panama Papers. The Panama Papers led to investigations on General Hayat, which then led to his murder. In order to follow the money, she needs access to the Panama Papers, which means she needs to call in a special favor.

Opening an encrypted email, she contacts an old friend from college who works with the International Consortium of Investigative Journalists (ICIJ). ICIJ represents a group of four hundred journalists from over one hundred organizations in over eighty countries investigating the Panama and Paradise Papers, a combined twenty-one million leaked documents spanning tens of thousands of accounts. ICIJ publishes as a group to protect the individual identity of journalist members. The leaks disclose a shady world of offshore finance, money laundering, and tax evasion by prime ministers, CEOs, criminals, dictators, and cartel lords.

To her surprise, she gets an almost immediate response. Her friend now uses the alias of "Alice" because she's peering through the looking glass. Alice has agreed to meet, but not in Mexico City; she wants a location several hours away on the Gulf Coast, which means she needs to leave now. While she packs, a new text from *Delores* pings her encrypted phone.

Phoenix: K1 bad news. Follow $ to LASSG, JPdM a sponsor. Keep distance. Sleeper cell alert for solstice. Possible War. No heroics. SIT [stay in touch]. Love, Delores.

For once, she's ahead of her brother on following the money, but his suggestion to consider LASSG had not occurred to her. Cozumel would be great cover for an arms deal. That said, she has no intention of keeping her distance, not when she's so close after so long a search.

Delores: K1 linked to broken arrow. Arms deal? Need a buyer + Panama Papers. OTR [on the road] SIT. Love, Phoenix - Send.

If Lucia wants to leave Mexico City, she needs an escape plan. In fact, she needs several plans. Vacub Came will be watching for her, so she should give him lots to see. With an unsecured browser, she books a flight to La Paz, then a second bus ticket to Acapulco, a third airline ticket to Puerto Vallarta, and then a fourth flight to Dallas, Texas. All trips take off around the same time, but from separate stations or airports at least an hour drive from each other. A set of decoy trails for him to follow, allowing her escape in the opposite direction by car.

Packing only a single encrypted laptop with Xavier's classified application, fake passports, and extra cash, Lucia checks the corridor video cam for an all-clear. After relocking the safe house, she takes the urine-tainted elevator to the garage. Unlocking the roll-up door, she finds an older-model white sedan with tinted windows, so mundane it's the most invisible car on the planet.

Riding on a high of adrenaline and Coca-Cola, she can feel herself getting close to finding the men who murdered her parents. The hunt is on, and she forces herself to endure the spasms of unease that she is both the hunter and the prey.

In the middle of the night, she turns onto the highway east toward the Gulf Coast town of Veracruz, where she will meet with Alice and peer with her into the looking glass.

Chapter 24

The Confession

The last-minute itinerary forces Sophia and Estefan to change planes again in Cancun. Deboarding the plane, with little luggage, she and Estefan walk to the new gate.

"Who are we meeting, and why do you trust him?" Sophia needs to know more. Tight-lipped about the plan on the flight down, Estefan claimed he didn't want to jinx the contact, a ridiculous superstition, in her mind.

"My son, Miguel," he admits.

It takes a moment for the name to register. "Wait, a minute, Miguel Martinez the treasure hunter is your son?" She read about him years ago but never imagined there was a family relation.

Estefan cringes through an embarrassed smile. "Well, not exactly my career choice for him, but he has experience handling cartels and bureaucrats. His crew can get us in and out of Roatan without attracting undue attention. I checked with a colleague on his ship to learn that he recently docked temporarily in Belize, which is our next stop."

Sophia ponders the situation. Actually, not a bad plan; it would keep the whole affair within the family and avoid the rumors and police spies stationed at Coxen Hole.

Sophia changes the subject. "What happened between you and your son?"

She pries without apology, a habit she learned from Carmen, a rather nosey *buyei*. He barely mentioned his son during the family history, and only referred to him with a remorseful tone, leading her to worry about extra emotional baggage. After believing she was the last Martinez, she now has a family with an older cousin reminiscent of Papá and his famous son, but something isn't right about the situation.

He draws a deep breath. "Miguel was nine when his mother died," he begins. "A few years before your father disappeared."

Sophia can relate to the anguish of losing a parent so young, so she listens quietly with a bit more empathy over yet another example of family tragedy.

"Olivia, Miguel's mother, was injured in the assault that followed my visit with Dr. Colon," he confesses with his eyes cast down to the table. "She died of complications at a rural Belize hospital. Had we been in the States, she would have lived, so Miguel blames me for her death, and I guess on many levels, I still blame myself. For several reasons, most of them my own failures, we drifted apart."

Taught by her *buyei* to respect the sacred moment of spiritual *agufesera*, or confession, as a time of healing, she listens and waits without trying to fill the awkward silence.

"Her death devastated me," he continues. "I plunged into my work to distract me from my unhappiness, dragging Miguel around the jungles like a piece of equipment. How could I help Miguel rise above his melancholy when I was sinking in my own? Instead of a sports team or a school prom, I carted my son to Third World villages, ancient temples, and remote caves. Like a reckless fool, I often led us both into mortal danger when he should've been learning to dance or play a musical instrument. What I had hoped would be a shared adventure turned into a mutual nightmare and a deep wedge between us."

Her empathy for Miguel rises. Papá abandoned her to chase after an insane mythical treasure, and Mamá was too sick to comfort her.

He lifts his gaze with a weak smile. "What's not to love?"

Sophia tries to imagine the experience. As a child, Carmen kept her safe and nurtured. Now Carmen's overprotective cocoon has been violently shattered, and she feels unwillingly thrust into an uncertain world. Like a good Garifuna, she feels compelled to endure the suffering, but her Spanish blood boils with resentment. In the end, she can't see any difference between one kind of abandonment and another; they both leave deep, lasting scars.

"Miguel should feel blessed to have a surviving parent, even a flawed one," she responds.

"If you can convince my son to see life that way, then I will owe you a great debt," Estefan confesses.

As they approach the new gate, other passengers already board. Taking a place in line, Sophia happens to glance behind her to realize that her creepy stalker from Dallas stands right behind her, startling her with a slight jump. The stranger never smiles but simply leers at her with a dead expression. His gaze sends shivers up her spine.

Sophia not so subtly shifts positions in line with Estefan, feeling a bit foolish to act so paranoid of a stranger in a public place. After insisting on the window seat, she dismisses the anxiety as her lingering asandiruni, her premonition of something evil on the horizon.

Chapter 25

Plunder Port of Call

Plunder Lust, Port of Belize, Belize
June 19, 10:03 a.m. | 44 hours to Mayan chaa

Miguel feeds on the kinetic energy generated when the *Plunder Lust* docks at port, and both the crew and ship plug back into civilization, united in one purpose: to prepare the ship for sea again. No one enjoys shore leave until the crew addresses core ship needs to refuel, restock, repair, and replace broken or worn-out parts necessary to get the ship ready for an unexpected quick departure. Not that he expects one, except that over the years, he's learned to expect the unexpected.

The science team head to the local farmer's market to refresh food stocks. An overwhelming crew vote banned Ben from the galley for life, so Mai and Brenda drew up a new menu with fresh vegetables and fruits to augment the ship's supply of canned or frozen whatever. While Hansen, Moses, and Jackson hunt down ship supplies and used parts for a forty-year-old vessel, Ben and Dave work on engine maintenance with the parts they have in stock.

As always, Xavier gets a pass from other ship duties to focus on security. Brilliant at monitoring multiple channels of chatter across radio, law enforcement, military, and Dark Web networks, Xavier needs the extra quiet to investigate some disturbing news from his sister Lucia that may relate to the chaa warning they picked up a few days earlier.

In the meantime, Miguel does his best to entertain the Belize harbormaster, Captain Remi Borealis, who showed up early, insisting on an impromptu inspection. As captain, Moses would normally deal with these tours, but with Moses gone, the job falls to Miguel. After a mandatory inspection of the storage and engine rooms, he leads Captain Borealis by the cannon lab to meet the attractive Cambridge archaeologist, eager to show *Plunder Lust* as a legitimate research vessel, a tough sell considering the poor condition of the ship.

"Captain Borealis," Darcy greets him with a pleasant smile, handing him a photocopy of her permits. "We're under contract to the Panamanian government for a historic salvage near San Lorenzo," she explains. "While Hurricane Stephanie forced us to abandon the site, we are under a deadline and eager to return as quickly as possible."

Her story more or less aligns with Miguel's version, but it sounds more believable with the British accent and blue eyes. The harbormaster hands the permit back to Darcy and then casts a long, dubious glance at Miguel.

"Hey, didn't you used to be that big-shot American treasure hunter?" he asks.

The term *used to be* hits Miguel like a cannonball to the gut, and the humiliation of having it said in front of Darcy burns even worse. Instead of searching for Morgan's treasure, instead of following his dream, he babysits a bunch of scientists. He's becoming his dad. No, even worse, he's becoming the laborers who worked for the professor. A shame he hasn't felt in a decade wells up inside.

"Yeah, that used to be me." Miguel chokes out the admission, instantly wanting this smug asshole off his ship.

The older man glances around at the dingy paint and the rusted corners of steel. "Tough times, eh?" he chuckles.

Miguel knows he's hoping for a bribe to get dock rights for a few days, but Hansen took the last of the petty cash to buy black market explosives and ammo, planning for the worst-case scenario back in Panama. Without warning, Moses bounces into the lab, holding up a small bag of weed, sporting a huge grin as if he's already sampled it. Startled, Moses's surprise quickly lights up into joy.

"Ya, Remi," he shouts as he reaches out to embrace the shorter, middle-aged official, somehow making the weed disappear in a flurry of long arms and dreadlocks.

"Moses, mi amigo, I haven't seen you since *Blue Oasis*." The official smiles wide at the scrawny Jamaican, referring to the bordello Moses captained offshore of the Cayman Islands.

Moses looks at Miguel with a big smile. "Nah, mon, I land a good ship. Good friends, no bullets, no—" He stops midsentence to glance at the makeup-less scholar in her McCartney T-shirt, men's Levi's, and curly auburn hair pulled back into a ponytail. "No hookers, mon," he finishes the sentence as the two men burst into laughter.

Darcy scowls while Miguel laughs along the best he can through the pang of truth. He's a used-to-be, pimping out his ship to a bunch of geeks, a laughingstock for locals. Remi lets him slide on the bribe, handing him a two-day dock pass.

With a tap to Moses's shoulder, Remi nods at the exit. "Since you've already been to the Frog, come buy me a drink," he suggests with a wink. Moses probably scored the weed at the Wet Frog.

Smiling, Moses looks over at Miguel. "Ya, Skipper, I'll fuel up da ship when I get back." Without waiting for permission, Moses and Remi disappear down the steel hallway, echoing laughter.

A free dock pass helps to wash the bitter taste of humiliation off his tongue, but not very much of it. Exhaling a sigh of relief, Miguel tries to make the best of his humiliation. "That's why I hired that man."

"You mean his pot smoking with local officials or his familiarity with popular brothels?" Darcy chortles back.

"Exactly." Miguel smiles widely.

Turning to face Darcy, he drops the smirk. "Look, I meant to tell you before we left Panama, but Xavier spotted a Nacon scout on San Lorenzo. Now, don't worry, I've already talked to the guys, and we can handle it. Once we're back, we move to night dives with an armed watch."

"What?" she exclaims. "Why would the cartel care about my empty ships?"

"Well, they don't know the ships are empty," Miguel explains. "They only know the *Plunder Lust* by reputation." He chokes down the tarnish on that reputation and omits the violent history with Golan, seeing no need to frighten her further.

"For how long?" she retorts. "What happens when they discover your ploy?"

"We change tactics. Look, my guys can handle it," he insists, preferring to avoid the details he hasn't sorted out yet.

"This is a bloody nightmare. We're going to lose the contract." She rubs a palm over her forehead, pivoting away with a slight tremble of anger.

Miguel reaches out to take her by the shoulders, turning her around for an embrace. "Look, I know you're worried about the deadline," he concedes. "Okay, so we pull double teams. One of the other five ships has to be a Morgan ship. We'll find the proof. It'll be okay."

Looking down, she shakes her head into his chest. "It's more than the deadline, Miguel. I'm worried about us. What happens to us if we fail," she confesses.

He didn't see that one coming. He's not even sure what that means. Unsure what to do, he holds her tighter. "Okay, so we don't fail. I'm a lucky guy. We'll make it work, both of us, together." He offers the only words he can think to say.

Stiff and unresponsive, something else must be on her mind. "Miguel," she mumbles into his chest, "we need to talk."

"Yeah, sure, okay." Miguel pulls back with a sudden sense of dread freezing his heart. When a woman needs to talk, then a man needs to hide; it's never good news. Never. Maybe she also sees him as a failure or wants to fire him. Sure, they've had a few setbacks, but nothing they can't work out. Maybe she's still mad about the stupid video.

Before she can speak, Hansen barges into the lab. "Hey, Skipper, hi, Dr. O'Sullivan," he says. "Skipper, Moses bugged out on me. We need your help to unload and store these crane parts and sparklers." Sparklers are the ship code word for ammunition and explosives.

"Yeah, sure, I'll be there in a minute," Miguel deflects, anxiously turning back to Darcy.

She lowers her eyes, spinning away. "No," she demurs. "Go ahead. You should go help Hansen. We can chin wag a bit later. It's, hum, it's not urgent, really."

With her back to him, she goes to work without another word. He stares a long moment, unsure what to say or do, and no clue what's behind all of her mood swings. In truth, he's afraid to know. He only knows the premonition of a coming shit storm that keeps getting stronger. Pushing it aside, he heads to the main deck. The ship needs come first.

*

Tulu Cantina, Port of Belize
June 19, 6:16 p.m. | 36 hours to Mayan chaa

Putting aside the numerous setbacks of Panama, Darcy postpones her conversation with Miguel for a more private moment, kicking herself for bringing it up earlier. They all need a distraction, so she offers to treat the entire crew to dinner to boost morale.

The boisterous cantina bustles with a blend of tourists, merchant seamen, and locals hoping to swindle the visitors. Most of the crew takes to the dance floor to blow off steam, with Mai and Hugo showing off a bit of swag for Dave and Juniper. Ben and Brenda secretly collaborate to out shark a pair of local pool sharks, while Hansen keeps a protective eye on everyone.

Near the bottom of a second pitcher of beer, Darcy sticks to water while sharing laughs with Jackson, Hansen, and Miguel, like old times. More relaxed than she's been in a while, she sets aside her irritable behavior as the byproduct of stress and unbalanced pregnancy hormones.

"Okay, gentlemen—" She raises her finger in a mock disciplinary expression. "As soon as we're back in Panama, we switch to a new wreck site," she demands, "and I don't want to see a single wet arse until you find my proof."

"Yes, ma'am," Hansen agrees, sipping his beer while bobbing his head to the music, watching the women on the dance floor.

"Sure," Jackson smirks. "If you stop dropping cannons on me, we're cool."

Darcy glances to Miguel sipping his beer, lost in thought. "Captain, are we agreed?" She presses him for alignment in front of the crew.

Miguel slowly puts down his beer. "Yeah, sure, new site, wet arse, need proof, no worries."

After a beat, he turns to meet her gaze. "You know, I just can't figure out where the hell I've seen those damn symbols." He glances at Hansen. "You know, on the shell Captain America found."

Darcy groans, more mocking than mad. To be honest, she's also curious where he could have seen such a rare script. He grew up in the region, so it could have been anywhere.

"Go ahead, Skipper," she teases. "We're at the pub, and you're full of piss and beer, so talk it out of your system. Tell us about the mystery symbols."

Miguel flashes a huge grin, kissing her on the cheek. "Thank you, Duchess, for your permission to speak, but there's nothing to tell," he replies with a shrug. "That's the problem; it's tickling the crap out of my brain. I remember a skinny old dude holding a paper with those symbols in one hand and a handful of raw gems in the other, but I can't remember who or where or when, and it's driving me freaking nuts. I've always thought it was a dream. I'm too damn young to go senile," he complains when his phone buzzes in his pocket.

"Yo, Xavi, what up," he answers with a worried expression. "Got it, thanks." He turns to the team. "Sorry, folks, party's over. We need to get back to the ship."

"What? Why?" Darcy objects. "The crew are enjoying a wonderful time."

"Tell you on the way," Miguel deflects.

Not offering an explanation, he gets up, motioning to Hansen, who chugs his beer. Jackson follows the big man's lead until his eyes bulge. Of all the times for Peter Pan to get serious, she never would have guessed she'd see it happen inside a pub.

Chapter 26

Late Night Call

Plunder Lust, Port of Belize
June 19, 8:07 p.m. | 34 hours to Mayan chaa

Miguel would trust Xavier with his life, so he takes the heat from the whining crew. Xavier picked up signals about a snatch-and-grab operation going down tonight. Even though the signal did not mention a target by name, Xavier urged Miguel to get his largely American crew back to the ship.

"Weather report?" he asks Moses as he enters the bridge.

Feet up on the console, leaning back in the captain's chair, Moses smokes a roach, blowing it out the open bridge door. "Stephanie downgraded to a tropical storm ova Ecuador," he reports. "Very wet." He takes another hit.

Miguel doesn't like wasting time in harbor. "Good to hear." He claps his hands in delight. "Have the ship ready to shove off by daybreak."

Half-asleep, and quite stoned, Moses groans, blowing out his breath with a slight cough. "Ah, no skippa, it be a rough sea so soon after da storm, and you have a hung-over crew. You have a lot of unhappy faces hang in da head, mon."

Miguel smirks. "Yeah, you're right. A little fresh ocean air will do the crew good. Purge them of the demon rum."

"Ah, you be an evil man, skippa," Moses complains, climbing out of his chair.

"Yeah, I know, but let's keep it a secret," Miguel rejoins with a grin.

"No worries, mon, everybody knows," Moses grumbles, heading to start refueling, the task he put off to enjoy his drinking and smoking binge. "Everybody knows."

With time to kill, Miguel heads to the mess hall for a mug of coffee, only to be greeted by the savory aroma of sizzling chicken strips over fresh onion, garlic, peppers, tomatoes, and cilantro. He breathes in deep through his nose to appreciate the wisdom of banning Ben. Mai and Hugo have teamed up in the galley, working together without a word between them. Mai grabs Hugo's ass, then points to a pan starting to sizzle. He attends to the pan with a smile. Good teamwork.

Brenda and Ben huddle together in the corner to split their profits, laughing loudly over the humiliation of the local sharks losing to a woman. Hansen entertains Juniper and Jackson with a story of how he met Miguel and Darcy at a biker bar in Tampa. Miguel smiles at the fond memory.

Right on cue, Darcy enters the mess hall, unaware of his gaze. He watches her pick at the cheese, make a cup of tea, and wait for more chicken to finish. Sometimes it only takes one glance at his amazing girlfriend to remember who anchors him. His grandfather once told him it was better to be lucky than either wealthy or handsome. Miguel has always been lucky, and he considers Darcy his undeniable proof, at least he did before he was a "used-to-be."

His cell phone vibrates in his pocket, giving him a startle. Others stop their conversations to gaze at the unexpected late-night call.

He looks at the number with a groan. "An LA area code." He shows it to Jackson.

Jackson and the caller are peers at UCLA, and while Jackson claims to play Switzerland in the decade-long estrangement, his suspicions impulsively flare.

"Did you call him about the symbols?" he demands, unable to imagine any other reason for a call.

"What? Whoa. No, dude, like, no," Jackson responds, more from hurt than guilt.

"Maybe he's sick," Darcy suggests with a worried expression. Miguel hasn't told her much about the professor, preferring to avoid the subject entirely.

"Come on, man, it's your dad. You gotta answer," encourages Hansen, a devout Christian believer in the power of forgiveness.

Miguel groans and clicks. "Hello?"

"Hi, Miguel, it's your dad," the awkward voice shouts above a noisy background.

His eyeballs roll up. "Okay," he replies, unsure how to respond, still in shock as enormous walls of distrust instantly erect into a maze of unresolved traumas and emotions.

"I've just landed in Belize, at the airport, and I, I need to meet with you. It's, uh, it's urgent. A family matter of life and death," the professor pleads.

The voice instantly pulls up decades of buried anger, blame, arguments, and questions that have no answers. Miguel does not want to talk, much less meet.

"I'm fine, Professor," he says. "Thanks for asking."

Miguel checks his watch, not interested in a family crisis. Besides, they aren't even a real family, not anymore. Out of the corner of his eye, he spots Hansen turn to Jackson, mouthing the word "professor?" Jackson shakes his head in a "not now" subtlety. Miguel ignores the exchange, growing more anxious, wishing he were already at sea and out of cell range.

"I'm sorry for your troubles, Professor. Listen, we're ready to shove off, so it's not a good time," Miguel lies, knowing they have until dawn. "Good luck with—"

"Son, please," his dad interrupts. "This involves you too." He offers a nontransparent tease.

"Why are you calling?" he snaps.

"I can't tell you over the phone." The professor hesitates. "But I need to see you tonight."

"And how the hell did you even know I was in Belize?" Miguel asks, looking at Jackson, who shakes his head, denying any role.

"Please, son, your mother would want us to at least talk to each other," the caller implores.

"Whoa, I can't believe you went there," he retorts.

His mother had always been the peacekeeper in the family. After her death, his father grew distant and obsessed with work. Miguel was little more than excess baggage on one hellish misadventure after another. He rebelled by putting as much distance between them as possible. When he dropped out of college and used his mother's inheritance to buy *Plunder Lust*, it created a wide rift between them. Sadly, even after all these years, invoking her memory works.

"Okay, Professor, I'll agree for her sake," he concedes. "Meet me at the Iguana Reef Cantina outside the Port of Belize. You get fifteen minutes."

He hangs up the phone, storming out of the galley without a word of explanation to the crew staring at his back. The professor can attract trouble like a magnet, and the lie about family makes no sense because they have no extended family; he's the last of the Martinez line. His gut tightens with apprehension. Miguel has no interest in the professor's latest mystery or the gravestones lurking behind it.

Chapter 27

Cantina Contact

Belize International Airport, Port of Belize
June 19, 8:16 p.m. | 34 hours to Mayan chaa

After a tedious delay in Dallas and an unnerving change of planes in Cancun, Sophia and Estefan arrived at the Belize International Airport to endure a slow customs line, only to face a twelve-hour layover until their morning flight to Roatan. Surviving the second muscle-aching overnight flight in three days, Sophia consoles herself that she will be home soon, although still unsure how to rebuild her life, much less her crumbling house.

Stretched far beyond her normal limits, she's learned little that might explain the full extent of the family history, why Montego hid the relics, or why others will murder for a dagger she would gladly sell. Grateful to dispel the notion of a curse, having found nothing mystical or evil about the relics, she's also happy to cast off the idea of a hoax.

After Estefan had stepped away to make a call to his son Miguel, rather doubtful he can arrange a meeting so late, she curled up in the crowded gate area, clutching her bag. On the other side of the seating area, the leering pervert from their flight keeps gazing in her direction, jerking away when caught. Accustomed to the lustful leer of men, many of them drawn by her almond eyes and mocha skin, this feels different. Exposed in such a public place, it's doubtful she will get much sleep, but her heavy eyelids close just for a moment to rest.

"Sophia, Sophia," whispers Estefan, nudging her awake. "Sophia, we need to go. He's agreed to meet with us, but we need to go now."

Startled and disoriented, she must have dozed off, more tired than she wants to admit. Checking her watch, she sees that only five minutes have passed. Looking up, she's thankful to see her travel stalker has gone. Eager to get far away from the leering creep, she agrees to leave the airport, and doesn't care where she goes.

*

Iguana Reef Cantina, Port of Belize
June 19, 8:34 p.m. | 34 hours to Mayan chaa

Sophia and Estefan share a booth in a boisterous cantina near Belize harbor, waiting for a snack, a *café*, and a mystery visitor. While it feels good to be on familiar ground and away from the leering creep, she's anxious about meeting a total stranger.

"What makes you think he will help?" she asks the obvious question nagging her since his confession in Cancun.

"I'm not sure he will," Estefan admits. "To be honest, we haven't spoken much in a decade."

Her shock at that confession doesn't have time to sink in before an unkempt man with a two-day beard and shaggy dark hair appears at the entrance to the open-air cantina, scanning the crowd. He stops when he spots Estefan but looks startled to see her. The earlier phone call may have left out a few details. Estefan stands to greet him, but there's no hug, no handshake or affection between the two men, who stand apart with tense, unresolved resentments that radiate between them like a furnace.

"Miguel, please meet Sophia Martinez," Estefan introduces, "a distant cousin from Isla Roatan, the home of Papá Joaquin. We were there once, when you were a boy, if you remember."

Miguel raises an eyebrow to stare with a blank expression she can't read.

"Sophia, please meet my son Miguel. He lost someone precious once, so I believe he may understand your crisis." Estefan gestures toward his son, who shoots his father a suspicious glower.

She extends a hand to shake but draws back when he doesn't return the gesture. His eyes narrow as he takes the opposite side of the booth, forcing her to sit with Estefan.

"Clock's ticking. What's this about, professor?" he demands. "You said it was a matter of life and death."

Estefan nods and inhales. "Someone murdered Sophia's grandmother to steal ancient artifacts found hidden in the family home on Roatan. Not finding the relics, the raiders will try again, putting Sophia's life in danger. The university has agreed to study the items, but we need your help to get them to a secure location."

Miguel stares a long moment, then shakes his head. "Let me get this straight," he says with a snort. "We don't talk for nearly a decade, and then you call out of the blue because an obscure family member I've never met has a black-market relic and needs an illegal transporter to avoid Nacon."

Surprised at his response, she develops an instant dislike for the man, who seems distrustful and completely self-absorbed, a typical pirate. Longing her entire life to be part of a family, she never imagined having to deal with one she disliked.

"Nah." He sits back and folds his arms. "Sorry, Professor, it doesn't add up. How does this involve me? What are you not telling me this time?"

Miguel acts more suspicious than Sophia expected. Nonviolent by nature, raised with a keen spiritual awareness, she may no longer believe in silly superstitions, but she knows a man with *iganu,* an inner anger, and his unexpected ire frightens her. Working with him will be a bad idea.

Estefan changes expressions from hurt disappointment to surprised alert as he leans across the table to whisper. "We're being watched."

Sophia scans the cantina, and quickly spots a man with eyes on them diverting his gaze. Her heart sinks. "He was on our flight," she whispers. "I saw him watching me at the airport before we left."

Without a word, Miguel stands up to grab her wrist and practically drags her from the cantina to shove her into a waiting taxi, climbing in afterward, followed by Estefan.

"*El puerto, embarco tres. Andale,*" barks Miguel, slapping the back of the seat.

The cab darts into traffic on the busy commercial boulevard. Sophia looks out the rear window to see the stalker run out of the cantina into a black SUV pulling up. Blocked by traffic, following a light change, they gain a small lead.

"You never were very subtle," says Estefan. "I ordered food."

"Your fifteen minutes are up, Professor," retorts Miguel, pointing to the taxicab driver and then staring out the window.

She clutches tightly to her bag, percolating in dread, and keeps a close watch for the danger behind them. Unsure what's going on, she only knows that as of this moment, she's lost control of her situation, with two men she barely knows. Her internal panic escalates into a furious squall of foreboding.

Chapter 28

Big Shove Off

Plunder Lust, Port of Belize
June 19, 8:57 p.m. | 34 hours to Mayan chaa

The taxi pulls up to the dock with a skid as Miguel leaps out, throwing extra cash at the nervous driver, and not waiting for the change.

"Let's go. Move it, move it," he shouts at the professor and his new friend.

A few tourists still stagger out of the open cantinas at the far end of the pier, but otherwise the industrial dock remains quiet.

"Hey, Xavi," he shouts. "Xavier!"

Xavier sticks his neck over the bridge rail.

"Lock down, now," he orders. "We may have visitors."

Xavier draws back quickly. Turning back to the professor, he doesn't disguise his apprehension. "Look, I really, *really* hate to say this, Professor, but you and your friend better get on board. It's probably the only safe place."

"I will not," Sophia resists, clutching her bag.

151

"Sophia, we agreed to ask for his help," interjects the professor. "We should do as he asks."

Miguel ignores them, pivoting back to the gangway. "Moses!" he shouts.

The skinny Jamaican sticks his long dreads over the rail. "Ya, skippa," he replies in a stoned deadpan.

"Prime the mains, and finish fueling later. We shove off in five minutes," he commands.

"Ya, skippa," Moses replies, his wide eyes seeming to yank his locks back over the rail.

"I'm not getting on a boat full of strangers until you tell me what's going on," she objects.

Miguel growls his frustration. "Look, I don't know what he told you, but there's probably something he forgot to mention." He points an accusing thumb at the professor. "I don't know you, and I really don't care what trinket you found, or stole, or whatever. Your shadow is a Nacon thug, or did you miss the neck art? I don't play games with Nacon."

Swinging back toward the gangway, he calls from over his shoulder. "Get on the ship or you're on your own, but I'd avoid the airport. They'll be waiting."

At the top of the gangway, he meets up with Hansen. "What's going on?"

"Trouble," he summarizes. "Let's hope I'm wrong, but I want all guns on deck until we're out of port."

"Aye, skipper," Hansen replies, trotting off to the gun locker.

Entering the bridge, he finds Moses on ship intercom. "Ya, Ben, I need your skinny ass on da dock now, mon."

A moment later, the engines rumble to a rough start, common for old diesels until they warm up. Hansen enters the bridge, handing Miguel an AR-15 assault rifle with an extra magazine, handing a second one to Moses, who straps it over his shoulder on his way to the dock.

"Gather the science team," Miguel orders Hansen. "Nobody leaves the mess hall until I give an all-clear."

Hansen nods and continues on his way to arm Hugo and Xavier. Brenda passes him on her way onto the bridge.

"What's going on?" she inquires, looking anxious.

Miguel knows her father was a marine who taught her how to shoot, but instead of giving her a gun, he hands her the radio.

"If you hear shooting, press that button for harbor police. Tell them we're under assault, and then hide." Her eyes widen, but she nods and takes the radio.

Miguel checks on the defense team. Hansen, Hugo, and Xavier each check their weapons, taking up strategic spots on the upper deck, behind the crane, and behind the bow windlass. A still-drunk Ben stumbles down the gangway in his boxer shorts and a tank top. After a gangly spin of the situation, he heads for the stern, while Moses works on the heavy bowline.

Vulnerable at dock, Miguel needs the ship at sea to even the odds. Back on the bridge, the diesels are warming, but the fuel gauge reads only one-half tank—not ideal, but enough. As soon as Moses and Ben are back on board, they'll shove off. He can drop the professor and his bad-luck charm in La Ceiba, where they can finish refueling.

On the main deck, the professor and his cousin have boarded the ship. A cousin seems like such a weird notion. His whole life, he thought he was the last Martinez, an only child with no extended family. Instead, he built his own family of close friends and crew.

Darcy greets the visitors near the top of the gangway, where their voices drift up in the quiet.

"Dr. Martinez," says Darcy. "What a splendid surprise."

Darcy knew Miguel had gone to meet the professor, but there was never a plan to bring him back, much less with a guest.

"Yes, well, a surprise for all of us," replies the professor. "Oh, you're Dr. O'Sullivan, Darcy O'Sullivan. Jackson has said so much about you, all good of course."

Jackson and the professor both work at UCLA as colleagues. Miguel can imagine them talking about his Cambridge teammate, but he wonders what else Jackson has spilled about Darcy, like her fling with the captain. The professor reaches out a hand that Darcy gently swats away to move in for an embrace, more affectionate than she normally treats strangers.

"Dr. O'Sullivan." He turns. "I'd like you to meet Sophia Martinez, a distant cousin from Roatan."

Darcy reaches out for another unexpected hug. "Well, I'm not sure what demon Miguel riled up this time, but I've seen the crew in this mood before, so we may all be safer and more comfortable in the mess hall. Perhaps one of you can explain what the bloody hell is going on."

Ignoring for the moment that his girlfriend automatically blames him for the commotion, Miguel checks on the dock, where the only activity pulses from the *Plunder Lust*. Moses has the bowline freed, while Ben has disconnected the fuel line. They both start work on the heavy stern line.

Before he can jump to the conclusion that he overreacted, two Humvees screech around the corner at the end of the pier. Racing past the still-open cantinas, the vehicles force pedestrians to leap aside with a scream.

"Heads up!" shouts Xavier.

Miguel cuts the ship and deck lights, still leaving Ben and Moses exposed by lighting on the dock.

"Find cover now," Hansen calls down.

"Harbor Master," Brenda shouts into the radio. "We're under deadly assault, dock three, hmm, *Embarco tres. Ayudanos!*" screams Brenda.

Before the Humvees fully stop, a half-dozen armed commandos jump out to rush toward the ship. Hansen, Xavier, and Hugo open fire, but the Humvees and dock containers provide the attackers with cover.

Miguel watches in horror as Ben takes a bullet to the chest, throwing him backward into the water. Moses gets the heavy stern line free a split second before a bullet to the back of his head slams him like dead weight to the dock. The assailants return fire, forcing Hansen to pull back as others storm the gangway.

Miguel instinctively shoves the port bow thruster up to full power. So close, the prop wash splashes a two-foot-wide water funnel onto the dock, tripping an attacker. Hansen rains down a volley of bullets to keep him down. With the ship pulling away from the dock, the gangway drops into the harbor, taking the two attackers who had nearly reached the top with it. Hugo and Xavier pepper both waterlogged assailants with gunfire. The commandos are wearing Kevlar vests, so it's not clear how many shots are lethal.

As the bow swings into the main channel, Miguel spins the helm hard to starboard to line up the rudder, avoiding other ships by mere feet as bullets continue to ping the hull. Lining up with the channel, Miguel pushes the throttle to race *Plunder Lust* out of the harbor, creating a wake that causes a fortune in property damage. Out of range of the attackers, Hansen joins Miguel as Brenda crawls out of hiding.

"Take the helm," he orders Hansen.

Miguel calls up GPS navigation charts of the narrow Belize Channel that cuts through the coral reefs into deeper water, then turns the screen to Hansen. "Can you get us through the channel without running aground?" The chart contains a few turns.

"At this speed," responds Hansen, "only one way to find out." The Texan studies the chart and then gazes to the buoy lights ahead as Xavier and Hugo enter the bridge.

"Hugo, go help Dave in the engine room. As soon as we're at sea, I need a welding crew on those bullet holes near the water line," barks Miguel. Hugo nods then vanishes.

He swings to Xavier. "Can you make us disappear but still track if we're being followed?"

Xavier shakes his head. "Sorry, for a ship this size, invisible will be impossible."

"Make us invisible," he commands.

Xavier nods and goes to work shutting down any system that can easily give away their position or identity of the ship, including the radio, GPS, and Hansen's navigation charts. Hansen will have to use the navigation lights alone for their high-speed escape. If he leaves the narrow channel or misses a turn by as little as fifty feet, they'll run aground.

"What in the Sam blazes was that about?" exclaims Hansen.

"That's a damn good question," barks Miguel, storming off the bridge toward the mess hall, followed by Brenda and Xavier. "Let's go find out."

Chapter 29

Death is Complex

Plunder Lust, Offshore Belize
June 19, 9:17 p.m. | 33 hours to Mayan chaa

Sophia struggles for control over her palpitating heart and hyperventilation. For several minutes, the entire ship exploded in loud cracks coming from every direction. Low-wattage infrared lighting has replaced the momentary darkness, giving the ship a tense battleship atmosphere. Overwhelmed by the ferocity of the assault, unlike anything she has ever experienced in her life, trembling and shaken, she simply can't conceive of what would make an old dagger worth so much death. The unspoken shame of bringing such evil to these strangers swells in her throat.

"Stay calm. Wait for the all-clear." Dr. O'Sullivan tries to ward off crew panic. "I'm sure Skipper will be here soon to—"

"Two of my men are dead," shouts Miguel as he storms into the room, striding up to Estefan. "Why the hell are people shooting at my ship?"

"—enlighten us." Dr. O'Sullivan finishes her thought.

Still trembling, Sophia stands up next to Estefan, strangely unwilling to back down from Miguel's anger, feeling the disgrace.

"I honestly don't know anymore." Her voice catches. "A curse, ancient relics, a treasure, a hoax, a crazy ghost, or hell's revenge. Take your pick of the absurd explanations."

Near a breaking point, she simmers in humiliation and shock. She only wanted to regain control of her life, but with each new step forward, with each new person involved, the power of the curse expands. And with each new death that follows her, any illusion of control unravels.

Miguel continues to glare at his father. "Curse, what the hell is she talking about?"

"We don't believe in curses." Estefan shuffles his feet.

"You don't believe in curses," snaps Miguel. "I believe two of my friends are dead. Now what the hell is going on?"

"It's complicated," Estefan deflects.

"Death is complex," he shouts.

Sophia holds her tongue, feeling the resentment and anger burning between them, making her want to hide, wishing she could undo the past few days, that she would have tossed her bag into the ocean.

Miguel glares down his father until Estefan pulls out her images to place them on the table. Others grasp at the pictures to scan or distribute. Eyes quickly settle on the broken tortoise shell image with odd symbols.

"Holy crap, now that's freaky weird." A shaggy Waldo reaches into a nearby cabinet to pull out a small envelope. He lays a tortoise shell next to her shell image. The two shells could almost be top and bottom of the same shell, with similar symbols, except for color tone.

"How is that possible?" mutters Darcy, turning to Sophia with a questioning gaze.

Shrugging her shoulders, unsure where either shell came from, Sophia dares a question. "What do they say?"

"I did a little research last night on Hansen's shell," a petite, preppy blonde interjects. "The script may belong to the El Mirador family, but I'm guessing more primitive." That means nothing to Sophia.

"What's in the book?" a stern, shaved-head Hispanic asks.

"Good question," responds Sophia. "I was hoping Estefan could help me read it."

All eyes turn in her direction, each of them darkened by the trauma of death. The battle to keep her quest private has been lost; the heartaches are no longer hers alone to bear. Either way, she owes them complete honesty.

"Maybe you could all help," she says.

Reaching into her bag, she pulls out Estefan's book and removes the jacket cover to reveal a box made to look like a book. Inside the box, a cloth covers a grimy, tattered leather book. The revelation earns a hurtful glare from Estefan.

"I needed to know I could trust you," she explains. "Besides, you said it was all madness, and if they stopped me at Customs, I wanted you to be innocent." His expression softens.

Putting on gloves, Dr. O'Sullivan lays the book on a clean cloth spread out on the table. An Asian woman darts away and returns with an illuminated magnifying lens. Geeky Waldo puts on his own gloves as Dr. O'Sullivan opens the cover with padded tweezers.

"I think it's Spanish with words I don't recognize," notes Dr. O'Sullivan, peering through the magnifier.

"K'iche," interjects Estefan. "The odd words are likely K'iche."

Dr. O'Sullivan nods acceptance, since K'iche was the indigenous language from Yucatan to Honduras, and still spoken.

"There's a clean corner on the front cover," notes Dr. O'Sullivan.

Waldo leans over her shoulder to read. "It's a name, Pedro Montego Cortés de Alvarado."

Sophia notes the name of Cortés, remembering Papá's name for the Spanish ghost. The connection intrigues her. Maybe she misjudged the situation; perhaps these people can help.

"It appears someone wrote on the paper, covered it in blood, and then etched in the blood." Dr. O'Sullivan grimaces. "It's tough to read with so many scratches and layers."

"You never answered my question, Professor," Miguel redirects. "Why are my men dead?"

For a heartbeat, Sophia feels compelled to explain how she unleashed a curse and confess that his men are dead because of her shameful disobedience to her buyei and her foolish dismissal of an asandiruni.

"I can only speculate," says Estefan. "The dagger and shell script appear quite ancient."

"How valuable?" the shaved head inquires.

"Six, maybe seven figures," guesses Estefan with a shrug.

Sophia startles at the revelation. She never thought to ask about a value, assuming a few thousand at most. For hundreds of thousands or millions, then sheer greed alone could be enough of a motive for so much death. Even so, it still doesn't explain the family history of death, disappearance, or dementia. Long ago, no one would have cared about an old dagger or had a reason to hide it.

"That's it," challenges Miguel. "You sure there's nothing else?"

Relieved no one has mentioned curses, and glad she held her tongue, Sophia doesn't understand why Miguel acts so suspicious of his own padre.

Estefan sighs. "There's a slim chance it involves the missing pages of the book."

Sophia shoots him a surprised look. "You said the curse was madness, meaningless."

The whole reason for her trip was to learn the secrets of the supposed key, the three pages he inherited. He lied to her.

"Again, that word; curse," notes Miguel. "What are you not telling me?"

With a sigh, the professor reaches into his case to pull out laminated copies of the cursed pages, along with smaller versions of the light-spectrum images, and sets the pictures on the table, where the crew distributes them.

"I inherited the original pages from Papá Joaquin," explains Estefan, looking toward Miguel. "Like the book, blood and etching cover the pages with two or three layers. The last layer contains incoherent, mad gibberish that ends simply, *Cortés*."

The name her Papá gave as the curse of Cortés must have come from the separated three pages and not the book, which had been buried in the wall.

"What gibberish? Why are my men dead over gibberish?" presses Miguel, his eyes burning through Estefan.

"You need to remember," deflects Estefan, "Papá Joaquin suffered from dementia for many years before he died."

Sophia takes in another case of family dementia with a sad resignation to her likely future. Miguel waits with an unflinching glower.

"Joaquin told crazy stories of deep caverns and lunatic spirits guarding a terrible secret, a cursed treasure of the damned," he admits.

"Rafé told me the same stories," interjects Sophia. "How is that possible?"

Estefan glances down as if he doesn't want to answer. "I've always dismissed the stories as superstitious folklore," he replies. "Yet, Joaquin swore he'd seen the treasure with his own eyes. Joaquin and Rafé were brothers, so perhaps at some point they were there together." Estefan suggests a scenario she had not considered, but if so, then Rafé was quite young.

"Are you saying his crazy stories are true?" she retorts, surprised.

"No, of course not," he responds. "The story never made sense. I mean, who protects a treasure instead of taking it to spend? Still, for whatever reason, Joaquin claimed he brought the curse to America to end the legacy of tragedy in the family."

"Well, it didn't work," snaps Sophia, sounding more irritable than intended.

"My point is," Estefan redirects, "that during the search for your father, there were men from the mainland looking for Rafé's lost treasure. Whoever was looking for treasure then may suspect the book contains clues."

"I don't get it. You're saying Moses and Ben are dead because of a family legend of treasure?" Miguel asks.

"No, I believe the dagger to be the target," clarifies Estefan. "The Belize museum likely sold Sophia's information to a private collector who wants the artifacts at any cost."

"Well, that's just great," interjects Miguel. "The most obsessive private collector in this region just happens to be a homicidal Nacon wacko." Scowling with arms folded into clenched fists.

"So, what's your plan, Estefan?" asks geeky Waldo, breaking the awkward tension.

"Get the artifacts to UCLA and release a PR statement to remove the target off of Sophia," he explains.

"Yeah right, like Nacon stays current with the latest museum PR," shaved head laughs sarcastically. "Once you have your relic, what happens to la señorita?"

Sophia has been so busy trying to hand off the relics and go back to a normal life, she downplayed the prospect of remaining in danger. His comment makes her unsure how to handle a new reality.

"Too late, Professor," interjects Miguel. "We just left several dead PR statements in Belize."

"A regional arrest warrant will be issued by morning," notes the intense skinhead.

Miguel shakes his head. "Okay, I've heard enough. We have a choice." He paces. "I say we head back to San Lorenzo, where a paid contract waits. We contact authorities and tell them the truth that cartel pirates attacked our ship, and we defended ourselves. Yada, yada."

"Or," he gestures to Sophia, "we go to Roatan to retrieve artifacts so we can smuggle them to America with Nacon pirates hot on our ass."

"Won't we need the relics to prove our story in Panama?" a tall brunette points out.

"If we help Sophia out of danger," interjects Darcy, "we would be doing the right thing for family."

Miguel turns away from her scornful gaze without responding.

"Skipper, San Lorenzo will be the first place that authorities come look for us, not to mention the Nacon scout already waiting. We may tell our story from inside a Panama jail, or worse," notes the intense skinhead.

"There's a Nacon scout in Panama?" the blonde woman repeats, looking frightened.

"I agree with Brenda," adds Waldo. "We need the artifacts as leverage."

"I agree with Xavier," the Asian woman adds, pointing to skinhead.

The discussion heats up over avoiding jail in Panama versus avoiding cartel bullets. Sophia steps back, avoiding the conversation entirely, almost wishing they would vote not to help. The whole situation has grown beyond her control, like a curse. This was supposed to be a private family matter, an easy way to pay for the roof, a little factual history to dispel a dark stigma. Now, people she never even knew are dying, as Carmen predicted, a shame she's not sure how to self-forgive.

Miguel cuts into the conversation. "Okay, that's enough. You may not believe in curses, but you sure as hell should believe in a vicious Nacon. Cast your vote as a crew—Panama or Roatan."

After the vote, Miguel hangs his head with a sigh as the only one in favor of Panama. Sophia doesn't even know all of their names, and yet strangers who just lost two friends have chosen to risk their lives to help her. Overwhelmed with gratitude, she feels the tears slowly track down her cheeks, feeling unworthy. She's scared to death, and they show a bravery she can only envy.

"I don't know what to say," she confesses, her voice catching in her throat.

Estefan silently puts an arm around her like Papá used to do. Closing her eyes, just for an instant, she feels as if she were in Papá's arms, sensing her gubida encouraging her to have faith.

"Okay, your choice becomes your problem," says Miguel. "Nacon will come after the ship, so we need more fact, less folklore, and a plan."

Turning to Darcy, he points to the images. "How fast can you get real insights on that stuff?"

"Split into two or three teams, at least a week, longer without access to research libraries," she responds.

"Without knowing the script, we may never be able to read the shell," interjects Waldo. "But linguistic libraries would help."

"We'll be in Roatan by oh-eight hundred tomorrow," states Miguel. "You have until oh-seven hundred to present your best shot."

When the crew grumbles, Miguel shoots a cold glare with a raised eyebrow as a reminder that they voted themselves into this situation. "Oh-seven hundred," he repeats.

Dr. O'Sullivan turns to Estefan. "In that case, I can work with Dr. Martinez on the book."

Estefan nods in agreement. "Jackson, why don't you lead a team to examine the tortoise shell and blade."

Sophia notes the name. Jackson nods, turning to the preppy blonde woman. "Juniper studied pre-Xinca dialects. I could use her help," Juniper replies with a quick, perky nod.

Miguel turns to Sophia. "You work with Brenda and Mai to profile everything you know about Roatan."

Happy to make note of everyone's name, and contribute, she corrects him. "Actually, we're going to Isla Barbareta, a few kilometers east of Roatan."

Miguel nods. "Okay, then include both. I need you to run down geology, history, maps, wrecks, underwater charts, legends, and folklore. Everything you can find out."

Miguel picks up an on-board intercom to call the bridge. "Hansen," he says, "you're promoted to captain. Congratulations. Set a course for Isla Barbareta. Avoid shipping lanes, and stay off radar."

Turning back to the frightened crew, Miguel looks each one in the eye, ending with Sophia. "As of this moment, you're all fugitives from the law and a target for cutthroats," he states the blunt truth. "Be back here at oh-seven hundred sharp, and have your game face on."

Miguel pivots to storm away, not even speaking with his padre as Sophia watches the dejection fall over Estefan's face. Carmen used to say that no one can hurt you like family. Given that she never had any family, it was hard to imagine, but she can clearly see the deep wounds abiding between these two men, who both need a good buyei to help them reconcile and heal.

"Well, Estefan, Sophia," says Darcy with a sigh, "Hugo makes a killer coffee. Either of you interested?"

"Killer coffee is my favorite kind of killer." Estefan accepts with a one-sided grin.

Sophia shudders at the gallows humor but accepts the offer, hoping these strangers can help end this ordeal before anyone else perishes. It's a choice to have faith, not an easy choice, maybe not even a rational choice, but it's her only choice.

Chapter 30

Unity Gala
(Cha'an Hun)

Private Island, 78 miles north of Colombia
June 19, 9:24 p.m. | 33 hours to Mayan chaa

Juan Perez left Golan and Gerhard aboard *Túumben Epoca* with more than enough hardened mercenaries and firepower to abduct an entire village. He'll accept no more pathetic excuses. Once he grips the maker's blade in his hand, Shay can dump the bodies out at sea.

Forcing the distraction to the back of his mind, he focuses on the lavish Unity Gala, personally greeting each of the thousands of guests who have been arriving throughout the day to his remote island paradise. Ninety kilometers north of Colombia, the seventeen-square-kilometer island features a contemporary eleven-thousand-square-meter mansion with twenty-four guest rooms and twelve private beach bungalows, surrounded by lush private gardens, two pools, and tennis courts. Access to the island is limited to a secure helipad or a guarded marina where more than thirty yachts currently sit at anchor. The island has become his fortress, his retreat, and his temple.

Guests mingle, laugh, and drink from several bars set up around the estate or dine on gourmet cuisine stations spread throughout the grounds. A concert plays near the beach, where guests dance barefoot in the sand. A few guests swim within the pools or protected lagoons.

While many of his guests have known the true Juan Perez over the years, few knew him intimately. A well-known recluse, the womanizing eccentric remained a public enigma, his cherished privacy becoming a deadly liability. Years ago, he and the true Juan Perez noted how much they looked alike, almost like brothers. Friends and business partners for well over two decades, the true Juan Perez eventually grew suspicious of the ultimate goal, and then he grew a conscience. In the end, he became unnecessary, a loose end to trim.

Now he wears the face, the wardrobe, and the enigmatic *suavite* of Juan Perez de Menendez, with the combined resources of two empires at his command. He vows to himself that each guest will leave the gala convinced he or she shared an evening with the magnetic mogul himself. To take ownership of the identity, he will entertain them, win them over, and gain their trust.

"Señor de Menendez," greets Argentine banker Bernard Mieglitz, "your insights into the power of economic unity are quite insightful. Lanza was wise to seek your counsel for LASSG."

"Nonsense, Señor," he dismisses. "True insight was your proposal to such a lovely woman to be your wife." He kisses the hand of his blushing spouse.

With gracious compliments, he woos the elegant women dripping in gems, chuckles at their banal jokes, or offers his own one-liner to charm the elite guests. After anarchy consumes the continent, they will welcome him when he restores the peace with a vision of unity.

For most of his life, these very same people referred to him as an animal or a cancer to eradicate. Tonight, standing in a new skin, wearing tailored clothing, indulging his guests in luxury and free alcohol, they not only accept him, but they fawn over him, compliment him, and all but lick his shoes. The excitement tingles every nerve in his body. He will fulfill the prophecy of Chilam Balaam.

Scattered throughout the estate, HD screens play promotional videos featuring Juan Perez in cameos. Each video promotes the dignity of the many pre-Columbian civilizations stretching from Patagonia to northern Mexico, with a montage of compelling, emotional images. and a subtle expectation for a new beginning, a coming solstice, the Mayan chaa, a day of solemn rebirth for the cosmos, and a hope of the future.

The Peruvian ambassador to the United Nations approaches him near the beach cabanas. With excellent relationships at the UN, the ambassador could be useful during the political transition, longer if he performs well, and remains loyal.

"Señor de Menendez," he greets with a cheerful smile. "The snobs on Cozumel attended the wrong celebration."

Like many of his guests, the ambassador did not make the coveted invite list for LASSG. In a couple of days, each of the offended will fall to their knees in gratitude.

"Thank you, Ambassador Pupae," Juan Perez bows. "I am honored you would attend my humble alternative."

The ambassador came from the private grotto museum, where Juan Perez had his curator develop an incredible exhibition of five hundred priceless artifacts, featuring a hastily prepared but elegant presentation of the death mask and elongated skull of the snake king god, the mythical Kukulkan. Separately, an elaborate multimedia presentation highlights the Polpul Vuh myth of creation and the Chilam Balam prophecies of rebirth.

> Then it will happen—darkness. Bolon-Yokte will descend to the great waters. The Thirteenth Bak'tun will be finished (on) Four Ajaw, the Third of Uniiw (K'ank'in). Darkness will occur.
> —Chilam Balam.

Bolon-Yokte was an ancient god associated with the underworld, conflict and war, dangerous transition times, social unrest, eclipses, and natural disasters, like the dangers ready to unleash. Now, his Bolon-Yokte war council will bring the same.

"I must confess to being overwhelmed by your inspirational collection," praises the ambassador. "The skull and death mask of a mythical god, truly a one of a kind."

Juan Perez smiles, hearing exactly the praise he expected.

"Thank you, Ambassador." He draws the man closer as if to reveal a secret. "I know a dealer in Cuzco who could offer you an incredible bargain on the elongated skull and skeleton of a Paracas queen still within her burial wrap, her auburn hair and jewelry intact."

The diplomat's eyes widen. As they talk over the arrangements, Juan Perez gently leads him to one of the bungalows, where an orgy hums with moans and squeals of ecstasy. Nudging the middle-aged man toward the door, a naked, petite Latina takes care of luring him in further. If the ambassador resists cooperating with the UN, a copy of the video will persuade him; his wife controls all the money. For years, he manipulated people from a distance, behind the scenes or through others. To exercise a direct, personal control thrills him.

After socializing for hours, Juan Perez retreats into the island security office, where over 1,350 cameras and 750 hidden microphones feed an enormous wall with dozens of display screens. A handful of security guards sit at a massive control board.

"Where's Golan?" he barks, the polite persona of Juan Perez unnecessary here.

"Still detained on the other mission, sir." The lead soldier reports, avoiding eye contact.

He bites down his irritation. "Find Fredrick Gonzales."

The soldier pulls up the master view of the palace and gardens. Gonzales, a pharma executive, asked too many personal questions earlier, referring to a private conversation not in the profiles. After locating the executive near the pool, the soldier zooms a camera and turns up a nearby microphone. He talks privately with an Argentine admiral, not a member of his council.

"I asked him about a private moment that he and I shared several years ago, but he ducked the conversation entirely, like he couldn't remember," explains the executive.

"I'm sure it was just a senior moment, like the rest of us," dismisses the admiral.

"Perhaps." He lowers his voice. "Or he is not the actual de Menendez, maybe a security double. He looks a little different, have you noticed?"

"Nonsense." The admiral laughs and changes the subject.

Juan Perez has heard enough. "Eliminate them both," he instructs the soldier.

"Yes, sir." The only acknowledgment of a death sentence, with two names jotted onto a pad. Vacub Came will deal with the targets later, making sure the deaths appear accidental.

An exquisite beauty with a backless dress wanders from the noisy casino room onto the balcony overlooking the small private harbor. A diplomat's trophy wife, she had been flirting with him earlier. His second yacht rests in the harbor, much smaller than *Túumben Epoca*; he reserves the elegant sixty-foot sailing yacht for his personal use only. There are no cameras on the ship, only a guard at the marina gate.

Exiting the security control room with a lustful grin, he gives a parting command. "Keep recording every conversation, and filter out the trash later."

The media team will work for months to review, filter, and catalog the terabytes of content. Nothing can stop Buluc Chabtan or the coming epoch. Juan Perez heads toward the marina, where a randy goddess wanders the docks.

Chapter 31

In Plain Sight

C hico borders on a full-blown panic. The enormous dark ship silhouette has returned outside the eastern reef, waiting like a crouching panther preparing to strike. Mari and the kids huddle together a few meters behind him with no laughter tonight, only frightened whispers and prayers. A medical boat came yesterday to patch Rafé's wound and dose him with antibiotics. After sleeping most of the day, he awakened still weak, but ironically more lucid than he's been in years.

"What do they want?" Papá asks.

"They come for me," Rafé snarls.

"Why?" retorts Chico. "What'd you do?"

"I know the secret," replies Rafé.

Chico thinks he refers to the legend of treasure, but he knows the island better than anyone does, and the legends of lost caves are nonsense.

"Take the children in the canoes and hide behind the large rocks near the tide pool, but leave me your jug of acid," Rafé directs with sharp eyes and a calm voice.

Before Chico can argue, Mari herds the children toward the fishing canoes. A few minutes later, Papá stands waist-deep in water, handing him the night-vision goggles left by the mercenaries.

"No matter what happens," Papá states in a whisper, "stay out of sight. Keep the children safe."

Chico swallows hard and nods. Within minutes, he and the family are floating in wooden canoes, sheltered from view behind large rocks and mangrove. From his hiding place, Chico uses the night goggles to watch Rafé and Papá hide in plain sight. With snorkeling gear, they float several meters off the beach in the shallows. Even with night goggles and knowing exactly where to look, Chico struggles to see the two tiny tubes sticking out of the water. A jug of industrial-strength acid floats behind Rafé, tied to a string.

After an hour of damp night air and raging anxiety, Chico spots a large military zodiac quietly row into the lagoon and swoosh up onto the beach. Six commandoes leap out in silent teams of two, weapons ready to invade each shack. With no one home, the assailants turn on the lights to conduct a search.

"Why are they searching our home?" whispers Mari, looking angry and frightened.

"I don't know," he whispers. He suspects they're looking for something Sophia showed Rafé on her visit, but he never got close enough to see.

While the soldiers rip up their shacks, Rafé and Hector rise out of the lagoon next to the zodiac. Using a fishing knife, Rafé places dozens of shallow cuts along the main seam of the inflatable craft. Papá follows him, pouring the powerful industrial acid along the cut seams and over the engine fuel lines.

"What are they doing?" asks Mari.

"I think they're sabotaging the boat," he guesses.

"How will that get them off our island?" she whispers, anxiety raising the pitch of her voice.

He shrugs. "You should ask *el loco*."

Out of acid, Rafé and Papá snorkel to the distant side of the cove, where they climb into a canoe tied to a mangrove. Silently they paddle toward the main reef channel that leads out to the open ocean. On a moonless night, the pair of old islanders must know the path intuitively. Chico can't be sure, but it looks like they're dumping something into the water. When finished, they paddle back to join Chico in hiding.

"What were you doing out there?" Chico asks Papá.

"Inviting friends," he says with a smirk.

Not finding what they wanted in the shacks, the mercenaries split up to inspect the cove and jungle paths, flashing light beams dancing through the trees and coconut palms bordering the cliffs. Twenty minutes later, the commandoes head back to their zodiacs, having failed to find anyone.

"Rafé," whispers Hector, "what do they want?"

Chico glances over to see the old man jerking his neck, lapsing back into his dementia.

"Sophia hid them," Rafé twitches, and stutters, "in, in, in the, in the rock."

"Rafé, concentrate, what did Sophia hide?" Chico asks again, wondering what rock.

"She hid, she, she hid what was hidden," stutters Rafé, snapping his fingers.

Chico hangs his head in frustration, turning in time to see mercenaries toss hand grenades toward the empty shacks.

He yanks off the goggles just as explosions shatter the huts into a thousand splinters, blasting three fireballs into the air. With stifled tears, Mari suckles the toddler as the girls' gasp and weep, covering their mouths to avoid making noise. Chico holds Victor and his youngest boy close, each of them stunned to silence, shivering from shock as flames devour everything they own. Rafé rocks back and forth, snarling.

The assailants leap into their zodiac and power up their engine to scramble out of the inner lagoon, no longer concerned with stealth. Reaching the tight channel, they slow to navigate using bright floodlights. Even with the floodlights and the night goggles, it's hard for Chico to see that far in the distance, but something isn't right. The vessel sits low to port near the engine. A loud pop and a hissing noise drifts across the lagoon, followed by loud curses.

"What did you dump in the water?" Mari asks again.

"Shark chum." Papá sneers. "Real stinky."

From a half kilometer away, the sound of terrorized men shouting at each other drifts across the water. Chico hears more popping and hissing, evidence of the burning acid eating into the sliced air seams. The engines sputter to a stop as the acid burns through the plastic gas lines. The sight of guns firing into the dark water look like lightning bolts on the night vision. A third seam pops, then a fourth seam hisses to increased shouts of panic. Machine gun fire fills the lagoon as the commandos chase off the finned invaders, only adding fresh blood to the scent. The mercenaries will be lucky to reach the end of the reef alive.

Devastated and horrified beyond words, the family rows silently back to shore. Holding each other close, traumatized, and weeping loudly, they can only stare as flames light up the cove, reducing their humble huts into ash and cinder.

"Now what?" Mari worries, a tone of hopelessness in her voice.

"We do what we have to do," groans Chico. "Even if we don't like it."

He has to convince his family to escape from their paradise lost. The curse of the Martinez has returned to Isla Barbareta.

Chapter 32

Worthy
(Baler Ko'oh)

Private Island north of Colombia
June 20, 12:15 a.m. | 30 hours to Mayan chaa

Satisfied after his invigorating tryst with the amorous diplomat's wife, Juan Perez returns to the central mansion. While the gala winds down, hundreds will spend the night in one of the guest rooms, bungalows, or anchored yachts, ensuring the party continues through the chaa. Guests lounge around the pools or fire pits drinking, and entertaining each other, while two bungalow orgies rage on, oblivious to the hidden cameras. His staff will serve drinks and gourmet desserts until dawn, when they will switch to serving breakfast and fresh Colombian coffee.

The gala has been a complete success, and it's just getting started. The next two days will be the most rewarding of his life. When the time comes, these elite guests will welcome him to quell the anarchy of the masses, and he will accept his destiny.

An encrypted call from Golan vibrates his phone, instantly souring his elevated mood as he slips into a secluded room, closing the door for more privacy.

"What's taking you so long?" he demands.

"We were ambushed," reports Shay.

"Ambushed!" he roars before biting down his rage so guests won't overhear. "How? Where?"

"Team Beta found Barbareta abandoned. A complete search of the shacks and island turned up nothing—no relics, no old fool, no family, nobody. On the return trip, the inflatable sank in shark-infested waters, probably sabotaged," Shay spits out the news.

"Sank," Juan Perez bellows, lowering his voice a growl. "Idiot, if they sabotaged a zodiac, they were still on the damn island."

Shay has no answer. Too many bungled assaults have the locals expecting an attack.

"What happened in Belize?" Juan Perez demands.

"Team Alpha advanced on the airport, but the target, reported to be sleeping, had disappeared. We quickly tracked her to a nearby cantina, but before we could close in on her, a stranger helped the bitch escape onto a beat-up salvage ship," Shay explains. "There was a firefight."

"Hold on, you said an armed salvage ship. What ship?" he demands, suspecting the worst news. He knows only one salvage ship with enough *cojones* to shame Golan. "Tell me the name."

Silence hangs on the line until Shay finally admits the truth. "*Plunder Lust.*"

An intense rage explodes within him. That rusted piece of junk and her American scab rat captain have been a thorn in his side for years, like cockroaches he can't seem to crush. *Plunder Lust* was last reported in Panama, so he can only assume Hurricane Stephanie chased them north, but how did he come to rescue the woman?

"Losses?" he snarls.

"Six on Barbareta, three in Belize, two Hummers, and another zodiac," Shay sputters.

"And yet you dare to come back alive," roars Juan Perez before biting his tongue, veins bulging in his neck.

It's inconceivable how a woman getting off an international flight or an aged lunatic could defeat a dozen of his best men. Beyond incompetence, beyond poor planning, failures that could only be supernatural, cursed. Then the truth opens up like a sudden revelation. Shay and Gerhard are crude tools, blunt instruments, and idiots unworthy of retrieving such a sacred blade. The blade of the maker is not just a piece of obsidian and not just another artifact; the blade of the creator holds the power of creation and death. An omen to prophecy, meant for him and him alone. Of course, it should have occurred to him sooner. Only he can reclaim the sacred obsidian. The spirit of the Creator demands that he prove himself for the right to rule an epoch.

"Wake up the flight crew, and send the ship coordinates. Tell them to prepare for immediate takeoff," he snarls. "I will lead this mission myself, and you two idiots are coming with me."

He hangs up, struggling to control his explosive fury. With twenty-nine hours remaining to chaa, the safest plan would be to hole up on the island, spend time with his patrons, and watch the celebrations live. Yet he dares not fail the Creator's test or lose his sacred blade to the American. The Sikorsky will take at least three hours to rendezvous with *Túumben Epoca,* and another hour or more to arrive on Barbareta, which will give him a little time to rest on the trip. Rushing back to his private suite to change clothes, he works through the plan.

Cozumel will lock down for LASSG tomorrow. Naval patrols already actively ping sonar sweeps for a submarine wild goose chase. Sleeper cells stand ready for the signal of Buluc Chabtan, which remains safely buried, ensuring the new epoch will arise. In fact, no one can stop that from happening, not even him.

While Tomas Flores and that annoying reporter are loose ends to clip, he has confidence in his brother, Vacub Came. With a deep breath, he accepts the one final task before his plans of power are complete, a test of worthiness. With the power of the sacred obsidian, together with the wisdom and spirit of the Creator, he will fulfill the prophecy of Chilam Balaam for a new epoch.

Born Felipe Roué Gutierrez, the bastard son of a Mestizos drug mule and a cartel prostitute, his birth name now feels more like a past life or a bad dream. Beaten and neglected like an alley cat, he learned to survive at a young age. A lifelong chameleon, a master at blending in, he learned to change his look or his profession on a whim. A doctor, a concierge, a police officer, a tarot-card reader, a yacht captain, and a dozen other identities veiled his true persona and his growing empire.

In a stroke of genius, he faked his death, only to resurrect himself as Hun Came, the highest lord of death in the underworld of Xibalba, an identity chosen to drive fear into the hearts of his superstitious enemies. Like a demon with no past and no face, he built the persona of a savage, invincible immortal roused from the grave to reap vengeance on anyone who dared resist him. The demon ghost haunts every leader in Latin America. With unashamed violence, he gained power, and with power he made fortunes, bought an education and then influence. Now he craves a legacy.

He stands ready to claim his destiny, while his ex-partner, the real Juan Perez de Menendez, continues to languish in a forgotten, derelict prison cell, deep in the jungles of southern Colombia. One of them went to Harvard, living an entitled life of privilege, while the other was born of desperation, spit on, kicked, and worked tirelessly to write his name into history. Soon, the original Juan Perez will no longer be necessary.

Aware of the transformation needed within his own psyche, he throws back a tall shot of tequila. With a change of clothes, he storms out of his private suite, down a secret escape tunnel leading to the helicopter pad. The route will avoid his guests. From this moment forward, he must shake off the docile, diplomatic persona of Juan Perez and shed him like an overweight cloak. Only the unhinged savage power of Hun Came can reap the vengeance his enemies deserve.

Taking off, he throws back another shot of tequila before closing his eyes. They speed toward a rendezvous with *Túumben Epoca*, and his fate. If the blade of the maker will empower him, then by power and force, he must seize it. The American junk boat captain has crossed him for the last time. As if destiny were tying up all the loose ends for him, he vows to himself that this hunt will end today.

Chapter 33

Kinetic Spark

Plunder Lust, 15 miles offshore Isla Barbareta
June 20, 6:42 a.m. | 24 hours to Mayan chaa

Utterly exhausted after working with Mai and Brenda all night to prepare an overview of Isla Roatan and Barbareta, Sophia can't see how any of it will help against a deadly adversary. Grateful that she's no longer alone, and humbled by so many bright minds willing to help, she still feels traumatized by the violence. Overly fatigued and stressed by her lingering asandiruni, she's eager to hand off the cursed items to Estefan and return to what may be left of a normal life.

Preoccupied, she enters the bridge and encounters a huge, muscular man at the helm, partially blocking her way, a giant with crew-cut sandy-brown hair, deep dimples, and laugh wrinkles around his light-brown eyes. Startled speechless, she flushes, stalling at the doorway.

"Ma'am," he smiles wide, tipping his US Navy SEAL cap, bulging his T-shirt sleeve until it nearly rips. No one has ever called her *ma'am.* Does she look that old?

"You must be Ms. Martinez, Skipper's cousin." He extends his enormous hand. "We haven't met. I, I mean I heard about you, you know, that we had special guests an' all," he staggers with a thick East Texas accent.

He may be the one stuttering, but butterflies are playing havoc in her abdomen, keeping her silent, timid of saying something foolish, blushing, and breathless. She hadn't thought of herself as a special guest, more of a semi-willing abductee.

"I'm Brunk, hmm, I mean, Hans, uh—" He stutters, turns red, and draws a sharp breath. "I mean Hansen, Captain Hansen at your service, ma'am."

Miguel and Xavier stop working at a navigation table to turn with wide eyes toward the stuttering hulk at the helm.

Sophia blushes from the attention and changes the subject. "Do you have a ship-to-shore radio? I'd like to call the Woods Hospital in Coxen Hole to check on my friend Emilio," she asks, oddly self-conscious to mention Emilio as a friend. "My cell battery died."

"Nah, ma'am, you don't wanna do that," he replies with a raised eyebrow. "Ship-to-shore will register through the local harbor office with an open channel. We need to keep a low profile."

He plucks a cheap phone from his pocket. "Here you go. Try my burner phone. It's untraceable and supposed to cover the whole region."

"Thank you, Hansen—*Captain* Hansen." She grins, stepping out onto the bridge balcony for more privacy, feeling his gaze follow her. Both anxious and aroused by the attention, she tries to focus on her call. After several rings, the line finally picks up.

"Hola," she answers, lowering her voice. "I'm looking for an update on Emilio Eldon? Betty Girl, dis be his aunt Millie," Sophia lies, doing her best to sound like the old woman, a tad ashamed at yet another deception.

"Oh, hi, Mrs. Eldon," the nurse replies. "Good news, Emilio woke from his coma this morning. Dr. Morales is with him now. Would you like the doctor to call you?"

"Oh no, no, child," she dismisses. "Good news be answer to prayer."

She disconnects with a tremendous weight of guilt lifting from her shoulders and a silent prayer that the shadow of death has ended. Reentering the bridge, she finds it impossible not to notice Captain Hansen's boyish face light up, radiating an involuntary blush over her cheeks.

"Thank you," she says, handing back the phone.

His massive hands wrap around hers a bit longer than necessary, sending a spark of excitement to her heart and elsewhere. She can't imagine it was intentional, but the feeling was unmistakable. Could he feel it too?

"Everybody okay?" he inquires, sounding sincere.

"My friend Emilio woke up from a coma. I don't know more because the doctor was with him," she replies.

"Hallelujah," he spouts with an honest grin. "Well see, now that is great news." His response catches her by surprise. He certainly doesn't look spiritual.

"Sophia, come give us a layout of where we're going here," calls Miguel, interrupting the kinetic spark connection.

With a deep breath, she readjusts her attention to the chart table. "There's a crescent cove on the east side of Barbareta where Rafé and Chico live." She points to the spot. "Navigation buoys mark a shallow sea to the west." She points between Isla de Morat, Isla Santa Elena, and Isla Barbareta. "A ship this size will need to anchor in deep waters outside the eastern reef," she notes, placing a magnet marker on the chart.

Hansen steps over from the helm to gaze down from over her shoulder. So close, she can sense his presence, not touching her, yet thrilling her in ways she hasn't felt since high school.

"Once we're anchored, what's the best route to navigate the coral reef?" Xavier pulls her attention back to the chart. "It doesn't look easy."

"It's not," she agrees. "You need to take inflatables around the southwest edge of the reef to enter the main channel." Her finger traces a path on the chart. "Over half a kilometer each way."

"Sounds like you know the island well," interjects Hansen, earning a glance from his shipmates.

She peers up to the towering hazelnut eyes behind her. "I spent summers on Barbareta as a schoolgirl, and my uncle still lives there. He's an old loco, but a kind soul deep down." She reveals more than she intended.

Hansen smiles. "Yeah, I getcha. I have an aunt like that. Lindsey. We call her Loopy Liddy. She once danced a can-can on the front lawn in nothing but her bathrobe. A boy can't unsee somethin' like that." He chuckles at the recollection.

She imagines the scene, joining his chuckle and becoming aware of his effortless ability to make her feel safe, not just in a physical sense, but with a gentle humility.

"Remember, we're here to grab the artifacts and run, right?" Xavier reminds them, looking restless.

"No time for family visits, or scenic tours." Miguel flashes a glare at Hansen. "Or trips down memory lane."

Chastised, Hansen turns his attention back to the helm.

"Once on the island, where are we going?" asks Xavier.

Sophia points to the eastern shoreline. "The basalt cliffs on the east end. I hid my backpack in a rock crevice invisible from the ground."

Miguel taps his wristwatch. "Okay, debrief time," he reminds them. "Hansen, you got the helm. Xavi, Sophie you're with me."

After Miguel leads the way off the bridge, followed by Xavier, Sophia lingers. "May I ask you a personal question?" she says with an unexpected quiver in her voice.

Hansen's eyes widen. "Uh, yeah, sure."

"Do you have a strong sense of smell?" she asks, thinking of Carmen's theory of stinky fish and late-blossom romance.

He scrunches his nose. "Well, no, I guess not, no not really. I mean, my daddy smoked too much, and then I worked the oil rigs," he confesses, looking worried. "Should, should I?"

"No." Sophia smiles with another rapid flush. "No, that's perfect."

Unable to think of something else to say, she waves goodbye to her captain. The huge sailor smiles until his dimples crease, and he waves back like a schoolboy. Heading toward the mess hall, she becomes aware of a flush of forgotten desires. After a decade of numbness toward men, her heart palpitates. Something about that man ignites something long dead within her. *Have faith, girl*, she tells herself. *Have a little faith.*

*

Plunder Lust, 15 miles offshore Isla Barbareta
June 20, 6:58 a.m. | 24 hours to Mayan chaa

Xavier pulls Miguel aside on their way to the morning debrief for a private update. Overnight, Xavier had used an encrypted satellite signal to reach his contacts at CISEN for insights on the sleeper cell alert and the attack in Belize.

"What did you learn?" asks Miguel.

"More than I expected," Xavi replies, his facial muscles taut. "Belize police found the damaged Hummers near a private airfield. A chopper arrived minutes after your padre's plane landed, and left minutes after we blew out of port," Xavier summarizes.

"Tail number?" asks Miguel.

"Unmarked," Xavier replies with a frown.

"Pretty expensive muscle for a last-minute grab on an island girl." Miguel doesn't like the news and puzzles over the desperate tactics.

"Nacon may be pushing up other deadlines before the chaa," Xavier reminds him.

"Yeah, but why?" Miguel retorts.

"Funny you should ask," says Xavier. "Lucia uncovered evidence of a stolen Pakistani nuke. CISEN confirms both Mexican and US navies are conducting sonar sweeps of the Gulf and Cozumel. Lucia tracked funds to the media guru de Menendez and thinks an arms deal will go down at the summit, but I have a bad feeling that Nacon would never sell a nuke."

"Holy crap," replies Miguel. "A nuclear Nacon puts a dangerous spin on Buluc Chabtan."

"Like continental extortion," agrees Xavier.

"Yeah, now I'm getting your bad feeling," says Miguel. "After we're done with this little sideshow, I think we should head to Antigua and lie low until this all blows over."

"After this mission," replies Xavier, "I'm taking personal time away."

Stunned, Miguel waits speechless for an explanation. Xavier never takes time off. With a Nacon price on his head, *Plunder Lust* has been his safe refuge for nearly four years.

"Okay, brother, you're scaring me," says Miguel. "What's going on?"

"Lucia's in deeper trouble than she'll admit," explains Xavier. "Nacon put a target on her back, and I need to find her first before the region blows up."

Miguel met Lucia once when she visited *Plunder Lust* to check out her brother's new friends and escort her cousin Hugo to join the motley crew. A super-intense woman, attractive, smart, and a little scary all at the same time, she struck Hansen as a prettier version of Xavier.

"What if it's a trap to pull you out of hiding?" asks Miguel.

"Doesn't matter. If I don't go, Lucia will get herself arrested or killed," replies Xavier. "I'd never forgive myself if something happened to her."

Miguel takes a deep breath over the disappointing and sorrowful news. He's never had a sibling, unsure what he'd do if one of them were in danger. Xavier and Hansen are the closest that he'll ever get to brothers, and he'd run into the fire for either one of them.

"Well, okay brother, do whatever you need to do," offers Miguel with a bit of a heavy heart. "Just remember, *Plunder* will always be open for you and Luci."

Xavier laughs. "*Gracias, mi amigo*, but good luck ever getting Lucia to hide anywhere, and let's be honest, you're not exactly the Ritz Carlton."

Miguel grins. Yeah, he'll be back, but if Lucia's right about the nuke, the world may be a different place.

Chapter 34

Inquisition Executioner

Plunder Lust, 14 miles offshore Isla Barbareta
June 20, 7:08 a.m. | 23 hours to Mayan chaa

Already late for the morning debrief, Miguel and Xavier enter the mess hall, where most of the science team hang over their coffee mugs, disheveled and leaning into each other like a bunch of rag dolls. Jackson staggers into the room with semi-open eyes. Too sleepy even to try getting coffee, he falls into a corner bench, leans against the wall, and shuts his eyes. Feeling sorry for him, Mai gets up to pour a mug, sets it on the table in front of him, and waves the aroma in his direction.

"You look like shit," she says, going back to her seat.

"Uh-huh," he mumbles. His fingers creep across the table until they tenderly fondle the mug handle. Without opening his eyes, he slowly drags the aroma of roasted java to his nostrils, inhaling in a long, lingering moment before taking a blind sip.

Darcy arrives last, having slept as little as the others, yet she looks showered and fresh, pouring hot water over a bag of tea with a tad of cream and honey, and then signals to Miguel.

Inhaling a deep breath, he takes command of the room. "Last night a Nacon ambush gunned down Moses and Ben. Good men, good friends who didn't deserve to die," he states.

The room suddenly falls silent and attentive. He avoids eye contact with the professor, whom he blames for knowingly bringing a curse on board his ship. He'll deal with that insanity later.

"Don't fool yourselves," he continues. "Nacon will not stop until they get what they want. If you want to stay alive, we need to confirm what they what and why they want it so badly. More importantly, we need an advantage, something to use as leverage."

"Last night was a kidnapping attempt on Sophia," explains Xavier. "We need to know why."

Her eyes lower, taking the news with a brave face, less hysterical. Maybe Miguel misjudged her, but then again, the day is young.

"Okay, let's get going," says Miguel. "You're not briefing me, you're briefing each other. So, be factual. Be complete. Be quick." He sits down and waits for someone to begin.

Xavier leans in with a snicker. "*Muy inspirador.*"

Miguel ignores the snarky comment as Darcy and the professor exchange glances.

"I suppose we'll start," states the professor, gazing at Jackson. "Dr. Healy can follow if he can open his eyes."

Darcy stands to address the group. "As we noted yesterday, the book belonged to someone named Pedro Montego Cortés de Alvarado. While we found no official record of that name, we suspect a family connection to General Pedro de Alvarado y Contreras, conquistador of Guatemala, or more likely his half-brother, Diego de Alvarado. Both men sired a number of illegitimate Mestizo children of mixed heritage."

"Records indicate Diego died in Peru during 1556," the professor cuts in. "It would have been customary for the Franciscans to conscript any orphaned male Mestizo to the monastery at Mani. Ironically, to avoid violence themselves, the Inquisition monks forced their Mestizo disciples to perform the horrific tortures and executions."

Miguel ponders the mindset of someone raised to hate himself enough to torture his own people. Traumatized, demoralized, sick, and demented, a man jaded by human suffering that probably started with his own.

"We don't have multispectral tech, but we teased a bit of information from an X-ray," explains Darcy, laying a series of page images on the table for others to examine.

"During a 1565 Inquisition raid on Cozumel, Cortés writes of a pillaging a hidden temple of thousands of artifacts. During the raid, something drove him into a furious rage, causing Cortés to massacre the local village until the shaman cursed Cortés with a bloody spittle to his face. Within days, a hurricane left the murderous Mestizo shipwrecked, a sole survivor drifting for months before he marooned on a tiny island with a spring-fed waterfall and sinister caverns."

"Sinister, what do you mean?" asks Mai.

"Cortés spoke of horrific visions and hallucinations," replies the professor.

"In places, his writing grows so ragged in thought, delusional, and violent, it became too disturbing to read," interjects Darcy.

"We're dealing with the mad rantings of a sadistic lunatic," says the professor.

The description causes a few to take another gulp of their coffee and shift in their seat. Sophia combs her hand through her short hair with a deep breath.

"Isolation often led men to madness," the professor clarifies. "We cannot give credibility to his delusions, other than to note that he suffered severely from them."

"When Cortés ran short of paper, he covered the page with blood and then etched over the dried blood," Darcy interjects. "He may have survived for decades after he marooned."

"I found drawings that look like devices or booby traps," says the professor.

"If Cortés marooned alone, why build traps?" asks Xavier.

"Where did he get the materials?" asks Mai, looking confused.

Darcy shrugs. "Impossible to tell; maybe part of his delusions."

"Where did he get the blood?" asks Juniper.

"Likely Cortés himself," responds the professor. "The pages I inherited tested positive for human blood, although too contaminated to extract any viable DNA."

"What about the curse?" Dave asks. "What did you mean by mad gibberish?"

The professor takes a deep breath before answering. "Cortés was psychotic by any measure. The log speaks of things he could only have imagined in fits of delirium."

"Estefan, what does the curse actually say?" asks Sophia. "You never told me."

"Well, as I said before, the curse itself has no meaning." The professor tries again to deflect.

The room grows silent, waiting. Even Miguel wants to hear this one. The professor gives in with a sigh, lowers his chin, and closes his eyes. With a deep voice, he recites the English translation from memory.

"Through the jaws of death, both wicked and blessed will ascend Jacobs's ladder. Under a baptism of thunder, betrayal awaits with a sting worse than death until scavengers feed on your bones. Grovel in shame to escape the winged horde until you face the pale death of innocence and awaken the weeping of the doomed who shed their own blood. Between the cherubim of fire, an unquenchable lust will choke your lungs until you cough up your own blood. There will be no redemption for the glittering shame of Spain lost in the heathen hell and stained with the blood of maidens. Raise your hands to heaven in vain hope the raging torrent will not drag you screaming into the cold abyss. A narrow path of life leads to a bottomless, nameless tomb where the razor-sharp teeth of demons shred your soul. Damnation flows red over the abomination of the bloody altar, burning with the stench of death. Rise above the sacrifice of desolation to discover your dreadful fate. With my blood, I vow this eternal oath of penance. By my own bloody hand, I condemn my soul to the heathen hades. Cortés"

As a boy, Miguel remembers Papá Joaquin mumbling a few of those phrases when he thought no one was listening. He considered the words part of his dementia. When the professor opens his eyes, a few of the younger crew stare at him as if he had written those words himself.

"Joaquin passed away only weeks after handing me those pages. His dementia was too advanced to explain any of it," he recalls. "Months later, I took my family on an expedition to Belize, where I lost my guiding light." His voice cracks, turning to Miguel, correcting himself. "We lost her."

The professor sucks in air to push down his emotions, allowing Miguel to turn his gaze away and subdue his own upwelling. A link to his mother's death accelerates his growing disquiet, like reliving the worst day of his life. Her death devastated him as a boy and hardened him as a teen. He blames the professor, not some macabre tirade written by a psychotic henchman.

"For many years, I tried to find a context for such a horrific treatise, believing there had to be some tradition or legend or document, but I finally convinced myself the curse had nothing to do with my devastating loss," the professor justifies. "I concluded the pages were the ramblings of a dying madman, meaningless. I had all but forgotten about them," he gestures to Sophia, "until she walked into my lecture hall two days ago."

It suddenly occurs to Miguel that the professor dragged him around the jungles of Central America to a hundred dusty lost libraries in a desperate attempt to explain his mother's death. No, even worse, to blame her death on a sick curse. Impulse, pride, and bad decisions led to her death. He lost both parents that year, along with any hope of ever being a family again. *Yeah, maybe that does sound like a curse.*

"Okay, enough," he barks, angrier than necessary. "I doubt the cartel is looking for a crazy curse."

He points toward Jackson and Juniper. "Tell us about the dagger and script," he says, desperate to move off the morbid topics and dark memories. Besides, he's curious about the symbols. At the tip of his memory, like a dusty vapor, he needs to know where he's seen those odd symbols.

Still waiting on Jackson to open his eyes, Juniper stands to face the group.

"With only the pictures to study for the dagger, and Hansen's half of the shell, it limited our evidence gathering." Looking to Jackson, his eyes still closed, she sighs and faces the group, looking a tad shy.

"Made of green obsidian from the ancient mines near Teotihuacan, Mexico, the Aztecs discovered Teotihuacan abandoned a thousand years before the Spanish arrived. Teotihuacan means 'City Built by the Gods,' but no one knows who build the pyramids, the mines, or why they were abandoned."

She pauses to check on Jackson, still looking asleep. "The blade looks razor sharp, with signs of dried blood. While primitive, the artisanship and stylistic motif of a winged serpent are exquisite, with a possible connection to the snake kings of El Mirador," Juniper describes. "Or perhaps a pre-classic god cult of Kukulkan."

"Glyph," mumbles Jackson, eyes still closed.

"Oh, yeah," responds Juniper. "There's a glyph designed into the motif, and easy to miss, but it could be one of the symbols on the shell. Perhaps a name, but I'm not positive."

"Carbon," Jackson says, leaning against the bulkhead.

Juniper looks a tad nervous. "I carbon dated Mount Hansen's tortoise shell, but I need to retest."

"What date did you get?" asks Brenda.

Juniper sighs and hesitates. "12,900 to 13,050 BPE."

"That's impossible!" Mai exclaims. "There were no civilizations before the Olmec. Even the Snake King Dynasties from El Mirador only date to 6,000 BPE."

"Hold on, Juniper may be right," Estefan cuts in. "While the date may be unlikely, it would not be impossible. In fact, recent light-detection radar scans in the El Mirador basin of Guatemala have discovered over 61,400 previously unknown structures. While we can interpret nearly 85 percent of classic Mayan, we can only read 5 percent of the older El Mirador script."

"Dr. Martinez makes a good point," Brenda interjects. "During 2013, a team from Northwestern University discovered the complete skeleton of a teenage girl located in the Hoyo Negro cenote cave system of the Yucatan. Found

130 feet below sea level, the skeleton carbon dated to 13,000 BPE when the grotto was over 270 feet above sea level. The same caves also included altars, offerings, and the remains of a giant sloth, a creature that went extinct during the Younger Dryas."

"Interesting theory," interjects Juniper. "Hansen's shell was found on a ship called the *El Oro de Isabella*, so I did a little research. Owned by a wealthy landowner named Joaquin de Leguizamo, Bishop Diego de Landa chartered the frigate in 1565 for an Inquisition mission to find the lost library of Chilam Balam."

"Are you saying Cortés was on that ship?" asks Darcy.

"No, well gee, maybe," Juniper says. "I'm saying the relic Hansen found could predate other known scripts because it escaped the Inquisition. The wreck in Panama may open up a new phase of pre-Columbian history. Sophia's shell may have come from the same source."

Miguel suddenly understands why the professor risked his life for a distant relative. The old man is still willing to put others at risk for a pre–Younger Dryas civilization theory and now Moses and Ben are dead. The idea burns like bile in his stomach until he realizes with a sharp sting of truth and a wave of nausea that he and the professor are the same. While the professor will risk lives over history and ideas, he has lost men over fortune and fame. The man he fought so hard to escape is the man he became anyway. He refuses to linger on the comparison. Not the time or place, but damn, that one burns.

Jackson opens his eyes to squint from the daylight and sits up straighter. Done with his coffee, he gazes into the empty mug. "If the date proves correct, it's the oldest known writing in the world, older than the Sumerians by six thousand years. Priceless, worth killing to own, you know, for some people, if you're into that kind of thing."

"So, the shell is really old and could also be worth a lot of money," says Miguel. "Any guess on the glyph name?" He is hoping for more on the strange symbols.

"A guess, sure," Juniper states with a shrug. "Maybe Xibalque."

"The hero twin of mythology," responds Sophia, her eyes wide in surprise.

"Don't dismiss her," says Darcy. "Mythology often evolves from true historical events and people. They thought Troy was a myth until they discovered it. Dwarka was a myth until they discovered the city several miles offshore in 2012. The myths come from someplace."

"I agree with Dr. O'Sullivan," Xavier interjects. "This makes sense."

"You do?" Miguel gives Xavier a curious look. "It does?"

Xavier continues. "Of course, think about it. The leader of Nacon calls himself Hun Came, One Death, a mythical lord of Xibalba, the underworld of death and fear. Forget for a moment that he's a homicidal criminal psychopath; Hun Came has financed tens of millions to build his private relic militia. *El loco* Hun Came would kill anyone to get an actual relic tied to a mythical Xibalba."

"And now we're back to crazy talk again," says Miguel. He changes the subject. "What about the islands? What did you learn?"

Miguel doesn't dismiss Xavier's theory. In fact, it does makes sense, but it also raises the stakes from a valuable relic to a psychopathic obsession. It's harder to fight crazy.

Mai stands to address the crew. "Sophia, Brenda, and I took a look at the geology and history of the Bay Islands," she begins. "There was a lot to cover; we only scratched the surface."

"Sixty kilometers north of Honduras," interjects Brenda, "Roatan sits at the southern edge of the Belize Barrier Reef, the second-largest reef system in the world, extending north 680 kilometers past Belize, the Yucatan, Isla Cozumel, and Cancun, ending at Isla La Mujeres."

"As part of a reef survey during 2013," Mai says, "divers discovered roads offshore Belize at a depth of 160 feet that ran straight for a half mile, disappearing into the depths near the Cayman Trench. Divers discovered similar roads in the sixties offshore of Roatan Island. Ancient Pliocene reefs and underwater caverns surround the island."

"Volcanic in origin," explains Mai. "The nearby Utila volcano last erupted around 9,000 BPE. Thousands of years of eruptions honeycombed Roatan with caverns and ignimbrite deposits, many underwater."

"Interesting, but not relevant," Darcy redirects the conversation. "Move to more current history, please."

Sophia stands, looking uncomfortable. "My ancestors," she says, turning to Estefan, "*our* ancestors, arrived with a 1531 Spanish massacre of the Paya and Peche tribes to build the Spanish fort Castillo de Augusta. The massacre ended an ancient indigenous pilgrimage to the island, but no one ever learned the reason for such a perilous journey."

"How did the Spanish lose control of the island?" asks Juniper.

"The British privateer Edward Morgan seized control of Fort Augusta in 1641," replies Sophia. "Overnight the island transformed into a stronghold of five thousand pirates, prostitutes, and merchants. With an offer to join the pirates or die, another ancestor named Manuel chose a life of piracy and bought a plot of land on the ridge above Oak Ridge, where our family home still sits."

"How did the legend of treasure begin?" inquires Xavier.

"After the sack of Panama, when Spanish gold shipments dried up, so did piracy," explains Sophia. "When the pirates left the island, they left a legacy of abandoned women and orphaned children. Another ancestor named Paulo was one of those orphans." She gathers her thoughts. "Somewhere on the east island, Paulo discovered a cavern haunted by *duprees* or evil spirits which contained a terrible secret he swore never to reveal, even after three of his four sons disappeared."

"Stop there," snaps Miguel. "Sorry, but the story doesn't sound credible. If an old book and blade are what Paulo considered stolen treasure, then the tale sounds like a waste of time. More likely, common folklore that grew with pints of ale or generations of dementia."

Sophia's eyes fall to the floor. He didn't mean to hurt her feelings, but the idea of his poor family protecting a sacred treasure doesn't fly. While he fears the loss of his own mind someday, it won't be today, not with this nonsense.

"Again, I doubt the cartel will be interested in ghost stories. What else you got?" Miguel urges them to move on.

"Well, it's more in the folklore category," interjects Brenda. "A treasure hunter named F. A. Mitchell Hedges excavated near *Isla Santa Elena* between 1907 and 1911."

"Hedges," Sophia reacts with surprise. "Joaquin and Rafé's papá, Franco, worked for him. Carmen claims he was a liar and a thief."

"Didn't Hedges claim to discover Atlantis or something?" asks Mai.

"I don't know what he found," replies Sophia. "But Carmen remembers Franco cleaning thousands of shards and broken pottery bits."

"He may have discovered the remains of the pilgrimage you mentioned earlier," the professor points out. "What happened to those shards?"

"Gone," Sophia confesses. "Carmen claims Franco's sons destroyed them after Hedges disappeared from the island."

"You're missing the point," Brenda interjects. "Hedges left the island because he also found six million dollars in gold, over 280 million in current dollars," she teases out. "Now that sounds like cartel bait."

"Not if it's already been taken by Hedges," Xavier counters.

"Xavier makes a good point, and given the island history as a pirate base, the stash could have come from anyone, most likely Captain Coxen," Miguel points out. "Okay, what else you got?" he asks, hoping someone saved the best for last.

"Well, that's it," Darcy says. "We only had a few hours to research."

Miguel stares stunned at the room of scholars and genius IQs. Two men down, and he's not an inch closer to finding a defensive advantage. Hell, he hasn't even found a believable one.

The mess hall ship phone rings. He picks up, knowing its Hansen on the bridge. "What?" he answers in a foul mood.

Hansen ignores it. "Hey, Skipper, we've arrived at Barbareta, so I'm checkin' high-definition sonar for a good spot to drop the hook. Boss, I think there's a ship down there. In fact, I think I've seen two. You better come take a look."

"On my way." Miguel hangs up, leaving the mess hall without an explanation.

Sophia runs after him. "I'd like to check on Emilio again."

Miguel nods in agreement, suspecting she wants to check on the captain again. Entering the bridge, Hansen studies the high-definition sonar screen.

"What'd you find?" he asks.

At Hansen's first glimpse of Sophia entering behind him, the big man brightens, sits up straight, and turns his full attention. "Hi, Sophia," he greets, ignoring Miguel.

"Hello, Hansen, Captain Hansen," she replies with a shy smile.

"Yo, Big Rig, what did you find?" repeats Miguel, a little louder.

"Oh, yeah," replies Hansen, returning to the screen with Sophia stepping up behind him. "I was gliding along the undersea plateau when I noticed clusters that I thought could be cannons."

Hansen shows Miguel the saved image. The new high-definition mapping technology provides a detailed rendering of the sea floor, making the clusters easy to see.

"So, then I slowed down, and pulled up a little," explains Hansen, changing the screen.

A second image hints at the ribs of another ship covered by hundreds of years of sediment. It's hard to tell, except for a few angular shapes that shouldn't be there.

"That's when I called the mess," Hansen concludes.

"Good job, Captain," replies Miguel, patting the massive shoulder. "Good job."

He turns to Sophia. "These ships weren't on any of the marine survey maps I've studied. Are you aware of any wrecks off Barbareta?" he asks, trying to hide the excitement in his voice.

"All the known wrecks are near Oak Ridge, Coxen Hole, and French Harbor," she says.

Two unknown ships may mean nothing, likely old fishing boats, yet Miguel's instincts are tickling. "Okay, anchor farther up," he guides Hansen.

Sophia borrows Hansen's burner phone again, retreating to the bridge balcony for privacy. Miguel gambles the cartel will look for Sophia on Roatan and may not even know about her uncle on Barbareta. With any luck, they can be gone before anyone knows they were here.

While Hansen drops the hook, Miguel powers up the radar to check for ships headed in their direction. Scanning a seventy-five-mile radius, he spots a small cruise ship southeast of Roatan heading slowly away from the island, and too large to be a cartel attack vessel. Nothing else moves in their direction. If the cartel arrived by chopper in Belize, it's possible they were not prepared to track them by sea. He may have slipped off their radar, at least for the moment.

Sophia reenters the bridge with her eyes welling, looking distraught.

"What happened?" Hansen asks before she can speak.

"Emilio has disappeared from the hospital." Her voice cracks.

"Oh no, Sophia, I'm so sorry," replies Hansen, his eyebrows scrunched.

Nacon may be taking out the witness. His time window may be smaller than expected.

Xavier shows up at the bridge, looking on edge. "Shore crew ready."

Not knowing what to expect on the island, Miguel took Xavier's advice for extra shore crew and firepower. Hugo and Dave will join Miguel and Xavier. To his irritation, the professor insisted on joining them. The old man is dead weight, can't shoot, and another target if things go wrong.

Miguel looks to Sophia. "Okay, let's make this quick. Go with Xavier."

Sophia lingers at the doorway, her eyes locked on Hansen. His forehead wrinkles, looking as if he wants to say something, but he waits too long until she spins to leave, and his face falls.

Relieved she's gone, Miguel turns to Hansen. "Listen up, Romeo," he says. "This trip will take an hour to grab Sophie's stuff and get back. Check out those wrecks with eyes on. Keep a low profile from Darcy, and make it quick. I want to weigh anchor as soon as we're on board."

"Aye, Skipper." Hansen nods.

Treasure hunting often means keeping secrets, and he would prefer not to tell Darcy he's checking out a treasure lead when he's supposed to be committed to her project. A little research on an old mystery shouldn't hurt anyone.

Chapter 35

Go Ask Alice

Downtown Veracruz, Mexico
June 20, 7:41 a.m. | 23 hours to Mayan chaa

Anxious and alert, her skin tingles with anticipation. Lucia waits in a corner booth of El Cafersito, a small café located in the market district of Veracruz, a local favorite with a traditional ambience and a noisy early morning crowd. Wearing a red wig stuffed under a wide-brim hat, large sunglasses cover half her face, while her eyes stay fastened on the entrance.

When they met in college, the woman behind the Alice alias was a British journalist by the real name of Camille Adelson who once interviewed Lucia for an article on orphans of the drug wars. Now in her fifties, Camille has worked in Latin America for nearly thirty years. With a recurring column at the BBC Latin America desk, she's a fearless believer in uncovering the truth, no matter where it leads, a mentor, and a role model.

Camille enters the café and at once spots Lucia in the rear booth. With a deep-set frown, she sits, never allowing her eyes to leave the front door.

"It's not a good idea for us to meet," complains Camille. "You look absurd, by the way."

"Your idea, and it's great to see you too." Lucia ignores the paranoia, even though she shares the same uneasiness. It's her way of dealing with the stress.

Camille doesn't seem amused. "This is no joke, Luci," she says, looking haunted. "My husband died of a drug overdose four months ago, except that he wasn't a drug user."

"I'm sorry to hear that, Camille. I really am. I didn't know." She offers her condolences, empathizing the best she can. "But I have to follow up on this lead," she says, confessing her own obsession.

"I know. That's the only reason I came," responds Camille with a frown.

"I need everything in the Panama or Paradise Papers about Juan Perez de Menendez or Pakistani General Basri Qamar Hayat." Lucia lays her need straight out.

It takes Camille a flash to digest the request. Taking her eyes off the door to stare at Lucia, she finally replies. "I can't help you."

Disappointed and confused, Lucia has to ask. "Can't or won't?"

Camille thinks for a moment and sighs deeply. "I'm not telling you, because you're inquiring about the wrong name, and because the right name will get you killed."

Lucia doesn't hesitate. "You mean Felipe Roué Gutierrez?"

Camille's eyes swell with damp remorse as she places her palm on the table, pushing toward Lucia, who lays her palm on top of Camille's hand.

"Can I say anything to change your mind?" Camille pleads.

Resolute in her decision and desperate for justice, Lucia shakes her head with a beseeching in her own eyes. Camille's eyes redden, wet with tears.

"I love you, Luci. Godspeed," she replies. "But please don't call me again."

Camille slips her hand away and turns to go. Lucia considers going after her, and perhaps even trying to persuade her to work together. She doesn't. Underneath her palm, where Camille's hand had rested, lay a flash drive.

Motela Bahia, Veracruz, Mexico
June 20, 8:12 a.m. | 22 hours to Mayan chaa

Lucia doubles back three times on the way to her motel, paid for in cash under a fake ID—another lesson from Xavier. Habitually turning on the TV news and lowering the volume, she reaches under the mattress to pull out her laptop. Her hands tremble with anticipation as she plugs in Camille's flash drive. The flash contains hundreds of folders filled with tens of thousands of files with financial reports, corporate papers, wire transfers, and ownership transfers worth tens of billions in transactions, spanning decades. A quick search produces hundreds of offshore accounts belonging to Felipe Roué Gutierrez. For a dead boy, he amassed lot of money.

It would take months, if not years, to study each file manually. Opening Xavier's analysis program, she uploads the massive volume of new files. While the application absorbs the new data, she uses a weak Wi-Fi connection from the motel café downstairs to locate a death certificate dated forty years ago. One of dozens of bodies found after a fierce cartel battle in Nicaragua, Felipe's body carried an ID but was missing a head. Did someone use the name of a deceased person or confuse an ID? On the other hand, was it possible the police got it wrong, and Felipe Gutierrez never died?

Lucia leans back to consider the fresh angle. No one has ever photographed the infamous Nacon drug lord Hun Came. Even those of his own cartel don't know the identity or face of the notorious chameleon. Folklore calls him a man without a face, a ghost, brought back from the dead. If Felipe Roué Gutierrez and Hun Came are the same man, then the connection could be chilling.

Xavier's application completes processing, revealing a steady flow of funds between Felipe and Juan Perez de Menendez, going back decades. The missing connection between the two names turns out to be a simple one—money laundering born of either greed or extortion. Then she finds the key evidence she needs to confirm her core theory, a series of payments totaling $500 million to the same Pakistani company that recently lost a container en route to Panama. She has a name for the ghost and has confirmed that the ghost successfully smuggled a nuke into the region.

Xavier had encouraged her to consider a link to the Cozumel summit, and she found it. As a sponsor, Juan Perez could use the cover of the summit to broker a nuke deal, perhaps on behalf of his partner Felipe, or rather Hun Came. Preoccupied with developing her new theory, she nearly misses the next news story, unmuting the volume just in time.

"Breaking news, the award-winning BBC investigative journalist Camille Adelson was found dead in her hotel room of an apparent drug overdose. Authorities believe Ms. Adelson was visiting Veracruz to meet a person of interest, suspected of selling her the tainted narcotics. If you see this woman, contact the police immediately," states the newscaster.

Behind the newscaster sits a grainy café image of Lucia in her sunglasses, hat, and long red hair, alongside her official reporter image. Lucia turns off the TV, shaken to the core. A spike of remorse jams at her heart, knowing that she somehow led them to Camille. Then a second spike sinks in deeper that Vacub Came has already tracked her to Veracruz. The room spins until she can't breathe. Losing her balance, breaking out in a sweat, she runs to the bathroom to heave.

After rinsing her mouth, her eyes lift to see a terrified woman with mascara running down her cheeks in the mirror. On impulse, she pulls out a pair of scissors, exhales a deep breath, and cuts off her hair, all of it, until she looks like a pretty boy with a rag hairdo. Washing her face of makeup, she changes clothes and slips down the stairs onto the street. Wary of onlookers, she hides her face until she slips into a used clothing store a few doors down.

Within seconds, a black Ford SUV pulls up to her motel, skidding to a stop. Two men race into the lobby, only to bolt out a moment later with a key to her room and guns ready. They're not the police, and neither of them is the assassin, meaning the murderer has others at his command. With her heart pounding, she turns to the salesclerk, trying to shine her best camera smile, hoping she can hide her distress.

"Where is your men's section?" Her voice quivers.

Xavier once taught her, *"If you want to haunt someone, you need to become a ghost."* To become a ghost means Lucia Vasquez must die. If so, she wants to die on her own terms, starting with a new look and a new gender.

Chapter 36

Flip-Flop Armada

Old French Harbor, Isla Roatan
June 20, 8:15 a.m. | 22 hours to Maya chaa

Chico coasts up to the wooden pier of Old French Harbor, pursued by a thick fog of black exhaust. Barbareta no longer has a home, yet it took him an hour to coax Mari and the kids onto the seaplane. Rafé and Hector refused to surrender the island, both of them gone loco.

Mari leans out of the cockpit door to throw a line to a young dockhand who coughs, waving at the smoke until the breeze wafts the residue away, leaving an oily stain on the boy. Opening the cabin door, Mari leaps onto the dock, pushed by a wave of six children spilling out behind her. Running up the pier toward the road, eager to get away from the rattling beast, she chases after the little ones. "*Prisa, prisa,*" she calls, making a game of the horrid experience.

Once Mari catches up, they'll head to her sister's home in Punta Gorda. Her nephew Timothy died of an overdose last week, so they can cram into Tim's room until a better option can be found. Worried about the influence of drugs on his eldest boy, Victor, he has no choice; his paradise has been lost.

Shuffling to the rear of the plane, he unlatches a fuel knob and swings around to the nearby pump. When the dockhand comes over to help, Chico brushes him away.

"No, I got this," he says. "I need you to go get Dr. Morales at Woods Hospital."

In the commotion on the lagoon last night, he lost his cell phone. Knowing better than to involve the sellout Capitan Boyles, Augusto has access to emergency vessels. Besides, someone may need to tranquilize Rafé. As a leading member of the island council, Augusto will know how to call the navy.

"Tell Augusto we were attacked again. Hector and Rafé are in danger. I need help to get them off the island," he calls.

The attendant races away and then pivots back, looking puzzled. "Why would anyone attack Barbareta?"

"Go!" he shouts.

The boy jumps on his Vespa and putters off toward the hospital. By the time Chico finishes topping off his tank, a small group of divers, fishermen, and shop owners crowd the dock, heading in his direction. He suspects the dockhand has been spreading rumors, which spread like a virus on Roatan, mutating until the rumors themselves are spreading rumors. More islanders show up in groups.

"What happened?" asks the owner of a dive shop.

"Narco soldiers shot Rafé and then blew up our huts," he explains.

"Why?" another asks.

"Over something Sophia found, I think, but then Rafé sank their boats and fed a bunch of their men to sharks," he replies with a stammer.

"He what?" retorts a voice. Even in his own ear, the story sounds absurd.

"Do they have Sophia?" A woman calls out.

"She's hiding from el Capitan," yells another.

"No, the cartel took her," someone shouts another theory.

"Why take poor Sophia?" another woman calls.

"I don't get it. What do they want?" another asks.

Chico has been wondering the same thing. Why would someone attack the

Martinez family on Roatan and Barbareta? Only one chilling answer keeps coming to mind.

"They want the lost Martinez treasure," shouts someone at the back of the crowd, echoing Chico's unspoken fear.

"Ah man, not that crazy hoax again," complains another.

The dock boy returns, looking proud of the crowd he created with his rumors. Pushing his way to the front, he climbs onto a boat bow.

"I think Nacon wants to set up a drug distribution center on Barbareta," he shouts his theory.

"Not here," someone yells. "Not on our island."

"Keep the scum on the mainland," shouts another.

The discussion grows bold and heated, sparking rumors that fly as fact, sparking new unfounded rumors. The crowd quickly swells to over a hundred agitated islanders.

Augusto shows up at the dock looking perplexed by the swelling, excited mob as he maneuvers his path to speak into Chico's ear. "I got your message, but it looks like we have a bigger problem here." Augusto refers to the crowd. "What's going on?"

"Dr. Morales, what happened to Emilio?" a voice calls out from the crowd. "Rita would only say he's not in his room. Did he die?" A hundred voices fall into a hush, waiting for an answer.

Facing the crowd, Augusto raises his palm. "No, no, Emilio awoke from his coma very early this morning."

Spontaneous cheers erupt at the news. Augusto calms them down with his hand. "A witness to a crime with his attackers still on the loose, and Sophia missing, I moved him to a secure but secret location. Now you should all go home before anyone else gets hurt."

Big Uti, a large Garifuna named after the nearby Utila volcano for his size and temper, stands up on a dock box, nearly cracking the fiberglass lid, motioning to the crowd to let him speak. "I'm not going anywhere," he bellows in his deep, resonating voice. "Many of us come from conquistador, pirate, or Garifuna *gubida*. We are survivors, independent and strong. Our island must never fall under the Nacon shadow like on the mainland."

The approving hoots of the crowd follow. "Threaten one of us, threaten all of us."

"Ah, hell man, we don't even like Rafé," a voice calls, eliciting laughs.

"Yeah, but we love Carmen, Sophia, and Emilio," comes a reply.

"Hey, you forgot Chico and Mari," another voice admonishes, to Chico's vigorous nod of agreement.

The crowd continues to build steam until someone chants, "Our island, our home!" The chant repeats and builds until the wooden dock shudders from foot stomping.

"I pledge my entire dive fleet to exterminate those rats!" Big Uti hollers above the chaos.

"My fleet as well," calls another, and then another.

On the heels of Timothy's death, Carmen's death, Emilio's coma, and Sophia's disappearance, the community teeters on the edge. The assault on Barbareta sparks a wildfire from a dry kindling of fear and rage. Men spin off to get weapons or alert the private fleets at Coxen Hole. With mayhem on the docks, Chico's heart sinks. They could be heading into a massacre.

"What's happening?" he asks Augusto. "I only wanted help to get Papá and Rafé."

Augusto's face turns pale. "Let me see if I can calm this down before it gets more out of control," he offers. "Go get Hector, and leave Rafé if he won't cooperate."

"It's time to call the navy," Chico calls to Augusto as he slips back into his cockpit. Augusto raises an eyebrow but doesn't respond.

With a grimace, Chico cracks the engines until they explode into a noisy, smoking thunder that pushes the crowd away but fails to discourage their plans. He needs to get Papá off Barbareta before an angry armada invades his peaceful lagoon to save a paradise already burned to the ground.

Chapter 37

A Ghostly Silence

With a hand over her mouth in shock, Sophia guides the overcrowded zodiac through the complex reef channel, now littered with torn-up boats, debris, and oil slicks. Icy waves of remorse shudder her shoulders, trying to imagine what happened, and terrified for the lives of her friends. Miguel signals his men to keep silence as they prep their weapons and watch the coastline, fearing an ambush.

Even from a hundred meters offshore, the charred remains of the humble huts look like a debris field of splintered wood and personal belongings. Horrified by the destruction, a silent tear rolls off her cheeks, tasting salty on her lips. What kind of evil did she unleash?

Closer to shore, the deafening quiet, absent the playful sound of six happy children, shoots a frigid chill through her heart. Sophia wants to scream out for Rafé, or Chico or Mari, but Estefan motions her to silence.

Someone may still be on the island.

"I've been here before," whispers Miguel. "A weird old fisherman used to live here."

"I mentioned that we once stayed on Barbareta when I introduced Sophia," whispers Estefan.

Sophia finds it interesting that Miguel may be just now remembering the experience, as if he had blocked it out, or as Estefan mentioned, the island was only one of too many places to remember.

"His name is Rafé," she corrects him, "and he still lives here." She silently prays that Rafé survived the assault or may be in hiding.

"Really," he replies. "The dude must be like two hundred years old by now."

Sophia tilts her head at the notion. "More or less." A shadow of self-reproach falls over her like a dark fog. Cursed, she's become a contagious disease, infecting everyone she touches and loves, leaving behind a shadow of death. No one was supposed to get hurt from seeking the truth. She just wants the nightmare to end.

On the beach, Xavier, Hugo, and Miguel fan out with AR-15 rifles, ready for an ambush, while Dave guards Sophia and Estefan. Running to each hut, Sophia breathes a sigh of relief to find only charred, smelly rubble, and overturned fishing canoes filled with bullet holes. Debris covers the beach like bombs have exploded, but the there are no bodies.

Back from his rapid scan, Miguel looks anxious. "We're clear, now go get your stuff."

"Maybe Chico took everyone to Roatan?" she speculates, although it sounds wrong. Mari and the kids hate that stinking beast.

"We're exposed," Miguel urges again. "Get your stuff, and let's go."

She shoves down her disquiet to dash to the eastern basalt bluffs, followed by the others.

"Stay here," she directs.

Without hesitation, she scales the steep bluff, knowing exactly where to place her hands and feet. Born with an athletic body, she has climbed this ledge a thousand times since she was a child. Ten meters high, she reaches her arm into a crevice invisible from the beach and draws out a knapsack, tossing it over her shoulder. Inside the crevice, her childhood diary still rests within a rusty lunchbox. Pages filled with the secrets of a terrified and lonely ten-year-old struggling to understand her parents' death and her battle with depression. Deeply conflicted, she almost wants to read her old traumas, somehow wishing her childhood insights could make sense of her current ordeal. Exhaling her remorse, she leaves the diary in place and carefully descends.

Still a few meters off the sand, a screeching noise startles her a second before an explosion shatters the seaward bluff. Blown off by the blast wave, she falls screaming into the unexpected, clasped arms of Xavier and Miguel. Collapsing together into the sand, they instinctively roll over to shield their heads from the small debris raining down.

"*Andale!*" exclaims Xavier, leaping to his feet.

"Coconuts," shouts Miguel in the same instant, pointing at the dense coconut grove where they can take visual cover.

The rest of the group struggles to their feet and bursts into a sprint. Grabbing her bag, she chases after them, her heart pounding in panic, her head throbbing from the blast, knowing what the others will soon learn—there's nowhere to hide.

*

Plunder Lust, Isla Barbareta
June 20, 9:20 a.m. | 21 hours to Mayan chaa

"What the bloody hell was that?" shouts Darcy, yanking down the binoculars.

Focused on watching the shore team, the small tactical missile blindsided her until it screamed past the bridge, leaving a silvery stream of vapor before exploding against the distant sea bluff. From the aft balcony, they spot another ship several kilometers out to sea, moving in their direction. A much bigger, faster ship with a rocket launcher mounted on the bow.

The science crew scrambles onto the bridge. "Where's Hansen?" asks Brenda, surprised not to see him.

"Inspecting something below," replies Darcy. "Try the engine room."

"I already checked," reports Mai. "He's not there."

Darcy doesn't have time to consider the problem before the ship radio lights up.

"Get the ship to sea now," shouts Miguel, sounding out of breath.

Darcy grabs the radio, panic-stricken. "No," she argues. "Get back to the ship. We're not leaving without you."

"No time," Miguel insists. "It's too long around the reef. Get *Plunder* out of range from those rockets. I'll call when it's clear."

Jackson grabs the mic. "Miguel, we can't find Hansen."

"Shit," Miguel says. "Shit, shit, shit," fades away with his panting. "Get him on the dive channel. Tell him to haul ass, but get away from those missiles," he shouts before the radio dies.

"Miguel," Darcy yells into the radio. "Miguel! Oh, bollocks."

*

Ocean Floor, Offshore Isla Barbareta
June 20, 9:21 a.m. | 21 hours to Mayan chaa

Hansen figures he can get to the depth of 155 feet to investigate the wreckage and be back on board before the shore party returns to the ship. So far, the dive has been worth the risk, confirming several old cannons coated in coral. Recent storms have exposed the remnants of ship timbers, and even more promising, the tip of a Chinese bronze, greened by age, peeks from the sand. It would be great if the skipper won a contract to salvage here, then maybe he and Sophia could get to know each other. He can't shake her hazel-green eyes off his mind. No, maybe it was her smile. Yeah, it was definitely her smile—and her eyes.

Sure, the science team women are pretty, but those girls are scary smart, a bit intimidating for a good old country boy. Besides, Momma wouldn't want him dating a teammate. Even so, he's been part of an all-male crew since he was a teen. His daddy always said God would put a woman in his path when he was ready. Oh Lord, let him be ready for Sophia.

The unmistakable metallic clanging of heavy chain rattling up into a steel hull catches him by surprise, shaking off his daydream. *Plunder Lust* weighs anchor, and that can't be good. Hansen wears the top-of-the-line full face dive mask with communication gear. He flips on his intercom switch to hear Darcy yelling.

"—water, now. Hansen, Hansen, where are you?" shouts Darcy in a panic.

"No need to yell—" responds Hansen before she cuts him off.

"Another ship is shooting missiles. Get your arse up here." Darcy uses her tough professor voice, sounding scared.

"No can do, ma'am. I'm too deep, and it's too risky for you to wait for me. I'm ordering you to get the ship out of the line of fire," replies Hansen.

He immediately changes direction back toward *Plunder*, kicking into a fast swim. With 152 feet to ascend, he checks his depth and sets his timer. He doesn't have the time or the air to debate.

"Hansen, no, we can't leave you," retorts Darcy.

"Ma'am, if I come up too fast, I'll get the bends," he explains. "If you wait, we're either hostages or dead. They don't know I'm here, which gives me a tactical advantage."

"Screw tactical advantage, Hansen. We need you on the ship," she pleads.

"Dr. O'Sullivan, you're in command of the *Plunder Lust* and all souls aboard," he says. "As captain, I'm ordering you to haul ass, and get your ship and crew out of danger," he uses his own authoritarian tone.

"But Hansen," she rejoins.

He cuts her off. "Look, Doc, I know you're scared, but listen up. I need you to drop a marker buoy with twin firecrackers taped to the weight. Then take *Plunder* out to sea at least five miles with an arc to port. Approach the island from the north rim. I'll meet you near the peninsula," he pants.

The last of the anchor chain begins to capstan into the ship as the engines rumble to life.

"Hansen, I can't do this alone," pleads Darcy.

"No choice, ma'am. Now remember—two firecrackers on a buoy," he reminds her before turning off his headgear.

He can't lose *Plunder Lust* on his first day of being captain. Besides, Skipper and Sophia are still on that island. He's not sure how yet, but he needs to do something. He can't lose Sophia, and while he knows how crazy it sounds, he can only hope she felt it too.

*

Plunder Lust, offshore Isla Barbareta
June 20, 9:44 a.m. | 21 hours to Mayan chaa

Darcy furiously slams down the ship radio. An emergency comes up, and the fearless crew of the *Plunder Lust* is not even on the ship. *Why was Hansen diving anyway?*

"Jackson, get us out of here, full speed," she yells, racing off the bridge toward the dive lockers.

A demolition expert in the US Navy, Hansen keeps a range of prepackaged C4 explosives on the ship in watertight packets with detonators that he affectionately calls firecrackers. Brenda and Juniper follow her to find the locker door secured with a typical padlock, until Brenda grabs a nearby emergency fire ax and swings it down until the lock snaps. Grabbing two of the demolition packets, Darcy sprints back to the transom, while Juniper grabs a roll of duct tape.

"Whatever you're doing, do it faster, people," shouts Jackson over the deck speakers.

Darcy grabs a small buoy pole on the way, taping the kits to the weight. Brenda grabs the pole from Darcy's hand and races to the transom to toss the buoy as far behind the ship as she can throw. A half mile behind them, an enormous mega-yacht heads straight for their anchorage.

"I don't get it. We're leaving them?" asks a worried Mai.

"We're following orders," Darcy admits, biting down her dread.

"We have company," Brenda warns, pointing to an eighteen-foot zodiac emerging from behind the huge ship. Darcy grabs the deck binoculars. Two armed mercenaries head straight for them.

"Oh, bollocks," Darcy gripes. Picking up the intercom, she hits the switch for the bridge. "Pedal to the metal, Dr. Healy."

Brenda turns to Darcy. "I'll be right back."

Chapter 38

Jacob's Ladder

Isla Barbareta

June 20, 9:48 a.m. | 21 hours to Mayan chaa

Panic-stricken Sophia paces the sand, trying to think of options but she keeps coming up blank. The enormous ship dwarfs the ragtag salvage, which still seems slow getting underway. From behind the yacht, two attack zodiacs with at least a dozen men head toward the protected lagoon channel. They have twenty-five, maybe thirty minutes before the invaders land.

Just as Carmen had warned, death continues to pursue her relentlessly, but she still isn't sure why. All of this violence for a dagger or even revenge seems inconceivable.

"Go on, Darcy, go. Move the damn ship already!" shouts Miguel.

"Skipper, we need to find better cover," says Xavier, scanning the cove.

"Hugo, check out that trail, pronto," orders Miguel.

Hugo races off to check the old commercial dock trail, while Xavier and Miguel debate their options of using machine guns to cut into the jungle or hiding in trees. Hugo returns with the bad news that the trail dead ends. She could have saved him the trip. Sophia notices Estefan, quiet and by himself, reading a laminated copy of the curse.

"Reading, really?" she asks.

Estefan ignores the rebuke. "Is there a waterfall on the island?"

Her surprise changes to curiosity. "Over that ridge in the next cove, but it's a dead end, a tide pool between two bluffs."

"Is there a ladder to get there?" he asks, getting up to trot in that direction.

"Well, I wouldn't call it a ladder exactly," Sophia tries to explain, jogging to catch up, followed by the others.

Arriving at the base of the rocky bluff, hidden behind an old diesel generator shed, Sophia pulls on a vine to show a set of footholds notched into the steep rock. The notches zigzag over the ridge, not obvious until you look right at them. The first time her papá showed her the notches, she was too little even to reach them.

"Rafé claims Franco found these steps as a boy," she explains. "No one knows who cut them."

When the others hesitate, she scales the bluff, listening to the grunts that follow her until they all reach the top of the ridge. Under a tree canopy, they have a camouflaged view of the crescent beach lagoon that stretches for eighty meters, edged in by another basalt bluff. Behind the cove, the hills rise covered in thick virgin jungle. Out in the channel, two large zodiacs with a dozen mercenaries maneuver their way to the beach.

Trapped like an animal, Sophia nervously runs her hands through her hair, her eyes darting everywhere, looking for something she may have forgotten. Down within a jungled ravine are two modest waterfalls welling from a natural spring. The larger waterfall, less than two meters high, empties into a deep pool before cascading over a second, smaller fall that spills into an ocean tide pool. Behind the upper fall, a volcanic peak rises up, covered in thick jungle.

"I thought they would be bigger," mumbles Estefan, looking toward the falls.

"What do you mean?"

"I'm not sure," Estefan confesses. "I expected the falls to be more thunderous."

As if to respond, she hears a familiar rumbling cough approaching the island from the west. She can't see Chico's plane from the narrow ravine, but she knows that disgusting sound. His timing couldn't be worse, but at least the hideous noise offers renewed hope that the family survived.

"Not now Chico. Go away," she pleads, sounding like Rafé in her own ear.

A second later, several loud cracks of gunfire explode from the lagoon, and then the engines cough to an eerie silence; no explosion or sound of collision, just a heartbreaking silence.

"No, no, no, no!" exclaims Sophia in shock and sorrow.

Her vision spins until she falters to her knees. An instant oppressive weight of six children made fatherless or even worse, the lives of an entire family fall over her soul.

"*Bungia feruduna*, Father God, forgive me," she sputters, softly weeping, her nightmare only growing worse.

Miguel turns to Estefan. "Okay, Professor, cough it up—why are we here?"

For the Spaniard's revenge, Sophia wants to respond, but that would only sound crazy.

"I'm not sure," Estefan confesses.

Chapter 39

Firecrackers

Offshore Isla Barbareta
June 20, 10:07 a.m. | 20 hours to Mayan chaa

Hansen cuts the firecrackers from the buoy line, hearing the low rumble of powerful engines long before the enormous shadow spreads over the ocean floor. A few moments ago, someone on *Plunder* shot two men from a high-speed inflatable, leaving both bodies floating in the water, one bleeding from his chest and the other from his neck. The stray zodiac circles in an aimless loop above on the surface. Impressive shooting that must have been Brenda, except the blood will attract sharks.

Unable to protect the ship during a moment of crisis rips at his conscience and pride. Without better options, he turns his focus on neutralizing the threat. Swimming toward the stern of the massive ship, he gradually rises from 152 to 135 feet, then 100 feet, then 70 feet, holding steady at selected depths until the nitrogen levels in his bloodstream can equalize. At midship, he discovers an empty submarine stall, ringing his alarm bell even louder.

Ships with missiles and hidden submarines don't bring good news or an amateur crew.

With all the extra exertion, his air supply depletes faster than expected. Past his safety zone, he reaches the massive twin screws, thirty feet in diameter. He attaches both firecrackers to the eight-inch stainless-steel starboard prop shaft coupling where it enters the engine room. With a ship this large, he's not sure his firecrackers will have enough bang, but if he can dislodge or jam a single shaft, then he might disable the ship. He'll only get one shot.

Completely timed out, with zero oxygen, he kicks his final twenty feet to the surface, lunging from the water loudly sucking in air. Thankfully, there are no guards near the transom. The crew may be overconfident or undermanned.

After catching his breath, he climbs onto the spacious transom deck near the tender garage. Removing his heavy dive gear, he replaces the empty air tank with a fresh one from the ample ship inventory of top-of-the-line gear to prepare for his escape. The garage has four Jet Skis but no keys, likely stored in the master's suite. A new zodiac waits for an engine, making it too slow for an escape.

With a peek through the scuppers, he estimates at least eight crewmembers wearing military-style uniforms with no insignias, meaning narco mercenaries. Well-paid, well-trained professionals not interested in dying for the cause but willing to make good money killing for it. The safe choice would be to stay in hiding until *Plunder* returns.

That plan changes a moment later when a patrolling soldier steps down to check out the wet spot where he had climbed out of the water. Hansen has no choice but to grab him from behind, place his hand over the man's mouth to prevent a scream, and snap his neck.

"Forgive me, Father," he prays, despising himself as he seamlessly executes the well-trained maneuver, triggering a momentary flashback of an incident in Yemen.

He shudders off the memory to carry the limp body off the deck and stuff it behind a Jet Ski, removing the handgun and radio; he hides the detonator near the garage exit. With a dead soldier, it's only a matter of time before they conduct a search. Reluctantly, he needs to go on the offensive, starting with gathering intelligence on who's behind the attack.

A corridor leads him to a master's suite so grand and spacious that it reminds him of a Saudi prince. On one wall hangs a photo of the yacht owner, smiling with General Panera. Interesting, Panera forced Xavier out of CISEN Mexican Intelligence. The face of the owner looks familiar, a media mogul, but a mogul with a private militia and a secret submarine. Either way, knowing Panera could be involved raises his suspicions. Xavier could be in danger.

The suite door slams open abruptly, spilling three soldiers with targeting lasers aimed at his chest. Hansen looks up to notice the camera casing in the ceiling corner with motion detector. *Another careless mistake*, he silently chides himself. He raises his hands for them to take the gun, radio, and shin knife before they stiff punch him in the gut. Zip tied at the wrist; they shove him to another room where the bloodstains won't matter.

*

Plunder Lust, 7 miles offshore Isla Barbareta
June 20, 10:18 a.m. | 20 hours to Mayan chaa

Darcy struggles with an immense guilt over abandoning Hansen, Miguel, and the shore team. With the immediate missile threat gone, she needs a better plan than to circle back and hope for the best. On the bridge, Jackson operates the helm, taking the ship out of the rocket range as ordered.

"Faster, Jackson, we're going back," she orders.

"Hello, not a speedboat," he retorts, looking pale and sweaty. He nudges the throttles forward until the entire hull vibrates.

Brenda and Juniper run into the bridge, anxious and alert. "I took care of our unwanted guests," boasts Brenda.

"Truly amazing aim," says Juniper, "but we should contact the US Consulate before this situation gets out of hand."

"Girlfriend, we passed 'situation out of hand' with bodies in Belize," deadpans Brenda.

"What are we going to do?" Mai paces the bridge bordering on frantic.

Darcy gazes at the island and then the trembling team as her heart beats out of her chest and she hears her father's stern voice in her head. *A leader stays calm and resolute.*

Exhaling a deep breath, she states in the calmest voice she can muster, given she's ready to cry, "Work together, and try to do what Miguel would do. Juniper, contact the US Consulate. Jackson, stay on course. Everybody else, brainstorm. We're not helpless, for God's sake, we're scientists."

Juniper races to the communication station. "Mai," she calls out, "I need your help to get signals up or something. They have a satellite, right?"

Mai rolls her eyes. "Give me a minute," she groans. Dashing to Xavier's workstation, her fingers rap at the keyboard.

"I say we send up Oliver," Mai says. "If I can hack the ship sat signal, we can send a video feed and direct the feed to an IP address; take this show live."

"Send to where?" Brenda asks.

"Everywhere." Mai replies as she powers up onboard systems. "We go viral. YouTube, Snapchat, Instagram, TikTok, Facebook."

"Actually, I have a special IP in mind," replies Juniper, writing it down from memory.

Mai works feverishly while Brenda races to the aft deck to set up Oliver, and Juniper powers up the radar and radio.

On the edge of desperation, Darcy will face her shameful regrets later, but not now, not in front of the others. She can't lose Miguel this way. More than ever, more than she ever realized until this very moment, she needs Miguel. More than tenure, more than her estate, she needs her shabby captain, the father of her unborn child.

Chapter 40

Corner the Rats
(Peets' Ch'o')

Túumben Epoca, offshore Isla Barbareta
June 20, 10:29 a.m. | 20 hours to Mayan chaa

Hun Came rested little on the flight to rendezvous with the *Túumben Epoca*. Enraged over the cash, men, and unwanted attention this relic acquisition has cost him, the risk of losing his sacred dagger to the American captain churns his stomach with vitriol. With so little sleep, and time running out before the chaa, his mood hovers between savage and a psychotic rage.

The slow trip to navigate the reef channel gives him a close-up view of Shay's disastrous failures to capture an aged lunatic. Two zodiacs destroyed, one burned to a char that hangs off a coral crest, and the other sitting at the bottom of the shallow channel. Equipment and debris litter the sandy floor, while fuel slicks and floating debris cover the surface. There's no sign of the missing eight men except for bits of shredded clothing and weapons on the bottom. A handful of sharks still patrol the reef, looking for leftovers. An inconceivable disaster.

Had he taken the time to deal with this himself in the beginning, he would be back on his own island, relaxing and preparing for the chaa celebration with his guests. Exhaling to steady himself from a rising tide of fury, he concentrates on his worthiness and the prophecy of Balam. Yet his thoughts betray him, yanking his imagination back to retribution, bloody, vicious retribution.

Once on the beach, his commandos silently fan out with hand signals to clear the craggy cliffs and burned-out huts of any targets who may be hiding. Six people were on the beach thirty minutes ago, but now the cove looks empty, abandoned. *Scurry, little cockroaches, scurry*, he thinks.

Shay finds the *Plunder Lust* zodiac at the far end of the beach, shredding it to pieces with his AK-47, the blasts reverberating across the lagoon. Hun Came wants the rats to feel trapped and panic, but nothing happens.

Posting a guard by the two shore boats, he sends the rest of the squad to search the hiking trails. The teams return minutes later, finding no one. Dismayed by how the targets could disappear, he orders a closer inspection of the coconut grove where he last saw the woman.

Before they can obey, the distinct sound of gunfire draws their attention back to the *Túumben Epoca*. Pulling up his binoculars, Shay looks to the bay beyond the ship.

"There's a damn swarm of mosquitoes out there," he mutters.

Hun Came takes the binoculars. Over thirty boats and recreational craft surround *Túumben Epoca*. It would be laughable if it didn't mean so many eyewitnesses, attention he wanted to avoid, another cost of Shay's incompetent failure.

The ship radio crackles to life. "Commander Golan, we're under attack, dozens of targets. We need to leave," reports Captain Melon.

"I'm not leaving without my blade and blood to pay," snarls Hun Came.

"Shoot them," Shay orders. "Sink them all."

Hun Came blazes an aggravated look at the Syrian but can offer no better command. Millions' worth of missiles used up on a joke flotilla. The whole situation has gotten out of control, but he will not leave this island defeated by the American rat or that island puta, especially over something as precious as the blade of the maker. Even so, the optics of his ship being involved in such a violent incident will not be easy or cheap to cover up.

The hissing screech of a missile targets a dive boat, exploding seconds later as men leap overboard. The architects designed *Túumben Epoca* for entertainment, not battle. Retrofitted with a rocket launcher, she's not a bona fide warship, and he didn't leave his best men on board.

"Vessels are moving from all directions. There's too many for the guidance system to lock and too small to target manually," complains the captain. "We need more firepower on deck."

"Go end this," he barks at Shay, seething at the escalating cost and attention. "Get the ship to sea, and hunt down the *Plunder Lust*. Sink that rusted piece of scrap. I'll hunt these rats and call you when they're dead."

With six soldiers, Shay scrambles out of the inner lagoon, slowing to navigate the long, complex, and cluttered maze channel to the open ocean. Left with six men, plus Gerhard, Hun Came lacks the overwhelming advantage he wanted, but it will be enough.

A radio crackles. "I found footprints behind the coconuts."

"Hurry." His pulse quickens. Vengeance and retribution boil in his blood. His destiny calls.

Chapter 41

El Bautismo de Truenos

Isla Barbareta, Barbareta Falls
June 20, 10:34 a.m. | 20 hours to Mayan chaa

The sound of missile explosions and machine gun fire echoes in the distance. A wake of dead souls keeps adding up from a curse Sophia unleashed in disobedience. Waves of guilt magnify until they block her vision of anything else. Trapped with murderers behind her and no way to escape, she feels herself falling inward, her emotions shutting down little by little. Drained of tears and self-pity, her Pandora's box of relics has unleashed a demented evil she simply can't begin to fathom, leaving her nerves on that frayed edge where insanity takes root.

Standing guard on the ridge, Dave signals them for silence. Mercenaries approach the coconut grove. If the assailants find the step notches behind the old generator shack, then another gun battle will erupt. With wide, desperate eyes, Sophia scans the gully.

"We need to hold the ridge," whispers Xavier.

"Agreed," replies Miguel.

"Is there any way behind *El Bautismo de Truenos*?" Estefan still gazes at the unspectacular rocky waterfall with a puzzled expression.

Sophia twists to face him, confused, scrunching her eyebrows together. "Maps call them Barbareta Falls; only Rafé calls them El Bautismo de Truenos." The term baptism of thunder never made sense for such a small fall.

Lifting her gaze to the falls, she shakes her head. "As a child I played in the larger pool with Papá," she replies with a twinge of melancholy. "Believe me, behind that water is nothing but rock."

"Under, what about under?" asks Estefan.

"Under," Sophia repeats, pausing to think. "Under," she mumbles again.

The question triggers something new, a forgotten memory, vague, fragmented images cut in and out of her awareness with one vaporous image dissolving into the next. In her mind, she swims with Papá in the pool when he disappears under the water, staying down a long, long time. Growing frantic, she recalls Rafé chuckling, his laughter sounding wicked at the time. For years, she thought the memory was a dream, a metaphor for her abandonment.

"Si, maybe under." She points to the larger pool.

Miguel straps his rifle on his back, takes out a waterproof penlight from Xavier's pack, and without a word slips into the pond, adjusting to the cold with a shiver. Expelling three deep breaths, he dives beneath the waterfall, and with a kick, he's gone. One minute. Two minutes. Three minutes. After eight minutes and counting, her anxiety swells. She notices Dave peer down anxiously from the ridge.

Estefan's forehead crinkles in worry. "No one can hold their breath that long."

Sophia remembers the same reaction as a child, yet her confidence dissolves into the terrifying dread that she unwittingly doomed Miguel. Suddenly, he bursts through the water like a whale breaching, gasping for air. Dave twists his head with a horrified look as if the noise could give them away. It takes a moment for Miguel to calm his breathing.

"There's a tunnel two or three meters below the surface," he admits in a whisper, turning to his dad. "Swimming through sounds like rolling thunder. Only wide enough for one person, it's long, and black as hades," Miguel conveys with a grimace. "There's a current. I had to grab the rocks on the bottom to pull myself." Still treading water, he grins. "The tunnel ends at an internal cavern."

The professor smiles in vindication.

"We're not the first ones to find these caves," says Miguel with a raised eyebrow. Holding up a handful of inexpensive fluorescent light sticks, he tosses them over. "There was an old knapsack full of these."

Sophia remembers Chico saying her father had purchased light sticks before he disappeared, and he used to carry a surplus army knapsack on his boat. A connection to her father's disappearance captivates her instantly, inflating her courage just enough to brave the tunnel.

"Come on, we need to hurry," urges Miguel.

She follows Estefan into the long, watery tunnel, illuminated only by a dim green light stick. Kicking hard and pulling on rocks until her lungs are ready to burst out of her chest, she senses Xavier push at her from behind. If she dies now, she will take him with her. Then a terrifying idea jolts her. What if the dead will stop following her only once she's dead? Her lungs scream for air, her kick loses power and her panic rises.

*

Caverns of Cortés Isla Barbareta
June 20, 10:46 a.m. | 20 hours before Mayan chaa

Miguel lurches out of the dark lagoon, gasping for air, and climbing quickly over the rocky edge into the pitch-blackness. He cracks a few more light sticks to guide others just as the professor breaches the water, followed seconds later by Sophia shooting up behind him, gasping desperately for the stale, dank air, coughing and gagging. As soon as she climbs onto the ledge, Xavier and then Hugo blows out of the water, urgently coughing.

Phosphorescent neon-green light gives the cave a creepy, amusement-park ambiance, but the sticks do nothing to warm the penetrating chill. Shivering uncontrollably, dripping onto the stone with hair matted to their heads, Hugo and Xavier quickly remove their packs and then shirts to wring out excess water before checking their weapons. Miguel sits by the lagoon to remove and wring out his shirt and soggy socks, ignoring his damp shorts but shaking his shaggy hair. Sophia turns modestly toward the darkness to remove and squeeze out her blouse. The professor pours water from his bag, holding up laminated copies of the curse, shaking off the excess water.

"Where's Dave?" asks Miguel.

"He was behind me," replies Hugo.

Several more minutes pass in grim silence. "I need to go after him," Miguel announces preparing to reenter, unspeakable remorse gnawing at him. Dave was planning to go home next month, maybe reconcile with his own dad.

The professor grabs his arm. "It's too dangerous," he says. "What if they caught him? If they see you, we're all dead. If he drowned, it's too late."

"I agree with your padre," Xavier adds with deeply saddened eyes.

Miguel chokes down a terrible guilt that morphs quickly into a suppressed anger at his cursed father and cousin. Pulling out the ship radio, he suddenly realizes the swim ruined it, along with his cell phone. "Ah, damn it."

"And the dead will follow you," whispers Sophia, staring down at the rock.

Miguel spins to glower hard at her without blinking. "Why would you say that?" he barks. "Three of my men are dead since you boarded my ship with your goddamned curse, and who the hell knows what's happening on my ship?"

"I'm sorry, *feruduna*, forgive me," she demurs, lowering her gaze. "I didn't mean to say that out loud. It was," she chokes, "Carmen's warning when I found the book. I am to blame, not you. I unleashed the curse. The death follows me." She turns away.

Miguel bites his lip, feeling bad for coming down so hard.

"Easy, Skipper." Xavier places a hand on his arm, calming him down. "Blame Hun Came, not his victims. I say we hole up here until its safe."

"When will that be?" snaps Miguel. "*Plunder* is out there. Darcy's out there."

"So is Hansen," Xavier reminds him. "Under the circumstances, better a war hero than either you or me."

Miguel blows out a deep breath. Xavier has a point. He has to put his faith in Hansen. It was a foolish, rookie mistake to send him on the dive, and even sloppier to think the ship on radar would continue heading south. Rather than blaming Sophia, in truth, he should be blaming himself.

Taking a break from his pity party, he refocuses on the new dilemma. Scanning with his light, he sees the cavern expands up from the narrow pool, branching into at least a dozen tunnels. As the dull light washes the grotto, the walls and floors wiggle to life. Thousands of insects' scatter into hiding with a scratchy-clicking noise that reverberates on the stone, eliciting an involuntarily shudder. Xavier kicks a centipede off his boot, stomping on it fiercely.

"Be careful," warns Sophia, her eyes wide with fear. "Centipedes and dragon spiders infest the island caverns, but the nastiest are the gray whip scorpions, very painful and deadly."

Air moves as if they've awakened something. A distant mournful chatter builds like the shrieks of forgotten souls echoing in the shafts, coming from out of the blackness, getting closer. Pulling his gun, Miguel braces himself, staring wide-eyed into the void. With a sudden whoosh, countless bats swarm, swoop, and flutter around them, squeaking, diving, and flapping. The team duck and cover their heads, shouting profanities. Hugo grabs a strip of planking to swat them away as they bite and scratch Xavier, who curses in response. After several dreadful moments, the torrent of flying rodents dissipates.

"What the hell was that?" Miguel still swings his hands around his head.

"Dinner," responds the professor. "I saw bats with centipedes or spiders in their mouths. Disturbing the bugs must have sounded like a dinner bell."

"*Quitatelo*," screams Hugo. "Get it off!" He twists, and turns frantically to dislodge a large bat, still clinging to the back of his damp shirt.

Miguel snatches a nearby cutlass sticking out of the sand. "Stand still."

Hugo freezes long enough for Miguel to knock off the bat with the blade and then blow it away with his gun. The blast echoes until the labyrinth responds with a long, low groan.

"Bloody winged demons," a hoarse voice whispers behind Miguel's ear.

He swings around, expecting an attack, but no one is there. Shocked, spooked, and confused, Miguel stares into the darkness, his veins turning to ice.

"You okay?" asks Xavier, looking concerned.

"Yeah," Miguel says, his pulse racing, certain he heard someone whisper. "Yeah, I'm fine."

"Where did you get that?" asks the professor, pointing to the cutlass.

Miguel looks at the seventeenth-century cutlass tingling mildly in his grip. Sticking the cutlass back in the sand, he checks his palm, wiggling his fingers.

"I picked it up from over there." He points with his light.

Only then does the crew take notice of the dozen or more skeletons and skulls scattered around the upper lagoon chamber. The rotted clothes and weapons appear late seventeenth century, while the haphazard way the bones lie in place suggests a battle. Scattered between the bones are crates of supplies such as rope, planking, and iron stakes; kegs of gunpowder; tackle; or what may have once been food.

"A storeroom," speculates the professor. "There was a battle for control."

"Control for what? Why would someone bring so many supplies through the falls?" Sophia challenges the idea.

Over to the side of the lagoon, near the underwater tunnel, lies a large pile of stones. "It could have been a way to escape," Xavier surmises.

"Escape from what or whom?" She challenges again. "How else did they get in?"

Miguel had researched the island of Roatan, but he never paid much attention to the small sand cays or privately owned Isla Barbareta. Now he's found two unknown wrecks and an unknown cavern with supplies. His instincts tingle, but he shoves it aside; not the right time.

From somewhere deep in the caverns comes the sound of mad, maniacal laughing that transitions into screams of agony, returning to hideous laughter, cutting back to tormented howling, and then dying abruptly. A shudder grips Miguel as Xavier and Hugo cross themselves, whispering prayers.

"The Spaniard," whispers Sophia with a tremor in her voice. "He smells Martinez blood."

"I thought you didn't believe in curses," says Estefan.

"I'm becoming a convert," she replies.

No one notices the faint light glowing from within the lagoon pond until a man with a machine gun leaps out of the cold water, gasping for air.

They've been discovered.

Chapter 42

Phantasm Ambush
(Emboscada Pixano')

Caverns of Cortés, Isla Barbareta
June 20, 11:02 a.m. | 19 hours before Mayan chaa

Sophia screams and covers her ears. Xavier and Hugo force the diver back into the wet tunnel with an explosive volley of gunfire that echoes harshly on the stone until the diver disappears.

"Take all the light sticks," Miguel orders. "Throw one down each of those main tunnels," he says pointing to the labyrinth leading outward.

Everyone grabs at the sticks as Sophia loads them into her backpack with the relics. Light sticks make it possible to navigate the cavern but also make them easy targets. Unlike a flashlight, they can't turn a light stick off once broken.

"Down here, quick." Estefan points to a low, narrow tunnel that would force them to crawl on their hands and knees.

"I don't think so," protests Xavier.

"We shoot it out," replies Hugo, shivering, also reluctant.

"No time to argue," Estefan insists. "We'll use my light stick." With no further discussion, he disappears into the dark tunnel.

"Ah, geez," Miguel complains. Turning to Sophia, he points to the professor's disappearing feet. "Okay, you next. Follow el loco."

"With the bugs?" she exclaims, also resisting, her fear of guns battling with her phobia of insects.

Ignoring her, Miguel joins Xavier and Hugo in defensive positions behind rocks and empty barrels. Sophia holds back at the tunnel entrance to scan the surface for anything that wiggles. Someone had sprinkled a dark powder across the floor of the crawl space, raising her suspicions of a trap. When the second commando emerges from the water shooting wildly, Miguel's crew send him back down the tunnel. With little time for a breath, he'll be lucky to make it alive, assuming he's not shot or dead already.

"I hate to say it," Xavier mutters, "but we don't have the ammo to keep this up. The extra magazines were in Dave's pack."

"Down here," Sophia calls, watching the professor crawl ahead unharmed.

Miguel growls and then nods to his team. "Go on, follow the professor. I'll cover."

Hugo obeys the order to follow the professor and then Xavier who curses as he enters the tunnel. She continues to hold back, petrified. Lastly, Miguel heads for the tunnel.

"Why are you still here?" he snaps. "Move it."

Reluctantly, she scurries ahead of him, holding her light stick in her teeth to crawl faster, hyper-aware of every shadow or movement. As Miguel follows behind her, the sound of mercenaries bursting out of the lagoon with a barrage of gunfire echoes throughout the caverns. With no return fire, they quickly take charge of the main cavern.

Ahead of them, Estefan's green light casts a grim shadow, and the tunnel reeks of sulfur or maybe gunpowder. Sophia fears the longer they wait, the higher the risk someone will find them or worse. The surrounding darkness sparks an odd memory of Mamá teaching her that "when life is completely dark, you carry the light you need within you," as if she knew she would someday face this moment.

"Stay together. We only have one copy of the curse," whispers Estefan.

Sophia hates hearing that word, *curse*, especially here. Voices of the attackers grow more distant behind them. The distraction of light sticks worked.

Ahead, Estefan finds a small alcove where they can stand. One by one, they emerge to stretch out their legs and necks. From the lagoon comes the sound of shouting and then gunfire. Sophia shudders, imagining more bugs or bats. Estefan immediately finds a corner and goes back to reading his laminated papers, holding the dim light to the page. Not the first to be here, Xavier finds an old oil torch and lights it, sticking the light in the sand next to the professor, trading him for the dim light stick.

Miguel pulls out a compass to get a bearing. "The rock must have magnetized lodestone," he grumbles. "I can't get a reading."

"The team said the islands were volcanic," Xavier reminds him.

"Sure." Miguel pockets the compass. "But I didn't plan on exploring them."

"According to legend, Mitchell Hedges claimed to have a compass malfunction when he found gold," Sophia notes. "But he was supposedly walking on the beach near Old Port Royale."

"He lied; gold isn't magnetic," interjects Xavier.

"Exactly," Sophia replies.

"Are you saying Hedges found his gold down here?" Miguel raises an eyebrow.

"I'm not sure," she says with a shrug. "Our ancestor Franco worked for Hedges. If this place was a family secret, maybe Franco leaked the secret."

Island history recorded Franco's death as accidental. Sophia wonders if the stories were completely accurate. A puzzle strikes her. "If a compass won't work here, why would someone hide a broken compass?"

"It's not supposed to point north," Miguel and Estefan both answer in an unplanned but symbiotic unison.

Estefan gazes up to Miguel. "Son, I'm so sorry for getting you into this mess," he says. "I've always put curiosity ahead of safety, one of my biggest failures as a father. But honestly, how could anyone know it would turn out like this?" he confesses. "Please, forgive me."

Miguel looks surprised, awkward, and uncomfortable with the sudden intimacy. "Save it, we're not dead yet. We're getting out of here."

Estefan smiles. "I may know a way," he teases, getting everyone's attention.

"As we discussed," Estefan begins, "Cortés went mad within the caverns, building booby traps and dead ends for imaginary enemies."

Xavier and Hugo fold their arms at the mention of traps. She shares their unease.

"Sophia, I may have been wrong about the curse being meaningless," Estefan admits. "I'm now coming to see the curse like a riddle or a macabre guide."

"Like a key?" Sophia replies, thinking of Carmen's words.

"To be honest, I never understood it until we arrived here, but yes, like a key," he agrees.

"The only way through is through," mumbles Sophia, thinking aloud.

"Excuse me," Estefan retorts.

When the others turn to her, she explains, "When I was growing up, Rafé would repeat that saying over and over. I always took it to be a metaphor for enduring tough times, but he repeated it like it was a lesson he wanted me to learn."

"Your uncle may be right," says the professor with a grin. "The curse may be a set of clues or markers."

"Hold on," snaps Miguel. "We're not looking for a secret, or a key, or a clue." He checks the eyes of his men. "We're getting out the same way we got in—under the waterfall."

Estefan looks crestfallen. "I suppose you are right," he concedes. "But consider what we've experienced so far. From the jaws of death, the wicked and blessed will ascend Jacobs's ladder. Through a baptism of thunder, betrayal and a sting of death await. Don't you see it?"

Sophia's face lights up with insight. "You're saying the jaws of death are like the reef sharks, and the steps over the ridge are like Jacob's ladder."

"Exactly."

"That would make the baptism of thunder ending in betrayal and stings the water entrance under the falls leading to deadly bugs," Xavier surmises.

"Yes, precisely," Estefan says. "I chose the low tunnel because the next line speaks of groveling."

"What are you suggesting?" asks Miguel, folding his arms.

The professor takes a deep breath. "Cortés wants to guide us to a secret, or maybe another exit."

"Away from traps, or right into them." Xavier raises an eyebrow.

"Ah, hell no," retorts Miguel. "Not signing up for the grand tour. We're leaving the same way we got in. Just waiting for the right time."

Sophia quivers at the idea of following sick clues into this blackness. While she agrees with Miguel, she steps away from his negative spirit, accidentally snapping an ancient bone, the sound echoing on the rock. Then she hears something unexpected, soft sobbing.

The professor moves his torch toward the sound, which emanates from a low niche in the alcove. At the edge of the light, where shadow begins, the dusty image of three women, dressed in the tattered remnants of what were once fine dresses slowly appear. The image looks vaporous and transparent, like a hologram made of ultra-fine dust particles with a gritty dinginess, heavy in shadows and decay.

The women appear sick, sunken in their cheeks and eyes, starvation thin, huddling together for warmth. Once proud, joyful maidens now reduced to their final desperate moments. One maiden kisses her two listless sisters on their dusty foreheads, and with a long, sharp blade, hidden under her skirt, she slices their necks. Sobbing with no tears, she allows them to rest in peace. When the apparition tries to slice her own throat, she lacks the strength. Instead, she leans back against the cold stone, bleeding out slowly. Her grimy, sorrowful eyes look up suddenly to hold Sophia's gaze directly for what seems an eternity before the dusty particles dissolve into darkness.

Only then does the team notice the decaying dresses and bones lying in the sand near the knife. Stunned by the horrific hallucination, Sophia feels violated, and defiled, as if the vision had penetrated her thoughts with an intimate and terrifying telepathy.

"Face the pale death of innocence. Awaken the weeping of the doomed who shed their own blood." Estefan repeats the next line of the curse to confirm his theory.

Miguel walks over to the bones, looking curious. "So, why were you girls in this dark crud pit when there were plenty of brothels in Port Royale?"

Sophia can think only of the knowing gaze. "They had names, parents, siblings, and dreams," she mutters, still stunned and trying to comprehend the vision.

"Estas cavernas son blasfemadas," Hugo whispers, falling to his knees crossing himself. These caverns are cursed.

As if to say *amen* to his testimony, another hideous, agonizing howl reverberates throughout the cavern, echoing into a hundred demonic responses. Sophia hates that word, *cursed*, loathes it from the core of her being, but struggles to think of a more rational explanation.

"Hugo," whispers Miguel, "go check out the lagoon. I think we've overstayed our welcome."

Hugo nods, eagerly scrambling back into the tunnel. After several moments, the sound of a gunfight, and then a massive explosion rattles the cavern, shaking rock lose from the ceiling and pushing a cloud of dust up from the shaft.

"Hugo." Xavier drops to his knees, shouting, joined by Miguel. "Hugo!"

After a deafening moment of silence, they hear a distant cough. The choking grows closer until Hugo emerges with dirt clinging to his still-damp clothes and hair. Miguel and Xavier help him up, dust him off, and offer him a drink from a canteen.

"What happened?" Xavier asks with a more nurturing tone than she heard last night.

Hugo takes another sip of water before responding. "They posted a guard," he begins. "He saw me and fired. I returned fire. One of us must have hit gunpowder."

Shaking his head to shed a coating of dirt, he coughs. "The explosion buried the lagoon exit. I had to dig my way back."

No one speaks, and hardly anyone breathes; the implication is devastating and clear. There's no turning back. Her heart sinks with the truth. With a fatalistic determination to unravel the enigma, she turns to Estefan. "What does the curse say next?"

Chapter 43

Phantom Battles

The deaths of Moses, Ben, and Dave cut Miguel like a dull knife. Gritting his teeth, he forces the fury in check for the sake of his men. Losing his cool now would only make the situation worse. He desperately wants to be on his ship, far, far away from this ghastly black hole. Without enough ammo for a real gunfight, survival will rest on staying ahead of Nacon in an unknown labyrinth with boobytraps. Those are not good odds for anyone.

If he were completely honest, he'd admit that his rage may be tempered somewhat by a piqued curiosity. He remembers now where he's seen those symbols—here on this island, from the old man, Rafé. *The key will fall to you, boy*, the old man promised at the time. *You will unlock the secrets of the treasure.*

For years, he thought the whole memory was a dream to encourage him to find Morgan's treasure. Then again, this whole nightmare could just be another one of the professor's poorly planned misadventures that end at the grave of someone he loves.

"I think I have it," the professor announces. "Cortés discovered three entrances. A watery entrance he enlarged, which sounds like the lagoon. A sea cliff entrance where—"

"Wait," interrupts Sophia. "The family legend claims Paulo found a sea cave but then hid the entrance afterward. What if Cortés leads us to a destroyed exit?"

"We're screwed," answers Miguel, uninterested in sugar coating their chances.

Estefan raises an eyebrow and continues. "There's a final exit above a place he calls the Temple of Desolation."

Miguel grows impatient. "Get to the point, Professor. How do we get out of this pit?"

Estefan hesitates. "Well, I'm still not sure what the next line means."

"Well then, why not share it with the class," prompts Miguel with impatient sarcasm.

The professor sighs. "*Between the cherubim of fire, an unquenchable lust will choke up your lungs until you cough up your own blood.*"

Another malevolent, sadistic howl cackles somewhere, sounding distant, echoing ominously on the countless rock walls. Miguel shudders each time he hears the hideous, inhuman voice. Swallowing his apprehension, he heads toward the only exit from the alcove.

"Okay, let's go find us an angel orgy of chain smokers, or whatever the crazy riddle dude said," he jokes, an attempt to mask his terror.

Now that he's here, he has no idea what loco Rafé really meant, but so far, his boyhood dream keeps turning into an unimaginable nightmare.

Caverns of Cortés, Isla Barbareta
June 20th 11:38 a.m. | 19 hours to Mayan chaa

Hun Came listens to the feverish, fiendish howl and malicious laughter bouncing off the rock walls, generating a hellish chorus of echoes. The second demonic call since arriving in the caverns sounding more bone-chilling than the first. Deeply superstitious, he grows claustrophobic in the darkness, edgy, and anxious to get this mission completed so he can escape this utter blackness. He expected to confront the American on a boat or a beach, not this place.

"Ignore it," he exhorts. "The American plays juvenile mind games." At least that's what he wants to believe, except that the voice does not sound human.

An explosion had pulled him back to the waterfall entrance to find his posted guard crushed under rubble. Even worse, the blast covered the watery exit. To dig out could take hours or days and would turn them into easy targets, a set up for an ambush. The tactic of placing lights in many tunnels distracted him long enough to destroy the exit. If the shrewd American destroyed this exit, there must be a second exit.

If he finds the American parasite, then he'll find his blade and a way to the surface. He has them trapped and outgunned. His tongue tingles with the sweet, metallic taste of revenge.

"They're not going far, and they're not moving fast," he reminds his men.

"Stop it! It's in my pants, stop it," screams a soldier.

He slams the butt of his machine gun against his leg and thigh, stomping and shaking his leg, only stopping after hearing the crunch of a shell. With quivering hands, the warrior takes his knife to cut open his wet pant leg. An eight-inch, dark-gray whip scorpion falls out dead, leaving the man's leg bruised and bleeding. Pale and sweaty, the soldier turns to the side and heaves.

"Find the American cockroach, and we find our escape," growls Hun Came, not waiting for the man to finish.

He continues to lead the systematic examination of tunnel dead-ends until a passage takes them deeper into the honeycomb. Muted sounds of distant conversations cut in and out of the cavern walls, pulsating from the stone. Distant, then close, and then gone, it's futile even to attempt to distinguish the language; the voices sound out of phase or distorted.

"Keep moving," orders Hun Came. "It must be the bats."

Soon a spacious chamber opens up, branching in several directions and cluttered with so many human bones, they crush them under their heavy boots. The vague, undiscernible whispers from the narrow passage become louder. In the shadows, at the edge of light, dusty images engage in a fierce battle, but they wash out under a direct beam.

Scattered among the countless bones are small stashes of gold bracelets, rings, and chains; clumps of corroded silver coin, the original leather bag that held them having deteriorated. Random clusters of raw gems lie near finger bones with gold rings. Jade that may have once been part of a necklace encircles a detached skull. Handfuls of treasure are everywhere, never claimed by the victor, as if there were no victor.

He and his men instinctively drop to their knees, filling their pockets and emptying their field packs of supplies to load them with gold. The men put chains on their necks, rings on their fingers, and jewels in their packs, pockets, and socks.

"Dr. Gerhard," shouts Hun Came. "Your ridiculous family legends were true. Where did all this come from?"

"I'm not sure," he confesses, filling his pack with lascivious greed.

Han Came doesn't care; the fortunate surprise will offset the cost of Shay's failures and compensate his men for the extra risks. He'll come back to salvage all of it later.

The sporadic shadows grow more persistent as the disembodied voices grow louder until he can hear men groaning and dying in battle. The sound envelops the soldiers, surrounding them, growing shriller until it nearly deafens them. Shining their powerful flashlights around the grotto, they only chase the horrific battle scene that dances between the light and shadow.

Mesmerized by the intensity of the grisly apparition, he inhales the pungent, sweaty stench. As if stepping through a portal, a wraith breaks out of the shadows to charge at Hun Came, holding a spiked club high over his head. Instinctively, he raises his pistol to shoot the dusty ghoul, only making it snarl and charge faster. He fires again but the specter collides into him, evaporating into a dusty cloud and covering him in a layer of grime.

Startled by the unexpected attack, and terrified more than he can admit, his heart pounds like a jackhammer. Glancing to where the apparition first appeared, he sees the body of one of his soldiers, lying face down, shot in the back of the head. The ghoul had tricked him into shooting his own man. He trembles, speechless.

With the soldier's death, the noise, and chaos of battle turns silent, yet within seconds, the alarming sound of clicking grows from a dark crevice behind them. The smell of fresh blood draws an enormous swarm of ravenous gray whip scorpions. A commando lays down a volley of gunfire, but it only scatters the approaching surge of thousands and doesn't slow them down.

"That way." Hun Came points to higher ground. "*Andale.*"

From higher ground, he watches scorpions encase the dead soldier, ripping holes in the clothing, crawling underneath to devour his flesh, causing the lifeless body to twitch under the voracious attack.

"Keep moving," he says, turning away his gaze.

Shaken by the gruesome experience, a bitter desperation to prove himself worthy sinks into his heart; to find the sacred blade, and extract a bloody retribution quickly, so he can find a way out of this insanely hellish hole.

Chapter 44

Cozumel Incognito

Isla Cozumel, Quintana Roo
June 20, 11:54 p.m. | 19 hours to Mayan chaa

Lucia pulled every favor she had left in the business to be on the last ferryboat to Isla Cozumel, arranging to cover for another correspondent. After her narrow escape from Veracruz, she kept up the ruse of being a young male. With an urgently purchased masculine wardrobe, she added a fake mustache and sideburns to a pair of stylish glasses. Her new name is Anton Sanchez, a columnist for the *Guatemala Flores Gazette*. With fake press credentials and a valid LASSG invitation from the real Anton, she hopes the ruse will fool summit security.

As part of the online registration, she requested interviews with Director-General Tomas Flores, Genera Francisco Panera, and the new Banco de Mexico Nacionale CEO, Señor Tito Pena, but still awaits interview schedule confirmations. Not available as an interview option, the man she really hopes to meet is Juan Perez de Menendez, the spider at the center of the web.

Convinced that Hun Came and Juan Perez are using the summit to broker a nuclear arms deal, she hopes to pin down the buyer. If Vacub Came catches her, then the truth will die with her. With so much at stake, she decided to submit the story in segments, sending her first segment to the API distribution network from a bus stop café Wi-Fi. As a backup plan, she also sent a copy to her ex-husband, Marco Vasquez.

Marco now works for the *Washington Post* and is remarried to a respectable and attractive NSA analyst. In retrospect, she made a huge mistake in separating from her college sweetheart, realizing far too late that she should have followed him to America. At the time, she was afraid the move would end her search for justice over her parents' death. She now grasps the truth that Marco was trying to save their marriage, using the foreign job as a last hope of saving her from a life-consuming obsession. Even Xavier had encouraged her to follow Marco to America. Maybe she never really deserved such a good man, but in her lingering, passionate dreams, she still loves him and remembers his touch. She can only hope he has no bitter feelings and still knows a good story.

Within her first segment, entitled "Nacon—A Jesuit-Style Takeover," she starts with the massacre of the Salazar de Aguilar family to gain board control over the Banco de Mexico Nacionale. From there, she paints a picture of enterprise takeovers, reaching into banking, media, internet, energy, and military. She uncovers the *Panama Paper* evidence, showing Lanza on the take for $100 million in bribes. She exposes a scheme of money laundering by Juan Perez de Menendez to finance a Jesuit-style Nacon infiltration within business and government. She promises her readers more revelations to come in a next segment, if she lives that long.

At the Playa del Carmen ferry security checkpoint, she presents her press credentials and media invitation. After thirty minutes of scrutiny, luggage searches, computer swipes, delays, and whispered conversations, she fears they've discovered her ploy. Without explanation, the guard waves her through. Two more checkpoints to go before she reaches the summit. At the next Cozumel ferry terminal checkpoint, the guard waves her forward to board a military bus to her assigned room. On the way, she passes a newsstand and impulsively stops to browse.

The *Cozumel Insider* headline catches her eye. "Ixchel Village Leader Found on Cocodrillo Reef," which is the same disappearance that grabbed her attention a few days ago. Her senses prickle. Police recovered his body on a reef with a gunshot wound. Suspicious by nature, she instantly wants to connect the murder to the arms deal, but she's not sure how.

Her phone pings with a secure text from Xavier, timestamped from 1:21 a.m. that morning, delayed by spotty cell services or possibly a location offshore.

Phoenix – Offshore. Ship under NC [Nacon] attack. Avoid Cozumel=war. Do not pursue K1. We meet – work together. SIT [stay in touch] – love, Delores.

Her stomach tightens, thinking of Xavier under attack. His offer to meet alarms her, knowing it could endanger both of them. The warning to avoid the island comes too late, although she doubts that she would have listened anyway. Xavier's theory of war makes no sense. Nacon would gain nothing by invoking a war. Extortion or her theory of a lucrative arms deal makes more sense.

Delores – On Cozumel now. War makes no sense. Arms deal more likely. Lost K1. Island locked. Need to ID buyer. Justice, brother, justice. SIT – love, Phoenix. Send.

Arriving too late to get a nicer room at one of the summit beach hotels, the bus drops her off outside the conference area at an older adobe cabana-style duplex motel backed up to a natural banyan tree forest. The quaint, rustic room features a basic TV and slow internet. Perfect.

Lucia sits at the worn desk and opens her laptop to finish segment two but then changes her mind. Unable to identify a plausible buyer creates roadblock to the story. More important, the mystery of the murdered local leader, keeps nibbling at the edges of her instinct. After hiding her PC and locking her cabana, she catches the next bus to the Temple of Ixchel.

Chapter 45

Glider Bomber

Plunder Lust, 4 miles offshore Isla Barbareta
June 20, 12:05 p.m. | 18 hours to Mayan chaa

Darcy ignores the vibrating hull as she scours the horizon with binoculars, hoping the old ship engines hold together without a mechanic. With fuel sitting on empty, she may not even reach Hansen, much less have enough fuel to escape. Even worse, there's been no sign of him at the end of the peninsula. He didn't make it to the rendezvous point. Anxiety bleeds into a full-blown panic as she considers and then second-guesses what Miguel would do.

"Maybe he's hiding until we get closer?" guesses Jackson.

"If Hansen didn't make it, then someone stopped him," Darcy replies.

"I say we ram their transom," Mai suggests.

"Well let's put a pin in that one and work on options that won't sink both ships," counters Darcy.

"Thank you, God!" exclaims Jackson. "So, what's our plan?"

"I don't have one yet," Darcy replies.

"Ready," says Mai. "I've reestablished all ship electronic systems and hacked into the satellite signal. The signal piggybacks an array of video feeds from the bridge, the mess, and Oliver. Then we bounce off a Google Earth satellite and reroute to a live YouTube account. A second signal will route to Juniper's IP address." Turning to Juniper, she asks. "Okay girl, for real, where does your IP go?"

Juniper ponders a moment before answering. "The US Senate Intelligence Committee POD, a secure hearing chamber."

Darcy drops her binoculars to gawk at the graduate student, flabbergasted at the audacity.

"Tres cool, Juni," says Jackson, nodding his head in approval.

"I interned there last summer," she explains, turning aside to avoid any further discussion.

Grateful for whatever help they can get; Darcy dismisses for now the question of why an anthropologist would be a Senate intern.

"Okay, I'm not sure what's going on here," Juniper changes the subject, monitoring radar. "A swarm of little dots are surrounding a big dot. Can you see them yet?"

Darcy focuses the binoculars on the bay just coming into view. "Well, to be quite frank, I'm not sure what I see." Still a few miles away, it looks like a bunch of little boats buzzing around the mega yacht.

"Who are those people?" asks Juniper.

"I don't care," Darcy responds. "We're not leaving Miguel and Hansen a second time."

"Okay, let's assume we can find Hansen. How do we go after Miguel?" asks Jackson. "The shore team has the only zodiac."

"One miracle at a time, please," she replies. In truth, she hopes Hansen will have a plan, forcing herself to believe he's okay.

Closer to the scene, the chaos becomes more alarming, with several boats sunk or destroyed, scattering debris across the bay. Missiles and sharpshooters on the large yacht force the other boats to keep their distance. The mega-yacht delays departure, suggesting their shore party remains on the island, although she's unsure if that means good or bad news for Miguel. Still kilometers away from the scene, a group of boats turns to intercept *Plunder Lust*.

"Um, are we the good guys or the bad guys here?" asks Jackson.

"We're the outsiders, and nobody likes outsiders," Darcy clarifies. "Either way we're outgunned and outnumbered, so don't even think about slowing down until we see Hansen."

Brenda enters the bridge, rushing to peer over Mai's shoulder. "Oliver's ready for launch."

Darcy joins them as Mai powers up the industrial custom drone from the comfort of the bridge. They watch Oliver ascend above the deck before banking toward the battle, continuing to climb. The drone camera pans up in time to capture another missile fire toward a commercial fishing boat a mile away. Mai pivots the camera to track the white vapory trail until it detonates in a fireball as men leap overboard. Darcy checks the signal on Mai's computer. The video streams live.

Brenda turns to Darcy with a pent-up frustration. "We need to help these people. Let me go, I know what I'm doing."

"None of us know what we're doing," she disagrees, but the sight of burning wreckage fills her with compassion, guilt, and then an apprehension that *Plunder Lust* could be next.

"Oh, hell, how many firecrackers are left in Hansen's locker?" she asks.

"Three," Brenda asserts. "All with detonators."

"How will you gain enough altitude to keep from being a target?" she asks.

"You ever do any sport fishing?" Brenda responds with a grin.

Brenda's idea sounds dodgy on every level, but she agrees to help. Within a few moments, they're both on the aft deck, with Brenda buckled into the harness of an oversized industrial hang glider latched to the deck. Facing into the wind, the ship velocity creates a steady flap of the wings. She wears a helmet with a GoPro camera strapped to the top and a ship radio duct-taped to the side. Three demolition packs with detonators set to impact are slipknot tied to the glider's control bar. Darcy buckles herself into a deck chair with a heavy-duty sport fishing rod holster, the thick line connecting to the glider at the other end.

"Are you ready?" Darcy yells out, unsure she's ready herself.

Brenda nods, eagerly kicking off the latch that holds her to the deck. Caught by the wind, the glider rises rapidly into the air like a giant kite. Allowing the fishing line to zing out of the reel with a steady tension, Darcy watches the glider gain elevation until it's no more than a winged dot in the sky. As the line reaches the end of the reel, she takes a nearby fishing knife to cut it loose. The hang glider flies free, halting for a second before catching an air stream and banking toward the battle, ascending even higher. A wave of second thoughts sweeps over her for allowing Brenda to try this barmy stunt, but it sounds like something Miguel would've done.

Running to the bridge, Darcy finds Mai engrossed in her workstation, with cables connecting everywhere. Juniper must have found a cell signal, pointing to her phone, mouthing the words *on hold*, and then her eyes light up.

"Hello, Consular Steel?" she replies. "This is not a prank. My name is Juniper Burns, daughter of US Senator Michael Burns. I am on the US commercial ship *Plunder Lust* off Isla Barbareta, east of Roatan. We are under attack, I repeat, there's an assault on Roatan, and American lives are at risk." She listens. "Consular, we're livestreaming the event to the US Senate and YouTube as we speak," she says. "Search for Roatan Invasion…. Good to hear, sir. The sooner the better," she replies. "I'll stay on the line."

Professional, articulate, calm but firm, Juniper does not take no for an answer. Turning to Darcy, she gives a thumbs-up signal. Darcy smiles to learn that Juniper has a secret superpower, an influential father.

By now, Oliver hovers a thousand feet above the enormous yacht. Body-armored snipers are positioned around the decks, targeting anything that gets too close, which would include the *Plunder* or Brenda. Oliver also reveals another zodiac of mercenaries navigating the reef to reinforce the battle.

With Brenda getting closer to the large yacht, Darcy picks up the radio connected to her helmet. "You okay up there?" she asks. "There's still a chance to keep going to the island." Guilt urges her to offer a way out of this insane plan.

"Not gonna happen," Brenda squelches the idea, still determined.

"Okay then, I see three targets on the ship." Darcy gives her the view from Oliver. "A helicopter on the aft deck, a communication tower midship, and a rocket launcher on the foredeck. If you can fly in from the transom toward the bow, you should be able to hit at least one of those targets," Darcy encourages, not wanting to put too much pressure.

"At least one my ass," Brenda counters.

The sound of bullets pinging against the high steel bow of *Plunder Lust* pulls Darcy's attention away. A small group of pleasure boats attempt to get *Plunder* to slow down so they can board. Darcy moves away from the windows, hoping the rusted steel hull is thick enough for the small-caliber ammo.

"Be careful," Darcy encourages Brenda.

"Roger that," replies Brenda.

"Plan B," Jackson stammers. "We need a Plan B."

His white knuckles grip the helm as a bullet pings the steel bridge housing. Nervous sweat drips from his forehead, ducking low, yet he stays the course to ram the larger ship, an act that will certainly sink both ships.

"Still working on Plan A, mate," Darcy replies.

If Brenda can disable the ship, they may avoid the tough choices. If they slow down, the islanders will board the *Plunder* and keep them from finding Hansen. Without Hansen, she has no clue how to rescue Miguel. Without Miguel, she'll be a single mother. The idea terrifies her beyond words, so she takes deep breath to stay calm. "Come on Brenda."

"Oh man," Jackson mutters, "Miguel is going be pissed."

Darcy doesn't give a damn if Miguel gets pissed, as long as he stays alive.

Chapter 46

Rusted Revenge

Túumben Epoca, Offshore Isla Barbareta
June 20, 12:47 p.m. | 18 hours to Mayan chaa

Hansen focuses on assessing the enemy strengths. He saw at least ten men on deck with high-powered rifles, a captain, plus the two men interrogating him. The body stuffed behind a Jet Ski doesn't count anymore. On a ship this large, there could be more. He counts them again to keep his mind off the painful blows coming to his gut and face. They won't kill him, at least not before their boss comes back. These soldiers are doing the prep work to tenderize him so he's more cooperative, ready to break. They're good, taking turns to land punches to his face, then his gut. The last punch bruised a rib. Even for a big man, that's unbearably painful. Since Hansen knows little, it's easy to play dumb, except playing dumb isn't working.

"Where's the dagger?" they demand.

"What dagger?" he replies as they pound on him again. Miguel told him

249

they were retrieving something but never said what. He tries to incorporate as much truth as possible.

"I was diving when my ship abandoned me," he complains. True.

"You killed Gonzales," they accuse him, pounding out their rage. Gonzales may be the body stuffed behind the Jet Ski. On the plus side, they haven't asked him about the detonator, meaning they haven't found it. Still, his chances of living long enough to use it fall rapidly with each blow.

Another punch lands to his face. "Tell us about the book."

"I only read the Bible," he tells the truth, spitting blood onto a valuable wall painting.

Another smash to the gut ignites the sharp stabbing of his bruised rib. The next punch could send a fractured rib into his lungs.

"You're lying," the mercenary grunts, pounding his face so hard, it sends a bolt of excruciating pain erupting from his jawbone.

As an ex-SEAL, they trained him in techniques to resist basic interrogation. But torture is not an interrogation. No training takes the agony out of a beating. That takes an inner strength he isn't sure he has anymore. Therapists call it posttraumatic stress syndrome, but he calls it the hell raging inside his head. Fury and defeat build up with each blow, sending him to a disconnected place, where he's somewhere else—in pain, but disassociated and apart from it, seething at himself to kill these dirtbags. Zip ties cut into the skin of his wrist, bleeding down his fingers, dripping onto the plush carpet. He teeters on the edge of consciousness.

Before they land the next blow, an explosion rocks the ship, followed by a call from the bridge as a second explosion detonates. Gunfire erupts on the decks above. Then a third explosion comes from the bow, shaking the entire hull with enormous secondary explosions as klaxon fire alarms blare across the ship. After one last punch to his face, his interrogators leave for fire duty, locking the door behind them.

He hangs his head, waiting for the terrible throbbing to subside, already knowing it won't. Taking a slow, shallow breath, hyperconscious of his fragile rib, he lifts his head with a blurred vision to pound the back of his right heel on the floor. A thick three-inch blade pops out from his dive booty. Using the toe of his other boot to kick off the knife boot, he then rocks his chair until he tips sideways to the floor, taking the brunt of the impact on the shoulder opposite his bruised rib. Stabbing pain paralyzes him, until he breathes in slowly, then again, taking a dangerous amount of time. With a patient swivel on his side, he finds the booty blade with his hands. Bloody, trembling fingers fumble and slip as he cuts the zip ties. With his hands free, he replaces his now-bloody dive boot and re-hides the blade.

With all hands-on deck and the sound of klaxon blaring above him, he holds on to a cabin ceiling beam and swings his foot to kick the door. There's no impact on the door but a jabbing pain in his side. He pulls back and kicks again, bringing an instant searing spike, but only a jiggle on the door. After resting with several slow, painful breaths, he pulls back for a third kick with both feet, that splinters the door outward. His head throbs, the room spins, and his ribs stab him like sharp needles. Adrenaline pumps through his nervous system with a hypervigilance that amplifies every sound and shadow. With no time to waste, he searches for the transom.

"Lord," he whispers. "A little help, please." It's time to leave, and alive would be good.

*

Plunder Lust, offshore Isla Barbareta
June 20, 1:06 p.m. | 17 hours to Mayan chaa

"Ace job, Ms. Kerrigan, positively ace," Darcy compliments on the radio, watching the hang glider fly past the yacht toward the island.

Mercenaries have abandoned their sniper positions to deal with the multiple deck fires, taking pressure off the civilian fleet. Banking toward the island, Brenda jerks her head, which swings the video image wildly.

"Crap," Brenda says, "they cut my starboard wing; it's shredding. I'm losing altitude."

She banks sharply toward the lagoon and directly into the line of fire from the zodiac full of mercenaries almost out of the channel. Darcy's stomach sinks, watching helplessly as her friend becomes a target.

Behind Brenda, an unexpected noise in the sky draws her attention. A derelict seaplane rounds the peninsula, trailing dense black smoke, with engines that sound like they're about to explode. The rusted junk dives toward the enormous ship in a kamikaze-style attack, then suddenly banks sharply to plunge straight for the zodiac taking aim at Brenda.

"What's that noise?" Brenda shouts, unable to see the plane.

Her GoPro pivots from the ripping wing just in time to witness machine guns shatter the windshield, and shred the wings of the derelict junk as it plummets toward the zodiac of mercenaries. Falling out of an open cockpit door, the pilot pulls a vintage parachute that doesn't fully open before he slams hard into the shallow water, barely missing a sharp reef outcrop.

"Hold on!" Darcy yells into the radio.

A split-second later, the garishly rusty seaplane smashes directly into the screaming commandos, exploding into an enormous fireball, shooting shrapnel in every direction. Brenda's already-damaged wings collapse from the blast, throwing her into a tailspin. Her screams fill the rapidly spinning GoPro video, while Darcy and Mai helplessly watch the camera splashing into the water, tossing and tumbling as it sinks to the bottom.

"Oh my God, Brenda!" Mai exclaims, her hand over her mouth, sobbing.

"Brenda," Darcy yells into the radio. "Brenda!"

Her heart shatters like crystal into a million pieces as static fills the radio. She's in over her head, beyond her limits. Hanging her head in defeat, she feels suspended between overwhelming heartache and shameful remorse. People weren't supposed to die.

Chapter 47

High Stakes
(Kimen Hunts'it che)

Caverns of Cortés, Isla Barbareta
June 20, 1:12 p.m. | 17 hours to Mayan chaa

S ophia runs her dirty fingers through her short hair out of nervous habit. The desperation in the eyes of the maiden specter still haunts her as if the spirit were telepathically pleading with her to end their suffering. Insane even to consider, vague in meaning, and impossible to forget, she imagines what must have occurred in this horrid place and then grows terrified to her bones that she will become a part of the tragic story.

Somewhere in this pitch-black maze lie the bones of Papá, an unknown number of her ancestors, and the Mestizo savage Cortés, along with countless others she can't even begin to fathom or explain. Tragedy upon tragedy for thousands of years seem buried within these catacombs. With each new discovery of bones, her heart stops just for a moment to see if they belong to

Papá, looking for his knapsack or his clothes or something she can recognize, before moving forward, feeling both relieved and disappointed each time. She recalls Rafé calling the book a testament of Hades, which sounded crazy at the time but now rings with a chilling truth.

The darkness leads her thoughts inward. A lifetime of shame, secretly wearing the label of "cursed orphan girl," has left her scarred with a relentless self-doubt, always feeling different and alone. Despite her cautious Garifuna response to life, she now finds herself trapped inside one of her own nightmares. For decades, she resented the family secrets that held her back from truly living life, seeking romance, or taking any risk for fear of triggering an evil she never understood. Now she wonders if every desperate, lonely hour had conspired to drive her toward an unavoidable fate. Why, so Cortés can reap an age-old revenge over some stolen junk? She struggles to make sense of the madness, but in this thick, impenetrable darkness, the madness runs wild. If she's going to perish, she desperately wants to understand the reasons behind her cursed fate.

A fatalistic acceptance of a dark destiny seeps into her bones. Dehydrated of tears, and shivering from the cold, a fierce determination flows hot within her veins that she will make it through as Rafé insisted. With little left to lose, she has little left to fear. She and her troubled cousins are the last chance to destroy the curse on the Martinez name. If she only knew how to destroy a curse.

*

Caverns of Cortés, Isla Barbareta
June 20, 1:33 p.m. | 17 hours to Mayan chaa

Deeper and more complex than he anticipated, Hun Came pushes through the honeycomb of bones, tunnels, and dead-ends. The extra weight of gold increases his fatigue, but he dares not order his men to abandon their plunder.

Gerhard keeps trying his compass, with no luck. They're lost, but he throws off the thought. Destiny called him here, so he must trust that destiny will lead him out. Still rattled by the savage attack of the phantom, he senses the presence of something evil within this labyrinth. The blade of the maker must possess immeasurable power to require so severe a test to possess.

Soon the high-pitched tone of whispering drifts from a crevice up ahead. He motions to his men to shut off their lights.

"Sneak up to the crevice and listen," he whispers to his lead soldier, thinking he hears the American.

After several tense moments in the darkness, the whispering grows more intense, and then an explosion of wings, squeaks, and a scream disturb the silence. Flipping on his flashlight, he watches the soldier fall backward into a pit of sharp wooden stakes, pushed by a horde of bats. Howls of anguish instantly erupt as two stakes spear his thigh and spleen. At once, the screams of previous victims rise up in a tortured chorus, filling the chambers with the echoes of agony past and present. Dusty images writhe in the narrow pit, wailing into the face of the injured soldier, adding unimaginable horror to his unspeakable suffering.

Transfixed by the morbid scene, Hun Came looks his doomed man in the eye, raises his gun, and shoots him in the forehead. Ironically, the rare act of mercy brings an immediate return to utter silence.

Pulsating with fury and a rising tide of panic, he pivots in a new direction. His tactical advantage dwindles with each man lost to this demonic lair. If the spirits called him to this maze, then maybe that fate intends him to battle alone. Either way, he's down three men and closing in on the chaa. He must prove himself worthy and escape before his flashlight battery dies.

Providence responds with a pale-green light that glances off a distant wall through a long chamber dripping in stalactites. The little cockroaches. Hushing his men to silence, they move silently toward the light. Savoring the intoxicating thrill of the hunt, he senses the spirit of the maker calling him, taunting him to take his prize and exact a savage carnage for his troubles. *Patience,* he steadies himself. Without overwhelming force, he must be careful to stalk the prey.

Caverns of Cortés, Isla Barbareta
June 20, 2:38 p.m. | 16 hours to Mayan chaa

A single gunshot ended the horrific chorus of screams, reminding Sophia that a raging psychopath pursues her like a nightmarish demon, but both her nightmare and her demon are real. The oppressive caverns turn out to be more of a labyrinth than she had expected, more than anyone had expected. No one had planned to find these caves, much less spend any time in them. Tunnels branch off in all directions, but Estefan continues forward, waiting for the next clue. They are completely unprepared, and yet she senses her destiny unfolding, as if she were ordained to journey here, unnerving her with the ominous implications and the looming question of why.

Before she passed, Mamá warned against the ghosts inside Sophia's head, the imaginary fears that would cripple her from experiencing life. Her childhood fears now seem silly as she flees a true evil filling her with a sense of regret for never learning how to live while she had the chance.

With each step, the encouragement of her *gubida* to have faith sounds more naïve and fragile. Too paralyzed to feel anymore, she falls into a deadened state of survival, just like when she was a child, a primal determination to make it through another dark hour. Mamá once said when the world looks too dark to hope, the light she needs will be inside of her. Unable to conceive of a darker hour, she reaches inside, deep, deep inside, until she finds a single glimmer.

Even if she dies here, she's not the last Martinez, and she's no longer alone. She lets out a deep sigh. Mamá was wrong. No glimmer of hope can save her.

Chapter 48

Reef Rescue

L ost on the enormous ship, weaving through the long corridors, Hansen listens to the klaxons continue to blare.

"Lord, keep the *Plunder* and Sophie safe," he prays in his head after hearing a huge explosion in the bay several moments ago. If they destroyed the *Plunder*, he's a dead man.

Disoriented, he enters the main salon by mistake, seconds before his interrogator steps out of an elegant gold-trimmed toilet room, buckling his belt. Caught by surprise, Hansen lands two powerful blows to his larynx, closing the commando's air passage. Instinct and training take over as the SEAL slams his boot-knife heel against the wall behind him, ignoring the sharp stab to his rib. With a downward yank on the collar of the choking man, he throws back his weight and kicks up with his boot blade, jabbing the soldier hard in the heart. Both men collapse with a heavy thud as blood instantly spreads over the expensive carpet, leaving both men deadly still.

Breathless and paralyzed by the penetrating, piercing pain, each wisp of air cuts like glass inside his ribcage. Forced to wait precious, dangerous seconds, he prays in silence, fearful of failing his crew and fearful of dying without air. Several moments pass before he can slowly force himself up and take the dead man's gun before turning to the transom corridor. Before he can take a single step, a second dog of war enters the salon from a different entrance, dazed momentarily by the scene. Hansen whips up the gun to shoot a single shot, dropping the soldier in the doorway. Anxious to leave before others show up, he shuffles as fast as he can toward the expansive watercraft garage.

From inside the garage, Hansen spots *Plunder* racing in his direction a quarter of a mile behind the ship.

Hallelujah, Lord, right on time, he thinks, too starved for air to speak. A second later, he realizes that *Plunder* races toward him at collision-course speed.

With only minutes before the collision, and no longer able to dive for an escape, he moves the small, engineless tender toward the open transom before he remembers the detonator and silently curses his forgetfulness. In the seconds that it takes him to return with the detonator, the zodiac has drifted a few feet away from the transom. With a mind-searing agony, he leaps toward the inflatable, clicks the detonator, and knows mid-jump he won't make it all the way.

From the corner of his eye, he spots a sharpshooter on the deck and hears a sharp crack of gunfire that sends a blazing bolt of fire into his shoulder in the same instant an explosion lifts the ocean in a cauldron, shuddering the enormous ship. He hits the edge of the zodiac, bouncing off with extreme pain, and then everything goes black.

*

Plunder Lust, offshore Isla Barbareta
June 20, 1:58 p.m. | 17 hours to Mayan chaa

"I see him, I see Hansen!" shouts Darcy. "Jackson, slow down. Stop the boat."

Jackson pulls the throttle back to neutral, instantly reducing the hull vibrations and speed, but 150 tons of momentum continues to push them forward.

Her joy quickly turns into frosty alarm when Hansen disappears behind an inflatable that has been pushed closer to the deadly reef by the underwater explosion. As the inflatable spins around, Hansen hangs with one arm entangled in the zodiac grab line and his head partly dangling in the water.

"Aim between Hansen and that ship, and don't you dare hit Hansen," Darcy orders as she runs off the bridge.

"What about the reef?" Jackson yells back in a squeaky voice, concerned with the narrow space between the ship and the reef.

Darcy doesn't answer but feels *Plunder* lean as Jackson adjusts course to evade a collision. They may all sink, but she's not giving up on Hansen, not a second time. She snatches two lifejackets on her way, and with a leap onto a capstan housing, she jumps over the railing, throwing the floatation devices in front of her.

Resurfacing with adrenaline surging through her system, she swims toward the wayward zodiac to find Hansen unconscious but still breathing. Placing a floatation unit under his head and a second one under his huge torso, she climbs into the inflatable with a long grunt. Unable to haul the enormous man into the boat, she lashes him to the pontoon like a harpooned whale, his head held out of the water by life vests.

Out of breath, she hadn't noticed the shark fins approaching the zodiac, drawn by the blood dripping from Hansen's shoulder and wrists. Grabbing an oar, she swats at a shark before she digs in to row, but can't pull away from the swell pushing her toward the coral. Terrified, she sees two small boats slip around the large ship and approach her with weapons raised. One sailor shoots a shark getting too close to Hansen, sending the wounded creature to dart into deeper water, leading a frenzy of other sharks chasing after the familiar scent.

Another man throws her a tow line and then points ahead, past the grand ship. Jackson pulled off a miracle to avoid the reef.

"Ace job, Dr. Healy, positively ace," he mumbles.

Careful of Hansen, the islanders tow her zodiac away from the breaking waves, while the second zodiac shoots at the hungry sharks which continue to follow. Above her, the sharpshooters on the deck have disappeared in an attempt to save their own ship.

As they approach *Plunder Lust*, the men towing her inflatable leap aboard the transom platform to help lift the heavy, unconscious giant off the pontoon. After resting a moment, it takes four men to carry the limp hulk to the mess hall, where they lay him on a long table, winded from their effort.

Escorted behind them, Darcy watches the eyes of Mai, Juniper, and Jackson react with shock over Hansen's bloody and bruised condition. Under armed guard, she motions with her palm for them to stay quiet. An awkward moment of silence falls in which no one attends to the unconscious ship mate on the table.

"This man needs medical help," Darcy demands, as nervous men raise their weapons in her direction. "What are you waiting for?"

From the aft deck entrance, a tall, boyishly handsome man hurries into the mess with a doctor's bag.

"They're waiting for me," he replies, motioning to the guards to lower their weapons. The man steps up to Hansen and opens his bag. "My name is Dr. Augusto Morales."

Salvation from the reef, and care for Hansen quiets her tongue if not her anxieties, at least for the moment.

"Did you see the explosion?" he asks.

Darcy shakes her head, signaling to her team to keep quiet. Instead, she tries to change the subject. "Nacon trapped our skipper and crew on the island. We need to go find them."

He ignores her. "Patient is unconscious and may have a concussion," he dictates into his smartphone video as he records the injuries. "There's bleeding from the nose and ears, with potential dental injuries. I note severe bruising to the face, ribs, and chest. A possible fractured rib on the left side, and what look like defensive wounds on both arms. A ragged bullet wound to the right shoulder, surgery and stitches indicated. Deep cuts on the wrists, likely from zip ties. I see no other open wounds, but he may have internal bleeding.

Immediate hospitalization is recommended," Dr. Morales concludes.

"Thank you, Doctor," Darcy softens, deeply disturbed to hear how much Hansen suffered so they could escape. "I agree he needs a hospital immediately." She tries cooperation instead of confrontation, at least for the moment.

Dr. Morales looks at her. "First tell me who you are and why people are dying."

Darcy avoids looking toward the cameras in the ceiling corner. They taped over the red lights to make them less obvious. She hesitates, anxious of sounding crazy, and unsure what words will help rescue Miguel, but she stays aware that the world is watching.

Augusto grunts at her silence. "So, is the enemy of my enemy a friend or foe?"

She finds his gaze and then her voice. "I assure you, Dr. Morales, we are not an enemy."

She waits a beat and then tries a new approach. "My name is Dr. Darcy O'Sullivan, a Cambridge archaeologist," she explains. "We came to help a local woman named Sophia Martinez to retrieve valuable relics she found after a recent earthquake. Cartel mercenaries attacked us in Belize and have now trapped Sophia and our shore crew on the island. You just saw a pilot and another one of our crew both crash into the lagoon, and they need urgent medical assistance. Frankly, Doctor, we're wasting time when we need to go save them."

Darcy makes a bet the locals will know Sophia or the pilot, and maybe it will give her more credibility. She desperately wants to be on the island to find Miguel, Brenda, and the others.

Dr. Morales studies her a long moment. "Thank you for your honesty, Dr. O'Sullivan," he replies, "but I have a few more questions."

Her eyes fall on Hansen, then her team, and then the guns. She's losing patience and time. Aware of the streaming video, she tries her father's approach of the pushy and impatient cooperation of entitlement.

"Well then, scurry on with it, Doctor," she snips. "Ask what you must, but lives linger in the balance, man. Let's not lose one with wasteful chitchat."

Chapter 49

Cherubim of Fire

Caverns of Cortés, Isla Barbareta
June 20, 2:17 p.m. | 16 hours to Mayan chaa

Another cavernous split soon opens to an ancient cut-stone archway. Sophia holds back, astonished to find man-made stonework so far below the surface.

"The stonework looks pre-Olmec," says Estefan, wandering in to explore.

Snapping another light stick for better illumination, he fans the light to discover thousands of small figurines and offerings, a primitive altar set up near a large buried stone ball, similar to those found in El Salvador with dozens of ancient skeletons encrusted with calcium.

"These offerings could be over ten thousand years old," Estefan says. "Untouched."

Intrigued, Sophia pushes through her fear to enter, watching each step, cautious of the calcified bones that litter the floor.

"Before the Spanish, the local Paya and Peche tribes considered the island a pilgrimage and a sacred place," she reminds them. "After the Spanish massacre to build Castillo de Augusta, no one cared enough to learn the reason for such a dangerous journey. I don't get it. After surviving an ocean passage, why would people risk their lives to come to this horrid place?"

"And why would Cortés lead us here?" asks a puzzled Miguel. "I thought we were escaping."

"I said it *could be* an escape," Estefan clarifies. "And there are more clues to follow."

Reaching down to pick up a carved jade idol, his eyes widen with amazement. "This looks like an icon to the god of Ahalpu."

"Ahalpu was a lord of Xibalba, the underworld," interjects Hugo, his eyes wide with fear.

"I know," says Estefan. "Which makes finding it here so fascinating. Many scholars believe the origins of the Xibalba myth came from the mountain cave systems of Actun Tunichil Muknal, or Altun Ha in Belize, where some of the earliest artifacts have been found."

Still astonished by the island history, Sophia gingerly steps over to gaze at the small idol, only the size of a thumb. Sophia imagines her father standing in this very spot, trying to understand why he came, and perhaps why she feels unwillingly driven to follow.

"Brenda said Mitchell Hedges claimed to have found Atlantis," Sophia recalls.

"Yes, on Santa Elena, although I suppose the cave systems may connect or could have connected at one time." The professor shines his light further around the grotto.

All around them, shadows of dust form another apparition. Her chest tightens, as blood drains from her face, and her eyes dart anxiously about the room. At the edges of the shadows, peasants lie against the walls, covered in ulcers, erupting with pus and blood, the ancient victims of a disastrous plague dying together, or perhaps pilgrims begging the gods for collective mercy. From out of the obscurity, the sooty shape of a primitive woman emerges, hovering toward Estefan. In a stupor, transfixed by her intelligent eyes, he watches the image approach. A young woman, covered head to toe with erupting and bleeding pustules, her clothes ragged and filthy, exposing a single dehydrated breast. The vision stops to examine the professor as he examines her, both of them curious and trembling in fear.

Paralyzed into silence and unable to breathe, Sophia watches, mesmerized by the interaction. Estefan stands rigid as the dusty pilgrim reaches out her bone-thin hand for the icon he holds in his palm. After taking the personal offering, the woman turns to stare a long moment into Sophia's eyes, then bows her head in reverence before dissolving back into dust, letting the icon fall to the sand. Estefan pulls out of his trance, shaking his head.

Startled by the penetrating gaze in the woman's eye, Sophia aches for the poor souls who suffered such misfortunes within these catacombs. Another intimate gaze, another unspoken plea unnerves her immensely, as if she were destined to end here. Her shoulders shiver from the thought.

"Over here," Miguel calls out. "I found something."

Toward the rear of the grotto, Miguel has found a tunnel entrance with a curious shape, a natural double archway in the rock with a vague wing shape.

"Between the cherubim of fire, an unquenchable lust will choke and devour you until you cough up your own lungs," Estefan quotes.

Sophia considers the shape. "Well, it's not perfect, but it sort of looks like an angel wing."

"What about the fire," Xavier asks, "and the choking?"

"You're right," says Miguel, stepping closer to scrape the rock, sniffing the oddly colored stone. "Someone coated these rocks with a blend of phosphorous and gunpowder. Anyone with a torch would kindle a white-hot flame with a thick, poisonous smoke."

"Could be a Cortés trap," Xavier points out.

"Or a Cortés warning," counters Estefan.

Turning to Hugo, still holding the torch found with the maidens, Miguel orders, "Put the flame out. Light sticks only from here on."

Sophia takes a deep breath, silently calling on her gubida for strength. Growing more terrified and more convinced with each step that they will be the last of the Martinez family to be lost without a trace. She follows her cousin, subconsciously holding her breath.

Chapter 50

Cozumel Cenote

Isla Cozumel
June 20, 2:27 p.m. | 16 hours to Mayan chaa

Touched deeply by the modest memorial of flowers and candles outside the home of the murdered community leader, Lucia absorbs the testimony of love this man created in life, making her own journey feel empty and in vain. If she died today, how few would even miss her presence, much less mourn the loss? Has she made the right choices in life? She and Xavier can't even spend holidays together without sneaking away to hide. Is the pursuit of truth or justice worth the sacrifice of love, family, or peace? Is it already too late, or can her fate change?

Laying flowers among the others, she hopes the act of respect will win over a sympathetic local willing to talk. Her ploy works. A petite elderly woman with high cheekbones, wrinkled lips painted red, and wavy gray hair, wearing an elegant black lace dress, undoubtedly reflecting the woman's former beauty and high style approaches her.

It doesn't take long to learn that Eugena had lived next door to Señor Santos her entire life. Excited about a recent discovery on his property, he wouldn't discuss the details until he called an expert. A few days later, he disappeared. Soon afterward, a sequence of helicopters buzzed low over Eugena's house, heading into the jungle. The police dismissed the disappearance as senility and ignored her report of air traffic.

Lucia shows Eugena her press credentials and asks permission to check out the Santos property. With Eugena's blessing, and the loan of a machete to protect against hanging snakes, she takes off toward the thick wall of green to find a narrow path.

A longer hike than expected, she grows annoyed at the constant buzzing of mosquitoes and the fear of squirming branches. At last, the path opens into a clearing, where a small backhoe sits next to a fresh pile of dirt and debris. A section of the clearing shows the telltale signs of helicopter wash in the low vegetation. Pulling out her phone to take pictures, she uses a map application to pinpoint her precise GPS coordinates. Her instincts tell her that someone murdered Santos over this pile of dirt, but she's at a loss to explain why.

Hot, thirsty, and puzzled by the new mystery, she heads back through the jungle path. After thanking Eugena, she takes a taxi back to her cabana to find an angry-looking Mexican Army guard waiting outside her door. Her pulse quickens as she attempts to act casual.

"Señor Sanchez, you're not allowed to roam the island without an escort," the soldier barks.

Lucia remembers to use the lower register of her voice. "My mistake. I thought an escort was needed only within summit grounds," she lies. "I went to pay my respects at a local memorial."

"Media must stay in their rooms," the guard informs her as if she should have known.

"My apologies," she says, bowing her head. "It won't happen again."

Worried the guard may have ransacked her room, she breathes a sigh of relief to find it untouched. Closing and chain-locking the door, she dashes to the bed to pull out her computer, finding it safe. Through a crack in the open window, she listens to the guard talk on a radio.

"Anton Sanchez has returned to his cabana," he reports. "Si, I'll wait."

While her guard waits for his ride, she boots her laptop to check email and finish her story, although her little adventure provided no useful information. Opening email, she finds the official LASSG interview schedule tool has declined all of her requests with the same language: *Media schedule has been canceled by the interview candidate.*

With no interviews, she has no reason to be on the island, which may explain her new guard. Logging into the summit website, she learns that none of her interview candidates even registered for their rooms, including Juan Perez de Menendez. Very strange that key event planners and sponsors are not even on the island, last-minute no-shows. Even more important, without the presence of de Menendez, her theory of an arms deal crumbles into sand. If not an arms deal, then that leaves one terrifying alternative, the one Xavier warned her to avoid. War. The Pakistani nuke isn't for sale; it's a game-changer, and she suddenly knows why a man died to cover up a jungle sinkhole. They intend to massacre the leadership of an entire continent.

As if to confirm her revelation, a text message pings from Delores. Another delayed send, time-stamped at 7:45 a.m. He must be offshore or remote.

Phoenix – Extreme caution. War=Cozumel. GFP = mole. Where RU? Will come soon. SIT. Love, Delores

GFP means General Francisco Panera, the man Xavier used to work for at Mexican Intelligence. Out of curiosity, a quick search of the Panama Papers finds General Panera's name only once, on the board of the same Pakistani company which lost a shipping container offshore Panama. Panera betrayed Mexico, but what would Juan Perez have to gain from war?

In a desperate search for answers, she does another review of the Papers and stumbles onto a few payments she didn't notice before, three wire transfers of $50,000 each to a plastic surgeon in Singapore under a Felipe account. Why would a drug lord, known for being invisible, want plastic surgery? Then her instincts flare red hot.

Searching online photos of Juan Perez spanning the last three years, including recent shots taken at Los Pinos with Lanza, she finds only minor differences that could be weight or lighting, until she notes a difference in the ears, not something plastic surgery can change. Looking closer, she sees that his eyes are larger and set further apart, another limitation of cosmetic surgery.

Covering her mouth from the epiphany, she bursts into astonished laughter at the sheer audacity. Juan Perez and Hun Came may have colluded to launder money at one time, but now they are merging. Rather, Felipe appears to have hijacked the identity of Juan Perez. Why would a wealthy drug lord with a successful secret identity want to take over the public identity of a corrupted media mogul? What happened to the real Juan Perez? Why set a bomb under Cozumel? Her new revelation explodes with a thousand new questions she has no time to answer.

Anxiously pacing her small room, she walks through the revised scenario forming in her mind. Hun Came spends billions to develop a continent-wide mole network, then buys a nuke from a corrupted Pakistani general with the help of corrupt Panera. Cartel assassin Vacub Came stages a Pakistani murder to look like suicide, transports a warhead on a Malaysian freighter, but then steals the warhead before Panama inspections. A helicopter puts the warhead within range of the Caribbean, explaining the naval sonar sweeps, a red herring for a nuke already smuggled into a cenote. Brilliant and evil. She opens a new encrypted text.

Delores: UR right. Cozumel=Ground zero. K2=HC=JPdM. Island locked down. Will try to raise alarm. No matter what happens, I love you. SIT. Phoenix. Send.

Without wasting time, she sits with a jittery knee and nervously stabs at the keyboard with her mind racing faster than she can type, sensing every second fall away. She needs to rewrite and then send her second story before raising an alert. *Insane Nacon Leader Declares Nuclear War.*

A dozen new revelations press on her mind as the sound of a heavy diesel truck approaches to pick up the guard. When the engine turns off, the hairs on the back of her neck rise up as she leaps from her seat.

"*Estupida,*" she curses herself, folding her laptop into a shoulder case, then darting to the bathroom window to roughly shove out the screen.

The guard wasn't waiting for a ride; he was waiting for backup. Her door pounds twice with a loud demand to open. Climbing out of the window, she falls to the ground over a bush, ripping her shirt as the door continues to pound. A giant banyan tree sits behind the cabana, leading to a garden that opens to a park. Kicking off her leather-soled men's shoes, she tosses them as far as she can throw and then scrambles into the tree. With a loud crack of wood splintering, soldiers burst into her room. Easing herself down off a long tree limb, she lies flat on the cabana-style roof, hidden by a Spanish tile facade. Her heart pounds loudly in her ears while a wave of nausea sweeps over her.

"He left by the window," shouts a voice. Seconds later, she listens to the sound of men rounding the building when a soldier calls out, "He ran to the park."

They must have seen her shoes. Daring a quick peek, she sees soldiers' fan out, searching in every direction. Lying back on the roof, she tries to slow her rapid breathing. If she stays on the roof, they'll find her. Staring up into the thick, long, tangled limbs of the banyan tree, she gets an absurd idea. Risking another glance, she confirms there are dozens of banyans in a natural interconnecting grove lining the park. The long, thick branches touch or intertwine with each other for at least a hundred meters behind the older duplexes, apartments, and shops lining the road.

A few minutes later, she scurries to hide behind a wide trunk. Soldiers have returned from the park without success. One smart *muchacho* climbed the banyan behind her cabana to check the same roof she vacated only moments ago. Motionless behind the thick trunk, she waits until someone calls the men to hurry, and the rumble of diesel fades toward the summit.

She dares a glance between two trunks. Clear. Even with the truck gone, a guard likely waits in her cabana. Forced to abandon her new wardrobe, she continues to climb through the camouflage of the banyan canopy until she reaches the back of a local bodega. Careful to check for the army, she clambers down to enter the rear entrance barefoot. Buying some flip-flops, she calls a taxi and then tries to reach Xavier by phone. No answer, and no message service, so she texts him again.

Delores – U OK? Cover blown. Need to escape. Urgent. – Phoenix. Send.

Xavier has always been there to take care of his little sister and prepare her for the dangerous path she stubbornly chose for herself. To have him fall silent in her true hour of need is unsettling. When the taxi arrives, she gives him the only safe address she knows.

Knocking on Eugena's door a few minutes later, she holds out a small bag of groceries and a bottle of tequila. The old woman's surprise evaporates into confusion.

"I know who murdered Señor Santos," explains Lucia. "Now I believe the entire island may be in danger. I need your help."

Eugena stares in astonished suspicion, trying to digest the words.

"Would you let me explain over dinner?" Lucia offers. "I'm starved."

Eugena doesn't respond or smile but cautiously opens her door enough to let Lucia inside. Looking toward the street, she closes and bolts the door. The walls of her small adobe home feature a portrait of Jesus, the Virgin with Child, a third of Pope Francis, and a fourth of President Lanza. A side table features her late husband and her grandchildren. Lucia notes Eugena's priorities.

After a quick meal and a few shots of tequila, Eugena is ready to listen. Lucia confesses her true identity, explaining the murder of her parents and her long history of tracking the cartel, leading her to the discoveries of the past week. Starting with the massacre of a family, a mole at Los Pinos, and plots against her presidente, she discusses the insane cartel leader who calls himself a pagan god. With her phone, she shows Eugena the jungle sinkhole and explains the significance of a murdered Pakistani general and a stolen warhead. Lucia needs to raise an alarm to evacuate, but she needs Eugena's help.

Lucia waits to see if Eugena will demand that she leave, call the police, or agree to help. She takes a huge risk in revealing so much, but she's running out of time. Even in her own ear, the story sounds absurd, so she understands when Eugena gets up in silence to clean her kitchen, using the normal activity to process the devastating news. After several awkward, silent minutes, the old woman wipes her hands dry and sits down again with a weary plop, looking older than she did only moments earlier.

"I remember Cozumel before anyone knew of drugs or cartels," she reminisces. "My granddaughter still lives here and wants to start a family."

Lucia resists the urge to push. Taking a long moment of prayer, the old woman sighs deeply. "What can I do?"

"Thank you," exhales Lucia. "Do you have an internet connection?"

"No." Eugena shakes her head sadly. "Only at the café."

Disappointed, Lucia hates the risk of going out in public, but she has no choice.

"Good enough," she accepts. "Before we go, I need some time to finish my story and a change of clothes."

Booting up her computer, she hurries to finish the last story segment, while Eugena looks for clothes that once belonged to her deceased husband. Once Lucia completes a reasonable unedited draft, she embeds the file into an email to Marco, including access to her online research, photos, and the sinkhole GPS. Giving research to another journalist is not normal, but she trusts Marco, and it will be her only way to reach back from the grave, in case.

In clean seventies-style clothes and shoes, Lucia dons a fedora in hopes the new disguise will keep her invisible. While Eugena places a café order, Lucia logs on to the local Wi-Fi network to send her email. Waiting on a slow connection, she tries to reach Xavier again. It's not like Xavier to go silent this long.

Delores, where are you? Must evacuate. Please confirm UR ok. Phoenix. Send.

The café connection grinds tediously slow as the sound of a heavy diesel rumbles in her direction. Her pulse quickens as she silently urges the file to move faster. Seconds later, an army truck parks in front of the café, blocking any retreat, as soldiers leap out with guns raised.

Lucia spins around to see a soldier glaring at her from behind the barista, his weapon aimed. They were expecting her. With a quick glance down, she notes the file upload reach 90 percent as armed men storm the door and immediately place her in handcuffs.

"Lucia Vasquez," they shout, "you're under arrest."

They know her real name, not good news. With a quick peek, the file finishes sending at 100 percent a second before a different soldier closes the lid, taking her PC and cell phone. In closing the lid, he engaged the encryption software.

Eugena looks stunned, torn between betrayal and helplessness. Pushed out the door and shoved between two guards, Lucia can only pray that the poor, sweet woman doesn't suffer for the secrets that she now knows. Then she prays Xavier doesn't come looking for her. It will be a trap.

Chapter 51

Lost Shame of Spain

Miguel continues to lead the team through an extremely long, noxious-smelling tunnel until it opens into a vast chamber, four or five meters high and fifteen or more meters broad. Dozens more skeletons and weapons litter the cave floor, with several dark crevices on the far walls leading in multiple directions, another central chamber.

"Whoa," he exhales, taking in the image of ship spars buttressing the roof, unimaginable how they got here. His heart leaps like a boy at Christmas, stunned speechless and afraid to believe his own eyes.

"Holy Mother Mary," Xavier mumbles. Hugo follows after him, silently crossing himself.

"*Hijole,*" whispers Sophia, her eyes wide with amazement as she combs her fingers through her hair.

"There will be no redemption for the glittering shame of Spain lost in the heathen hell and stained with the blood of maidens. Greed and avarice condemn your soul to the darkness of the abyss." Estefan recites Cortés from memory.

Hundreds of small crates, wooden boxes, and ironclad trunks are stacked, decayed, or haphazardly scattered everywhere. Some overflow with silver, gold jewelry, raw gems, and personal items such as jade brushes or gemmed mirrors. Between the crates are the remnants of wooden bins containing silver ingots or coin corroded green or black or overflowing with tarnished silver chandeliers, lampstands, gold platters and goblets, and even a six-foot golden crucifix. Rows of magnificent Chinese Ming Dynasty vases as tall as a man rest alongside dozens of even taller exquisite Ming bronzes. Tons of long ivory tusks and thick rolls of silk line another wall. Several large paintings wrapped in cotton fabric lean against the crates, everything under an inch of dust.

"Touch nothing," warns the professor. "I'm uncertain how yet, but the visions seem connected to touching belongings or bones."

"How convenient," Miguel gripes, shoving his hands into his still-damp pockets.

"Who could have imagined the family legends of treasure were true, much less so magnificent?" whispers Sophia.

"I'm guessing the cartel pirates on our heels," replies Estefan.

"Speaking of pirates," Miguel turns to Xavier, "that was one hell of a ship, and definitely not Shay Golan's normal crew."

Most of the time, Golan came in fast and furious on high-speed inflatables with lots of guns. Miguel has never seen the super-yacht before, especially one with a rocket launcher.

"*El fantasma loco* himself, desperate for his Xibalba relic before the chaa," Xavier repeats his theory.

"Loco ghost is right. Hey, I thought Luci tracked Hun Came to an arms deal on Cozumel. What's he doing here?" Miguel wonders aloud.

"Wackos are notoriously unpredictable," Xavier responds. "Besides, like I said, I don't buy Lucia's theory of an arms deal, which is why we need to get out of here."

Miguel realizes the diversion for Sophia may have cost Xavier his only chance to rescue his sister. Like the professor, he foolishly led his team into danger, a shame that hangs on his shoulders like a wet coat. He's no better than the professor, and the truth bites deep.

Shoving down his emotions for another time, he returns his attention to a short stack of gold coins coated with centuries of dust. He blows one layer of dust at a time until he reaches the surface and his eyes light up. "1669 King Philip of Spain."

Sophia steps over to look. "That's the same coin Carmen had."

"Call me crazy, but I bet these are the same coins old Rafé showed me as a kid," replies Miguel. "I was meant to find this treasure."

Several broken crates lie empty or contain a remnant of a few hundred gold coins. "I think we've discovered where Mitchel Hedges found his gold," concludes Estefan, looking in the same direction.

"So, Hedges *did* betray Franco," Sophia confirms the common folklore.

Miguel doesn't care about Hedges or family folklore; his mind turns to a different legend.

"Moses's family claimed that after Morgan cheated his men in Panama, he escaped an intense battle with the other crewmen," he recalls. "Since only one ship made it back to Jamaica, everyone assumed the battle was at sea, but that theory never explained how Morgan lost the treasure, crew, and slaves on board his own ship," he reflects aloud. "What if the revolt happened down here, where he buried the plunder?"

"You mean where he buried his crew," replies Xavier, gazing at the scattered bones.

"And the innocent women," Sophia interjects.

"Why bury a plunder and then abandon it?" Estefan wonders.

"Maybe he was ashamed of killing so many people," replies Sophia.

"I doubt it," says Miguel. "Morgan murdered many more for a lot less, but he did have a well-known reputation for being hyper-superstitious," he mumbles. "And I bet this place would have scared the British piss out of him."

"I'm not too happy to be here myself," muses Sophia.

Miguel can't contain it any longer. "I can't freaking believe it, but your glittering shame of Spain is the lost plunder of Panama. Boys, we found it," he shouts, forgetting the need for stealth.

Eagerly pacing every aisle, peering over the amazing treasure, he avoids touching, but it takes real effort to control the urge, already planning how he can excavate later. All these years, he's been looking for two wrecks, and it was buried next to crazy old Rafé all along.

"I don't get it," Xavier interjects, also roaming the loot, followed closely by Hugo. "If Cortés stranded in 1566, how could he defend a treasure that wasn't here until 1672, over a hundred years later?"

"Xavier has an excellent point, although both the Spanish and then Edward Morgan were here earlier," replies the professor. "There may be more to this mystery beyond Morgan. This may not be the lost shame of Spain."

"Okay, forget the shame of Spain," says Miguel. "We found Morgan's lost plunder. Don't you get it? We're going to be rich."

"Only if we can find an exit," Xavier reminds him.

"Si, una salida," agrees Hugo.

"Wait a minute," says Sophia. "I thought you weren't looking for treasure, only a way back to your ship."

"You're kidding, right?" Miguel raises an eyebrow. "I've been looking for this booty my entire life. Look, I didn't bring us here. You did, or Cortés did, or whatever. Don't blame me if your creepy riddle led us right to my destiny."

He can already feel the tides of respect and reputation changing back in his favor. Swallowing the guilt of losing three men, he reminds himself that he hadn't planned to find trouble or treasure, but he found both, and he's not about to walk away from either.

"Sophia is right," interjects the professor. "Remember the warning. *Greed and avarice condemn your soul to the darkness of the abyss.* There may be a price to pay for craving or removing this plunder. Maybe that's why it's still here."

"Well, Hedges sure got away with a chunk of it," Miguel says.

"And Franco Martinez paid with his life." Sophia folds her arms, stepping back away from the trunks.

"This place has brought generations of suffering for my family—for our family. I lost my papá to this blood ransom." Her voice quivers. "Why," she bites down, "so I could be orphaned? This gluttonous horde has caused far too many deaths, and I don't want to be one of them."

"She's right," agrees Xavier. "We need to keep moving."

As much as Miguel hates to admit it, Xavi may be right. Grief, dread, and fatigue fill the eyes of the others. The thought of leaving the plunder of a lifetime for a psychopath to find fills his gut with bitterness. One crate would set him up for life. Hell, one pocketful of gems would get the lawyers off his ass. If they survive, he can come back with the right team and equipment. None of this will mean anything without Darcy or if they die here. Taking a few deep breaths, he forces his obsession into submission, realigning his focus on escape. Otherwise, his destiny will be to die a very rich man in a very dark pit.

"We should hurry before—" Sophia's words are cut short, followed by a muffled scream and the shuffling of feet.

Hairs on the back of his neck rise as Miguel spins around, dropping, and then stepping over his light stick in the sand. He backs into the shadows against a crate, feeling behind him for something he saw moments ago.

A stout, middle-aged man with cold eyes and a silk shirt stands behind Sophia. One hand clutches her mouth, gold-jeweled rings on every finger. His other hand holds a long knife against her throat, while gold dangles from his wrist. Mercenaries block the tunnel entrance, slowly creeping into the chamber with weapons raised, but their eyes are clearly distracted by the alluring riches.

The professor ducks behind a bin of gold and blackened silver platters. From behind the cover of crates and darkness, the metallic clank of chambered rounds echo in the rocky hollow. Red target laser dots shimmer off the gold-laden chests of the two forward commandos; just Xavier and Hugo saying hello. Sophia whimpers as the blade presses against her throat.

"Careful now," the intruder cautions.

Miguel recognizes the face of a famous media mogul, a Latin Rupert Murdoch type, but he can't think of the name. It doesn't matter, his gut knows the truth, that he faces the deadly Hun Came. Edging into a state of hyper-alertness, his breathing slows, his eyes narrow, and he waits for the right moment. He'll only get one shot. With any luck, this will end today. If not, they will end together.

Chapter 52

Demonic Daggers

Caverns of Cortés, Isla Barbareta
June 20, 3:46 p.m. | 15 hours to Mayan chaa

Sophia watches Miguel slip into the shadows to hide. Terrified and furious, the sharp blade presses against her neck, encouraging her to stay silent. The sweaty, dirty hand drops, allowing her to breathe, but her eyes dart between the two Martinez men, waiting for somebody to do something.

The psychopath carefully nudges her forward. "Dr. Gerhard, explain my good fortune."

A thin, nerdy man with glasses slips from behind the commandos to approach the crates with his hands raised. "I never imagined anything so breathtaking," he confesses in a French accent.

"I remember you," Estefan finds his voice. "You were with the rogue search party when Antonio disappeared, the one we chased away."

"What can I say?" the man smirks. "The legend of a lost treasure protected by a family of lunatics intrigues me. I must say, I underestimated the lunatics."

Sophia winces at the derisive description of her family, a stigma that stings even in the darkness. The newspapers in Carmen's closet spoke of strangers searching for the Martinez treasure; the Frenchman must have been one of them.

"What do you want?" Estefan asks with a tremble in his voice, rubbing a gold platter, perhaps trying to conjure an apparition, a distraction.

Sophia hears a mild chuckle behind her. The man's breath feels hot and damp against the back of her neck, the cold steel of the blade reminds her that a sudden move could mean instant death.

"At first I only wanted the creator's blade," he replies.

The Frenchman continues to examine the plunder with his mouth open in amazement, carelessly snapping a bone under his foot, ignoring the offense, transfixed by the astonishing wealth. Audible whispers seep from the darkness as the wandering intruder picks up a jeweled hairbrush to admire.

"Then I wanted to skin the insolent puta who dared to get in my way," the drug lord hisses, licking her ear while his free hand gropes her breast, forcing an involuntarily shudder.

Her eyes dart to Miguel, who remains without expression, watching the eyes of her captor, his hands hidden behind his back.

"But now," the voice rises, "now I will take it all—my blade, my vengeance, and my reward from the gods." He bellows loudly in her ear, ringing of delirium.

"Si, si, it all fits. Destiny has prepared a reward for my perseverance," he says. "An offering to the coming epoch; the riches pillaged by invaders offered back again."

"The creator's blade," Estefan redirects the conversation, as the voices grow louder. "You must mean the green obsidian." He shakes his head. "Someone misled you. It was a fake."

"He lies," says Gerhard. "It bears the glyph of the creator."

"Creator," repeats Estefan. "Oh, I see, you mean the cult of Kukulkan." Estefan stifles a laugh. "You sold him what he wanted to buy. Clever, I guess, until you get caught."

Estefan's seed of doubt twitches the blade at her throat, releasing an unintentional whimper from her lips. She can't imagine why he would antagonize the man with a blade to her throat.

"The maker's blade holds the power of creation and death," the attacker spits into the back of her neck. "I will resurrect a new epoch over the ashes of Euro-trash like you. Give me my blade now, and I will let your puta live."

Another bone snaps under the Frenchman's foot, making the disembodied voices grow louder, finally catching his notice and stalling him in his tracks.

"*Buluc Chabtan ko chaa.* On the solstice comes war," Miguel finally speaks from the shadows. "You must be the cracker jack with a Pakistani broken arrow," he taunts. "Too bad we alerted the authorities."

"Moron, I own the authorities," the drug lord laughs. "*Koo chaa po epoca.*"

"On the solstice comes the next age," Miguel easily interprets. "You must mean the prophecy of Bolon-Yokte. Let me guess, on Cozumel, right." He smirks ever so slightly, obviously pleased with himself.

The hand holding the blade twitches at her throat. The drug lord laughs again, but this time more menacingly. "Nothing can stop Buluc Chabtan from rising, nothing."

"Well, that may be true," Miguel taunts back, "but dude, what a total pisser to know that you're gonna miss the fireworks for the sake of a trinket."

Sophia can't believe Miguel toys with her life in such a flippant manner.

"Give me my blade, or you will all die," shouts the drug lord.

"Release my cousin," replies Miguel, "then I'll negotiate."

"I trusted others to kill you in the past, Captain," rumbles the voice behind her. "I won't repeat that mistake today."

"Bold talk for a dead man walking," retorts Miguel. "You don't get it, dude; you're trapped like a rat in a maze. I sealed the waterfall entrance, and now there's only one exit left. If we don't leave, you don't leave. If she dies, then you die. Let her go now, and I promise to let *you* live," Miguel counteroffers.

The apparition expands around them, raising her anxieties even further. A hot growl breathes on her neck. Miguel's lying. He didn't seal the lagoon on purpose, and they have no proof of another exit. Why would he risk her life with a lie?

"You're bluffing," growls the man behind her.

"You're trembling," snickers Miguel.

"Give me my dagger, or I will slice her throat," he threatens, his tension and anger increasing.

"So much as scratch her, and you will die here and now," Miguel threatens back with a terrifying calmness to his voice.

"I will gut you like a dog," comes the desperately angry retort.

Miguel chuckles. "You don't have the cojones, wanker," he taunts. "But if you really want a shot at me, then let the girl go and come at me, bro. We have a score to settle. You and me, mano a mano, winner take all."

Her whimpering grows as the tension rises, and the blade nudges harder against her skin.

"No one needs to get hurt," the professor interjects, reaching for her backpack hanging around his shoulder. He had asked to look at the relics earlier, and then held on to the pack.

Murmured out-of-phase voices grow louder, floating in and out of audible discernment as shadows move freely between the lights. The apparition intensifies, filling the darkness.

"Don't do it, Professor," warns Miguel. "He'll take the blade and still try to kill us. We know too much, and the Nacon don't tolerate witnesses. Isn't that right, Hun-Dung?"

Anger rises in the rumbling growl from behind her, frightening her with its savage energy.

"Yeah, I know who you are," scoffs Miguel, raising his voice above the chorus of laments vibrating off the walls. "Lame-Came, or is it Scum-Cum, Death-Dude, ah, whatever, we just call you wacko jack."

The man's grip tightens as the voices grow louder. "You just signed your death warrant, pig," hisses the voice in her ear.

Mercenaries dart their gun lights to chase the visions that dance between the shadows. Miguel seems oddly unaware of them, intently focused on the evil that holds her in its grasp.

"Get real. You came here to kill me. I'm just having fun with it," quips Miguel.

Between the flashlight beams, a vaporous slave woman approaches the Frenchman, still holding a gemmed hairbrush. With imploring eyes, the ghostly maiden reaches for the beloved reminder of a life she once led. Drooling in fear, Gerhard drops the brush, backing away until he trips into a bin of silk rolls. Thick clouds of dust burst into the chamber, enriching the ghoulish mirage as another slave specter elicits ethereal screams that spark a violent spectral uprising.

The hand holding the blade trembles. "Shoot anyone who tries to escape," he shouts.

"Last chance," shouts Miguel over the deafening shrill.

When Sophia looks back, Miguel has a Glock aimed to the side of her face with the hot, stinky breath. His other hand holds another sword ready to slice the gold-laden arm holding the knife. His icy gaze burns past her to the malevolent snarl behind her. The power balance has shifted, yet she remains dangerously stuck in the middle. Her heart pounds like a *Dugu* drum, while the ghastly hallucination rages around them, reverberating in her ears.

Unfazed and laser focused, Miguel cocks his gun. Anxious of his aim in the poor light, she involuntarily turns her face away. Her short, sad life flashes before her eyes, a lonely life of fear, uncertainty, and hiding, only to end here as a hostage to a lunatic obsessed with a cursed blade.

"Give, me, my, blade," he demands in a rage filled stutter.

"Let go of the girl," replies Miguel.

Within the chamber, another bloodcurdling fiendish shriek of madness erupts, so close that she can feel the terrible lamenting within her head and chest. Just when the nightmare could not get worse, like a slow-motion video, she notices a change in Miguel's eyes the instant he shouts, "Fire!"

Before the word leaves his lips, machine guns explode within the rocky chamber to ricochet off the gold laden mercenaries who dive for cover. A stray bullet nicks the corner of the poison-coated tunnel, spraying bits of white-hot phosphorous onto a third soldier, instantly igniting his clothes in flames. Real screams of terror join the phantom howls as the flames ignite the entire toxic tunnel in a blinding-hot flash.

Pulling away from the heat, the drug lord trips over a pile of bones. In a split second, Sophia pushes the knife away from her neck, just as Miguel swings down the cutlass to slice the same arm, provoking a howl of misery behind her. Her other fist slams hard into her attacker's groin, while her head drops to push back with her butt as a gun blast sends a hot bullet whizzing past her hair to graze the cartel lord's ear in a splatter of blood and another tortured shriek.

Dropping the sword to snatch her wrist, Miguel yanks her forward as the drug lord falls backward into the bone pile. Two apparitions instantly leap from the bone dust to attack the cartel leader with a savage ferocity, stabbing him repeatedly with spectral daggers, evoking husky screams of terror.

The whole experience takes mere seconds before she and Miguel are running for an exit.

"Time to go," Estefan shouts as he follows after them. Xavier and Hugo lay down a final round of repressive fire before chasing after Estefan.

With a fresh light stick, Miguel charges ahead, leaping over rocks.

"Son, slow down," Estefan calls. "What if we took the wrong tunnel?"

Miguel keeps moving as fast as his light stick will allow. "We're not stopping for a damn study break," he calls over his shoulder.

After several twists and turns, Miguel and Sophia emerge into an opening and stop. The professor soon catches up, out of breath, with Xavier and Hugo pulling up the rear. A three-meter underground river blocks the way forward, with water running fast over a rocky bottom. A tattered, moldy rope bridge hangs partly in the water. They've hit a dead end.

"How about now, can I study now?" pants the professor.

"Hugo, Xavier, guard the tunnel," barks Miguel, turning to the professor. "Okay, what next?"

Estefan hesitates then quotes from memory, pausing between breaths. "Raise your hands to heaven in vain hope, for you will be dragged screaming into the dark abyss."

Miguel shines his light up "to heaven," or rather the cave roof above the tattered rope bridge. Someone had pinned a thick rope to the ceiling using iron pegs hammered into the stone. Rusted by the damp air, the iron could be hollow and the rope rotted.

"Oh, cool," quips Miguel. "We took the right tunnel." He shakes his head angrily and joins Xavier to check the tunnel.

Backing up to a rock wall, Sophia holds her arms to fight the uncontrollable shivering from the shattered nerves of coming so close to death. Rocking herself back and forth, she mumbles childhood prayers as her mind flashes back to the cold, biting feel of the blade and the hot, stinky breath on her neck. Wishing she could wash off the sense of a pure evil who groped her, she trembles and rocks. Certain she was going to die, she braces herself with the truth that she still may, and still desperate to understand why. She wants to be brave, faithful, and full of light, but not nearly as much as she just wants out of this hellish ordeal.

*

Caverns of Cortés, Isla Barbareta
June 20, 3:52 p.m. | 15 hours to Mayan chaa

Still lying in the musty pile of decay hyperventilating, Hun Came fights to regain control of his psyche. Checking his shirt, expecting blood, he finds no more than the splatter from his ear and arm. While the gold kept the slice to his arm to a shallow gouge, a touch to his head sends a searing sting that tells him part of the ear is missing. Disoriented and terrorized, he feels the phantom blades still vibrate within his chest. His horror and rage blend into a toxic brew of savage revenge.

The noxious tunnel echoes with the sound of his burned man choking to an unnatural end. The two surviving soldiers shamefully rise to their knees, gathering the gold and gems that had fallen from their pockets. Cowards, he will deal with them both later for not spraying the room with bullets when they had the chance, but then again, he should have sliced the puta's throat.

At the far end of the chamber, Gerhard wanders without his glasses, his eyes wide in horror. Covered head to toe in thick dust that clings to his damp clothes, he stumbles in the uneven shadows cast by flashlights dropped in the sand.

"Go away," he begs, spinning in a new direction. "Leave me alone." Gerhard backs up and then pivots to dash down an aisle only to stop and pivot again.

Hun Came picks up the flashlight to shine it around the chamber but sees no danger. Even the apparitions have evaporated into dust, and the voices have silenced. The Frenchman stops, turns in a new direction, and then stops again.

"What do you want with me?" he pleads to no one there. "Go away."

Gerhard backs up, whimpering, waving his arms in front of him, guarding against an unseen evil. His hands reach into his pockets to empty them of treasure.

"Here," he offers. "I don't want it. Take it. Take it all, I'm sorry. I didn't know." The man has lost his mind, hallucinating.

Then Hun Came hears it, the barely audible, malevolent sound of cackling jumbled with the whoosh of a foot dragging in the sand. A vile stench of decay permeates the cold, dry air as Gerhard backs up against one of the thick posts blocking his retreat. The sound of wood clunking into place echoes throughout the chamber. Without warning, a cutlass lashed to a heavy spar swings down rapidly from the dark ceiling to sever Gerhard's head before he can even scream. The blade digs into the wood with a loud clunk that echoes as the head bounces off the post to roll in the sand. Blood spouts from the neck as the body twitches before collapsing and continuing to convulse.

The entire cavern instantly resounds with another hideous, maniacal wailing that vibrates within his chest like a burning acid, changing from torment to scorn before stopping suddenly. Pulling himself up with the remaining two men, each of them pale and shaken, he moves in the direction where the American disappeared. More terrified than he has ever been in his life, he can't show fear in front of his men.

"Shoot to kill," he orders.

Chapter 53

Angelic Silhouette

C hico floats in and out of consciousness, unsure where he is or what happened, only certain that every muscle in his body throbs in agony. Images are fragmented, foggy, and sharply, intensely painful. The huge ship returned … a terrifying sea landing … wings shredding … scorching heat … hard water. The memories drift aimlessly, unconnected from any meaning or each other. Aching, floating backward as thick black smoke rises to the sky, and then a throbbing blackness detonates in his head.

Struggling to open his burning eyes only makes a piston pound into the back of his skull like an anvil. A brief glimpse, the afternoon sky filters through the swaying shade of coconut palms. How did he get here? All goes black again.

Cold water drips on his chest as he struggles to open a quivering eyelid, burning, and driving the iron pistons even harder until it feels like his skull will explode. A wet tangle of dark hair dangles over him, obscuring a face in shadow.

"Señor, Señor," says an American female. "You okay? Señor, can you hear me?"

His head detonates into a painful, pulsing blast. Then darkness.

*

<hr />

Plunder Lust, Offshore Isla Barbareta
June 20, 4:49 p.m. | 14 hours to Mayan chaa

Darcy does her best to stay calm. She's grateful that Dr. Morales moved Hansen to the *Plunder Lust* sickbay bunk, but the situation remains unacceptable. He should be in a hospital. A medical emergency boat from Coxen Hole won't reach them for another hour. When it does arrive, the vessel will prioritize the numerous local dead and wounded on the bay. It may take several hours before they can attend to Hansen. Unwilling to risk his care any further, she bites her tongue as her agitation escalates.

She and Jackson do their best to make a story of midnight assaults in Belize, mysterious bloody books, family curses, ancient daggers, and a missile-shooting mega-yacht sound credible. She lays out the photos, bloody book, and Hansen's tortoise shell as evidence to the bizarre tale.

"Do we sound crazy yet?" asks Jackson.

"Oh, si, you passed loco a long time ago," Augusto reassures them. "You sound like a Martinez."

Darcy tries not to evade the truth, well, most of it. The entire island fleet saw Brenda bomb the ship, which Darcy explains as self-defense to end the carnage. Witnesses saw Hansen dive off the transom the same instant an explosion occurred under the ship, but she will only admit that she had abandoned him, chased off by the missiles. Her hope of avoiding legal trouble evaporates with multiple deaths across two countries in less than twenty-four hours. Even so, she grows restless over Miguel and tired of the questions.

"With all due respect, Dr. Morales, we're wasting time. We should be searching for our crew," she insists.

"I assure you, Dr. O'Sullivan, that men already search for Sophia and your friends," Augusto replies. "I daresay they know the island better than you do."

A commotion on the aft deck grabs their attention as an islander races into the mess hall to murmur something into Dr. Morales's ear. They both leave as the guards at the door stiffen. Darcy shares a glance of foreboding with her team as her pulse quickens.

A few uneasy minutes later, Augusto returns. "Dr. O'Sullivan, would you join me a moment, *por favor*."

Escorted to the aft deck, she spots a group of men standing over a body on a stretcher. A sudden, icy spasm grips her heart, shooting a chill through her veins. Bracing herself for the worst, she cautiously approaches. Men separate to reveal the ashy, lifeless body of Dave, with a single bullet hole through his forehead.

An involuntarily gasp escapes her lips before she covers her mouth, spins away, fighting the impulse to burst into tears. Relieved it's not Miguel, a wave of guilt and shame washes over her for the very same relief. The news will devastate Dave's father, who wrote recently in hope of a reconciliation. Slowly raising her gaze, her eyes fall onto the bruised legs, battered body, and weary face of Brenda.

"Brenda," screams Darcy, leaping across the group of strangers to embrace her colleague. "Thank heaven, I thought I lost you."

"Yeah, for a minute there, I was definitely toast," she agrees.

"This young woman rescued the pilot," Augusto interjects. "A good friend of mine."

Pointing to Dave, his demeanor softens. "I'm very sorry for your other friend. We found him in a tide pool over a ridge from the main beach," he explains. "There was no sign of the others, but we're still looking."

"Thank you, Dr. Morales," says Darcy. "Thank you for bringing them both back."

A few hundred meters beyond the transom of *Plunder*, a third of the stern of the megaship now sits under water, listing hard to starboard. The fires are suppressed, but the warriors on the ship have abandoned their sniper rifles, as well as any delusions of saving the ship. Wearing life vests, they cling to the forward port-side rails, shouting for the armada to come save them, but not one islander dares.

"What about them?" Darcy asks.

Augusto glances over. "You mean the ship that murdered a dozen of my friends in cold blood? They can sink or swim. Let the navy deal with them," he states. "If they ever arrive."

Even as he speaks, they hear the distinctive whump-whump-whump of a Honduran reconnaissance chopper in the distance. A few minutes later, the chopper hovers over the sinking yacht to assess the reports of an invasion. The scene now looks more like a massive rescue and salvage operation. A naval patrol boat will certainly not be far behind.

Augusto frowns, disappointed at their arrival. "Too bad, I was hoping they would sink."

Darcy panics, sensing her last chance to save Miguel slipping away. Turning to Augusto, she gently rests her hand on his arm. "Dr. Morales, I beg of you, let us go help look for our crew before the navy locks us behind bars for a battle you know we didn't start. You may know the island, sir, but I know Miguel." She gazes hard into his eyes, trying to find his heart. "Please, Doctor, before any more lives are lost."

Chapter 54

Dark Abyss

Caverns of Cortés, Isla Barbareta
June 20, 5:04 p.m. | 13 hours to Mayan chaa

After an unsuccessful search for an alternate route back to the main labyrinth, Sophia studies the moldy rope above her head with a growing sense of unease.

"Maybe they're gone, and we can go back the way we came," she suggests, grasping at straws.

"Light coming," Xavier whispers from his guard post.

"Too late." Miguel points to the rope. "Now or never."

Sophia had volunteered to go first out of guilt, but now her bravery evaporates like one of the apparitions. Reaching up to grab the thick, damp line, digging in with her fingernails, she shuffles across the gap, pausing to rest at the midpoint over the rapids where the rope creaks and her breath catches. With a frantic scurry, she drops off at the end, blowing out her tension. After snapping another light stick to guide the others, she leans against the solid rock to wait for her heart to stop racing.

Miguel motions for Estefan to go next. Heavier and slower, the middle-aged academic hesitates when the rope pops several strands at the weak point. A few shuffles later, he drops with a grunt, moving quickly to snuggle for comfort and warmth, like Papá would do, which strikes her as an oddly comforting gesture in a dark, cold place.

Across the water, something startles Hugo into opening fire in the dark passage.

"Cease fire!" yells Xavier. "Cease fire!"

With the silence of the gun comes another horrendously caustic laughter and intermittent scream to fill the cavern with echoes. With each inhuman howl, she hears Carmen's prophetic voice that death will follow her until she destroys the curse, but the old *buyei* never taught her how to destroy the curse.

*

Caverns of Cortés, Isla Barbareta
June 20, 5:24 p.m. | 13 hours to Mayan chaa

After the tormented scream, Miguel listens to scorpions stampede to make a noisy meal of the dead mercenary in the dark tunnel, cutting and penetrating through clothing and flesh. Xavier throws a fading stick onto the passage to make ambushes easier to detect. Miguel motions for a shaken Hugo to go next and then takes a post with Xavier for another standoff, his face anxious and hard.

"Give up, Captain," the cartel lord calls out. "Once again, your treasure is mine. I have you trapped with no food or supplies while my men dig out the lagoon. I ordered your ship sunk. No rescue will come for you, cockroach."

He's lying. He has no outside contact, certainly not this deep in stone. At least a dozen men arrived on the zodiacs earlier, but there were only a few men in the toxic tunnel, so he could have men working on the lagoon. He refuses even to imagine *Plunder Lust* sunk. After his mom died and the professor grew lost in his own world, Miguel mastered the art of compartmentalizing his emotions until he could deal with them in private. Hansen once told him that soldiers often did the same during the heat of battle, and just as often suffered PTSD in the aftermath.

"Hand over my blade now, and I will let you live," offers Hun Came.

Xavier shakes his head; another lie. Nacon never allows witnesses to live—ever. Besides, Sophia, Estefan, and her backpack rest on the other side of the river. No way that either is coming back now. The path beyond the bridge must lead somewhere. Needing to stall, he plays along with the intimidation game.

"Wow, that the best taunt you got? Kind of weak, if you ask me," Miguel responds. "Okay, let me try one." A smirk emerges. "You've lost at least three men, and the rock has cut you off from your ship. You piss away battery power chasing after a dagger delusion, while all that gold around your neck slows you down. Booby traps riddle this entire hellhole, but we've got the only map to the last exit. Go ahead and enjoy the treasure until your light dies or until the shadow demons come after you again. I'll come back long after the scorpions have picked your ugly-ass bones clean to salvage *my* booty. Oh yeah, and I've still got your sacred dagger, Scum-Dog."

"Oh, snap," Xavier calls aloud. "No chaa for you."

Miguel laughs, joining the refrain. "That's right, dude, no chaa for you."

Miguel's also bluffing. They have a curse, a grotesque, abstract, confusing riddle written by an insane Inquisition executioner that he can only hope leads to an exit. All part of the mind game, only a stall tactic. He leans against the wall listening to the guttural growl reverberate on the rock. Not every day you get to smack down a drug lord. Damn, that felt good, but of course, it would feel a whole lot better if he actually had an escape plan—and the treasure.

"Filthy little cockroach," the drug lord spits back. "I already watched a missile blow your rusty piss bucket into scrap. Before this day ends, you will watch me slit your friends from throat to crotch, and then I'll cut you like chum for the scorpions to eat you alive. By dawn, I will change history for a thousand years."

Hugo makes it across, stepping away from the water's edge to take his turn huddling with Sophia and Estefan. Miguel nods to Xavier to go next.

"Okay, now see, that was much better," mocks Miguel. "I could really hear the rage that time. Grrr. Good growl. And rusty piss bucket, yeah okay, that one stung a little. But seriously, dude, with a nickname like One-Death, you're a bit of a letdown. I mean sure, you're ugly as hell, but a little makeup wouldn't hurt the brand, you know, like the 80s rock band KISS. And for some reason, I imagined death would be taller. Have you ever tried sole inserts or platforms, you know, for the ladies?" he scoffs.

Miguel falls back to his go-to move for masking fear: self-confident, snarky smart-ass. No question, he's terrified to the core, on edge, doubtful any of them will even survive, but he refuses to let it show, not to his men and certainly not to the psychopathic killer trying to intimidate him.

Two-thirds of the way across the river, the rope jerks loose from the pin, dropping a yelping Xavier into the rocky water. The professor and Sophia both lunge for him as Xavier grabs at the end of the wet cord, slipping until he catches hold only inches from the end. Pulling himself closer, Xavier can almost reach the professor's grip when he slips another meter. Estefan and Sophia both stretch arm in arm, wading hip deep into the water's edge while a wide-eyed Hugo lunges to help.

"Come on, Xavier," the professor encourages. "Almost there."

In a frightful instant, the ancient rope disintegrates, sending Xavier downstream, screaming into the black abyss, until his voice abruptly stops. Miguel staggers, fighting an urge to leap downriver. Xavier was like a brother. Even worse, the rotted rope, his only rope to freedom, now drifts in the water, half as long as it was only moments ago. He has only one chance, and it's a cursed slim one.

A malevolent laugh echoes down the tunnel. "Tick-tock, cockroach. Skin for skin, *pendejo*. I'm coming for you, and you will pay for your insolence."

"Suck on it, Dum-Scum," scoffs Miguel, unleashing a burst of bullets.

Buying a second or two at the most, he races to the river, tossing his gun across the water toward Hugo, who catches it in midair. With a running leap several meters upstream, he lands feet first in the shockingly cold, neck-deep water. The rapid current and mossy bottom instantly drag him downstream toward the fragile cord, illuminated only by one eerie green light. Grabbing at the slippery line, it passes quickly through his hands until he digs in with his nails only inches from the end. Hugo joins the professor and Sophia to form a human chain of arms until the professor grips him by the wrist.

Hugo, then Sophia, then the professor, climb the embankment, pulling Miguel to safety. While Miguel still climbs the rocky edge, gunfire explodes in the darkness, ricocheting on the stone. Hugo falls back to return fire but takes a bullet to his shoulder that spins him around with a painful yowl. While Estefan pulls Hugo to safety, Miguel grabs the dropped weapon and pivots on his back to return fire. Deafening blasts ricochet across the water, causing the cartel to retreat for cover. Miguel rolls for cover just in time before fresh fire pings off of the rock.

"I will have my blade and blood," shouts el loco.

Miguel ignores the taunt, done with the macho game. His eyes fixate on Hugo leaning back into Sophia's arms. Part of his shirt is torn off; she presses the cloth wad on the wound to slow the bleeding. Hugo's eyes are wide with the unmistakable dread of death, not just from the bullet, but also from the impenetrable darkness. On the other hand, Miguel could be seeing a dark reflection of his own inner terror.

"We better keep moving." He helps Hugo to his feet.

Without a rope bridge, Scum-Dung won't be able to follow, but it also means they are cut off from the only confirmed exit and the treasure he was destined to discover. Kicking himself for his delays, all he needed was a single pocketful of gems.

*

Caverns of Cortés, Isla Barbareta
June 20, 5:52 p.m. | 13 hours to Mayan chaa

"I should have sliced that puta when I had the chance," Hun Came scolds himself, climbing around the scorpions blanketing the body of his soldier, and then Gerhard. Unconcerned with the Frenchman's death, it was his erratic behavior before losing his head that unnerves him.

Spinning to take in the remarkable scene, he tingles with the hedonistic thrill of a half-billion-dollar bonus, but then chokes on the irony that his precious omen just escaped. And like the American said, the reward may be as fleeting as his flashlight battery. He has no choice but to come back after the chaa, buy or confiscate the island, and bring engineers to level the entire mountain. But first, he needs an escape. With the original tunnel still venting toxic fumes, he needs a new route. If he can make it back to the lagoon, they can dig out unafraid of an ambush.

The older American's hint that Gerhard had deceived him feeds a new dread that the blade is a red herring, a fraud, a hoax. The thought that he may have sabotaged everything he worked his entire life to achieve for a French con job saturates him with a bitter fury. Years of sacrifice, billions in bribes to build covert alliances in preparation for this hour, only to fail over a false omen, cuts deep.

Then a surprise. At the opposite end of the long chamber, near the vanishing edge of his weakening light, he spots someone moving; a cave hermit. A ragged stranger, ancient in age, rummages like a beggar. Not transparent like the other apparitions, he must be real, but he can't imagine how, unless the hermit survives on bats and bugs. Suspicious, he lifts the weakened beam to make sure the image doesn't wash out in the light.

Dreadlocks in his hair and beard drag below his knee. Long, twisted nails look unkempt for decades. Twitching his neck, he clicks his long nails, trying to snap his fingers. Mumbling Spanish curses under his breath, spittle drips down his beard in a demonic Tourette's syndrome. Lifting his eyes to Hun Came, the filthy face breaks into a snarl, and the crystal-blue hellfire eyes seem to self-illuminate. Without a word, the cripple hobbles into the void of a distant crevice.

"Wait," Hun Came calls, chasing after the hermit. "Sir, we need to leave," he shouts. "Stop, *pare*, we mean you no harm."

Chapter 55

Mayan Stelae

Isla Barbareta

June 20, 6:14 p.m. | 12 hours to Mayan chaa

Darcy does another 360-degree spin of the horrendous scene from the Isla Barbareta lagoon beach. It looks like a war zone, with charred huts in the foreground, a debris-strewn beach, then a smoking seaplane and zodiac wreckage over the lagoon. Beyond the coral reef, the Honduran Navy helicopter struggles against a growing wind to airlift commandos from the sinking, burned yacht. Two-thirds submerged, the transom must be resting on the sea floor, with only the bow of the giant ship remaining out of the water, held afloat by air pockets.

Surrounded by sea bluffs, coconut groves, and dense jungle, the picturesque cove has only a few narrow trails leading to other parts of the island. The *Plunder Lust* zodiac lies in the shallows, shredded by gunfire, but there's no sign of Miguel. Desperation and bewilderment rise to a fever pitch on how so many people could simply vanish. Dozens of islanders come and go in search parties, but so far, they've found zero clues.

Anxiety over the growing mystery churns acid in her stomach, although her nausea may not only be nerves. Fear of losing Miguel takes on a terrifying, dark turn. She can't lose him now, not like this, not without telling him that a child needs a father, even a flawed one.

She left Mai and Juniper on board *Plunder Lust* to watch over Hansen, while Augusto left an armed guard to watch over them. Mai continues aerial inspection with the sound of Oliver's whine skimming a few hundred feet overhead roughly every twenty minutes in a grid pattern.

"Mai, you there? What do you see?" Darcy speaks into her hand radio.

"Still here," Mai replies, sounding discouraged. "I'm tracking three teams hacking the jungle and two teams combing beaches. One insane team with Brenda climbing the sea bluffs where they found Dave, and Jackson's team on their way back from the commercial dock," she sighs. "No sign of Skipper or Hugo."

With twelve hundred acres of dense, virgin jungle and seven miles of coastline; it's not a simple task. Still, there's been no sign of a dozen people, and they had to go somewhere.

"On the plus side," Mai continues, "Juni has the US Embassy promising to connect her with someone who knows someone else who can decide something or other."

Darcy grins, only hoping Juniper's savvy can keep them out of prison. Given her new superpower of having a US Senator as a patriarch, it could go either way. In this part of the world, they could become hostages for someone's personal vendetta. For now, she concentrates on Miguel.

Nearby, Augusto attends to Chico, the pilot who saved Brenda, and whom Brenda saved in return. He suffered a severe concussion, burns, and bruising. Conscious now, he rests under a shady palm, complaining of a savage headache; sipping water, but asking for a beer, or a joint. Mainly, he scowls at the smoldering wreckage of his seaplane. Hector explains how Sophia's uncle Rafé had outfoxed two well-armed attacks over the past few nights. After helping Chico's family onto the seaplane for Roatan, Rafé refused to leave, and Hector could not leave his friend.

"Where's Rafé now?" she inquires.

Hector scratches his beard. "Well," he says, "after Chico left, I say to Rafé, we should take canoes to Roatan. Then he says, no amigo, we hide. You dig, and I swim."

"Dig?" Darcy repeats. "Dig where? Please show me."

Leading them with a smile, Hector approaches an overturned wooden canoe riddled with bullet holes and tilts the canoe back on its side. Under the canoe lies a meter-deep pit bordered by blackened tin roof panels blown off the night before. Even more surprising, an unconscious mercenary bound in thick spools of duct tape lies in the hole, with dried blood trickling down the back of his neck.

Hector smiles with pride and holds up an antique blowgun with a leather bag of darts. "*Mi saba* left me his hunting kit," Hector boasts. "It still works." A cherished possession, and likely one of the few belongings left after the fire.

"Is he dead?" asks Augusto, eyebrows raised in concern.

"Nah," Hector lets go of the canoe, letting it flop over the sleeping captive. "He'll sleep a day and then wish he was dead."

Augusto posts an armed guard in case the old narcotic wears off sooner than expected. Darcy needs an explanation to the crew's disappearance, but the canoe trick is not that answer. Disappointed, she pivots back to Hector. "Okay, now where did Rafé go to swim?"

Augusto and Hector exchange a glance. "I wish I knew," Hector responds. "Rafé can be gone for days."

"Nobody knows where," explains Augusto. "It started after Sophia's father went missing. Rafé made it home, but they never found Antonio. I believe that trauma triggered Rafé's dementia. He would disappear a few times a year, always returning wet and bruised."

"Where did Rafé say he went?" Darcy asks.

"To find Antonio," Augusto explains.

Hector shrugs. "Crazy, huh? After a while, we stopped looking for him."

"Well, our crew and those soldiers had to go somewhere!" Darcy exclaims in frustration.

Hector only shrugs.

"What about caves?" she prompts. "Isn't there a legend of caves?"

Hector and Augusto exchange another odd glance.

"There have been tales of caverns on Barbareta for generations, but no one has ever found them. The only known caves are located on eastern Roatan and Santa Elena across the bay, but Barbareta has none," responds Augusto.

"Unless the entrance lies underwater," Darcy offers an alternative view. "Maybe that's why Rafé's always wet."

Augusto and Hector exchange another look with raised eyebrows. "I never thought of that option," Augusto admits. "But we have miles of coastline; I wouldn't know where to start."

"Okay, how about other islands? Could they have swum or canoed to one of the cays?" she pushes.

"Well," Hector's eyes widen, "Rafé likes to visit Isla de Morat."

"Why de Morat?" asks Augusto. "There's nothing there except the old mangrove swamp." He stops and opens his eyes wide. "Oh, yeah, the old mangrove swamp, of course."

"Why would that be important?" she asks, eyebrows furrowed.

With a pained expression, Augusto inhales. "Rafé found his father, Franco, drowned in the mangroves of de Morat when he was a child. Since that day, Rafé has lived on Barbareta as an orphan, an outcast."

Hector shakes his head. "No, Rafé say he commune with *gubida* by the old Maya stone."

"Maya stone," Darcy blurts out in surprise. "One relic Sophia found had pre-Mayan symbols. The stone could be a clue. Can we check it out?"

Augusto shrugs, pointing to the high-end zodiac left by the lost mercenaries. "We'll use the large inflatable."

"Dibs," Chico whispers in a raspy, hoarse voice, rousing from his resting spot under a nearby palm.

"I call dibs," he says again, raising his hand so others can see, staggering to stand until Hector helps him.

Augusto gazes at the burned-out huts, the plane wreckage, then back to the brand-new zodiac, shrugging as if it made for balanced island justice. At that moment, Darcy gratefully sees Jackson's search party reappear out of the jungle path, sweaty and discouraged.

"Just in time, Dr. Healy," she calls out. "Field trip, you're coming with me."

Within minutes, Chico has settled into the cushioned captain's chair of his new zodiac. Seven meters long with twin 280-horsepower engines, crew seating for twelve, and equipped with a full range of radio, GPS navigation, radar, sonar, a built-in cooler, and awning for the pilot, Chico smiles. Checking the cooler for beer, he finds only water. With a shrug and a frown, he takes one.

Carefully navigating the wreckage for forty minutes, they enter shallows between Barbareta and Roatan with several sand cays and islands. With a huge grin, Chico opens up the engines to the skim across the shallow bay. The low, sandy profile of Isla de Morat palm trees lies a kilometer ahead.

"Do you know where Mitchell Hedges excavated when he was on Roatan?" Darcy shouts to Augusto.

"Sure. My grandfather and Franco Martinez both worked for Hedges," he replies. "Mainly they dug on Isla Santa Elena." He points to a larger island farther away to the southwest. "But they also dug on de Morat and Barbareta."

"What did they find?" she asks.

"Thousands of pottery shards, and small, broken tortoise shells with markings," he states, pulling out a personal necklace made of a thin leather strip, holding an ancient shard of tortoise shell, smaller than the one found by Hansen, with only a partial symbol.

"My grandfather gave it to me for good luck," he explains.

Darcy shares a glance with Jackson. "What happened to the artifacts?" Jackson asks.

"Lost, destroyed, no one knows, but locals blame Franco or his sons," explains Augusto.

She glances back toward Barbareta and then toward the island ahead of them. While she has little doubt Miguel could swim this far, she has less confidence in the others. This whole visit may be a long shot, but the only shot she has left, unless they want to put on dive gear.

Chico lines up with a shallow, sandy shore, and revs the engines enough to push the craft onto the beach. Taking an anchor line, he uses a nearby palm to secure his new baby.

"Okay, let's check the Maya stone," she directs. "It either has meaning, or we head back to Barbareta."

Augusto leans toward Jackson to whisper, "She always this pushy?"

"Oh, hell no," Jackson deflects with a snicker. "Normally she's like, way worse."

Darcy dismisses the remark with a smirk. She can think of no more powerful or more human reaction than an unrelenting focus on saving someone you love. Her father would do the same, a good man under his damnable crusty bluster.

Leading the way with a machete, Hector stops when his blade clanks on a round stone stela about a meter wide, then he clears the growth. Darcy falls to her knees to scrutinize the stone, grabbing a nearby twig to scrape off the lichen.

"Damn it," she curses. "Too weathered to read. Either way, I doubt it's Mayan. It might be Xinca or maybe the same as our mysterious script."

A few meters away, Jackson approaches several large, heavily weathered cut stones peeking inches above the sand, also covered with lichen.

"Hey, Darcy, these stones are granite," he calls out, sounding surprised.

"Granite?" she repeats. "The nearest source for granite must be over a hundred miles away, fifty by ocean."

"Why would they bring granite to a tiny sand cay with a larger island like Roatan only miles away?" Jackson asks a rhetorical question.

"Why indeed," she ponders the enigma.

A violent aftershock abruptly jolts the small, sandy island, shaking the tall palms like rattlers.

"Watch out for coconuts," warns Hector, racing to the beach in a zigzag. Dozens of heavy coconuts drop like mini-bombs, hitting the ground with a loud wooden thud, skull cracking if they hit someone.

With Jackson helping Chico, they gather on the sand to wait out the tremor. Overhead, swarms of bats emerge from beyond the palm trees to form an enormous dark cloud. There must be tens of thousands, creating shade on the sand.

"What's beyond the palms?" Darcy calls to Chico above the rumble.

"A large outcrop of basalt," he replies. "Then the mangrove swamp."

The island shaking ends, leaving only the sloshing sound of waves and the faint squeal of a bat swarm.

"Show me those rocks," Darcy pleads. "There may be a cave system under the island."

Chapter 56

Narrow Path of Life

Caverns of Cortés, Isla Barbareta
June 20, 6:23 p.m. | 12 hours to Mayan chaa

Rattled by the aftershock, and grateful the ceiling rock held, Miguel pushes forward on the narrow, winding path leading away from the river, his treasure, and the only known exit. Instead of a labyrinth of interconnected tunnels, the path beyond the broken rope bridge forces them into a single-file trek with parts of the tunnel looking hand-hewn from the rock like a mine.

His brooding thoughts bounce wildly between the loss of friends, especially Xavier, his growing concern over Hugo, and a scorching fury at Dum-Scum, which deflects his rage away from the professor. More than anyone, he rages at himself, teeth grinding over his stupid decisions and careless mistakes, drenched with a thousand regrets and missed chances he should have played differently.

Yet all thoughts, every thread of dread or hope or fury eventually leads him back to Darcy, the angel he doesn't deserve. His obsession to find gold before giving in to love was little more than a vodka tonic to quiet his own nagging sense of failure. It becomes brilliantly clear that he could never enjoy any treasure without her, certainly not for long. Yeah, he wants his reputation back, but not at the cost of losing his angel. Even if he has to follow her to frigid, damp, shit-food, snobby England, there are worse things than being a kept man—like being a dead man or a forgotten one. Within the quiet despair of a pitch-black catacomb, Miguel rediscovers his core truth and his guiding light. There's only one goal, one north, one clue, one hope to grasp. *Survive to see Darcy.* Find the words to tell her whatever she wants to hear, and then say it a thousand times over until nothing else sounds believable.

The path dead-ends at a deep vertical chasm, an ancient lava tube. Around the left side of the chasm, someone had carved a narrow ledge into the stone, three meters long and half a meter wide. Two meters above the ledge are three rusted iron rings hammered into the basalt with strands of ship rope hanging from each ring, looking dry-rotted. Beyond the ledge, the rocky trail continues with something etched on the far walls.

"The narrow path of life leads to a bottomless, nameless tomb where the razor teeth of demons will shred your soul," the professor quotes.

Miguel tosses a used light stick, which glances off the razor-sharp rock until it fades and ends seconds later with a splash. They're heading deeper, not to the surface.

"I'm starting to really hate this Cortés guy," complains Miguel.

"You may not want to say that aloud," cautions Sophia.

Silence and indecision grip the group.

"*Avanzamos*, we move forward," Hugo sputters, pointing to the ledge with his good arm. "We have no choice, Skipper," he asserts leaning against the wall, his face pale.

Miguel places his hand on Hugo's good shoulder. "Xavier and I have always been proud of you. It's my honor to have you on my crew." He squeezes. "Now, buck up, amigo. I want to keep you on the payroll."

Years ago, Xavier asked him to hire his young cousin Hugo, to help the boy escape the cartel-infested neighborhoods of Juarez. Welcomed to the ship as family, Hugo has proven himself a hundred times over in humble honesty and hard work. A quiet, shy young man with a good heart, Miguel has come to think of him as a younger brother.

Turning back to the narrow path, Miguel ties a light stick to his leading wrist, and exhales to calm his nerves. Taking hold of the first rope, he tugs hard to test the strength, shaking dust from the iron and the line, but they both hold tight. Inching his toes along the ledge, he holds on to the line with his leading hand, balancing against the rock wall with his trailing hand. Keeping his gaze forward, his cheek nearly scrapes on the stone as he steps deeper into the blackness with only the dim light tied to his wrist to show the way. The sound of his own heart pounding in his ear is almost deafening.

When his foot steps onto firm stone, he exhales loudly and then holds up his light stick to help others see. "Small steps, hug the wall."

Sophia goes next, the distance between rings almost too far for her to reach. When she makes it across, she moves past Miguel, several feet away from the edge, to lean her back against the solid rock, hyperventilating.

Stepping up next, the professor moves slowly past the first two rings, but at the third ring, the basalt ledge partially crumbles under his foot. He yelps from loss of balance, clenching hard on the rope.

"Careful," warns Miguel.

Eyes shift to the heavy iron ring that shakes off hundreds of years of dust but holds tight to the stone. Quickly regaining his balance, the professor rapidly finishes the last few steps and shuffles past Miguel to huddle next to Sophia, shuddering together as she whispers prayers, and he takes a turn to hyperventilate.

On the other side of the chasm, sweat beads down Hugo's forehead, his eyes wide in fear.

"Listen, amigo, I'm not gonna lie to you," Miguel says softly. "Reaching up to that line will burn like hell. Accept it. Just remember that the pain won't last, but you can; you can make it. You just gotta hold on."

"Hug the stone, and keep your eyes on us," encourages the professor, standing to help.

"Small steps," coaches Sophia, standing and holding out her light.

Hugo nods, reaching for the first rope with his wounded right shoulder, letting out an agonizing wail that quivers his lips until he drools.

"Hold on," Miguel urges. "Don't you dare let go."

After the surge of pain, Hugo takes a moment to breathe in rapid, shallow breaths, slowly taking deeper breaths. Gradually, he creeps along the ledge until he reaches the last ring, stopping to rest, his shirt and arm soaked in blood.

"You're doing great," Sophia encourages. "Two more steps."

Hugo reaches for the final rope, groaning with tears rolling down his cheeks. He's losing strength.

"Okay, hold up," calls the professor.

"Take a bigger step this time, over the crumbled section," guides Sophia.

Hugo can't see down but places his leading foot out farther.

"A little more," the professor encourages. "Okay, that should be enough."

As Hugo's weight shifts down, the basalt crumbles again. Thrown off balance, he reaches out for the trailing line with his good arm, but he's an inch too short. His full body weight yanks hard on his wounded shoulder and bloody hands.

"Hold on," shouts Miguel, reaching out a hand inches too short.

With an excruciating shriek, Hugo loses his grip, falling backward with arms flailing.

Miguel lunges to the ledge of the pit with an outstretched arm. "Huugggooo!"

It's too late. Hugo's terrorized screams join together with an unholy chorus, all of them ending with a sudden, deafening silence followed a few seconds later with a splash.

Devastated and unable to breathe, Miguel reaches his arm into the black abyss. In less than twenty-four hours since the cursed duo boarded his ship, he's lost nearly his entire crew. More than crew, more than friends, he's lost brothers, his only real family.

A deep, voracious black hole opens within his soul, pulling him over an event horizon of fury, blame, and remorse. Disconnecting from time and place, his mind plummets through a thousand images that saturate his marrow with icy sorrow until the air freezes in his lungs. Overwhelmed, he grows deadened, dazed. He failed Ben, and Moses, and Dave, and Hugo, and Xavier. He failed them all. Had he only left the professor and his cursed cousin in Belize, he would only be guilty of two deaths.

Suppressing the impulse to scream, he crams down the urge to rage against the professor, knowing it wouldn't help. Neither Xavier nor Hugo will resurrect. To survive now, to find Darcy again, they need to work together, and then he never wants to see either one of them ever again. A survivor instinct rises above the cauldron of wrath and heartache. Only one true choice, one true compass—bite his tongue, live to find an exit, and then find Darcy.

Without a word, he slowly pushes himself up, takes an enormous breath, and stiffens. With a loud exhale, he pivots forward.

"Pick up the pace," he grumbles. "I want out of this shithole."

"But to where?" Sophia wonders aloud, sounding panicked. "Where is Cortés leading us?"

"It doesn't matter," he complains.

"On a pilgrimage," replies the professor.

"How could you know that?" snaps Sophia.

"Behind you," notes the professor.

"Oh, wow!" exclaims Sophia.

Damn his curiosity. With a resentful sigh, Miguel turns back to look. Dozens of archaic petroglyphs and symbols lie scratched across a three-meter section of flat rock wall. A handful of symbols look like the shell shard; others look more preclassical Mayan, like an ancient graffiti wall reflecting thousands of years of visitors.

"Rafé must have etched these on paper, but why would he risk coming this far when the treasure was on the other side of the river?" Miguel wonders aloud.

"Excellent question," replies the professor.

"This symbol was on the shell." Sophia points.

Wrinkling his brow, the professor studies the etching. "Reminds me of a symbol noted in a paper on the El Mirador script. I'm not entirely sure, but I think it means *Ahaltocob Xiba.*"

"What does that mean?" asks Sophia.

"Desolation of Xi," replies the professor.

"Catchy name," quips Miguel. "Still think we're being led to an exit?"

The professor's silence gives Miguel the answer he already fears. "Yeah, that's what I thought." As Hugo noted, they have no choice.

Sophia furrows her brow. "Rafé said that Papá died beyond the gates of desolation or something, but I assumed he was hallucinating."

"Interesting," the professor notes. "I wonder if this whole place might be an energy gateway of sorts."

"What do you mean," Sophia asks.

He turns to Miguel. "You mentioned highly magnetized walls, correct?"

"Yeah." Miguel nods, unsure where the professor is heading, but recognizing the look of wheels turning. "And some of the objects carry a mild tingle."

"Yes, exactly," the professor agrees. "I noticed the tingle when I picked up the idol, but much less when I rubbed the gold plater. Each touch triggered an apparition, just as when Sophia stepped on the bone, and then the Frenchman."

"The images act like past shadows," notes Miguel, "replaying in a loop."

"Well, not always," interjects Sophia.

"Electromagnetic fields are essentially electron waves that transport energy," the professor explains. "The Earth has a number of known energy vortexes where magnetic fields intersect, sometimes resulting in gravitational variations or other anomalies."

"Get to the point, Professor," urges Miguel.

He takes a deep breath. "An extremely strong blast of electromagnetic plasma at the right frequency, in theory, could create a magnetic feedback loop, a temporal wormhole as it were."

"You mean something like a magnetic mirror?" Miguel responds, thinking of an article he read once about a magnetic trap and how scientists use the technology in fusion power experiments to contain high-energy plasma.

"Precisely," the professor confirms. "Analog tape uses magnetic patterns to record sound vibrations. What if a strong enough plasma event could capture other life-force energies? Instead of ghosts, what if we're seeing a past resonance trapped within the saturated materials?"

Sophia shakes her head. "What are you two talking about?"

The professor takes a deep breath. "I don't believe in ghosts or curses or voodoo, but I do believe something unspeakable happened here a very long time ago. An event so supercharged that it created a magnetic trap within the honeycombed cavern walls. We break the circuit, as it were, to release that stored energy, which appear as apparitions, when we touch or break saturated items."

"Plasma event—you mean the meteor impact?" Miguel asks, confirming the professor's motive.

He suspects the reason why the professor agreed to help Sophia, and the reason why his friends are dead was to prove a point about the Younger Dryas Impact.

"I am," the professor acknowledges. "In fact, we know the plasma and iridium field covered this island, which at the time would have been a small volcanic mountain range over a vast coastal wetland. The plasma waves would have vaporized and buried any civilization. In fact, I'm willing to bet these caverns were created by that very event. The magnetic energy still permeates the dense ignimbrite deposits in the walls."

"I think you're both missing the point," interjects Sophia.

Miguel turns with the professor to gaze at her.

"We found the reason for the ancient pilgrimage. Why people traveled over sixty kilometers of ocean for thousands of years," Sophia points to the wall. "A *Dugu*, a memorial."

"So, we're trapped in a graffiti-tagged tomb with reruns of death leading us on a path to desolation. Cool, just like growing up." Miguel frowns, shaking his head, still in a foul mood, turning back to the path. "Now keep up, or I'll leave you both behind."

Miguel doesn't intend to sound so angry, but the professor can turn the most tragic day into a history lesson, and he's not in the mood. He listens in silence to the banter behind him.

"Did you mean what you said about the dagger being a fake?" asks Sophia.

"Oh, no," replies Estefan. "But it's not Kukulkan. The historical Kukulkan was more likely a Phoenician who left Mesoamerica on ships with a promise to return. In fact, many of the elongated skulls of the Paracas in Peru contained DNA from the Black Sea area. When Hernán Cortés conquered the Aztecs, they believed he was the Chilam Balaam prophesied return of the bearded deity, sailing on ships of winged serpents."

"What name did you read?" she asks.

"Like Juniper said, Xibalque," he responds. "One of the hero twins from mythology. He and his twin brother, Hun Hanahpu, descended into Xibalba to rescue their father, protector of ancient knowledge. Xibalque defeated Hun Came, the Lord of Death, and cut off his head."

"Interesting coincidence, don't you think?" asks Sophia.

"I don't believe in coincidence," responds Estefan.

Chapter 57

Shadow Secrets

Caverns of Cortés, Isla Barbareta
June 20, 6:49 p.m. | 12 hours to Mayan chaa

For the first time in her life, Sophia sees herself as a victim of the family legacy she never wanted to believe, driven by a malevolent force into a dark, mysterious pilgrimage. While she now understands why so many generations came searching for treasure, it has also become frightfully clear why so few returned. Those who did return, such as Rafé, came out demented by the horrendous visions, a sad and ironically rational explanation to the family history of dementia. Lunacy may not be her primary concern, as it seems less and less likely they will find a way out.

All of the stolen relics have returned to the caverns, except for the cursed logbook itself. Together, she and her cousins will be the last of the Martinez lineage, an end of the curse, and a final victory for the Spaniard.

Stuck in her morbid thoughts and dreading her grim fate, step after rocky step she contemplates how her life has led her to this place and this moment.

Papá taught her long ago to have faith, but how could anyone hold on to faith in this place? Mamá used to say that in her darkest hour, she would carry the light she needed within her heart. Sophia always thought the advice was encouragement for the dark hour when Mamá would die. Now she knows her true darkest hour has arrived, yet the only light she can perceive is the knowledge that she's not alone, she's not the last Martinez. Her two cousins are with her, and even though they may die together, she won't die alone. Rafé claimed the only way through would be to go all the way through. Perhaps an option before the river, but now an imperative.

An epiphany slowly forms in the darkness, hollow like the dusty images, bare threads of thought that pull together until she wonders if maybe all of her gubida were correct. Instead of destroying the curse by her death, maybe the true way to defeat the curse will be to reach deep inside for the light of belonging, find a renewed faith in herself, her family, and her gubida, and then together reach the end to survive the ordeal. Maybe the secret is the ability to hold on to hope through the darkness of tragedy, hubris, and revenge. Maybe only a pure light of forgiveness can win over such an unspeakable evil of vengeance. Maybe she's grasping at straws.

It could be her bleak mood or her fatigue or suppressed trauma, but ever since the black chasm, she can't shake the sense of someone watching, stalking. She stops again to gaze behind her, holding up her light as the shadows appear to move. She's unable to tell if she sees wiggling bugs, another apparition, or her terrified imagination, but Papá's face almost forms within the darkness. Her heart pounds, expecting the apparition to approach, convinced now that Papá perished in this perdition. She longs to see his face or hear his voice, but nothing moves, and no spirit approaches; it's only her imagination running wild.

Turning back to the path, she hears a low, almost inaudible voice behind her. "Sophia."

Paralyzed, afraid even to breathe, she slowly turns around as ice seeps into her veins. "Papá," she whispers, her voice tight with fear and yearning. "I miss you."

Her heart pounds loudly in her ear as quivering hands slowly move the light stick across the shifting shadows on the craggy rock walls. Only silence, no face and no voice. The oddly comforting idea emerges that they will be together in death, until she realizes in an instant of horror that they would be together in hell.

"I just want to go home, Papá," she pleads. "I only wanted answers. Help me to have faith. Show me the way, Papá. I'm not ready to die."

She waits another moment in anticipation until the silence becomes deafening.

"Sophia, are you okay?" Estefan calls from the darkness ahead.

The solemn, intimate moment broken, she looks desperately one last time into the darkness and then spins forward.

"Coming." She hustles to catch up with the others.

They soon reach another dead end with a split in the path. The left shaft looks narrow with another unknown powder sprinkled along the rock. To the right, the path looks wider and easier to follow.

"What does your riddle say next?" asks Miguel, weariness in his voice.

"Nothing," replies Estefan. "Not about this juncture at least."

"Maybe you missed something," retorts Sophia.

"Maybe it doesn't matter," deflects Estefan.

There's a growing anxiety to every step. Their lives hang on an interpretation of what could be meaningless madness to nowhere. Estefan chooses the easy path.

"Hold up," warns Miguel, grabbing Estefan's shirt and pulling him backward.

"Sophia, let me see your broken compass." He points to an odd notch carved into the rock between the two tunnels. Very subtle, Sophia would have missed it. Miguel places the hexagonal compass box inside the notch. A perfect fit. Opening the lid, the broken needle clearly points toward the narrow passage.

"Oh, I get it," mutters Sophia. "Not supposed to point north."

Someone created the broken device to guide travelers at a critical juncture where there was no riddle clue, and then Montego hid the guide. She would have missed it, had it not been for Miguel, a glimmer in her light of faith.

Another sign she follows a path of her gubida, hopefully the path of those who made it out alive. As the last one to squeeze into the crevice, Sophia tosses her used light stick into the larger tunnel out of curiosity. An unmistakable squirming in the lime-green shadows tell her all she needs to know—snakes.

Soon bones litter the cavern walls around them. Tens of thousands of petrified bones penetrate out of the walls, jammed into the ceiling, and spike up from the floors, as if rammed there by an immensely powerful force. Someone had placed step stones on the path to avoid stepping on the brittle bones directly. Cold, stale air feels heavier with each breath, a sign the oxygen levels are dropping.

"What happened here?" Sophia asks in a whisper, not wanting to disturb the spirits.

"More evidence of the meteor catastrophe," Estefan points out. "I think we're looking at a tsunami human debris field embedded in the old stone."

"Hedges really did find Atlantis," says Sophia.

"Well, yes, the Mesoamerican version," replies Estefan. "The Mayans believed Xibalba was a dark, watery underworld of fear, death, and despair, ruled over by nine lords of death, including pus, blood, broken bone, razor, disease, and evil spirits. Sounds like the aftermath of a horrendous natural disaster."

"I think it sounds exactly like this place," replies Sophia, realizing how much this place helps her make sense of Rafé's *locura*.

The tunnel ends with stone steps descending, worn down in the middle. "Wow, how long was Cortés down here?" she wonders.

"These stones were foot worn ten thousand years before Cortés was born," Estefan speculates.

The steps lead them into another lagoon with nowhere else to go, another dead end.

"Cortés only wrote of one water entrance," notes Estefan, sounding confused.

"We have to go back," snaps Sophia. "We must have taken a wrong turn."

Miguel steps down to taste and then spits out the water. "Salty and stagnant."

Once again, he removes extra weight to lay it on the step.

"We're low on light sticks." Estefan stops him. "You can't waste time looking for another underwater passage. I agree with Sophia, we go back. We must have missed something."

Miguel continues to prepare. "We're in the right place," he insists.

"How do you know?" she challenges, her anxieties edging higher.

He points to a corner of the step leading into the lagoon, littered by a single used light stick.

"Whoever left the light sticks came this far," he justifies. "I want to know why."

"Or they died doing what you're thinking of doing?" argues Estefan.

"I need your old light stick." Miguel holds out his hand. "If I'm not back in five minutes, then I'm not coming back. Conserve your light. Find another way out," he instructs without emotion.

Near tears, Estefan grabs Miguel's arms before he steps into the water. "I've always been proud of you, son," he confesses. "Losing your mother nearly destroyed me, so I can't lose you too, not here, not like this. Please come back. We may not have lived like a close family, but by God, we'll die like one, together."

Miguel swallows hard, nods, and then turns to dive into the dark water, his green glow quickly disappearing. At first, Miguel came off as a crude, blunt, angry, and resentful pirate, only looking out for himself. However, she's coming to see a brave man who deeply loved his men. *Have faith*, she tells herself, *hold on to the light*.

Sophia and Estefan huddle close together. Shivering, their blood sugar low, they conserve the last of their own energy. In the silence and shadows, Sophia slips into a deep melancholy, reviewing her life in short, sad scenes, all of them darkened by someone's death. She regrets not traveling more, or learning how to cook better, maybe learn to dive, or pay more attention to Carmen's spiritual teachings. Sally once told her that she was destined to be a *buyei*, but she lacked the confidence. It would have been nice to meet Hansen, Captain Hansen, under better circumstances, and maybe even raise a family. She regrets every moment she doubted herself or didn't live to the fullest simply because of some dark legacy over her shoulder.

The light stick continues to fade, and with the light, her hope. "We have another one, right?"

Estefan holds up the last one. They've been wandering for hours. The early light stick distraction now seems wasteful. Unsure how to fill the unbearable silence, like a good Garifuna, she endures it in silence. No one keeps time, but it sure feels longer than five minutes by the time the light dies, plunging the lagoon into utter darkness except for a useless pale-green stick.

"We can't leave without Miguel," Estefan declares with a faltering confidence. Snuggled in his arms for warmth, hearing his voice in the darkness, she imagines Papá.

"Then we'll wait," Sophia whispers to a silent agreement. She wants to scream, *"I'm not ready to die!"* but the dark despair even swallows her voice.

As if *el diablo* himself were waiting to gloat, another screaming lament and mocking laughter echoes throughout the caverns above them. In the same instant, an eerie green glow emerges from the black water until Miguel bursts out gasping for air.

"Yes!" exclaims Estefan, reaching into the lagoon, but Miguel waves him off.

"I'm not getting out, you're getting in," he says with a grin. "You're not going to believe what's on the other side of this hole."

Chapter 58

Dark Cloud Rising

Darcy surveys the enormous basalt rock that erupts from the sand and spills into the mangrove swamp. Four meters high and three times as wide, inches of bat guano cover four major and several smaller crevices in the rock. An enormous colony of bats continues to hover over the island, blocking the sun, disturbed by the strangers checking out their front door. Gagged by the smell, Darcy holds her nose.

"Dr. O'Sullivan, are you there?" Juniper squawks over the ship radio.

Pulling the radio from her pocket, she answers, "Go ahead," sounding nasal.

"The Honduran Navy just arrived," reports Juniper. "I need you back on the ship."

"Stall them," replies Darcy, turning off the radio and replacing it in her pocket, continuing to study the rock.

"Who was that?" Jackson asks, walking up from the Mayan stone area.

"Juniper, to tell me the Honduran Navy has arrived," she relates the news. "Jackson, I need you to go back to *Plunder Lust* with Dr. Morales and pick up Brenda on the way. Tell them you're the acting captain. Explain our situation, but don't tell them I'm here yet."

Jackson's eyes widen while Augusto's eyes narrow.

"I need more time," she explains. "That many bats need an enormous cavern. Something big and dry must be under this rock, and so far, it's the only blasted clue we've got."

Beyond the shallow bay, boats of the island armada head west toward French Harbor, Oak Ridge, and Coxen Hole as the search teams disband. No one wants to face down the Honduran Navy. She needs time to play out this last-ditch hunch. The rock crevices are far too slim for humans to enter or exit, but she suspects the crevices connect a few feet into the rock. To verify her theory, she needs to bash away the hard basalt, and she only has an hour or so before dusk.

"Hector," she says, "I need you to stay here with me."

Leaping off the rancid rock, they walk back to the stelae stone. The mystery of the weathered granite nibbles at her instincts. There had to be a reason ancient people brought granite over an ocean. With a possible cavern under the sand, Isla de Morat fascinates her, knowing it could be nothing more than a desperate distraction.

Finding a large, broken coconut shell, she hands it to Hector. "Use the shell to dig like you did on the beach," she guides him. "Dig until you find the bottom stone, okay?"

Looking for his agreement, she sees annoyance dissolve into despair turn into a shrug, and then a nod of why not. She expects only a foot or two of stone at most.

Choosing one of the smaller broken granite stones, light enough to lift but hard enough to crack basalt, she approaches the large outcrop. An unexpected whiff of pungent ammonia catches her off guard, sending an uncontrollable wave of nausea that urges her to befoul a nearby bush. Once the nausea passes, she holds her nose to climb to the largest crevice. Raising the hard granite high, she smashes it down on the basalt, only managing to chip a layer of guano. Pulling up, she tries a few more times. A section of rock crumbles.

Already winded from the brief exertion, she wonders if her idea will be worth the effort. Peering into the crevice until her eyes burn convinces her the rock opens up further down. There's equipment on the ship that would make the job easier, but that would mean alerting the navy she was here, and that would mean an arrest.

Lifting again, she smashes the stone, then again and again. With each smash, she chips away a tiny fragment of her guilt, anger, and anxiety. Each chip of basalt chisels at her shame for not telling Miguel about the pregnancy. With every chunk of rock that crumbles, a bit of her self-pity erodes over a shattered career. Each new opening in the crevice renews a hope that Miguel could still be alive, still fighting to get home.

Out of breath, her heart pounding wildly, she climbs off the putrid rock to take a deep, clean breath. At least two major crevices connect. With a need to rest, she checks on Hector, who leans back waist high in the sand, also wheezing for air. To her surprise, the deeper stones grow larger, show less wear, and fit tighter together. Already at least three feet deep, the structure could be much deeper than she expected, perhaps even a tunnel, and extremely ancient. The stones are not the bottom of something, but rather the top of it.

Between breaths, Hector holds up an antique gold watch on a chain. "Look what I found," he boasts. "It has letters. FAMH."

"F. A. Mitchel Hedges!" exclaims Darcy. "Now we're getting somewhere." Although she's just not sure where.

Chapter 59

Orgy of Sacrifice
(Kinsik Ya'abo'ob)

Caverns of Cortés, Isla Barbareta
June 20, 7:16 p.m. | 11 hours to Mayan chaa

As hard as he tries, Hun Came can't catch up with the filthy old hermit. The disgusting cave rat must know his way in the dark. By the time he reaches the end of a tunnel, the old man is climbing over a pile of distant rock. After running and climbing the same rock, he spots the filthy gnome turning down an ancient lava tube.

"Stop!" he calls out climbing after him, his gold-laden commando panting to keep up.

The old man turns his head with a malice-dripping grin, his piercing eyes striking a frosty bolt of terror that seems unexplainable from a decrepit old lunatic. Without a response, he turns away into the shadows muttering. Everything about this place resonates evil; a pure, unbridled terror seeps into his heart like never before. Not the kind of branded evil that he projected for decades, or the ruthless violence of Nacon, or even the demented psychosis of Vacub Came, but an eternal vile malignance he can't even explain.

The pervasive pitch-black, claustrophobic tunnels play tricks on his mind, zapping his anxiety with high-voltage terror. For the first time in his life, he actually imagines the chance of failure, and the idea overwhelms his psyche with an all-encompassing distress. Not only did he fail to take revenge, but he failed to obtain his sacred obsidian. If he doesn't escape, he will fail to rise to power. Worst of all, he could die here in this dank pit alone and forgotten, a possible fate that was unfathomable only hours ago.

Soon, the path becomes uneven, sharp, and brittle, jammed with thousands of bones embedded within the rock. In fact, the entire tunnel exposes tens of thousands of bones jutting everywhere, like a tunnel dug through an enormous mass grave fossilized into the stone. Without warning, a spectral stampede of countless naked, ashen, and diseased people smashes into him, screaming and shrieking with unbearable anguish, a human horde climbing over each other to escape an unseen calamity. He shudders and staggers back with each fetid collision that splatters him in grime, blinding him and choking his breathing.

Then, as suddenly as it began, utter silence returns, leaving Hun Came and his final soldier coughing and shaking off the shock and grunge as the dust cloud cascades to the ground. Ahead in the tunnel, the cursing, twitching old man climbs a cut-stone stairway. The second exit.

"Señor, we need to get out of here. I can pay you," he calls again.

He desperately wants out of this place, secretly willing to give up on the dagger if he could only see sunlight again. He'll come back for the treasure later, once he's risen to power, and better prepared. Now he only wants a way out. Nothing matters if he doesn't escape. Rushing to the end of the shaft, he once again finds the old man gone, ascended on the ancient stone staircase.

After a long, steep, and exhausting climb that burns the muscles of his thigh, he enters a hand-carved chamber. In the corner lie the remains of a king or high priest with a jade necklace scattered around an elongated skull. A deteriorated jaguar skin covers the enormous bones, perhaps seven feet tall or more. Thousands of small offerings of gems, gold, and jade surround the bones. In the wall behind him, a library of hundreds of tortoise shells cascade over the shaman's remains like an offering of ancient knowledge from the temple itself, untouched by the flames of the Inquisition. A glyph carved into the wall reveals his identity, but he can't read it.

"Where are we?" asks the commando, who enters after him, sounding winded.

For a moment, he wishes Gerhard were there at least to guess an explanation. The room ends with two cut-stone archways leading to a balcony and the sound of trickling water in the distance.

"I don't know," he responds.

"Do you see a way out?" asks the soldier, his voice weary.

He hates to admit the truth. "Not yet."

Unsure where the old hermit disappeared, he's deeply disappointed that the steps did not lead to the surface. Through the cut arches, he discovers a platform carved into the side of a limestone cliff. Terraced steps plunge into a rocky lagoon infused with even more bones, or perhaps the same bones of the petrified tunnel. Twenty or more meters across and just as high, the enormous chamber must be an air pocket below sea level. Thick layers of volcanic ash and limestone have dissolved to reveal the remnants of an ancient city.

A colossal granite altar sits on the platform, still looking damp as if wet with the blood of a recent sacrifice. Mesmerized with the sight, soaking in the sacred origins of his people, he moves his palm over the stone, which tingles to the touch, emanating raw power.

"No, don't touch it!" shouts the commando.

Too late. A vibrant hallucination instantly bursts in every direction to encompass the full chamber. Cut into a mountain, the temple platform overlooks a natural harbor. In his delirium, he stands above a hundred thousand or more terrified people spreading in every direction. To the east lies a vast coastal wetland that stretches for hundreds of kilometers. To the west, an erupting volcano spews a river of lava, creeping unchecked through the city below, burning wooden markets and choking the air with a thick black smoke.

Eyes peer up at him with unspeakable desperation as throngs of men, women, and children scale the forbidden steps to evade certain death.

Their efforts seem utterly futile in light of the more dreadful perils approaching from the northern horizon. Beyond the harbor, the ocean has drawn back to the edge of the great trench, leaving hundreds of trading ships, fishing canoes, and sea creatures stranded. A massive tsunami builds to enormous heights. Ahead of the water, a white-hot furnace capped by a massive black cloud rips open the sky.

In an effort to hold back the inevitable, the high priest and his shamans engage in a despicable orgy of sacrifice. Drenched in blood, they continue to chant while they slice throats and shove the victims off the platform, sending the bodies to tumble down the terrace, adding to the sacrificed heap of humanity already at the base of the temple. Blood runs crimson down the terraced stone steps, failing to discourage others from choosing the sanctity of sacrifice over the approaching unknown horror. An entire nation suffering inconsolable terror as they face an inescapable annihilation.

So gruesome, grisly, and abhorrent is the sight that a wave of revulsion sweeps over him until he turns to vomit, polluting the heartless sacrifice left on the altar. Wiping his face on his silk sleeve, he lifts his gaze to catch the harsh glower of the high priest, who whips his scolding gaze back toward the ominous horizon. White-hot plasma towers to the sky. Behind the furnace, a mountainous wall of ocean and steam advances at alarming speed. From below, an overpowering sound of voices wailing in a mournful lament resounds with an escalating, deafening drone that he can feel reverberate within every fiber of his being.

The high priest throws out his arms wide to welcome his unavoidable fate, dropping the still-bloody sacrificial blade. In a reactive panic, Hun Came dives for the sacred dagger as it falls, catching the delicate glass before it shatters on the altar stone. In the same instant, an explosive hurricane blast as hot as the sun detonates the hillside forests of cedar and mahogany like a fiery bomb igniting over the entire region, instantly vaporizing countless souls. Hundreds of meters of burning rock and black ash bury the city only a few seconds before a powerful tsunami rolls over the entire smoldering mountain, sealing it with a violent shudder.

The overshadowing wave smashes the hallucination into a fine dusty mist, drizzling down the entire chamber, leaving only the echo of water dripping down the walls, and blackness.

Paralyzed by the vivid vision of utter devastation, he finally understands the true inscrutable destructive power of Bolon-Yokte, humbling him to think he dared to call such judgment down on his own. With an anxious glance, he finds his grip empty, the blade he caught gone, only part of the hallucination. Infuriation and shame churn in his stomach, feeding off the disgraceful scowl of the chief priest. Did he really come so far, plan this long, and achieve so much, only to fail? The thought strikes like a spear deep in his soul. If he's unworthy, then he can't count on destiny to lead him to an escape, saturating him with an instant icy terror.

Trembling, he stares into the gloom where the ancient harbor once nestled, surprised to see something move, an eerie green radiance. It takes several seconds to recognize the light stick. The Americans survived.

"*Matalos*," he bellows. "Kill them now!"

He pulls his handgun to fire several shots that miss in the darkness, until the glow disappears behind a wall. Enraged at the soldier who failed to obey his command, he turns to find him dead, blood pooling around a dark slash in his throat, as if sacrificed by the vaporous shamans.

From everywhere at once, another anguishing shriek of madness blares within the caverns, echoing off the stone into a chorus that reverberates inside his chest as it shifts from tortured agony to maniacal laughter, then back into frenzied torment. The sound vibrates with a destructive, painful intensity, eating like an acid. Just when the pain becomes unbearable, it ends with an abrupt silence.

Rage and determination rise up as he scurries down the terraced temple steps. The true blade of the maker has reappeared below. Fate has granted him a final chance to prove himself.

Chapter 60

Kiss of Death

Caverns of Cortés, Isla Barbareta
June 20, 7:28 p.m. | 11 hours to Mayan chaa

Soaking wet again, chilled to the point of shivering, and breathing rank, stale air, Sophia feels stunned, traumatized by the horrific vision of unbelievable human suffering and cataclysmic annihilation. An entire civilization incinerated into ash and bone. The tragic truth behind why the ancients would risk the treacherous pilgrimage, why they would carve a path into such perilous caverns to leave memorial messages on a wall. The tragic human side of the professor's sanitized video animation of an asteroid apocalypse. An appreciation grows for why Paulo wanted this place to be kept a secret—to keep it sacred.

Hiding behind an ancient wall, she holds herself, and rocks, more for warmth than fear; she's grown too numb. Instead of an exit, they've ended at a graveyard, probably their own, with a psychopathic killer still on their heels.

"Seriously, where's the damn exit?" demands Miguel. The horrific vision and return of the killer had doused his earlier excitement over finding the temple ruins.

"One final step," Estefan points to the temple platform.

"Damnation flows red over the abomination of the bloody altar burning with the stench of death. Rise above the sacrifice of desolation to find your fate," Estefan quotes the curse. "We need to climb above the altar."

"Gift shop, always put an exit near the gift shop," Miguel jibes, rubbing his hands over his grimy face with a growl, clearly frustrated.

"So how do we get past el loco?" asks Sophia, running her fingers through her hair.

Miguel shares a painful glance with Estefan, and with powerful emotions behind the eyes of both men, they stiffen to explain in a single word. "Lamanai."

"Lamanai," Sophia whispers. "What happened at Lamanai?"

Estefan looks to Miguel. "I lost my love, and Miguel lost his protective angel."

"Okay, I need a little more," she presses in a whisper.

"We were near Lamanai when raiders attacked our encampment, killing several good men," Miguel confesses, turning to his papá. "Much like the last few days." He turns back to Sophia. "Instead of giving them what they wanted, we escaped through the jungle."

"I don't get it. Sounds like you won," she replies.

Estefan shakes his head. "No, like today, they figured it out and gave chase. His mother, Olivia, was fatally injured during our escape," he admits with his eyes cast down. "Like your friends."

"I should have given him what he wanted at the rope bridge," admits Miguel, clenching his jaw.

He holds out his palm to Sophia for the knapsack now slung over her shoulder. "It may be too late, but we're out of options. Let's hope it diverts him long enough."

"Agreed," replies Estefan.

They both wait for her approval. The dagger could be worth millions, yet it's worthless if she dies here. She has the truth she came to find, and a family she never expected. *Faith, light, and perseverance,* she reminds herself as she hands over the bag and prays for a day when she won't wrestle with the crushing disgrace of so many deaths. If she dies here, that day will come soon. Now, more than ever, after years of depression, nightmares, stigma, and a crippling insecurity, she wants a new chance to live. A wishful thought, a silent prayer.

While Miguel and Estefan sneak around the wall to find a place to offer the compromise, Sophia waits in the darkness of the narrow stone niche.

"Papá," she whispers to herself, "I just want to go home."

Silently, another vision materializes across from her. Filthy, starvation thin, and deathly ill, one of the pirate scoundrels sits with his head lowered, writing in a logbook. The frail buccaneer closes the book with a heavy sigh and then hides the journal inside a crack of the ancient wall next to him. Slowly, the phantom lifts his gaze to hold Sophia in his eyes for a long, tender moment, and then with a weak smile, he blows her a kiss. At once, other apparitions appear from nowhere to lance him in the heart and throw his emaciated body onto a bonfire of other corpses. Smoke rises to the ceiling, filling the chamber with the stench of roasting flesh. Bothered by the smoke, hundreds of bats emerge in a fretful squeal to exit above the temple.

The vision evaporates into a puff of dust, lasting mere seconds, yet her soul floods with a deep remorse for the unimaginable suffering that occurred within this cold, sinister necropolis. Intrigued, she reaches into the nearby rock crease to pull out a real leather-bound logbook.

The touch of Estefan's hand on her shoulder startles her. "What's that?"

"*Arinaguni mafiougati,*" Sophia mumbles, thinking of Rafé's comment. "A testimony of Hades."

"Let's hope he takes the deal," whispers Miguel, coming up behind him. "Okay, we need higher ground, pronto."

Water continues to flow into the cavern from aftershock damage. Sharing one last diminishing light stick, they also share one fading chance to find an exit.

"Let's follow the bats above the temple," Sophia suggests, thinking of the vision.

"I think we should follow the Cortés hint to the altar," Estefan disagrees.

Miguel doesn't vote. The sound of a gun cocking freezes everyone in place.

"Yes," responds a gruff voice. "Let's all follow Cortés to the altar."

Behind Miguel, the drug lord aims his gun to the base of Miguel's skull with Sophia's backpack slung over his shoulder, returning for the kill, just like Miguel predicted. She can see the panic behind Miguel's stoic eyes and clenched jaw.

"Kill any of us and you'll die here, I swear to it," Estefan states with a cold certainty.

"Move," the brute orders, pointing toward the temple steps with a dimming flashlight.

Biting her tongue, she quickly falls behind Estefan to climb the chest-high temple steps, thinking of the earlier vision of the ancients climbing for their lives.

Then, with a powerful flash, she recalls the nightmare that had startled her awake on the day of Timothy's *dugu*, the dream that triggered her recurring *asandiruni*, her premonition. She dreamed of climbing enormous stone steps in the pitch dark toward a sacrificial altar where someone was destined to die. She had dreamt of this very moment.

"Papá, help us," she whispers, feeling a new level of terror seep into her veins. In truth, she needs more than guidance from her *gubida*; she needs a *masuseredati*, a genuine miracle.

Chapter 61

Desperate Twist

Lucia waits in a dark basement storage room with each wrist handcuffed to the arm of a wooden desk chair and a hood over her head to keep her from knowing her location. A hotel, judging by the passing sounds and smells of a large kitchen, she decides.

The door swings open, casting a wide shadow blocking the hallway light. The back of a huge hand swats across her face so hard, she swears a tooth loosens. A beat later, the door slams shut, and the light switch flips on before the hood rips off her head. Squinting, her eyes slowly adjust until she can make out the crisp uniform and deeply creased face of General Francisco Panera, the traitor.

"Señora Vasquez," growls Panera, knowing her identity. "We have your files, so we already know everything."

The general bluffs. No one could hack the encryption key so soon. They have the wall image but lack the critical last few days of discovery.

Panera lowers his face, stinking of stale cigar. "The police will charge you with the murders of José Juarez and Camille Adelson and the conspiracy to assassinate President Lanza."

"You forgot the murder of General Hayat," she retorts. "Or will the death of your business partner raise too many questions?"

The general draws up surprised. She learned about the Pakistani death after the wall photo. Panera connects to Hayat through the board of directors, a stolen container, and a nuke. His surprise confirms they haven't cracked her computer. The brute doesn't appreciate her humor, whacking her hard on the face, cutting her lip.

"Tell me the computer password," he demands.

"Go screw yourself, one word, all caps, with an exclamation point," she sneers, earning another hard smack.

"Who else have you spoken too?" he snarls.

"My brother Xavier, who sends his regards to the traitor. And oh yeah, the *Washington Post*," she admits with a snicker. "That's right. Soon the world will know your dirty secrets."

Years ago, after Xavier identified at least three Nacon moles inside Los Pinos, he refused to reveal the information to anyone except President Lanza personally. Instead, Panera forced Xavier to resign, but not before Xavier hid the report. Soon after, Nacon put a price on his head, leading Xavier to go into hiding on a junk salvage ship. Ironically, Xavier told her recently that Panera was one of the moles.

The powerful man's eyes narrow. "What did you tell them?"

Unsure if Marco convinced the *Washington Post* editors to publish a Latin American piece, she needs a bluff to play. "Everything," she claims, uncertain what that vague term might mean to the general.

He staggers back a half step, his eyes darting back, and forth. "Why are you here?"

"I heard the Cozumel Hilton made the best margaritas."

Panera laughs, looking down at her with contempt. "No, Señora," he snorts.

"You want to be a hero, but I'm afraid I have other plans for you."

Right on cue, there is a single knock at the door. "I invited a mutual friend," he scoffs.

As the door opens, Lucia's heart freezes in her chest. Vacub Came struts into the room, wearing the uniform of a Brazilian general and carrying a large, stylish Italian leather case. The large man lays the heavy case on a supply carton, using it like a makeshift table, pulling the carton and another chair close to Lucia.

She gazes on her father's assassin. Seeing his scars and dead eyes up close, Seven Death looks even more menacing, accelerating her pulse and tensing every muscle.

"What took you so long?" Panera grumbles, looking down on her with pity and disdain.

"Other loose ends," replies Vacub Came, keeping his eyes on her.

With a seven-key combination lock and a thumbprint, the case accordions open into an organized display like a sales presentation of stainless-steel torture tools with an assortment of drugs and needles. Printed labels define each tool or drug, with each device appearing more menacing than the last. A genuine sense of terror tightens in her chest.

"What did she say?" Vacub Came asks the general.

"She contacted an American paper," Panera hisses, "and her brother. I told you they were working together."

"Is that so?" Vacub Came burns a gaze into Lucia. "Then we may cut off the heads of two snakes tonight."

The idea of endangering Xavier sends an icy chill through her heart, but not as frigid as when the assassin lays a cloth on the carton with several empty syringes. Selecting a bottle from the case, he loads the first needle, tapping the syringe to remove the air.

Panera glares at her like a parasite to exterminate. "You should have snuffed out this bitch sooner."

"Then I would miss all the fun I expect to have tonight," the assassin deadpans.

Without warning, Vacub Came jabs the needle into the back of General Panera's thick neck, pressing the plunger half way before extracting the syringe. The huge warrior bolts upright, twisting to face the assassin, his eyes wide with confusion and alarm, his lips trying to speak but only drool. Quickly placing the needle next to the others, Vacub Came scurries to lower the burly general into another nearby chair.

With his back to her, Lucia stretches against the cuffs to use a fingernail to touch the syringe, managing to roll it under her palm before Vacub Came whips his gaze around, freezing her blood cold, thinking he had caught her red-handed.

"Don't worry, this will only take a moment," he taunts.

Turning back to the general, he pulls a folded newspaper from his case and opens it onto the paralyzed general's lap. Lucia glances down to see the *Washington Post* Latin America edition. Marco got her story on the front page, filling her with a bittersweet sense of triumph and vindication. If the *Post* published segment one, then the editor will certainly want to publish story two, successfully sent from the café hours earlier. The truth will get out, even if she doesn't. At least she won't perish in vain. Her father used to say that corruption of the world hinged on secrets. Expose the secrets, and you take the first step toward true freedom. She considers herself a freedom fighter.

"Hun Came hates loose ends," the assassin lectures the general. "You got sloppy with the Pakistani deal, then you failed to sink the freighter, and now your name is in the news. You've become a loose end who knows too much. Now you will be made an example for the others."

Paralyzed, powerless to speak or move, Panera's eyes open wide with fury and betrayal.

"I've injected you with a rare toxin," the assassin explains. "Based on an ancient Aztec formula to paralyze sacrificial victims, the toxin allows the victim to retain complete awareness of their experience. Exquisite in design, the muscles and the vocal cords paralyze almost instantly. Next, other organs such as kidneys, pancreas, liver, and bladder shut down, but more slowly, and much more painfully. Eventually, your heart will stop," he educates with a deadpan voice.

Turning back to prepare a fresh syringe from a different bottle, he continues. "Your mind will stay alert until the very end. Of course, you will experience excruciating pain as each organ dies, but you will be unable to scream."

Vacub Came finishes the syringe preparation. "Absolutely fascinating to observe. One can read so much anguish and regret in the eyes of a silent dying soul."

Panera sits slumped in a chair, drooling, his eyes wide with fear and rage.

"Oh, don't worry, General. Give it a few minutes for the full effect," the killer taunts before turning to Lucia with a malevolent smirk. "Enough time to enjoy watching Señora Vasquez share everything with me."

Trembling, she's more terrified than she wants to admit, even worse than the day her parents died. His eyes scan her body with a lustful ogle.

"Many powerful men find necrophilia to be the most erotic form of conquest over a beautiful woman," he coos, leaning on her arms and forcing a kiss.

Pulling back, he unbuttons her shirt, unhooks the front of her bra, and pushes his fingers over her breast to pinch her nipple.

"To ravage your motionless body, while you are unable to resist or scream, totally and utterly under my power," he whispers.

He stops pinching her nipple to move his hand down to caress her thigh, pushing up to her crotch, rubbing through the heavy zipper on the men's trousers. Lucia stares forward stone cold, willing him to stop, and unwilling to give him the pleasure of a response. Her strategy backfires, exciting him even more.

"*Si, bebe, si*, just like that," he coos, stepping behind her to nibble her ear, ending with a bite that causes her to yelp and pull away. He moves behind her back to the other side, unnerving her with anticipation.

"Then again, I could make you experience agony unlike anything you've ever imagined. As if your veins and organs were on fire from within," he hisses, sticking his tongue in her ear. "Or maybe I should crush your bones and ravage you like a bull on a rag doll."

Each mock sends a jolt of terror that trembles to her limbs.

He moves around to face her. "Oh, you'll want to scream or pray for me to kill you," he torments. "But you won't whimper a sound, will you? No, you troublesome little puta, not even a whimper."

Leaning on her arms, he forces his tongue into her mouth until she bites his lip. He yanks away, licking at the blood, leering down at her exposed breasts.

"It can be exhilarating to watch a woman fight the inevitable. I enjoy breaking a willful bitch into submission," he stokes her fear. "One agonizing step at a time, don't rush me."

Vacub Came turns to pick up the second needle, and with no preparation, jabs the syringe into her arm, making her flinch from the sting.

"Sadly, before I have my fun with you, we must complete our work," he teases. "I've given you something to encourage you to cooperate."

The drug burns through her veins with a sudden sense of relaxation, then dizziness, and nausea until her head swirls, her vision blurs, and her tongue tastes of metal.

Panera had brought her laptop, so Vacub Came sets it on his case and powers it up.

"Let's start with something easy," he states, "like your computer password."

Without even thinking, the words leave her lips. "Capital X, 051058, asterisk," she rattles off Xavier's birthday, sounding drunk to her own ear.

"See how easy that was, General," the killer gloats. "Is your phone code the same?" he asks.

"Yes," she hates herself for responding, knowing he will use her phone to trick Xavier, filling her with instant remorse.

A few keystrokes lead to several moments of silence as Vacub reviews her recent file activities, including her email log with the second story.

"Interesting," he mumbles. "You found the burial site of Buluc Chabtan, very clever, I didn't even know." He checks his watch. "By the time your story goes to print, there will be no cenote. I doubt there will even be much of an island."

"Boom!" she exclaims, her eyes wide in horror, the drug taking full effect.

"Don't worry about me." He turns back to her computer. "I will be on General Panera's personal helicopter long before dawn."

With a scowl, he opens a few more files, and then with a malicious smirk, he turns the screen to show her a picture she took on a trip to secretly meet with Xavier on St. Croix. The selfie image shows her and Xavier touching heads with silly smiles. In the background, on the bay behind them, an old rusty salvage ship lies at anchor.

"Has your brother Xavier been hiding on the *Plunder Lust*?" He points to the junky salvage.

"Yes," she admits, hating herself, sealing the death of Xavier and his friends.

He closes the laptop. "See, General, two snakes." Turning to Lucia, he taunts, "Nice work. Too bad you will be branded as a lunatic, a liar, a murderer, and a traitor."

"Maybe, maybe not, things could change," she teases, feeling loose from the drug. "I have a secret. Shhhhh." She hates herself for almost revealing the secret.

"And what is your little secret?" he asks with a raised brow, knowing the drugs will speak.

"Come closer, so I can whisper," she coaxes. "You know, secret stuff."

It takes every ounce of willpower to keep from blurting the news. She grips her fist and nods toward Panera. The killer huffs and leans forward.

"No, no, closer," she coos with a sexy, husky voice. "So, I can whisper in your ear. It's a dirty secret."

With an angry growl, he leans over to grab her breast and whisper in her ear. "Now tell me your little secret, bitch, before I choke it out of you."

"I took a syringe," she whispers back.

Before the words finish leaving her lips, she jams the needle into his inner thigh, pushing the plunger all the way. He startles back from the sting, swatting the needle away, then falls back against the wall. Wide eyed from surprise and fury, he slumps to the floor with his legs twitching, any effort to talk only making a gagging noise.

"See," she says. "Now I get to watch you die, you sick pervert." Elation and victory surge through her like an adrenaline shot of pure joyful disbelief.

Rocking her chair forward until it slumps over her backside, she waddle-walks over to the general and leans her head against the huge barrel chest. The back of the chair slams against the traitor's face as she sets aside his service pistol, and with a cringe, fumbles in his pockets for a handcuff key until she finds it. With a waddle back, she clunks the chair down to unlock her cuffs.

Grabbing the gun, Lucia spins to stand over Vacub Came, pointing the barrel at his skull. A lifetime vow of revenge only a trigger squeeze away, yet she hesitates, suspended, paralyzed with the gun sighting the sinister face of her nightmares. The savage, who executed her parents, murdered her partner and her mentor, who would have raped and mutilated her just for the enjoyment. Yet now, the monster slumps against the wall, unable to strike, like a caged and declawed tiger. Helpless, pathetic, worse than impotent; a snake poisoned by his own venom.

His eyes burn for her to pull the trigger, begging and daring her to finish him, dreading what the poison will do to his body. She grips the pistol with both hands, lining his sweaty forehead in her sight, the steel of the trigger feeling cool and smooth against her finger. She imagines the blast and his brains splattering against the wall. Then she imagines lighting his dead carcass on fire, the same way he murdered her parents. She takes a deep breath and cocks the gun.

She had imagined this moment for years, expecting to tremble from nerves or anxiety, but the narcotic gives her an eerie sense of calm and clarity. This man deserves to die, and he will die by his own vile toxin. A bullet will be redundant, an undeserved mercy, and a gory mess for some poor soul in housekeeping to clean. Xavier would not approve. She lowers the gun, inhaling and exhaling to clear her head. With a broad sweep of the pistol, she slams the side of his jaw, hearing a crack. He makes no sound, but he had to feel that one as blood trickles down his lip like drool.

"You can die slowly and painfully like the slimy worthless piss slug you are," she spits in his face.

With a deep breath, she flushes the anger and turns to Panera, the once-powerful general who ruined Xavier's career, betrayed his country, and now struggles to inhale. His eyes show less rage and more suffering, perhaps feeling his organs dying, his threats now meaningless.

"Lieutenant Xavier Alvarez served Mexico with honor, integrity, and distinction," she states with pride. "A shame he had the misfortune of working for a double-crossing scum like you. History will remember General Francisco Panera as the cowardly, corrupted puta of a delusional drug lord and a traitor to his people. Xavier taught me never to become the demon to destroy the beast," she recalls. "Shine a light on his deeds, and the beast will self-destruct."

Repacking her computer, she sets it by the door and then checks the storage room for housekeeping supplies such as cleaner and paper towels. With grunts, and heaves, she drags Vacub Came's limp torso toward Panera, shoving the killer's face hard into the general's crotch, and then hanging his thick arms around the general's heavy thighs, a rather unflattering pose.

"Hilarious," she giggles. "Of all the times not to have a camera."

Panera's eyes are too pained to show outrage, but the assassin's foot twitches, showing his incredible determination to fight back.

With a swift kick from behind to his testicles, she reprimands him, "Shut up, perv." The killer makes no sound, but the foot stops.

Wiping her prints off the used syringe containing the paralyzing toxin, she places it underneath Seven Death's dangling hand. An examination of the little case of horrors uncovers a useful concoction, a high-potency pepper spray with a chloroform base. Pouring a puddle of cleaner right by the door, she carefully avoids the slippery liquid.

"Wish me luck," she says with a grin.

With the aerosol spray in one hand, she pounds the door hard with her fist like a man. Stepping behind the door, she draws the gun as Panera's eyes fill with fear. The door opens a few inches, offering a narrow view of the compromising pose, stunning the guard long enough for Lucia to thrust the door wide with her heel, and point the gun and pepper spray into the guard's startled face. With his eyes wide in surprise, she sprays before he reacts.

With a scream, his palms swing up to cover burning eyes, while she grabs a shoulder to drag him over the liquid cleaner, causing him to slip and tumble face first into the ass and tender nuggets of Vacub Came, shoving his face into Panera's crotch, popping open the general's eyes. Then the guard slumps over and passes out.

"And the crowd goes wild. Yeeaaa!" she gloats with a drug-enhanced mock sports victory dance. "Lu-ci, Lu-ci, Lu-ci!"

Grabbing the laptop, she leaps over the puddle and locks the door from the outside, giggling over the scene and her astounding, remarkable surprise even to be alive. Roaming the basement corridors, checking for an exit, a sign for the Intercontinental Hotel finally gives her a clue to her location, brazenly the same hotel as President Lanza. The evening festivities and concerts should be well underway, so Lanza could be anywhere.

At a freight elevator, she punches the lobby button. The door opens into a hallway near restrooms and a lounge bar. Music plays as the well-dressed guests engage in passionate but polite discussions over the concept of economic unity. Tuned to an Evolucion station, the muted television channel features full coverage of the concert on the beach and edited versions of earlier interviews. Evolucion camera crews are everywhere, a feedback loop for attendees watching only positive news about themselves.

Forgetting her disguise, she steps into the women's restroom out of habit, tossing the gun and pepper spray into a trash can. The mirror reflects a disheveled, battered, pretty man with heavy bruises on his face, a bleeding lip, blood splatters on his clothes, and his breasts exposed. Removing the fake mustache and sideburns, buttoning her bra and blouse, she feels ridiculous now. Inside a locked stall, it takes a moment to gather her thoughts with a heart throbbing from adrenaline and a head pounding from the drug.

The *Washington Post* may have already gone to press for the morning. The second segment portrays the story of a dead man, Felipe Gutierrez, who resurrected himself as a cartel lord, delusional with his own branded mystique of immortal evil. From a maniacal drug lord, she tracks a decade of money laundering to the usurped identity of Juan Perez. Then she connects the Nacon lunatic to his sponsorship of Cozumel, a disgraced Pakistani general, US

DEFCON alerts, until she points back to Cozumel, describing the murder of a local leader over a recent sinkhole.

Lucia admits to the reader that the final segment of her story may never be written and concedes to herself that the news will publish too late to save the island. Without her phone, she can't even reach Xavier. On her own, trapped with two hundred thousand people, she needs a tactic to get immediate attention, ring an alarm, spread terror, and get people to evacuate. She needs to scare Lanza enough to cancel his own summit with the cameras rolling. She can think of only one approach.

A few moments later, with an increasingly painful drug-induced headache, Lucia emerges from the elevator onto the Presidential Suite hallway with her hands in the air holding a laptop. Armed guards respond at once to her unauthorized and tousled appearance with raised weapons and demands to freeze.

"I'm a reporter here to help," she announces. "Nacon has hidden a nuclear device under the island. You need to order an immediate evacuation," she says. "We have little time to save lives."

Chapter 62

Final Sacrifice
(Ts'ook Sacrificio)

Caverns of Cortés, Temple of Xi'
June 20, 8:02 p.m. | 10 hours to Mayan chaa

Keeping safely behind the cocky American, Hun Came fights the overwhelming urge to splatter his brains onto the stone steps. Climbing up proves more strenuous and time-consuming than climbing down. The chamber shows signs of collapse, and he needs to escape soon, hoping the American truly knows how to find one before the power of his flashlight drains completely. Anxious for the moment he can kill these swine, he first needs to see daylight and forces himself to remove his finger from the trigger.

Finally reaching the altar platform, winded from the climb, his captives pant and leer with revulsion at the dead mercenary pooled in his own blood, with gold and gems spilling from his pockets.

"Just like old times, eh, Professor?" quips the young American.

He shoots into the ceiling. "Silence," he shouts.

No secret codes or messages. The others will shut down if he kills the *pendejo* too soon. If he drags them along a little longer, then he can still sink a bullet in each of their heads.

"Old man, find the exit," he growls. "You get thirty seconds."

"It would help if we all looked," the old man argues.

"Twenty-nine seconds," he shouts.

Taking a deep breath and closing his eyes, it looks as if the idiot dares to ignore his command. Then his eyes flash open as he spins into a systematic inspection of the walls with his dimming light stick.

"There's a downward exit over here," he cries out.

"I came in that way," declares Hun Came. "Keep looking, twenty-six seconds."

A minor aftershock rocks the cavern suddenly, shaking his frayed nerves along with more loose rock that crashes into the lagoon as the water cascades down the walls in rivulets.

When the rumbling stops, he barks, "Twenty seconds," to keep up the pressure.

Unlike Gerhard, who blabbered nonsense with shameless begging, this one works like a savant, combing the seams until he pauses to study the ancient shaman bones.

"Fourteen seconds," Hun Came provokes him.

"Another archway leading up," he declares with a deep sigh, "but it's blocked. It may have been open in the time of Cortés, but not any longer."

"Ten seconds," Hun Came shouts, pointing the gun at the silenced American captain, eager to squeeze.

"*Asuera da inaruni y amuru*," the young woman lifts her head to shout a chant of some kind. "I spit the curse at you," she translates. "*Asuera da inaruni y amuru.*"

What curse? No one mentioned a curse. The old man races to peer above the platform.

"*Asuera da inaruni y amuru*," the woman repeats loudly, closing her eyes.

"Six seconds," Hun Came calls.

"*Asuera da inaruni y amuru*," she calls louder, raising her hands.

"Shut up," he shouts, shooting a warning shot above her head until she glowers in silence.

The old man holds up his hands. "Wait," he pleads. "At the temple of Characol, the sacrificial summit lies midway to the top of the temple. Cortés said to go above the altar, we need to climb higher."

Hun Came glances to the swelling lagoon. These dogs are slowing him down. He has a direction to escape, which is all they have and all he needs. The sacred blade of the maker lies in the backpack over his shoulder. He felt the tingling power of the true blade surge through him when he gripped it in his hand, confirming his worthiness and his destiny. His momentary self-doubt forgotten, the scorn of the high priest meant nothing, an illusion. He no longer needs these swine, especially the cocky captain.

"Enough!" he yells. Silence fills the room except for the growing sound of water.

"I forgive you, Dad," the American speaks softly, calmly to the elder. "Mom would want me to say the words. It wasn't your fault. I get that now. I'm sorry for the time we lost."

Tears well up in the old man's eyes. "You have to have faith, Miguel."

The unexpected sentiment dredges up a long-forgotten memory of when his own padre sold him and his younger brother Enrico to the cocaine growers to pay a gambling debt. He couldn't have been more than ten at the time, tearfully asking to know why they were being punished. He begged, cried, and pleaded until his papá turned away, closing the gate behind him. In that instant, his young heart became a frozen tundra in the steaming jungle; fertile soil for a lifelong need to prove his worth and demand respect with blood. When the day came to kill his own padre, the coward begged for mercy like a little girl. He shot him in the spleen, ensuring the bastard would bleed out slowly, painfully, and then he walked away to let the old coward die alone. Now he has yet another reason to hate this smug American.

"Good, now you can watch his face blast into blood and bone," he bellows, expecting them to beg for mercy.

The woman glares at him defiantly and calls again a loud voice, "*Asuera da inaruni y amuru.*" Raising her hands. "*Asuera da inaruni y amuru! Asuera da inaruni y amuru!*"

Infuriated, he considers shooting the witch first, when an unexpected sound, and a movement at the edge of the platform startles him, drawing his attention. One hand, then two appear, followed by the shabby face of the cave hermit climbing the stone steps, looking even more sickly and mad. His rotten Spanish colonial coat smells rank and pungent as if he stole it from a corpse. The degenerate twitches, cursing to himself in a harsh spittle of bastardized Spanish, stumbling forward with a menacing limp, dragging a leg across the stone.

Terrified beyond explanation, Hun Came pivots to shoot the miserable wretch. Dust explodes as the bullet penetrates the jacket, but the cave rat only jerks and hobbles forward. Escalating terror shreds his nerve as he shoots again, but the menace only snarls, drooling blood onto his ratty beard as he moves forward step by halting step. In a trembling desperation, he empties his clip, but the putrid zombie shuffles forward unfazed.

At the sound of the empty chamber, the American's elbow swiftly swings up to slam his bloody ear, jolting a shriek of pain from his lips that staggers him backward. The captain lunges toward the dead soldier in a tuck and roll, and then back into a standing position, holding the discarded machine gun aimed directly at his chest. But he doesn't shoot, only stares with wide, frightened eyes.

Now standing face to face with the malicious poltergeist, Hun Came inhales the stench of primal decay. With no breath or preamble, el diablo opens his mouth wide to bellow an unearthly, lamenting shriek and hideous mocking lament so piercing that it resounds within his chest like an electric shock, paralyzing him until he drools from quivering lips and unwillingly soaks his own trousers.

With a long-twisted nail, the phantom slices his own throat, releasing a trickle of blood down his dreadlock beard as an evil scowl distorts his face.

Before Hun Came realizes what has occurred, a skinny, leathery fist reaches from behind his back, gripping tightly to a razor-sharp fishing knife that slices his throat. Sharp pain and warm blood wash over his chest as he falls helplessly limp over the ancient altar, his bloody ear slamming hard onto the cold stone. A howling agony erupts in his brain, but his lips stay numbly silent, only drooling blood that spreads over the sacred stone for the first time in nearly thirteen thousand years.

Utter terror rips through him like a sniper's bullet. He's been found unworthy. Two hundred thousand will die at dawn on live television, but he will die alone and forgotten. His entire life spent hiding in the shadows, and now he faces an eternity consumed by it.

His darkening vision fixates on the haggardly degenerate who points his bony finger and laughs an uncontrollable, malevolent cackle. Behind the demonic hermit, an enormous horde of doomed spirits ascend the temple platform. The entire throng of hopeless souls charge at him with an indescribable screeching ferocity in an explosive, horrifying instant, and then there is nothing.

Chapter 63

Final Collapse

Caverns of Cortés, Temple of Xi'
June 20, 8:13 p.m. | 10 hours to Mayan chaa

Petrified speechless, Sophia tries to grasp exactly what just happened. The stench of death and the resonating, terrifying, lamenting howl still linger, vibrating within her chest. Shivering from cold and fright, she stares at the gaunt shadow slumping over the sacrifice at the altar, still holding the sharp knife dripping in blood.

For a split second, she sees the face of Papá, Antonio. Grabbing the dead man's discarded flashlight, her trembling hands lift the weak beam to discover the face of Rafé, hiding his eyes from the glare, twitching, and jerking his neck. A filthy bandage seeping with blood wraps his wrinkled old leg.

"Rafé," squeals Sophia, rushing to embrace her emaciated uncle. "*Gracias a Dios*, I thought I'd never see you again."

"You, you don't, you, don't, don't belong here," he stutters and twitches. "Not, not, you, why, how, why are you here?"

Estefan steps forward, extending his palm. "Rafé Martinez, we owe you our lives. Thank you. My name is Estefan Martinez, your brother Joaquin's grandson. This is my son, Miguel. We met once after Antonio disappeared. Do you remember?"

Rafé gives Miguel and Estefan a dubious assessment, distant and out of touch; he's overly stressed, pointing and jabbing at something no one else can see. For the first time in her life, Sophia understands how he lost his mind. Here in this hellish necropolis, his demented answers have a bizarre context she never could have imagined.

"Joaquin, Joaquin," Rafé mumbles, glimpsing at the group with questioning eyes. "Joaquin has the key."

"Now I have the key, and I solved the riddle of the curse," explains Estefan.

"How did you find us?" asks Sophia.

"I swam," he explains, expecting her to understand. Ironically, she does.

Rafé jerks his head, squinting at Miguel. "I remember you, boy. You, you save my treasure." He puts his hand gently on Miguel's chest. "You, you save, you save Sophia."

She wonders if Rafé witnessed the encounter in the treasure room, or if he may have been the presence that she felt following her in the dark.

"We'll celebrate later," says Miguel. "Now how do we get out of here?"

Rafé's eyes moisten. "Too late."

Sophia suspects the rising water has closed off the path back through the cavern. "What about the bats?" she once again suggests in frustration.

Rafé shakes his head. "Too small."

Miguel nods toward Sophia. "She might be right; it may get us above sea level."

Without a word, Rafé shuffles off, followed by the others. Before leaving the altar platform, Sophia gazes over the vast chamber of desolation. She can't explain why the drug lord went berserk, shooting into the open, but the terror in his eyes and the soiling of his pants were undeniable. Perhaps he encountered the dreaded Spaniard Cortés, called by her spitting of the curse on him as Carmen had done to the intruder. She's not sure how she got so bold, except maybe an impulse from her gubida, but a part of her imagines that Papá came to look after his little girl.

"Thank you, Papá," she whispers. "I forgive you too. I understand now why you risked everything. You didn't leave me for a treasure or to protect some ancient secret; it was for Mamá, for her cancer, but you got lost because you didn't have the key."

They were poor. Her papá must have discovered the caverns or heard of them from Rafé. Papá wanted the gold for medical care. For the first time in her life, his death has a true meaning. It wasn't a curse, and it wasn't abandonment; it was a sacrifice born of love.

Spinning to catch up with the others, she soon wonders if asking Rafé for guidance was such a good idea. He acts confused, taking them in one direction, only to change his mind and take an opposite route. Sophia keeps redirecting him, calling on him to focus, but he's overly tired, confused. Reaching a ledge where it's not clear how to move forward, Miguel shoots the machine gun into the air, dislodging a few stubborn bats.

"That way." Sophia points with the dying flashlight, seeing a bat head higher.

Climbing with her normal athletic agility, her energy has drained, leaving only adrenaline and panic. Miguel stays close as both the professor and Rafé lag behind. Reaching a dead end, a gap above them drafts air upward, but it's too high to reach.

"Give me a lift," Miguel directs Estefan.

Dropping to one knee, Estefan clenches his palms to give Miguel a foothold and lifts with a loud grunt as the sound of water grows louder.

"*Andale*," she yells. "Hurry."

Miguel groans his way through the opening, then drops an arm to pull up Estefan, needing Sophia to help push on his filthy shoes. Sophia goes next, easily pulled up by Miguel, and then she turns to reach down to help bone-thin Rafé. Deep in the caverns, a slow growing implosion shudders the walls. The roof of the temple chamber must be collapsing. Floodwaters rise rapidly in an enormous roar, pushing up a gush of fetid-smelling air. Sophia grabs hold of Rafé's hand to pull him up, but blood on his hands causes him to lose his grip, falling back to the ledge.

"Rafé get up!" she screams. "Andale."

Miguel drops down an extended arm to help. "Come on, Rafé, give me your hand."

Rafé struggles to stand, looking dead tired just standing there looking at them.

"Rafé, give us your damn hand!" she screams.

Surprisingly, he casually glances to his side, breaks into an enormous smile, and waves as if he sees a loved one. Looking up, he smiles warmly with clear eyes. "Antonio and I are very proud of you, but you must have faith, Sophia."

No sooner had the words left his lips than an underground surge of water smashes him from behind, washing him out of sight.

"Rafé!" she screams, falling partway into the crack until Miguel grabs her. It's too late; there's only rising water. Miguel pulls her up until she's on her own feet again, leaning against the cold stone and sobbing in heaving waves, devastated.

Miguel lifts her face to lock eyes. "Rafé would want you to keep moving. Can you do that for him?"

He's right. She nods tearfully, pushes off the stone, and climbs with what is left of her strength. After a frantic scramble upward another several meters, they dead end.

"In here," calls Estefan, climbing up into a small, dry stone niche that smells of bat guano.

"Is that sunlight?" Sophia whispers, finding her voice. A broken ray of fading dusk shines through a crack several meters above them.

"Beautiful, isn't it?" replies Miguel.

It would be, except there's nowhere else to go. The crevice above them is too tight to pass. They're stuck with a rank ammonia stench permeating the air, burning their eyes and lungs. Huddled together, crammed against the corners, the last light stick fades into uselessness, and the dark shadows envelop them completely. A moment later, the flashlight flickers off.

With a violent shudder of stone, the rancid air rushes out of the caverns in a powerful whoosh, followed by a torrent of water shooting up through the floor hole like a fountain. Quickly overflowing the small niche, the surge slams them against the jagged basalt to the sound of Miguel groaning.

Submerged and saturated by a cold, wet, toxic darkness, Sophia waits for the water to dissipate, praying for forgiveness, praying for Rafé's soul and for Papá's faith. But most urgently, with every ounce of faith that she can muster, she prays for her bursting, burning lungs to hold on to the last foul breath one more second, and for the cursed water to dissipate.

Chapter 64

Sinkhole Tsunami

Isla de Morat

June 20, 8:23 p.m. | 10 hours to Mayan chaa

Darcy bolts back as water gushes out of the rock crevice like a fountain; the rock trembles, and a shallow wave washes over the entire island. Hector screams until the water slides back into the ocean, leaving sand and palm debris everywhere.

Leaping off the rock, Darcy dashes to discover a large sinkhole opening over the shallow bay between Isla de Morat and Isla Barbareta, creating a giant whirlpool as the ocean floods the new void.

"Oh, dear God—" She feels gutted. Aftershocks must have collapsed the cave system. Her chances at a rescue have just sunk into the bay.

"Lady, lady, come back!" yells Hector. "Lady, run quick."

Rushing back to the basalt outcrop, she finds Hector clearing away debris from the lower crevice.

"I hear voices," he cries out. "I hear Sophia. They're under the rock."

Stepping closer, she can clearly hear a muffled Sophia screaming for help.

"Sophie, I hear you," shouts Hector into the hole. "Hold on, girl, we're gonna get help."

A redeeming surge of jubilation and urgency swells up in giggling bubbles as Darcy pulls out the ship radio. "Jackson, Jackson, come in," shouts Darcy.

"Yeah, I'm here," he replies, sounding stiff.

"Jackson, we found them," she yells. "Get a team over here ASAP. Bring the pneumatic hammer, the 3D laser rock scanner, a rescue tripod, the heavy-duty lights, oh, oh, and oxygen tanks with long tubes or something."

"Great news, um, the thing is," Jackson replies, "like, um, we're all under arrest, and like—"

The sound of a scuffle cuts him off.

"My name is Captain Ramirez of the Honduran Navy," interrupts a strange voice. "You and your crew are under arrest on the charges of manslaughter and destruction of private property. I am ordering you to return to your ship at once."

"Captain Ramirez," replies Darcy, "with all due respect, I'm not going anywhere as long as there's a breath of a chance to rescue our lost captain and crew. If you want to arrest me proper, Captain, then you can find me on Isla de Morat, but for God's sake, man, do the right thing, and bring the damn rescue gear, or their blood will be on your hands." She turns off the radio.

Chapter 65

Moment of Truth

Lucia needed fast, high-powered attention, and she got it. Arrested and cuffed again, she told her story to army officers, directed people to the *Washington Post* article, and opened her laptop for more transparency. Government security heads, generals, and admirals from a dozen countries cram into an executive conference room, questioning her narrative. Some call her a spy, a saboteur, a lunatic, or an agent of Nacon. She refuses to take the bait and continues to present her evidence.

During the heated discussion, soldiers confirm her claims about Vacub Came and General Panera, but instead of validating her story, the murder of a well-respected general and a mystery general raises suspicion even higher. Several suspect a hoax and demand validation of the outlandish claims of a buried nuclear device before taking any action. They fear the public humiliation of an evacuation in the middle of the night caught on camera. In

Lucia's mind, they're wasting time that will cost lives.

Without her phone, she doesn't have the exact coordinates but agrees to lead a team. Ten minutes later, escorted between two soldiers, she boards a military helicopter that takes off heading toward a jungle cenote clearing in the middle of the night.

Chapter 66

Comforting Thought

D arcy watches three zodiacs full of equipment and people whoosh onto the shores of Isla de Morat. Brenda, Jackson, Mai, and Juniper, along with Augusto and Chico bring the lights, tripod, rescue, and rock gear in crates. A second tender pulls up full of armed Honduran sailors with scowls. The third zodiac brings a surprise, a unit of US Marines accompanied by a slim, pasty, middle-aged fellow with a Panama hat and a cream cotton jacket.

Juniper escorts the Honduran captain, the pale stranger, and a US Marine captain to Darcy for introductions.

"Dr. O'Sullivan," Juniper states with a serious look. "Please meet Captain Ramirez of the Honduran Navy, who has orders to arrest us."

"Captain," Darcy nods politely to an ice-cold glare.

Juniper quickly turns her open palm toward the slim stranger. "Also please meet Consular Marvin Steele of the US Embassy. State Department has requested Consular Steele to personally represent us and negotiate on our behalf."

Before Darcy can reach out for a handshake, Juniper turns with a smirk to the US Marine captain. "Lastly, at the request of the Pentagon, please meet Captain Jack Diehl of the US Marine Corps, assigned to make sure all Americans are kept safe during the crisis."

"Thank you, Ms. Burns, well done." Consular Steele reaches out a handshake.

"Dr. O'Sullivan, we have a delicate situation here. Witnesses claim you sank a ship that belongs to Señor Juan Perez de Menendez, a very influential man, and a personal friend of Honduran President Hernández. Señor de Menendez was seen last night on his private island, so there are a lot of questions regarding his whereabouts and why his ship was sunk here," he explains.

"I have been ordered to assist in the rescue of your crew," interjects Captain Ramirez, clearly unhappy with the command. "Let me repeat that you are under arrest and will be held accountable for your actions pending a full investigation."

Captain Diehl stands behind the Consular, showing no emotion on a chiseled face.

"Gentlemen," Darcy replies, "I will answer any question and cooperate with any investigation, but right now we need to rescue our captain and crew."

Before anyone can object, she continues. "The whirlpool on the other side of the island used to be a cave system, which could collapse even further at any moment. Right now, we know of multiple people trapped, with at least one injury. We don't have much time, so if you're here to help, then I suggest your men grab those crates and follow me."

Darcy doesn't act like someone under arrest, and she doesn't care; she acts precisely how her father would act in this situation, an oddly comforting thought.

Within minutes, sailors and marines are hauling heavy equipment, while the science team sets up lights, oxygen tubes, cranes, and pneumatic hammers. Bats swoop down on the rescue team as they work, a near-constant nuisance kept at bay by the floodlights, netting, and occasional blasts of machine-gun fire, mainly using the concussive pops to chase off the sensitive ears.

She estimates they will need to cut fifteen to twenty feet of rock while avoiding a cave-in on the survivors, delicate work that will take all night. With a bit of luck, she'll reach Miguel by morning. Energized by the hope, she gets to work, determined not to lose her captain. If he can't sleep, then she won't sleep, and if she can't sleep, nobody will sleep.

Chapter 67

Choices and Regrets

Within minutes of arriving, dozens of military specialists converge on the site with Geiger counters quickly confirming a U-235 isotope and then going to work clearing the sinkhole. Feeling vindicated, Lucia has negotiated the right to stay on site as the exclusive journalist. Aware of the risks, she accepts death on her own terms but honestly hopes it doesn't come to that end. She is placed under the reluctant care of General Ramos Calderon, who orders her to stay in the helicopter, and out of his way.

With confirmation of a nuclear threat, President Lanza had no choice but to order an emergency evacuation. Using military Wi-Fi, she watches media footage of terrified political leaders and executives roused from their beds, drunk or still in nightclothes, rushing to private jets or choppers. Not a good look for any of them.

By the time they clear the sinkhole, the water in the cenote is dangerously murky. A high-tech crane stands over the open hole, lowering a motorized water sled into the water, while a recently arrived US Navy SEAL dive team prepare for a rebreather dive.

Above them, a continuous parade of choppers swoop over the island toward Playa del Carmen, where the military has set up an evacuation control point. Ferry vessels plan to work throughout the night. Other naval and nearby cruise ships are en route to assist in the urgent evacuation. Armadas of citizens escape from the local marinas in small crafts, many dangerously overloaded for crossing the busy forty-five-kilometer channel at night. Even with their best efforts, it will be impossible to get all 7,500 guests, 5,500 troops, 1,500 media, and 175,000 residents off the island by dawn. Once they arrive on the coast, the Quintana Roo roads designed for tourism have already gridlocked. Without adequate transportation, those transported from the island to the coast are trapped in the fallout and tsunami zone.

Admiral David Harris, the US Navy SEAL commander, a lean man in his fifties, paces outside her helicopter. "General Acker," Harris yells above the noise, talking on a secure channel with the Pentagon. "With all due respect, sir, my men are diving into a very dangerous situation already."

General Calderon and Lucia can only hear one side of the conversation.

"No, General, don't get me wrong," deflects the admiral. "The rebreather team will be mask down in five, but I can't understate the risks of sending them into that muck soup."

Listening for a moment, he shakes his head. He changes the topic. "What about the Pakistani? We need that code."

She learned during the heated debate at the hotel that even if they find the stolen warhead, they can't deactivate the device without a specific Pakistani code. Unique to each device, a deactivation code is not something the Pakistanis are willing to send by email or text. Officially, the Pakistanis are in firm denial that a warhead is even missing. Unofficially, a military jet has been dispatched with a Pakistani officer, but even at supersonic speeds, he may not arrive in time.

"I don't give a damn if you strap a ballistic missile up his ass," barks the admiral. "Get him here, or I'm pulling my men and calling the whole damn mission off."

The admiral disconnects and marches over to check on the cenote while he and General Calderon argue over the risks and tactics. With only a few hours left before dawn, her chances of making it off the island alive evaporate, giving her pause to wonder if she made the right choice.

In fact, at this moment, she questions many of her choices in life, such as choosing a career that fed her obsession or leaving a wonderful man to pursue a vigilante justice. Her refusal to continue counseling for childhood traumas or even her choice to leave the church where people didn't understand her, but at least they tried to care. She chose a life of isolation so others wouldn't see her fragility or judge her for her abiding, perpetual pain. Wearing a tough reporter persona was an effective way to cover up the inner core of a frightened, insecure, and lonely little girl.

With all her heart, she wants to talk with Xavier and tell him what an amazing brother, protector, and teacher he's been, even when she refused to listen. He was an anchor in her storm. Unable to say goodbye rips at her heart and could be her biggest regret in a life full of them.

Chapter 68

One Condition

Isla de Morat

June 21, 4:58 a.m. | 1 hour to Mayan chaa

S ophia leans into Miguel's trembling body, huddled together for warmth in the cramped niche. He suffered a bruised rib when the waterspout slammed them against the rock and may be slipping into shock. All of them are in shock, low blood sugar, dehydrated, bruised, shaken, bewildered, and far beyond exhausted, yet by some powerful miracle, they are still alive.

Drenched with the putrid water, overwhelmed by a thousand grisly images and sensations, a single moment replays in her mind, the moment when Rafé spoke of Papá's pride. She hasn't seen Rafé smile in decades, but he smiled wide and waved to someone he recognized. Could he see Papá? Did Papá's spirit whisper her name or confront the drug lord, or was it all a gruesome, hideous hallucination? Beyond depleted and emotionally numb, she can't help reflecting on one simple word, *proud*. She held on to her faith, found a glimmer of light, made it to the end, and now Papá is proud. Growing up alone, the pride of even a deceased parent feels like manna from heaven to a hungry soul. Her throat tightens, too dehydrated even to cry joyful tears. She overcame the curse.

Floodlights and muted conversations float down the shaft, intruding into her pensive reflections. The process of cutting several meters of rock has taken longer than expected. The hammer stops while an argument ensues, then pounds again, only to stop again for yet another debate. No one wants a cave-in, but even while the rescuers try to be careful, a constant flow of gravel creates a cone of debris. After a moment of silence, the loud, severe throbbing of pneumatic hammers returns.

Noxious-smelling water, poisoned with ten thousand years of decay, settles half a meter beneath their niche. Certain the flood would be her final moment; the floodlights above bring an incredible sense of being reborn. Papá, her gubida, heard her prayer.

Dazed herself, she can read the shock etched into the long faces and empty stares of both of her cousins, wondering how to ask the obvious.

"How do we explain what happened, what we saw?" she asks, uneasy with the potential scorn of being called crazy. She doesn't mention the *duprees* per se, but the graphic images continue to saturate her thoughts, impossible to forget.

"We don't," whispers Miguel. "Not to anyone, like ever."

"I thought you two had a theory of magnets, plasma, or something," she says.

"Magnetic mirrors creating a temporal wormhole," corrects Estefan. "A theory yes, but zero evidence. Without the caves to investigate and either prove or disprove the thesis, we would be labeled as quacks or worse."

"If we're honest," wheezes Miguel, "we're not sure what we saw."

Sophia can see his point. It was ethereal, disturbing, physical, intimate, and terrifying all in the same instant. Moments seemed to resonate from inside of her like a vibration on her mind, creating a hallucination. So much of it happened so fast, and always at the edge of shadows. Voices were out of phase and impossible to understand, and the impenetrable darkness distorted everything. Then there were the apparitions who connected with her on a personal, intimate, telepathic level she has yet to discern and still fills her heart with immense sorrow.

"I could live without the gossip." Sophia confesses her willingness to lie, swiftly getting a new perspective on Carmen's deceptions. "So, what do we say?"

"The simple truth," replies Estefan. "You found a valuable historic relic in the family home. A cartel wacko tried to steal it, killed Carmen, and then tracked you until they cornered us. Under duress, you recalled a secret that Antonio taught you as a child. The caverns were deep and deadly, and for the many who went in, few came out. Within the labyrinth, we discovered the reason for the forgotten island pilgrimage. However, the aftershocks imploded an air pocket and destroyed the ancient ruins. Rafé died a hero, and we were damn fortunate to be rescued."

Astonished, Sophia lets his summary sink in. "Wow. It's a little bit scary how you so easily explained the most horrifying day of my life in a matter-of-fact way that completely obscures the terrifying truth and reality of the experience," she replies, wishing it had been that simple.

"Yeah," snorts Miguel with a cringe, "welcome to my world. The man has a gift for spin. It's never what he tells you, it's always what he *doesn't* say that'll kick you in the ass."

Estefan grins. "Guilty, I suppose. I do tend to downplay the risks, but I agree with Miguel on this one. Leave out the specters or any mention of treasure."

Surprised at first, she can see his point as well. Any mention of the plunder would only inspire a new generation of fools to risk death for dreams, perhaps another reason behind the family vow to keep the treasure and the deadly caverns a secret.

"I'm sorry that you lost your reward," Estefan offers Miguel. "You worked a long time to solve the Morgan mysteries."

"Yeah, well, I sure as hell could use a pocket or two of those gems," he admits. "But we solved the mystery. Morgan buried hundreds of souls alive to keep a secret that he was too greedy to share and too superstitious and cowardly to reclaim."

"You were right," Sophia tells Estefan. "Cortés led us on a pilgrimage, a perilous journey where we each had to discover our own personal truth."

"Well said," replies Estefan, reaching into a pants pocket to remove a stone disc, several centimeters in width, featuring geometric lines and angles.

"Here's my truth," he notes with an impish grin.

"What is that?" Sophia asks.

"I found it lying next to the bones of the shaman," he explains. "I think it's called a Bac'tun Tae, a primitive astrological calendar. Unless I'm mistaken, the glyph there identifies the owner, Hun Hanahpu."

"That reminds me—" She hands Estefan her backpack. "I may have found an eyewitness account of what happened."

She had retrieved her backpack from the dead drug lord as they left the altar platform, placing the new book in the bag with the other relics. "It might be a bit soggy, but you have a way with old books. Maybe you can save some of it."

Never caring for the actual relics, Sophia found her answers—not the answers she expected but the answers she needed. Instead of disproving any notion of a curse, she learned how to overcome one. It took faith in herself, the light of family love and a dogged perseverance to keep breathing. A new, strange, warm emotion creeps through her heart—belonging; she has a family.

Finally, the rock crevice above has opened enough to lower a framed rescue harness to the top of the narrow space. Weary smiles spread across filthy faces, the ordeal almost over, although a new ordeal counts down a few hundred miles to the north on Cozumel.

"Okay," calls Darcy from the top of the shaft. "We've lowered down a harness for Miguel."

Miguel shakes his head. "One condition," he winces.

"What do you mean?" Sophia asks.

"I'll get in the harness on one condition," he wheezes the words with a painful, mischievous grin.

Staring at his bruised face, she has to ask, "Did you hit your head too?"

"Not crazy," Miguel replies then pauses. "Okay, maybe a little. Tell her, one condition."

"We're all tired and hungry, son," groans Estefan. "Is this really necessary?"

"One condition," he repeats.

Chapter 69

Rescue Reunion

Isla de Morat

June 21, 5:13 a.m. | 1 hour to Mayan chaa

U nder the hot lights, Darcy stands over the industrial field crane with a cable dangling in the jagged, rocky hole, tingling with anticipation to see Miguel again. Thankfully, Consular Steele and Augusto persuaded Captain Ramirez to transport Hansen by helicopter to the hospital in La Ceiba. That gesture may have saved his life. Now they have other lives to save.

"Before Miguel gets into the harness," Sophia calls up the shaft, "he has a condition."

"He what?" replies Darcy, dumbfounded and too fatigued for one of Miguel's cheeky pranks. Sailors and marines take a break to listen as Mai pulls out her phone to video the scene.

"Not the time for pranks, Martinez," scolds Darcy. "Get in the harness."

She can't believe the audacity. Her cheeks flush with embarrassment as sweaty sailors' snicker. A whispered debate echoes up from the cut rockshaft.

"He'll get in the harness if you agree to marry him," Sophia's voice calls out with an embarrassed exasperation.

"He wants—if I … what?" she stammers.

More whispered arguments echo up the shaft as sailors, and even the stone-faced marines' smirk and chuckle around her.

"I'm sorry," replies Sophia. "He may be going into shock or something, but he says he's not kidding."

"No one will blame you if you say no, dear. He may be delirious," calls Estefan.

The sound of mumbling floats up the shaft from below.

"One hell of a time to ask such a personal question," retorts Darcy. "And quite inappropriate." She wants to get mad over the sheer public humiliation alone, but there are too many eyes and Mai's video. A beat of silence passes. *Okay, two can play this game.*

"Well, it's rather difficult to say, really," Darcy teases out. "Marriage is a very serious decision one should never take rashly." Although she suspects that nuance may be completely lost on Miguel.

Darcy pauses a beat. "To be quite honest, I was really holding out for a chap with a nicer boat," she calls down with a simper, "or perhaps, someone willing to buy a bloody coat so he could visit his fiancée's family home."

Mai gives Darcy a thumbs-up as Jackson laughs aloud before stifling his chuckle.

"I say you call his bluff and let him sit here a while. He's been cranky all day," Estefan calls. "We don't have a condition. We're ready."

Darcy has no way of knowing why Miguel would ask such an important question now. The man has no sense of propriety, turning everything into a joke. She can't imagine he could have learned about her pregnancy. No one knows. He always spoke of finding his treasure before making a serious commitment to anyone. Is it possible the family legends were true? Despite the awkward situation, Miguel would not ask that question as a prank. She swallows her pride, embarrassment, and irritation. After almost losing him today, she won't test her fate again.

"Okay, yes. Yes, Miguel, I will marry you," Darcy calls into the hole. "Now get your broken arse into the harness before I come down after you."

Applause erupts from the sailors and marines, giving her an unintended blush.

The cable tightens. "Okay, he's ready," calls Estefan.

Jackson works the winch as the motor slowly drags the cable through the ragged gash, lifting the harness into the fresh blowing breeze. As soon as Miguel clears the rock, Darcy helps him out of the harness. Unable to resist, she pulls his filthy, weary face to hers for a long kiss as applause erupts again from the rescue team.

"You *do* know you're going to pay for that stunt," she whispers in his ear.

Miguel smiles a weak grin. "Yeah, I know. Did Mai get video?"

Celebration fades as work to pull out other survivors continues, and Darcy helps Miguel hobble off the rock over to the medical cot, where Augusto waits with a tired smile.

"Hola, captain, my name is Dr. Augusto Morales, Sophia's cousin. Thank you for bringing her home safely." Augusto offers a hand to shake.

"More of a family shipwreck really." Miguel accepts the hand with a flinch.

"Looks like you've had a rough day." Augusto grins, helping him to sit.

Miguel lifts his eyes to Darcy. "It could've been worse."

She couldn't agree with him more. Marines and sailors erupt in new cheers, pulling all eyes to Sophia emerging from the hole, looking as if she swam in muck.

"Chico, Hector!" screams Sophia, practically leaping off the rock. "I thought you were dead," she weeps as they all embrace together.

"Mari and the kids, are they okay?" she asks, to a vigorous nod from Chico, as she reaches out an arm to Hector with more tears of joy.

After a long moment, she pulls back. "I'm so sorry, Hector," she cries. "I had Rafé in my hands, I had him, but then he got swept away. I'm so very, very sorry."

Close friends his whole life, Hector breaks into fresh blubbering until they all bawl together, holding each other tightly. Augusto's eyes grow red, but he continues to care for Miguel.

Estefan emerges next to more cheers, greeted immediately by Jackson in the standard warm, thankful embrace of a colleague; a two-Mississippi hug, two back pats, pull back, and a friendly tap to the shoulder. Darcy grins at the universal male ritual.

"Estefan, great to see you, buddy. You had us all shitting bricks, dude!" exclaims Jackson, before he steps back, pulling his fingers to his nose. "Whoa, speaking of shit, like major shower time. Hold on, which way is downwind?" Jackson changes position.

"Jackson, it was amazing!" exclaims Estefan, ignoring the reaction, and excited as a student. "We were right—the ancient myths were based on the meteor impact. A remnant survived."

"Cool, dude, cool," responds Jackson. "I can't wait to hear the whole story over a beer. You know, after you smell better. Seriously, I'm talking a really, really long shower. Maybe a steam clean or a car wash," he complains, holding his nose, leading Estefan to another cot, handing him a protein bar and fresh water.

Estefan exchanges the protein bar for the Bac'tun Tae, devouring the bar in two bites before gulping the water. Jackson's eyes go wide, handing Estefan a second bar.

"Holy crap on a cracker, dude, we're gonna need like at least three pitchers for this one!" he exclaims. Estefan grins and nods. "Wait, is that, is that what I think?" He points to the name.

"Yup, you're holding the star map of a mythical god," Estefan beams.

The rescue crew realizes that no one else emerges from the shaft. Neither Xavier nor Hugo survived. Darcy watches the truth wash over Mai's face as she pivots into Brenda's chest with her hand to her mouth. Brenda gently holds her friend, who trembles in muffled sobs.

Turning to Miguel, his damp eyes sadly confirm the tragic news. Before he can ask, she conveys the other bad news. "Hansen's in a coma at a La Ceiba hospital," she tells him. "He saved us, Miguel. Hansen saved the ship; he saved everyone."

Miguel looks down, absorbing the information, then after a long moment, he lifts his gaze. "Then I guess I owe that man everything. I sure hope he takes an IOU."

At the mention of Hansen, Sophia scurries over to get an update and then arranges for transportation to La Ceiba with the consular. As soon as Augusto gives Miguel enough painkillers, he wraps a thick layer of gauze around his chest. Still sweaty from his rescue efforts, Captain Ramirez approaches them, joined by Captain Diehl, also sweaty and fatigued.

"We've just been ordered to Cozumel for an emergency evacuation," states Captain Ramirez. "I am authorized to release you into the custody of Consular Steele, pending the investigation. You and your ship are ordered to remain on Roatan until further notice."

"Thank you, Captain. They will be in my charge," Consular Steele accepts the responsibility. "Pass on my gratitude to Admiral Vega and President Hernández."

"Why are they evacuating Cozumel?" asks Darcy.

"Because megaship wacko-jack plans to vaporize the island at dawn," mumbles Miguel, apparently feeling the drugs.

"How could you possibly know that?" asks Consular Steele, looking surprised.

Captain Ramirez also stares, then checks his watch. There's not enough time for him even to make it to Cozumel, meaning his job will be to evacuate survivors.

"Long story." Miguel turns to Captain Ramirez. "Captain, do you have any way to find out if a woman named Lucia Vasquez made it off the island?"

"Lucia Vasquez, the reporter?" replies Consular Steele. "I believe she's under military arrest."

Miguel lowers his head with a short chuckle. "Yeah, that would be the right Luci."

Darcy stares, waiting for an explanation, but he shakes his head. "Xavier's sister; I'll fill you in later."

"I'd like to know a few of those details myself." Consular Steele raises an eyebrow. "Once you've rested, perhaps."

Captain Ramirez and his crew rush back to their ship while the marines stay behind to help repack gear. Unable to leave Honduras, Darcy forces herself to let go of any residual hope of completing the Panama project on time, which means her chances at tenure have fizzled overnight. She should be upset, but she's not. Instead, she helps Miguel toward Chico's waiting zodiac.

"Okay, Skipper, let's get you back to *Plunder* before I have to scuttle you both," she jokes. Miguel smiles just learning that the *Plunder Lust* still floats. It could've been worse.

Darcy lifts her eyes to the still dark northern sky and wonders if the worst may yet be on the way. If dawn brings a new crisis for the region, at least this time she and Miguel will face the crisis together. She needs to tell him.

Chapter 70

Cenote Cave In

Cenote Cocodrillo, Cozumel
June 21, 5:52 a.m. | 20 minutes to Mayan chaa

From the relative comfort of the military chopper, Lucia works on her unexpected final story about the courageous men risking their lives to save Cozumel. Admiral Harris stands over a communications station in near-constant contact with the dive team, while General Calderon paces the clearing, yelling final evacuation orders into a radio.

She details the terror of her abduction, her miraculous escape, and the hours after her surrender facing the mindless waste of time by politicians; fools, debating tactics to avoid looking foolish while innocent lives were on the line. Her story features a heroic narrative of the US Navy SEAL dive team, who disappeared into the muddy cenote waters to save an island not even their own.

After finding the device, the SEALs also found two dead divers. They started their return trip over forty-five minutes ago, now racing against the coming dawn. With still no word from the Pakistani officer, their chance of survival slips away with every passing second, making the heroic efforts so much more tragic.

Evacuation efforts to airlift diplomats and the media completed an hour ago. All nonessential military personnel, except for core evacuation and nuclear teams have withdrawn. The army had to subdue a riot at the ferry docks, while the private marinas have completely emptied. Jets continue to board at the airport. Navy ships previously conducting sonar scans are now hosting citizens and moving offshore. Tsunami warnings have gone out for the entire region down to the Honduran coast, including the Bay Islands. More ships head toward the area but are unlikely to arrive in time. So close to dawn, no new ships dare approach the island, but stand off a safe distance, waiting to assist survivors.

General Calderon estimates that roughly seventy thousand residents remain on the island. Most of the remaining citizens attend emotional prayer services in jammed churches or at the Mayan ruins. Lucia imagines Eugenia refusing to leave the island and attending one of those services at this very moment.

Her thoughts drift frequently to Xavier, with a growing uneasiness over his lack of communication since yesterday, but without her phone, she has no clue if he responded by now. If so, he must be worried sick by her last messages and her lack of response. Always her protector, Xavier alone truly understands the irresistible pull of her obsession and her endless battle with childhood trauma.

If Vacub Came was surprised to learn of his hideout, then perhaps Xavi is still okay and just out of cell range. If so, then he'll be devastated to learn of her fate. She had always imagined that once they removed the Nacon shadow of death, they would evolve into a normal family with kids and cousins and holidays together. Now, none of that will happen for either of them. She prays Xavier survives and can find some happiness, love, and forgiveness for a sister who ran into the fire. If only she could hear his voice, even one last time.

She ponders her padre, his lessons, and his passions. He once thought of becoming a priest until he met her mother. A stout, devout man, as a journalist, he taught her to pursue the truth, regardless of the cost. He would say that a life built on lies, even little ones, is a life cut short of its true potential. But his rigid moral code cost him his life and orphaned his children. Camille also perished before her time because of a neurotic need to speak the truth. Even Xavier lost his freedom to a slavish obligation to honesty and integrity. Truth may be overrated.

World news and the internet inundate the average viewer with an endless stream of misinformation in a digital tsunami of deception and delusion, while she paddles a canoe of truth upstream. History reprises the paradox that true cultural change requires sacrifices by brave men and women; a tragic and thankless fate for most. Will the world remember her sacrifice, or will she be one of those easily forgotten statistics? She smirks at herself, realizing how vain it is of her to consider.

She truly envies those able to live a life of naive acceptance of whatever they are told, whether from their church or school or government. They blissfully live each day as if their small life was all that really matters, and they share an enviable sense of peace from a false security. Ignorance may not exactly be bliss, but pursuit of truth or justice can be a personal curse. No one can live too long with their eyes open and not die or choke off inside from the corruption.

There is no lonelier place than to wake up one day and realize that while you may still believe in a few selected individuals, you've lost your faith in humanity overall. Her eyes have been open for far too long, and her heart has been dead for the same lonely eternity. No one wants to be alone, and she never wanted to be a hero. She only wanted to feel safe, like it felt before her parents and her spirit were charred black.

A flutter on the radio draws her attention to the communication station, where Admiral Harris stands rigid and tense. "Team Alpha, say again," he says into the mic. Squelch and static respond until she can hear, "… partial cave-in, visibility near zero. Our guideline broke, over."

Her veins turn cold, and the hairs on her arms stand up. General Calderon rushes over to the radio station, drained of blood with his eyes wide. "They can't make it back in time without a guideline. We need to evacuate the site before it's too late."

"Abandon my men? Like hell I will," snarls Admiral Harris. "I go when I take my men with me."

Two eyes burn into each other until Calderon spins, huffing back to his chopper to make a radio call in private, probably to complain about the irrational American admiral.

"Team Alpha, do you still have functional GPS? Over," shouts Harris into the radio.

"Affirmative," squawks the response.

"Use the GPS replay function to retrace," Harris orders. "Careful, boys, we only get one shot. Over"

"Roger that, over," comes the reply.

Harris paces behind the communications station, waiting for the report that his team cleared the muck. An unfortunate setback that will cost precious minutes, the same minutes that could mean life or death for seventy-five thousand souls, Lucia's among them. Minutes that could change history.

Lucia turns her attention back to her story to make sure she captures the disturbing turn of events as a way to distract her mind from the morbid, self-centered brooding.

Chapter 70

Intimate Confession

Plunder Lust, Isla Barbareta
June 21, 5:57 a.m. | 17 minutes to Mayan chaa

Without her crew, the *Plunder Lust* feels lifeless, hollow and empty like a rusty old shell. Miguel offered the professor, Hector, Chico, and family a cabin until the investigation completed. His ship has always been a refuge for those who needed to rebuild a life, and he sees no reason that should change now. After not talking for a decade, it looks like he and his dad will have ample time to catch up and maybe move past the past.

With a vow to return and check on his patient, Augusto headed back to Roatan aboard the med boat, which came back for him after filling the island morgue. Consular Steele and Sophia both returned to La Ceiba on board a marine helicopter, where Sophia plans to stay with Hansen at the hospital. A US destroyer has anchored ahead of *Plunder*. Expecting a possible tsunami, Captain Diehl posted a marine watch in case they need to move offshore quickly.

At the transom, Miguel takes a long hard look at the mega-yacht still glistening off the predawn water, hoping the huge wreck isn't sitting on top of the old wrecks, unsure if it even matters. Like his dad, he risked lives to check out a treasure, but it's over now. With Darcy at his side, they gaze toward the imminent catastrophe ticking down on the northern horizon.

"Do you think we'll see the explosion from here?" Darcy wonders.

"Who knows," he replies, "but I'm sure we'll feel the ramifications for years to come." In a few minutes, the world will change for decades.

Unsure what comes next, he knows that Darcy agreed to marry a broke, used-to-be salvage hunter, and from there life can only get better. After all, he's always been a lucky man.

On the way to his cabin, Miguel stops by Xavier's cabin.

"Give me a minute." He kisses Darcy on the cheek. "Meet you in the cabin."

After a momentary glance of concern, she smiles sadly and turns away. Over the years, Xavier had become one of his closest friends, like a brother. As he does during every mission, Xavier left his cell phone on the bunk. Now he understands why. The screen shows several recent messages from Lucia, and it rips at his heart knowing that Xavier missed the chance to save her. The shame he laid on the shoulders of the professor for so many years now falls onto him. If she's under arrest, then they probably evacuated her off the island by now, and confiscated her phone.

With a heavy sigh and a bitter tear, Miguel responds. He's not sure if she will even get the message, or when, but it would be better that she hears the news from a friend, someone who loved her brother deeply. Emerging moments later with moist cheeks, red eyes, and Xavier's cell phone in hand, he finds his cabin, where his fiancée waits patiently.

She nudges him into the hot shower to wash off the foul stench. He lingers a very, very long time to allow the steamy water to wash over his sore muscles, cuts, and bruises while a thousand dark haunting images flash across his mind's eye. Quivering from the terror, rage, shame, sorrow, and helplessness he refused to feel earlier, every suppressed emotion vent in spasms, jolting his nerves, jerking his muscles, and twitching his neck. Breathing erratically, his fists clench against the cold tile as steam purges him of the unexplainable, penetrating sensations. Aware of Darcy watching him through the glass, patiently waiting for his tremors to end, he forces himself to breathe until slowly the stench of purgatory washes away.

Cleansed body and spirit, at least for the moment, Darcy helps to rewrap the gauze and ease him into the bunk, crawling in next to him.

"When you proposed to me earlier," she asks, biting her lip, "did you know?"

Head on the pillow, Miguel can barely keep his eyes open. Her voice sounds distant, like an angel. "Know what?" He should pay attention; this sounds important, but his eyes won't cooperate. He's drifting.

"So, you really don't know?" she prompts again.

His eyelids flutter and close. "Huh?"

Her lips draw close to his ear. "You're going to be a father," her lilting, musical voice whispers, soft and tender.

The words must be a dream. A few hours ago, he was crawling through the blackest, most terrifying hellish catacomb on earth, and now an redhead angelic vision murmurs wonderful, and intimate secrets into his ear. Unworthy of the angel, no one can question his good luck. Ever since he was a boy, he's been destined to find lost treasure; engaged-to-an-angel lucky.

With an enormous effort, he manages to flutter open one eye with a weak grin. "Cool," he whispers, "a mini-you."

His eyes close, nodding off when her lips press against his. "So, Captain," she coos, "does this mean you found your treasure?"

The world may soon change, but he discovered his one truth, his one light, his true north, and he won't let her go.

"Yup," he mumbles, falling asleep. "Holding them both now."

Chapter 72

Mayan Chaa

S killed fingers flutter over the keyboard, polishing the final story of Lucia's life with a renewed sense of purpose. After hours of despair and morbid self-pity, she has come to accept her chosen fate, somehow sensing that she was born to be here at this moment. A lifetime of feeling out of place, a misfit, unlike the others, haunted by a past she could never change, she finds her true purpose in documenting the final heroic hours to save Isla Cozumel, so the world will remember.

"Ms. Alvarez," General Calderon approaches her. "We located the *Túumben Epoca*. The ship sank in a bizarre incident off Honduras. Interrogation of the surviving crew claim that Señor de Menendez went missing on a private island near Roatan, but a search turned up no one."

Disappointed, she had hoped they would arrest the dangerous psychopath before he escaped. Xavier mentioned a Nacon threat last night, and she wonders if the *Túumben Epoca* could have been that threat. Her gut tightens.

"Was there an American salvage ship involved in the incident?" she asks.

Calderon looks startled. "Actually, the report mentioned dozens of boats, but yes, an American salvage ship was involved," he confirms. "There were a number of casualties on both sides, but I'm afraid I don't have many details."

Lucia's heart sinks into her stomach at the news.

The general reaches into his pocket. "Also, we found your phone on General Panera's chopper. I thought you may want to use it for last-minute calls." Hanging his head, he turns back to the cenote.

A new text from Xavier sends a shot of joy into her weary heart until she actually reads the text, and realizes the message does not come from Xavier. Her elation quickly shatters into utter heartbreak and despair. With no pulse, her breathing freezes, she feels suspended in time, and her vision spins in vertigo. Lucia inhales a stammering, stilted breath as her trembling fingers types a response.

Yes, if I survive. Send.

Devastated by the confirmation of Xavier's death, Lucia barely notices the high-speed chopper approaching until it lands in the clearing. Using her phone, she livestreams the final moments for history. The helicopter door slides open to show an anxious Pakistani officer sitting under the dome light. Admiral Harris and General Calderon rush to confer with the new arrival, pointing to the empty sinkhole and the silent crane.

Clinging to a thick stainless-steel briefcase connected by handcuff to his narrow wrist, the anxiously sweaty Pakistani doesn't want to be here. No one does. She quickly adds a new scene to the ending of her story and checks the time; less than three minutes. Breathing deeply to calm her growing distress, she tries to stay present and alert, knowing she will be the eyes of the world.

A flurry of movement and shouting from the cenote grabs her attention, panning her video to capture the heavy-duty tripod whining to hoist a dark-gray watertight container the size of a wide coffin. Mexican soldiers rush to swing the container to the side of the hole, gently setting it down next to men with blowtorches, who immediately go to work cutting open the container seals.

With only forty-eight seconds remaining to dawn, she streams the video live to her official Facebook page, but her hands and the video tremble.

Leaping from his chopper and landing next to the container on his knees, the Pakistani opens his case with a biometric retinal scan and code key. As soon as torches wedge open the watertight container, soldiers open the lid to reveal a warhead.

The Pakistani connects a cable from his case to the warhead control panel and types a memorized twenty-six-character command sequence. When his trembling hands make an error, the panel flashes red.

Lucia glances down—twelve seconds remaining. She hits send to her story, now terrified she waited too long, but continues to stream the scene. The Pakistani curses, takes a deep breath and tries again, more slowly and deliberately. He only gets two tries, but she fears he won't make it in time.

The clearing goes silent as generals, SEALs, and soldiers bow their heads, mouthing silent prayers or crossing themselves. Above the treetops, the sky changes hue from dark marine to deep cobalt and then softer shades of blue.

Lucia hasn't prayed in years, but she closes her eyes as the dawn begins and the video continues to livestream. Soon all of her anxieties will end. She won't feel anything. All of her trauma, self-doubt, and loneliness will be gone; no more sleepless nights, no more nightmares, or fear of shadows hiding in the dark.

Her thoughts drift back to childhood, to a more innocent time with her papá, her mamá, and Xavier together at the shore, all of them safe and loved; her little moment of heaven on earth.

Chapter 73

Four Billion Men

Martinez Historic Home, Roatan
June 21, 9:41 a.m. | 3 hours and 34 minutes after Mayan
chaa–One Year Later

Sophia woke up highly energized and looking forward to a packed and joyous day ahead. It took nearly a year of rebuilding after the earthquake, but all of the remodeling finally feels warm, fresh, and home again. Comfortable and familiar, mixed with a new look for a new beginning, and completed just in time for a family wedding reception. Family, the word still sounds foreign, exotic, and somehow—magical.

A dozen buckets filled with the fragments of hibiscus and birds of paradise lie scattered around the kitchen, filling the home with an intoxicating aroma. Outside the enlarged kitchen window overlooking the terrace, she enjoys the new look of bamboo poles suspending white sails, casting overlapping triangular shade. Beneath the sails hang strings of white lights to create a festive atmosphere after sunset. Under the cool shade, tables with chairs wait for guests to arrive, each featuring a floral centerpiece. Emilio and his local reggae band set up a dance floor while Liz Beth sets up a cocktail bar against the rebuilt rock wall. Down in Oakridge, Mona and Mari create a Garifuna *Beluria* feast of chicken, cassava, and Hudut in coconut. All of her dear friends doing their absolute best to help her new family feel a traditional warm, Roatan welcome. From death came life.

As Carmen had foreseen, the money found a way to rebuild the house. Estefan arranged a generous stipend from UCLA to study the valuable shell and dagger, both of which were over thirteen thousand years old. Her newfound regional fame doubled her cruise line excursion business, especially for the new tours run by Emilio to visit Isla de Morat and Isla Barbareta.

When she rebuilt the wall, she re-hid the broken compass along with a written testimony of everything she had experienced within the pilgrimage to Xibalba, a way of purging the memories for a future generation to ponder. While Carmen died dirt poor, her uncle Rafé died surprisingly wealthy, owning the deed to an entire island, Isla Barbareta. Apparently, Montego bought the island around the same time he built the family home, a wise man who wanted to keep the family secret a secret from the family. Rafé inherited the island after Franco and his older brothers died or disappeared. She inherited the deed from Rafé, along with a La Ceiba bank-deposit box, which contained 394 gold coins worth thousands each.

In the cashbox was a note written by Montego, dated 1808, warning his descendants of the evils of greed that incur the wrath of the Spaniard. Montego urged his descendants to see the caverns as sacred, guarded by a pure evil. Before her ordeal, she would have completely dismissed that warning as superstitious nonsense, yet now she can never forget the unearthly screams, malignant laughter, or the final terrifying moments on the altar.

The inheritance carried conditions. The island must stay in the family and remain undeveloped, an oath passed down since Paulo, meant to ensure the sacred pilgrimage stays undisturbed. Montego had removed the curse pages from the book and included them as part of the inheritance until Joaquin took the pages when he fled to America. Sophia never imagined the family curse was a literal inheritance. Even the word *curse* has lost its sting, deflated of the imagined evil and replaced by a very real one, but an evil she overcame. Even so, she agreed with Estefan to keep the curse, the journal, and the island separated.

Through the same legal firm that protected Rafé's identity for so many years, she made all the arrangements with her new caretakers, Chico and Mari Lavoie, allowing Hector to retire. The entire Lavoie family will continue to live on the island rent free for life, limited to three hunts. With a handful of the inherited coins, she had her attorney rebuild the island shacks, adding a modern central kitchen, septic system, and showers. During construction, Chico found a second cache of gold coins and raw gems hidden under Rafé's hut, the treasure that went missing after Rafé returned home alone. When the island attorney didn't claim them for the owner, at Sophia's insistence, she encouraged Chico to buy a new seaplane. He bought a used red-and-silver Grumman that purrs like a kitten and swims like a swan. Encouraged by his good fortune, Chico earned his pilot's license, and Chico Air was reborn.

The front door swings open, leaving a six-foot-seven shadow that dims the room for a mere moment. Ducking under the door lintel, the mountain of a man strides over the flower buckets to catch Sophia by the midriff, lifting her off her feet as her wet hands push against his chest, getting his shirt wet, but he doesn't care. The real reason for Sophia's newfound joy in life; Hansen, Captain Hansen.

"Okay, sugar lips," he greets, stealing a kiss. "I got the Jeep all loaded up. Brenda and Juniper are headin' down to decorate the schooner," he explains, stealing another kiss she eagerly returns. "I'm gonna head over to *Plunder* and check on Skipper. You know, for last-minute best-man stuff."

"You mean, make-sure-he's-on-time stuff," Sophia corrects him with a kiss.

"Yeah, that's what I said." He kisses her again, lingering. "I'm mad, crazy, wild about you, girl."

His little saying that she never tires of hearing, a new twist on the word *crazy* she can warmly embrace.

"See ya soon," he promises.

"Not soon enough," she repeats her normal reply.

With a flash of his dimpled smile, her feet touch the floor, and he's gone, swift and agile for a man his size. After the battle of Barbareta, she spent weeks shuttling between Roatan and the La Ceiba hospital, while Hansen recovered from a concussion, cracked jaw, two broken ribs, and internal bleeding. Still weak, he needed a safe, quiet place to recuperate from his injuries and resurfaced PTSD, so she moved him into her semi-finished home to care for him, a huge leap of faith for both of them. Except for time spent together at the hospital, they had never really dated, and the home still had no roof. Even so, it took four long, tense months before she couldn't resist her urges any longer and seduced him one night on the terrace, unleashing a volcanic passion that still erupts with little warning.

Around her ankles, she feels the familiar warm, furry rub of the other new family member.

"Ya, Ziggy," she coos. "You just missed him. Snooze, you lose, *gato*." While Ziggy avoided Carmen like the plague, the stray tabby instantly attached to Hansen, sleeping at his feet and following him around the house. Perhaps another sign that they both belong here.

After the wedding, she plans to propose. A bold move, and not the least bit traditional, but it's perfect, the act of a bold woman freed from her shadows and no longer afraid of the unknown. Blushing off the kiss, she focuses on cleaning up for the wedding. Afterward, Big Rig had better have lots of energy saved; she feels an eruption rumbling.

*

Old French Harbor, Liberty Star Schooner
June 21, 7:18 p.m. | 13 hours after Mayan chaa–One Year
Later

Leaning back, Darcy sips champagne from a cut-crystal glass in the elegant captain's quarters on board the *Liberty Star*, a 127-foot three-masted schooner restored to her original elegance, and featuring the kind of master's quarters a proper bride should expect. The romantic honeymoon suite was a wedding gift from an anonymous and grateful citizen. Music on the main deck above intermingles with guest conversations, the clinking of glasses, and laughter.

Darcy wanted an evening wedding to capture the breathtaking Roatan sunsets and the coolness of the breeze. Of course, there was considerable discussion about having her wedding on the anniversary of losing so many dear friends. In the end, she and Miguel both wanted to redeem the tragic memories with layers of joyful ones stretching into the future. Each anniversary will be a triumph, a celebration of love, endurance, a rebirth, and rediscovery. Well actually, those may have been her words, not his.

A light rap on the varnished mahogany door precedes Brenda peeking into the cabin. Darcy holds a finger to her lips, then points to baby girl Morgan sleeping peacefully in a bassinet on the lush queen-sized bed, the gentle rocking of the ship having a tranquil effect on the infant.

"Your dress looks sinful," Brenda whispers.

"Why, thank you." Darcy smiles, standing to admire herself in the mirror, noticing Brenda blush in the reflection. The late-1920s satin gown features hundreds of strategically placed mini-pearls over white satin, so tightly fitting, shimmery, and sheer, it clings to Darcy's every curve.

"I discovered this dress in Hollywood years ago at a vintage store called Golly Esther," Darcy explains with a smile. "It once belonged to a silent film star. I've been saving it for years." Miguel will love it, others will be jealous or self-conscious, but she doesn't care; she's celebrating having her figure again.

"How's Morgan today?" asks Brenda, peeping into the bassinet.

"Delightful," Darcy boasts. "She has my sweet disposition until she's irritated, and then she sounds like Miguel." The sleeping infant features a tuft of Darcy's auburn hair.

The Honduran investigation ended in time for Darcy to fly to England to give birth. True to his word, Miguel came with her, and the scruffy sea dog fell in love with the manor house. He even bought a nice overcoat, gloves, scarf, earmuffs, and long underwear for the frigid fifty-degree weather. Adding a cane, he calls it the "Sting thing." With a few gold coins in his pocket, he learned to pull them out whenever he felt the need to impress the sedated London elite with an adventure story, just as Henry Morgan regaled the aristocrats of his day.

Mai pops her head in the cabin door with a light rap. "Oh my God, you look radiant!" she exclaims. Everyone points to Morgan with a scolding glance to stay quiet. Mai blushes.

"Thank you," Darcy replies, beaming. "Is Jackson ready?"

Jackson had begged for weeks to do the ceremony, even getting a minister's license online to make it legal. Miguel couldn't see the harm. Darcy caved in to the pressure.

"He looks like a church clown, but sure, let's call that ready," replies Brenda.

"I'm doing the right thing," Darcy asks, needing a little last-minute reassurance, "right?"

"If you mean a crazy-ass plan to marry Peter Pan, yeah, you're dead-on, sister," smirks Mai, smelling of wine.

"I hear you were granted tenure," Brenda changes the subject. "Congratulations."

"Thank you," Darcy replies. "So far, we've pulled over two thousand tortoiseshell scripts and hundreds of icons out of the sand. It'll take an entire lifetime to study them."

After Darcy lost the contract for Morgan's ships, she used Hansen's shell, ship's bell, and the log of Cortés to win a separate project, funded by Cambridge to excavate the *El Oro de Isabella*. The ship contained the ancient tortoiseshell scripts and idols from the lost library of Mayan prophet Chilam Balam. Thousands of years of missing pre-Columbian history, once they learn how to read them. She pours more champagne for everyone to celebrate with muffled laughter.

*

Old French Harbor, Liberty Star
June 21, 7:47 p.m. | 11 hours after Mayan chaa–One Year
Later

Sophia surveys the scene on deck with a wedding planner's eye. Guests mingle with drinks and laughter as Marley, Santana, Sting, and the Beatles rotate in play over the speakers. A red runner lined with flowers sets off the starboard side, reserved for the bride. Blue canvas drapes the deck from the forestay boom to the stern to create a shaded canopy.

A light breeze pushes on the massive hull, causing them to drift slowly toward the outer harbor. Hundreds of island vessels including powerboats, dive boats, fishing boats, canoes, and sailing yachts surround the beautiful schooner. The island armada has come to witness the wedding of the American and British couple who saved Sophia and sank the cartel invaders, considered local heroes.

Everything is perfect, except for the missing groom, but she has faith Hansen will get him here soon. With everything under control, she joins a conversation with Estefan, Jackson, Augusto, and Juniper. During negotiations between the US and Honduras, Augusto and Juniper stayed in touch. Working with the consulate during the investigation, Juniper developed a good relationship with Honduran President Hernández, who was grateful to be alive after the near disaster on Cozumel. After Honduras cleared the crew of *Plunder* of any charges, the US State Department offered Juniper a diplomatic post in La Ceiba. Since then, she and Augusto have become inseparable.

"After the failed attack on Cozumel," Juniper continues, "authorities raided the de Menendez island estate offshore Colombia, and found evidence of a vast continental coup, including corporate takeovers, military sleeper cells, extortion videos, thousands of stolen artifacts, and more. They even found and arrested the real Juan Perez. There were so many corrupt players involved that it created a ground swell of political change across the region, with thousands of arrests and hundreds of new elections. I thought it would be a good time to be a part of reshaping US relationships," explains Juniper, leaning back against a grinning Augusto.

"Congratulations again," offers a smiling Estefan. "The region sure needs fresh leadership."

Augusto turns to Estefan. "Speaking of fresh, I heard you published another book?"

Estefan smiles. "Yes, coauthored actually," he clarifies, "with Dr. Healy and Dr. O'Sullivan. It's called *Shadows of Xibalba—A Geologic View of Mayan Mythology.*"

"We're flying off the shelves at the UCLA bookstore," notes Jackson with a sardonic grin.

"What's your premise?" inquires Augusto.

Estefan takes a sip of his Pacifico. "The originators of the Mesoamerican calendar were an ice-age civilization from a land called Matwiil who were destroyed by the Younger Dyras Impact Event. At the time of the impact, Roatan was a mountain ridge surrounded by a fertile wetland, standing against a deep ocean trench. Asteroid plasma waves and tsunamis wiped out the civilization and transformed the mountain into an island. I theorize that a small remnant of survivors made it to Altun Ha and passed down the five-thousand-year calendar technology."

Augusto nods, seeming to understand the basic premise. Sophia remembers his lecture and video from a year ago and can never forget the horrific visions of the catastrophe within the catacombs. With a deep breath, Sophia sheds the memory to take great pride in her scholarly cousin and enjoy his deep, velvety voice, still warmly reminiscent of Papá.

"What perspective did Dr. O'Sullivan take in the book?" asks Juniper.

"Good question," remarks Estefan. "She demonstrated how stories from the aftermath of the meteor became the Polpul Vuh creation and Xibalba myths."

"Not sure I follow," Augusto admits.

"The Polpul Vuh claimed three cycles of creation before the Spanish arrived in 1518. Dr. O'Sullivan aligns each cycle of the long-count calendar to a mythical epoch of creation and then aligns those epochs to the destruction caused by known catastrophes starting with the 12,800 BPE impact. She then correlates the myth of Xibalba to the aftermath of a natural disaster with plagues, sores of pus, blood, broken bones, disease, starvation, and war over dwindling supplies. She postulates the characters of the Polpul Vuh such as Hun Hanahpu and Xibalque were real people in an epic battle for survival."

"Fascinating," says Augusto, turning to Jackson. "What about you, Dr. Healy? What part did you write?"

Jackson smiles. "Oh, dude, I got the cool part! I restored and translated a journal Sophia found in the caves that describes how a lost pilgrimage became a mass grave."

Sophia grins. "Oh yeah, I almost forgot about that book. What'd you learn?"

Jackson sips his Dos Equis and smiles. "Whoa, like a wicked-cool story. After the sack of Panama City, John Searles and the crew of the *Cagway* never returned to Jamaica. Instead, Searles took his cargo to the forbidden caves discovered by Edward Morgan, Henry's uncle, thirty years earlier when he conquered Roatan. Searles had no clue that Henry Morgan would also cheat his men and planned to use the same forbidden caves. Searles had already unloaded his cargo when Morgan arrived with hundreds of crew, slaves, and tons of cargo. Searles planned to hide, wait for Morgan to leave, and then move the entire plunder elsewhere."

Jackson takes another sip of beer. "When Morgan discovered Searles, a fierce battle erupted inside the caves that centered on control of the plunder. When Searles managed to escape, Morgan gave chase but destroyed the exit behind him, entombing over 450 souls alive."

"What happened to the people?" asks Juniper.

"At first, men died to control the treasure, and then they fought to control the dwindling supplies of food or access to clean water. Crude booby traps left by someone else killed others, while the wounded died of a scorpion infestation. After a while, men fought over any hope of an escape route, and then the final survivors died of starvation or cannibalism."

"If Searles escaped, who wrote the book?" asks Sophia.

Jackson takes another sip. "Simon Le Sueur, the *Cagway*'s first mate, who I think went insane during the ordeal. The dude spoke of evil spirits and hallucinations of devastation. I mean, this dude wrote some really weird stuff."

Sophia holds her tongue, realizing for the first time that Simon had also witnessed the same horrid visions and ancient duprees.

"Yeah, cool huh, get this," says Jackson. "In his last entry, Simon wrote about a vision unlike the others, a beautiful, angelic mulatto woman with hazel eyes who came to ease his pain and lead him out of purgatory. To win her favor, he planned to blow the angel a kiss. Is that cool or what?"

"Truly fascinating!" exclaims Augusto as he and Juniper glance to Sophia, who matches the description of the angel.

She can only grin and shrug, but the truth catches her breath. Simon Le Sueur had seen her before he died. Her mind tries to grasp how that could be possible, glancing to Estefan, who looks down, unwilling to discuss what they had witnessed. A wild thought occurs to her that maybe by ending the curse for her family, she also ended the curse on the other poor entombed souls, including the peasants, the pirates, and even Papá; maybe she freed them all.

"I'm confused," interjects Augusto. "If Morgan's treasure was loaded into the caverns, what are Hansen and Miguel excavating off the Barbareta reef?"

After Honduras and Belize cleared Miguel of criminal charges, he negotiated a contract to salvage the two ships Hansen discovered off Isla Barbareta, fortunately not destroyed when the mega-ship sank.

"Hansen believes that when Morgan escaped the caverns with a skeleton crew," she replies, "he was unable to either unload or sail the other two ships. Rather than let anyone else have the treasure, he sank his own ships."

The discovery enabled Miguel to pay off his debts, buy a second used ship, which he renamed the *Hugo Xavier*, rent a cabana on Roatan for his growing family, and make Hansen a full partner. Sophia grins to realize that with another island saga, another Martinez played a key role.

"Speaking of pirates—" Augusto points to the gangway steps. "Here comes the groom."

Chico brought them over on his new zodiac, which had pulled up quietly to the *Liberty Star*. Sophia can't help but love the new, stealthier Chico. Miguel has become one of Chico's best customers and a close friend.

"Estefan," she nudges, "you need to go escort the bride." She points to the captain's quarters.

"Oh, oh yeah." He gulps his beer and darts toward the stern companionway.

Hansen and Chico appear on the main deck with a pale, sweaty-looking Miguel locked arm in arm between them. Behind the men arrive a radiant-looking Mari and her beautiful eldest daughter, Cerra, who had agreed to watch Morgan during the ceremony. Lastly, Miguel's newest crewmember, Anton Sanchez, steps onto the ship.

After the political fallout of corruption and sleeper cells came the seemingly endless trials. With the trails came a string of Nacon assassinations to silence witnesses. Xavier's sister, Lucia Vasquez, the reporter who broke the story and won a Pulitzer Prize, vanished without a trace. The official report claims she disappeared into the jungle seconds after dawn on Isla Cozumel. Her ex-husband, Marco Vasquez, claimed the Pulitzer in her place. Not long afterward, Anton Sanchez joined Miguel's crew to replace Xavier as ship's security officer. Much like Xavier, Anton stays on the ship most of the time, avoiding public places, making today's appearance a rare exception, perhaps explaining the fedora and sunglasses.

Hansen and Chico make a beeline to the bow of the ship, where Hansen positions Miguel at the prow, standing guard behind him as best man. Chico and Mari find a spot next to Augusto and Juniper. At the forecastle, Jackson wears a black-and-purple satin robe purchased from an online store, looking comically monkish with his shaggy hair and Waldo glasses. Sophia queues up the music, Bob Marley's "One Love."

From the back of the ship, Mai and then Brenda emerges with graceful steps down the red runner toward the bow of the ship. A moment later, a beautiful bride appears on Estefan's arm. Sophia admires her new family, none of them more than a little crazy, and she can handle a little insanity.

Together, they stroll up the aisle as Sophia joins Augusto and Juniper in front to admire the moment. Brenda and Mai gracefully line up in place. *Perfect so far*, she thinks.

When Darcy catches her first good glimpse of Miguel, trembling and pale with large drops of sweat dripping down his forehead, she whispers to Estefan, "Is he okay?"

"He can't run. You got him in your sights. Take the shot," he whispers back.

With a raised eyebrow, Darcy ignores Miguel's nerves and proceeds to the altar. Sophia has seen Miguel face down deadly drug lords, horrifying apparitions, and certain death, making his nervousness now seem just a little bit comical and typically male.

"My son found a woman as beautiful, strong, and brilliant as his mother. Welcome to the family," whispers Estefan, kissing her on the cheek.

Estefan joins Hansen as the second groomsman, a testimony to how much Miguel has learned to forgive. Abuelita would call it *aharihabu,* a spiritual healing that binds a community.

"Good afternoon," Jackson starts the ceremony. "We're here today to join two dynamic individuals into one unstoppable force of energy."

Jackson admires the handsome couple. "A year ago, many of us witnessed this sea dog ask this world-renowned, brilliant Cambridge scholar to marry him. He was filthy, banged up, and pretty smelly," he jokes to a few chuckles.

"None of us would have believed she said yes, except well, Mai caught it on video." A few more chuckles percolate. "And then it went viral." Louder laughter erupts.

"Is this normal?" Augusto whispers to Juniper who holds her finger to her lip for silence.

Darcy takes Miguel's still-trembling hands.

"Now Darcy," Jackson says with a serious face, "there are four billion men in the world. There are tall men, attractive men, well-educated men, rich men, strong ones, smart, funny, good dressers, and nice smellers. I mean seriously, the possibilities of whom an incredible woman like yourself could attract are almost endless. Think about it." He pauses.

General confusion rolls over the ship. Sophia doesn't always follow Jackson's odd humor.

Augusto bends down to whisper again. "No, really, this doesn't sound right."

Juniper shushes him and reaches over to take his hand. "He's making a valid point."

Jackson continues. "I know, I know, too many choices can be confusing." He grimaces. "And let's face it, we all fear buyer's remorse, so I want to make sure you're really, really, absolutely, positively, no returns, no regrets, and one-in-four-billion sure you want to marry this one," Jackson says with a straight face, nodding toward the pasty, sweaty groom. Chuckles intermingle with hushed, horrified gasps.

Hansen leans down to whisper into Miguel's ear. "He's funny."

Miguel looks up with a numb, baffled stare.

Darcy gives Jackson a defiant gaze. "Oh yes, Jackson, I'm quite positive," she states with confidence. "I take Miguel to be my husband."

"Really?" he reacts. "Four billion is a lot of men. Your odds alone—"

"I know the math," Darcy interrupts him with a smile. "Move on."

Jackson grins at Miguel. "You dodged that one, dude."

Hansen leans down again. "Snap." Miguel just rolls his eyes.

"Now, Miguel—" Jackson gathers his thoughts. "Of the four billion women in the world, I gotta say, you're one lucky pirate. I mean, seriously dude, billions of women could visit *Plunder* and—"

"Jackson!" Darcy cuts him off with a forced smile.

Hansen chuckles, winning a rebuking glare from the bride. Sophia shoots him one as well, but he isn't paying attention. Choosing Jackson for the ceremony may have been a mistake.

Jackson turns back to Miguel. "Miguel, will you take Darcy to be your wife, no conditions, no regrets, and no complaints?"

Miguel gazes at Darcy, hesitating an awkward heartbeat.

"Ahoy," calls a pompous British accent.

No one had noticed the large, expensive yacht tender pull up to port, piloted by a tanned, pudgy man in a pink polo shirt, Bermuda shorts, and a yachtsman cap. "I noticed you were drifting. Should I call the harbormaster for you?"

Sophia glances downwind to see the prissy-looking superyacht still a hundred meters away. A self-entitled visitor not invited to the party who decided to crash anyway.

Juniper steps up to the railing. "Excuse me sir," she reprimands. "We're trying to have a wedding here, and you're being quite rude."

The man brushes her off, sipping his cocktail, probably not his first. "A wedding? Well then," he snickers, "I suppose you need more far help than I can offer you."

His comment pulls Brenda and Mai up to the railing, but he continues to blabber before they can reply. "You know, I've been married four times." He points to Juniper. "And that blonde with the fire in her eyes looks like a truly sweet number five."

He blows her a kiss as Augusto steps to the rail, and the stranger shuttles back to his yacht, leaving nearby guest boats to bob around in his wake.

Sophia spots Miguel pivot into an immovable Hansen, unwilling to budge an inch.

"I can swim," he whispers.

"Maybe later," says Hansen. "The man asked you a question."

Enormous hands spin Miguel back around like a ragdoll, wearing a nervous smile until his eyes lock with Darcy's, and his face softens.

"Yeah," he rasps. "Damn right I do. I take Darcy for my wife. No conditions, no complaints."

Darcy and Miguel exchange rings with still-trembling hands as Jackson puffs out his chest. "By the power vested in me by a church I found on the internet, I now pronounce you husband and wife." He holds out his arms like a rock star. "You may kiss the bride."

Hansen nudges the trembling Miguel a step forward until their lips touch and then linger much longer than she expected. A polite giggle spreads across the deck.

"Ladies and gentlemen," Jackson calls, not waiting for them to finish, "Allow me to present to you a very kissable Miguel and Dr. Darcy O'Sullivan Martinez."

He waves up his hands for applause that erupt on the ship, and across the bay of boats. The crew turns up the music as people on deck begin to sing and dance to Bob Marley's One Love.

Sophia nervously keeps her eyes on the bride until the kiss finally ends, and Darcy leans in to whisper, "You okay?"

Miguel takes a deep breath. "I am now. I thought he would never shut up."

Darcy smiles wide, simply nodding her head.

Hansen leans down. "Darcy, I've never seen a more beautiful bride, honest."

Sophia adores her polite gentle giant, but she sees a little mischief in his smile. With a wave, she tries to catch his attention, but he's not looking her way.

Darcy beams. "Thank you, Hansen."

Hansen takes a quick glance toward the sun resting on the hills above French Harbor. Sophia panics, trying harder to get his attention, shaking her head, and waving her hand. They discussed this several times. He should leave the couple alone; it would be inappropriate at a wedding.

Hansen wraps his huge hands around Miguel's shoulders. "Dr. O'Sullivan-Martinez, may I please borrow your husband for a few minutes? I promise to bring him back in one piece. You know, so we can go back to doing all the weddin' stuff."

"Okay, Big Rig, but he had better not smell bad." She grins. "I have plans for him later."

Hansen holds up breath mints with a big-dimpled smile and gently pulls Miguel out of her arms, pointing him toward the stern deck as the sun falls toward the hilltops of Roatan.

"Come on, Jackson," calls Hansen from over his shoulder. "Chico, come on, man. Hey, where's Anton? Anton, little buddy, light 'em up," Hansen waves to the new crewmember to join them.

Augusto stops Jackson. "What's all this about?"

"Ship tradition." Jackson shrugs. "Come on, join us."

Estefan, Chico, Hector, and Augusto, along with other guests, follow the groom to the expansive rear deck. Sophia doesn't spend much time on the ship, but Hansen once told her about the sunset ritual. She can't imagine why Miguel would allow this silly superstition during his wedding.

Embarrassed and annoyed, as any wedding planner would be, Sophia steps up to Darcy with a self-conscious apology. "I'm so sorry, Darcy. I told Hansen not to bother Miguel."

Others join Darcy with the bridesmaids to comfort the poor bride, joining in the offense at the ceremony interruption. Other guests join the men on the aft deck, each lighting up a cigar without saying a word or being gently hushed. Jackson, Hansen, and Anton hand out cigars, nodding silently as men pass around bottles of vintage rum, whiskey, vodka, bourbon, and tequila. They shush any talking, smoking side by side, drinking shots, and gazing at the sunset in silence.

"I've never understood this silent sunset ritual thing," complains Brenda.

"Some stupid macho bonding," snipes Juniper.

"I don't care," Sophia snaps. "It's not right for a wedding."

"At least they're bonding downwind." Mai pinches her nose, not enjoying the cigar odor.

"They're not even talking," Sophia points out, confused. Unwilling to make a scene at the wedding, she and Hansen are about to have their first fight tomorrow.

Darcy takes a deep breath. "As long as I've known Miguel, he's taught this ritual to his crew. One cigar, and a stiff drink at sunset in silent memory of loved ones lost along the way. No talking, just remembering, always at sunset, the moment his mother passed away," she enlightens her friends.

"For the longest time, I considered it nothing more than an anti-social excuse for a cigar, and a stiff drink without the need to engage with anyone," Darcy confesses.

Sophia contemplates the anniversary of so many deaths of family, and friends, and brave strangers, and can appreciate the desire to remember them. The Garifuna hold ancestors as sacred. Miguel made remembering them a part of his daily routine, a good Garifuna heart if she ever knew one. Yeah, he's a pirate, but he's also a good man. She had misjudged him.

Darcy stands in silence, looking every inch like a jilted Hollywood goddess of a golden era, then turns to her guests with a smile. "Excuse me a moment, ladies."

Without a word, Darcy sneaks up next to Miguel and reaches seductively into his coat pocket, earning an excited glance of surprise. Pulling out a cigar, she uses his cigar to light hers, and then turns quietly to gaze toward the silhouetted hilltops. Wrapping his arm around her waist, his gaze lingers on his beautiful bride a long moment before turning back to the sunset with a wide smile.

Within moments, Brenda steps up next to Jackson, pulling a cigar from his pocket. Juniper cuddles into Augusto's arm, sharing his cigar. Mari nudges next to Chico, refusing to smoke. Mai holds her nose until the whiskey passes, and then she takes two swigs. Sophia nuzzles under Hansen's arm to share his cigar. After a good hit of the bourbon, she passes the bottle to Anton, the prettiest man she's ever met. Anton smiles with a wink and a swig, passing the bottle on. Sophia wraps her other arm around the newest member of the family.

"You be home now, Luci girl, no need to be hiding who you be," she whispers into Anton's ear. "Ya girl, now you be loved, *mi itu*."

Silent tears roll down Anton's cheeks as she leans into Sophia for a hug, two orphans who now belong. The remaining guests stare in silence, unsure of what to do next until one by one, the entire wedding party and the entire armada turns to enjoy the sunset with a silent toast.

Under Hansen's protective arm, Sophia's thoughts drift to Papá and Mamá, young Timothy, and old Sally, and then she dwells a long time on cranky Carmen and crazy Rafé and the many voices of her gubida. In so many ways, the curse died with them, but not their voices of faith. Sophia will always live with the knowledge that each new day, and each new sunset that she gets to enjoy cost the selfless sacrifice of men like Moses, Ben, Dave, Hugo, Xavier, and Rafé; all of them heroes. From death came life, just as Mamá once promised. Nestled in the arms of a fresh beginning, her newfound faith only deepens.

As the sun falls behind the hilltops, the iridescent clouds of yellow, tangerine, and purple transport her to a magical place. Surrounded by the love of friends and family, she discovers where she belongs. Perhaps, now that she thinks about it, belonging is the only true treasure ever worth seeking.

THE END IS THE BEGINNING.

Epilogue

Backstories to Curse of Cortés

Curse of Cortés integrates multiple factual and historical events of the colonialization and inquisition of the Yucatan, which lasted from 1521 to 1565. The savage acts, which brought war, disease, and slavery, cost the indigenous peoples an estimated 150 million lives over fifty years.

There are two key backstories that did not make it into the body of the book *Curse of Cortés*, but which encompass significant elements of the epic.

The first story involves Chilam Balam, an actual Mayan prophet who foresaw the coming of the Spanish roughly thirty years in advance of the arrival of Hernán Cortés. The prophet also told of a darkness that would follow the end of the thirteenth Baktun, which occurred on December 21, 2012. Following his vision, legend claims that Chilam Balam hid a massive library before his death. That library has never been discovered and may have escaped the flames of the Inquisition.

The second story that lurks quietly at the heart of *Curse of Cortés* is the story of Pedro Montego Cortés de Alvarado, the insane Inquisition executioner who wrote the bloody logbook found by Paulo Martinez. While Pedro Montego Cortés is a fictional character, I pulled all of the key elements of his life from a book called *Ambivalent Conquest* by Inga Clendinnen. *Ambivalent Conquest* provides a detailed historical account of the savagely brutal days of the Spanish conquest, colonization, and Inquisition.

I wrote Curse of Cortés in part to expose the insidious evil done in the name of god or done in the name of superstition and ignorance. No act of hatred, oppression, bigotry, deception or violence in the name of any religion is true religion, but a perversion of truth. There are no exceptions, only deviant actors with silver tongues. In the end, the Curse of Cortés is about redemption from darkness.

This epilogue will provide a narrative account of the events that led Cortés into a such a demented and sadistic insanity.

Palace of the Jaguar

Tulum, Yucatan - 4 Ahau 5 Tumku (AD 1492)

Born of priestly descent, his elongated skull a sign of his birthright as high priest, Chilam Balam has come to enjoy the many honors of being *k'uhul ajaw*, the divine lord, the chief prophet of all the Yucatec kingdoms from as far north as Chichen Itza to the ancient kingdoms of the south in K'o, Labaantun, and the rugged Mosquitos.

He has chosen to escape the stifling heat of Coba to spend the summer at the priestly temple of Tulum on the Caribbean coastline of Quintana Roo, near the sacred lagoons of Xel Ha. The temple lies less than two days' journey by canoe to the sacred pilgrimage at Ixchel on Cozumel. The constant cool breeze, and the freshwater cenote made Tulum the ideal summer palace.

Away from the politics, vanities, and ceremonial demands of the daily Coba sacrifice, Chilam Balam prefers the tranquility of mediation and the study of the ancient codices. Originally from Chumayel, but trained by a master in Tizimin, Chilam Balam was blessed with the political savvy to forge priestly alliances across the multiple city-state kingdoms of the Mayans, Toltecs, Aztecs and other peoples of the region. His efforts to unite the spiritual leaders while declining a position of regional power has increased his influence greatly. He is not a ruler but a seer.

Excitement bubbles across the Tulum compound today. A group of scribes have just returned from a quest that has taken them two years. A treacherous, deadly journey from which, sadly, only a handful of the original travelers have survived. A journey that he commissioned, and whose deaths lay on his shoulders. As a result, the survivors will be generously rewarded.

Chilam Balam would have gone himself, the quest nothing short of a lifelong honor, except for his age and poor health. He sent them in search of the secret cave known only to the Peche of the ancient island of Roa. He sent them to search for the catacombs of Xibalba, to the tomb of Hun Hanahpu, the hero twin.

But he sought more than a legend; he sought a legendary script. Not just any script, he sought the most sacred of all scripts, the Xeb'utik Ilol re, the Eyewitness to the Flood. Written on a tortoiseshell stela, the shell gives an account of the day Bolon-Yokte destroyed the second creation of the world, and how the third epoch of the world began with death.

The surviving quest leaders, Mani and Aapo, have presented their findings to the delighted eyes of their *k'uhul ajaw*. With solemn respect, they have presented the large tortoise shell filled with an ancient form of the sacred script carved carefully on the polished interior, still legible, although the shell has yellowed dark with age.

"We found the shell next to the remains of Lord Hun Hanahpu, who guarded the ancient library in the catacombs of Xi, near the temple altar," Mani reports, his head remaining bowed.

"Many of our comrades were lost in the underworld. The nine death lords of Xibalba were vicious, my Lord. It took great sacrifice to retrieve the wisdom of the gods," adds Aapo respectfully. He can read terror flash over the eyes of his men. Legends of the terrifying spirits of Xibalba have haunted the dreams of men for ten thousand years.

He smiles, and *k'uhul ajaw* rarely smiles. Mani and Aapo have kept their eyes bowed, but a large bowl of reflective water lay between them, allowing them to behold their master without the insult of a direct gaze. He catches Mani smile in return, but only for a second.

The glyphs are so archaic that Chilam Balam isn't even sure he will be able to translate the stelae, until he finds the one glyph he desperately wants to see. "Xi Bal Xeb'utik, the Desolation of Xi," he reads aloud.

Since his youth, Chilam Balam has acquired a large collection of sacred codices for his personal studies. His library bears the accumulated wisdom of nearly eight thousand years of astronomy, math, sacrifice, and prophecy. Many of the codices in his collection were one of a kind, recopied and preserved from the originals. By comparison, the codex he holds in his hands is holy, written directly by the hand of a god. To read Xeb'utik Ilol re will be a spiritual revelation.

A shiver of excitement momentarily surges through him. Even though his students keep their eyes lowered, he can't imagine they had not already attempted to translate the shell themselves.

"You have done well, my children, but under penalty of death, you must never speak of what you have seen on this stele," he admonishes them.

"Yes, Lord," they readily agree.

Knowing they had not seen their wives in two years, he has compassion on them. "Now go and enjoy your wives, and commune with your children. Feast and celebrate, for you have been gone for many moons."

Under other circumstances, he would celebrate with them, but in truth, he wants to be alone to read the shell and ask the gods for a vision. After a simple meal, his faithful servant Xtaca enters the temple sanctum to light the oil lamps. He sets a fire on the temple summit overlooking the ocean to ward off the cool night air. Then Xtaca prepares a bowl of steaming mushrooms with sacred herbs and roots used only by the priests.

Chilam Balam hangs his head over the bowl to deeply inhale the steaming aroma. He sniffs raw tobacco through his nose and then returns to the bowl to blow out his nostrils and then inhale the steam again. Over and over, he repeats the ritual.

As the drug takes effect, he leans back to stare into the sunset reflecting off of the cobalt ocean, illuminating the distant clouds. Typical for Quintana Roo, the sunset radiates with spectacular color, shadow, and dimension in the distant clouds that tower to the sky. Tonight however, the splendid sunset has been cut in half by an ominous black storm system passing far to the south.

To the sage shaman, a split sunset is a bad omen. Just as the last ray of sunlight bounces across the distant horizon, instead of finding a flat line of cobalt, the light catches like a flash of fire as it reflects on the white wings of a large serpent rising out of the water and blazing for the briefest of moments before being swallowed by the twilight. Chilam Balam gasps in surprise.

He ponders the portent as the mushrooms allow his mind to ascend into the spirit realm. He falls into a deep trance to experience a powerful, vivid, and horrifying vision. The death pains of an epoch succumbing to the hand of archers, men riding beasts, famine, disease, and fire in the shape of a cross. Old gods and rituals crushed under the boot of new gods of armor and iron reeds that spit fire. His trance continues for hours, witnessing millions of deaths. At the end of the epoch, the vision takes a terrifying twist with the arrival of the nine lords of Bolon Yokte who bring a great darkness following the thirteenth Bak'tun.

Emerging from his trance with a frightful scream as if from a terrible nightmare, he stares with wide-open eyes, breathing heavily, still under the influence of the mushrooms. It takes Chilam Balam several moments to reorient himself to the familiar surroundings of his private temple, drawn by the aroma of the incense and the sound of the ocean.

From the palace promenade below the temple, he can hear the celebratory sound of music and laughter from the returning survivors. Disturbed from his vision, Chilam Balam gazes back toward the horizon, now saturated in deep sapphire blue with the light of the Sacbe, the Milky Way bright and brilliant.

He pulls the ancient shell in front of him, anxious to read. His eyes widen, and his heart races; sweat beads down his forehead as he imagines the revelations described in the script. By the time he finishes the codex, the sun has begun to rise. He now understands his omen and his vision. Chilam Balam knows what must be done; he needs to prepare before the coming of the burning cross. He needs to secure the secrets of his ancestors.

Xtaca enters the temple to extinguish the lamps, surprised to find his master still awake, but he bows to deliver a report. "The temple court servants are ready, My Lord. The sacrifice is ready, a slave captured from Tikal caught stealing our maize." Xtaca waits for his instructions.

Chilam glances down at the codex in his hand. He can no longer sanction the sacrifice of human life after reading about the desolation of Xi'. He understands only now how far the Maya have distorted the wisdom of the ancestors.

"There will be no sacrifice today," he insists as he stands. "Cut off his hand and set the slave free."

Xtaca stands a moment in shock, unsure that he really heard the command correctly. Chilam Balam looks on him with a mild grin, knowing he has just confused his faithful servant.

"No death today, Xtaca. I have seen a vision. The gods do not demand it," he assures. "Instead, summon my scribes and all of my servants. We must act quickly to obey the gods. The serpent is coming, and Kukulkan rides on his wings."

He thinks a moment. "Tell them to prepare for a journey. Collect every codex, idol, and sacred text in the palace," he commands Xtaca, who knows better than to question the reason behind any order. "We will leave in the morning," he declares before he dismisses the servant with a wave.

Xtaca hesitates. "Master, forgive me. How long of a journey shall we prepare to take?" he asks with his head lowered.

Chilam Balam considers for a moment. "A very long journey, first to Mani, then Chumayel, then Naj Tunich, and then Cozumel to the tomb of the hero twin."

Xtaca bows his head and pivots to obey.

Chilam Balam takes a long, lingering look around his beloved palace overlooking the surf of the Caribbean. His heart aches, but he is resolved in what must be done. He places a fresh deerskin in front of him and begins to write.

> *"In the time of 4 Ahau 8 Tumku a great desolation will come from*
> *the seas. A serpent with white blazing wings. A new epoch will come*
> *with archers, with disease, and with fire. Approaches our master,*

Itza. Your brother is coming now. Receive your bearded guests from the east, bearers of the standard of God.

"*Then it will happen—darkness. Bolon-Yokte will descend to the great waters. The Thirteenth Bak'tun will be finished (on) Four Ajaw, the Third of Uniiw (K'ank'in). Darkness will occur. It will be the descent of Bolon-Yokte of the Nine Strides to war and death. Then in the final days of misfortune, in the final days of tying up the bundle of the thirteen baktuns on 4 Ahau, then the end of the world shall come and the katun of our fathers will ascend on high ... These valleys of the earth shall come to an end ... I recount to you the words of the true gods, when they shall come.*" **Chilam Balam of Tizimin**

Codex of Cortés

Orphaned Mestizos | 1546 CE
Labutaan, Belize

I entered into this cursed, wretched life under the given Spanish name of **Pedro Montego Cortés de Alvarado**. Conceived by rape and born the Mestizo bastard son of conquistador Captain Diego de Alvarado and his Nahau servant girl, my na' Llana, who was a warm, kind soul. In contrast, my padre Diego was the lazy, drunken, illiterate half-brother of my uncle, Conquistador General Pedro de Alvarado y Contreras, who left a savage legacy across Guatemala, Honduras, and the Yucatan.

During his many raids of conquest, Diego would abandon us for long periods of time without provision. It was during those early years that na' Llana secretly taught me the Polpul Vuh and the ancient ways of my people. She compared the sacrifices of the Maya to the bloody cross of the invaders but feared the wrath of the Franciscans, who forbade any teachings, rituals, or idols of the old religion.

We lived in humble peace until Diego would return, and with him came an unrelenting drunkenness, sadistic cruelty with backhands to my face, boots to my knee, or straps to my back that seared deep into my skin and even deeper into my spirit. So na' Llana and I rejoiced the day we learned of my padre's death by the Inca. Sadly, our joy ended on a dark afternoon, when Fray Juan Pizzaro arrived with orders of the Bishop of Yucatan to rip me from of the arms of na' Llana. Tied together with other Mestizo boys, I listened to her mournful wails as we were marched out of the village like captives. For weeks we trekked until our feet bled, and we reached the monastery at Mani, hundreds of miles away.

With a shattered heart, completely terrified, they told me that I was destined for salvation from the demons of the Maya religion. My penance would be to serve the friars, their holy pope, and the Christ of the bloody cross. Like mi padre Diego, the monks demanded an unyielding, unmerciful obedience, with swift and cruel retribution. I endured the beatings much better than the other boys, having grown used to the inhuman treatment under Diego. They taught me to read and write in Spanish so that I would be more useful. In truth, we were Mestizo, half-bloods, filthy and polluted, little more than slaves to the Franciscans, savages to the colonials, and traitors to the Maya. I learned early that mine was a cursed destiny, born of the being born half Spanish; rejected by both cultures and by God himself.

*

Spark of Intolerance | 1562 CE

Mani, Yucatan

During the fall of 1562, a fellow Mestizo and I stumbled into a cave located in the remote hills surrounding Mani. Within the cave we found dozens of idols, shell scripts, and deerskin codices, all of them forbidden by the monks. In a wild race back to the monastery, I won the honor of reporting the hidden cache to Fray Pedro de Ciudad Rodrigo, in the hopes of gaining favor or extra rations. Within days, the Fray called on my help to load several mules with the taboo icons, to bring them back to Mani. It was not long before the bishop of Yucatan, Diego de Landa, traveled from Merida to investigate the discovery. A lean man with cold, dark eyes, the bishop immediately reminded me of the dark soul of mi padre Diego, striking a deep fear into my heart.

I must confess, I never imagined that my small act of obedience would ignite such a wildfire of religious fury, yet within months, Bishop de Landa had destroyed hundreds of the treasured idols. With a fierce, righteous indignation, de Landa began to torture local villagers to force a confession of other hidden caches of idols or codices. Many of the tortured blamed my betrayal for their suffering, and they cursed my name for the loss of their sacred icons. Yet, Fray Pizarro absolved me of my sin.

Over the next few years, as my body grew strong, my spirit grew dark and fierce. Soon Fray Pizarro conscripted me to execute the brutal interrogations and tortures of their holy inquisition. I became the masked face of terror for all of the New World. In the name of the Catholic God of mercy, and under the direct orders of the monks or the bishop, I committed unspeakable atrocities against my own people to satisfy the unquenchable zeal of foreign holy men. On direct orders of Bishop de Landa, it was my own hand that lit the bonfire that destroyed tens of thousands of ancient and sacred codex scripts. Ancient writings of math, astronomy, architecture, and mythology with some codices thousands of years old, and yet all of them deemed the work of the devil by Bishop de Landa.

I silently wept over the ashes, until I was ordered to force feed those same ashes to the children of the shaman to coerce his confessions of yet more hidden idols. So saturated in unholy malevolence and scorched by the flames of intolerance that my very soul became seared as black as a Franciscan robe.

*

Judgement Cometh | 1565 CE

Tulum, Yucatan

The judgment for my sins came late in the summer of 1565, when Bishop de Landa sent me with Fray Luis de Villalpando to find the lost library of the Mayan prophet Chilam Balam. Widely respected among the people, my na' Llana had taught me how the prophet saw the coming of the burning cross decades before the conquistadors arrived.

"Approaches our master, Itza. Your brother is coming now. Receive your bearded guests from the east, bearers of the standard of God." He remembers her reciting the prophet.

After a vision, legend claims that the aging prophet hid his private library of ancient scripts, idols, and codices within two days' journey of Tulum, and so our quest began at the Temple of Tulum on the shore of the Caribbean. The local shaman, a respected man with four wives and twenty-two children, received us as honored guests, yet he strongly denied the legend was true.

Callous and distrustful, Fray de Villalpando challenged the man, but when the holy man refused to cooperate, I was ordered to mutilate the healer's naked wives one by one with lacerations over every part of their body, including their intimate parts. With each slice, the shaman was given a chance to repent, and with each refusal, I cut another wound. Both Fray de Villalpando and the shaman ignored the countless screams and desperate pleas until the women were so bloody that they were unrecognizable. Bawling in tears, the shaman still refused to give up the sacred temple location.

Undaunted, Fray de Villalpando ordered the shaman to witness as I fed the half-dead women to ravenous alligators, who fiercely fought each other over the bodies, tossing and ripping them until they were submerged under the water to tenderize. Heaving sorrowful sobs, growling his hatred, the shaman would not repent.

Even my own jaded heart raged at his cruel stubbornness. By order of the friar, I tossed all twenty-two children, two at a time, alive into a pit of wild, hungry dogs. Holding the shaman by his hair, I forced him to watch the mongrels rip the innocent lives to pieces until their screaming ceased beneath the devouring beasts. The shaman begged for death, cried for mercy, and pleaded to replace his children. Yet he would not betray the sacred temple.

Throughout the daylong, dreadful ordeal, the pious Fray de Villalpando stood solemn and silent, stone faced, refusing each and every cry for mercy. I confess to God that the barbarism of that day shredded the last fragment of my own humanity, slipping me over an edge of evil from which there can be no forgiveness, no redemption, and no absolution. Enraged by the shaman's willfulness, and disgusted by the cruelty of the monk, I held the man's feet to a fire until they were blackened and bloody stumps. Near death, in unbearable pain, the holy man finally relinquished his battle and agreed to lead us to the lost temple hidden on the island of Cozumel. By midnight, I had the brutalized holy man loaded onto our ship.

*

Cursed Spittle | 1565 CE

Isla Cozumel

Reaching the coast of Isla Cozumel by sunrise, we carefully bypassed the village and Temple of Ixchel, wishing to avoid a conflict. Marching deeper into the jungle we ended at a rustic wooden ladder that descended into a semidry cenote. Within the dark tunnels, I discovered a semi-submerged temple. Within the temple walls we found an archaic stone sarcophagus surrounded by thousands upon thousands of idols, scripts, and other offerings of clay, gems, jade, and gold. The sarcophagus and many of the offerings were far too old to be those of the prophet, yet stored nearby in pottery vases, I found thousands upon thousands of tortoiseshell scripts, tree bark, and deerskin codices. The secret library of Chilam Balam.

Instead of a celebration, the putrid stench of a rotting corpse filled the cenote and drew me deeper. Beyond the temple, to my utter horror, I found the half-naked victim draped over an ancient altar, left to rot, her bare chest still ripped open. Despite my years of vicious butchery, I quavered at the sight. Never in my most horrid nightmare did I dream of discovering the lifeless, murky eyes of my na' Llana. She once claimed to prefer the sanctity of sacrifice over slavery to the bloody, vile Spanish. The local shaman granted her a dying wish.

An uncontrollable fury erupted within me. Grabbing a nearby ceremonial dagger, I slammed the shaman's head onto the cold stone to face the lifeless eyes of my mother. Still defiant in his spirit, the battered shaman spit curses in my face. The bloody spittle sent a spike of icy terror through my black soul, as if el diablo had reached into my chest and crushed my still-pulsing heart. With a terrifying shriek, I slashed the shaman's throat with the obsidian blade left on the altar of the heathen god.

Horrified by such a sacrilegious murder in such a profane place, the Fray unleashed a vehement reproach upon me. Yet consumed by my fury, I ignored the hypocrite to lead the other Mestizos on a rampage to plunder the temple. When the local villagers learned, and foolishly resisted, I led the slaughter of every man, woman, and child.

By nightfall, a dozen mules of contraband were loaded into the cargo hold of *El Oro de Isabella*. I stood on the bow as we pulled anchor and set sail for Campeche Bay to get provisions before embarking to Merida. I still held the dagger firmly in my grasp, tingling with power and still wet with blood.

Saturated with shame, I wallowed in self-loathing over who I had become. Cursed as a child, then cursed by my own savage hand, and now cursed by the bloody spittle of the holy shaman, I am become the face of evil. I am the face of death.

*

Fury Unleashed | 1565 CE

El Oro de Isabella, Western Caribbean

By morning, an unexpected storm had descended upon our ship, and for another thirteen days, I witnessed no sign of sun, moon, or land. We were lashed by the seas until all souls on board fell into despair, claiming our cargo was cursed, when I knew the curse was on me.

Near midnight on the fourteenth day, an explosive crack of splintering timber violently shook the ship and tossed every man hard onto the port deck. We had run aground. Across the listing cabin, I saw the lifeless body of Fray Villalpando smashed against the bulkhead, his neck twisted unnaturally, dead. A glowing light disrupted my shock to notice candles had fallen over and set fire to charts and spilled wine, quickly spreading the flames.

As I raced to the main deck, the fierce howl of the gale and the sharp sting of rain made it difficult to see. Tangled bundles of broken rigging lay haphazardly across the slanting deck while surging waves crashed over the starboard rails, flooding the ship even faster. A snapped mizzen had fallen over the main companionway hatch, condemning dozens of screaming men still trapped below.

I spotted our only shore boat dangling over the leeward side of the ship, suspended by halyard lines. Two sailors wrestled to drag the boat closer to the ship, but they fought against the fierce wind that blew the dinghy away; a vain and useless struggle. In an act of desperation, I ran toward the railing, jumped onto a downed spar, and then leaped into the swinging shore boat. The powerful winds grabbed my body and slammed me hard into the wooden frame, injuring my hip and leg and forcing a howl of pain that was swallowed by the deafening screech of the wind.

Other sailors on the deck joined in the useless effort to drag the shore boat with me inside, back to the ship as flames spread quickly below deck and across the rigging. Deaf to the cries of the crew, I swung down my cutlass to chop the halyard line, dropping the shore boat into the churning ocean. Shouts of obscenities and curses fell down from the ship's rail. As fire spread on the ship, the powerful winds drove the heavy hull harder onto the ragged reef. Those same fierce winds drove my shallow shore boat over the reef and back out to sea.

As justice for my black soul, my triumph turned instantly into panic when I realized the shore boat had no oars. Back on the ship, now burning with greater intensity, the silhouette of men holding up the oars, their curses swallowed by the storm, confirmed my dreadful fate. With dead eyes, I watched *El Oro de Isabella* sink beneath the swell. The flame-engulfed top mast was my last sight of the doomed ship. And then I saw nothing but darkness and the cresting of waves crashing into my little boat.

*

Castaway | 1566 CE

Western Caribbean

Adrift for weeks, I no longer expected to survive, nor did I deserve the mercy. I had become the evil that I once loathed, the evil that na' Llana loathed. Cursed from birth, I carried that curse with me into life, until it dominated my soul and doomed anyone who crossed my path. Drifting, dehydrated, and near starvation, I sank into a fitful, tormented sleep.

In my delirium, I stood over a motionless na' Llana, dead on the heathen altar with the cursed blade still dripping blood in my own hand as if I had murdered my own mother. Then suddenly, I stood alone on Judgment Day before the Catholic God, condemned for betraying my people, condemned for my inhuman savagery, and condemned for such evil in the name of holiness. As I pounded on the heavy iron gates of hades, pleading for leniency, I could hear the screams of those I tormented behind me. Desperate to escape their fury, with each slam of my fist on the iron gates, my body shuddered with an excruciating jolt of pain. The harsh screams and demonic howls grew to a deafening, moaning roar.

My own repetitive slamming jarred me and shook me slowly back to consciousness in time to witness lightning flashes and hear the deafening clap of thunder of another intense storm. Unsure if days or weeks had passed, I awakened to the dreadful sight of a nearly flooded boat. Surprisingly, I was not at sea, but somehow had wedged within a narrow sea cave. With each ebb of the tidal surge, the wooden shore boat slammed against the back of the rocky grotto, and rattled my sore, dehydrated, starving body to the bone.

Outside the cave, another hurricane howled across a narrow lagoon, but then came an even more terrifying sound from the rock crevices above me that penetrated deep into a cavern—the sound of a moaning shriek of human anguish calling to me. Wet and shivering, I listened to the hurricane-scream outside the cave and the inhuman screeches from within. Isolated between the world of the living and the purgatory of the dead, I was wanted by neither, and I was cursed by both.

*

A Blood Oath | Year Unknown

Caverns of Cortés

I can no longer remember or count the lifetimes I've spent wandering within this diabolic labyrinth. I have faced every demon and suffered every death. Every scream and each dying breath have been etched deeply into my soul, a just penance for my hideous brutality in the name of a false piety. My once-powerful body has been broken and then broken again. Now I am beyond years. I am dying. English intruders have discovered my sanctuary, my purgatory. They have gone now, but they will be back. I am no longer able to protect the secrets of the ancients, so I must carry my penance into death.

I have shed my own blood once again to write this testimony. I sacrifice myself with the same blade I used to sacrifice the shaman who cursed me; the same dagger used to sacrifice the innocent na' Llana, who cursed life itself. This cut will be my last. These are my final words of warning to those who would seek the truth concerning the shame of Spain.

> *Through the jaws of death, both wicked and blessed will ascend Jacob's ladder. Under a baptism of thunder, betrayal awaits with a sting worse than death, until scavengers feed on your bones. Grovel in shame to escape the winged horde, until you face the pale death of innocence and awaken the weeping of the doomed who shed their own blood. Between the cherubim of fire, an unquenchable lust will choke your lungs until you cough up your own blood. There will be no redemption for the glittering shame of Spain lost in the heathen hell and stained with the blood of maidens. Raise your hands to heaven in vain hope the raging torrent will not drag you screaming into the cold abyss. A narrow path of life leads to a bottomless,*

nameless tomb, where the razor-sharp teeth of demons shred your soul. Damnation flows red over the abomination of the bloody altar, burning with the stench of death. Rise above the sacrifice of desolation to discover your dreadful fate.

With my blood, I vow this eternal oath of penance. By my own bloody hand, I condemn my soul to the heathen hades.

Cortés

About The Author

Guy Morris a successful businessman, thought leader, adventurer, inventor, and published composer. During college, Guy was influenced by men of the Renaissance who were fluent in business, science, politics and the arts. After growing up on the streets, he earned graduate scholarships for his macroeconomic models, and won awards as an early webisode pioneer where he wrote the scripts that introduced the SLVIA, based on a true program that escaped the Livermore Labs. With three degrees and thirty-six years of executive-level experience in high tech firms, Guy's thrillers bend the fine line between truth and fiction with deeply researched stories, international locales and sardonic wit.

You find out more about Guy via his website:

guymorrisbooks.com

You can also stay in touch via the following social media:

instagram.com/guymorrisbooks
facebook.com/officialguymorrisbooks
twitter.com/guymorrisbooks